THE GLASS PALACE CHRONICLE

PATRICIA LE ROY

PIATKUS

Copyright © 1997 by Patricia le Roy

First published in Great Britain in 1997 by
Online Originals, London

This edition published 2000 by
Judy Piatkus (Publishers) Ltd of
5 Windmill Street, London W1
email: *info@piatkus.co.uk*

The moral right of the author has been asserted

A catalogue record for this book is available from the British Library

ISBN 0 7499 3154 X

Set in Bembo by
Phoenix Photosetting, Chatham, Kent

Printed and bound in Great Britain by
Mackays of Chatham PLC, Chatham, Kent

This book is dedicated
with admiration and respect to
Aung San Suu Kyi
and the struggle for democracy in Burma

Prologue

London

October 1990

Everything was ready.

She laid the syringe on the edge of the washbasin and stowed the instruments neatly away in her handbag. The sounds of voices and laughter filtered dimly down from the floor above. The party was in full swing. She had made the call from the basement storeroom five minutes ago. Even if Roland had heard the sound of the phone being replaced in its cradle, there was nothing he could do about it. The new exhibition had attracted a lot of attention and there were at least fifty people in the gallery. In any case, he had no reason to be suspicious. She brushed her hair carefully back from her face and applied fresh lipstick. Death was a friend: one should go to meet him looking one's best. There was a whole gram of heroin in the syringe, ten times the normal dose. She had left nothing to chance.

She sat down on the closed toilet seat and rolled up her sleeve. Since she had made her decision two days earlier she had been conscious of a vast inner lightness, as if a weight had been lifted from her heart. Subconsciously she had known for a long time that this was how it would end. Heroin was another country: it had no frontiers. No one escaped. There was only one way to get free of it. She had tried five times to give it up and she was weary of struggling. Even if Philip hadn't been coming back next week, she might have done it now anyway.

Someone tried the door handle. 'Just a minute,' she called, and picked up the syringe. Time was running out. Soon Roland would notice her absence and start fretting that there was no one to replenish the glasses and hand round the petits fours. She started looking for a vein in her left arm. Faintly in the distance came the sound of police sirens, growing closer. She was not afraid. Now at this moment, all she could think of was the shoot. Still she had a moment's fleeting regret for Philip. It was a shabby way to treat him after all he had done for her. But he had always understood her, better even than their parents, and maybe, after reading the note she had left in the flat, he would understand this too.

She found the vein on the third try. Now that the shoot was just seconds away, everything else was wiped out of her mind. Blood began to seep up into the syringe. The sirens stopped. There was a sudden silence on the floor above. Now. She pressed the plunger. Her heart felt as if it was being torn apart and her skull wrenched off her head. The flash, the glorious, the ultimate flash. And then the darkness hit her like a dead weight.

When the police arrived three minutes later and broke the door down, she had slipped off the seat on to the floor. She was lying on her back with her eyes open. The needle was still stuck in the vein. Her heart had ceased to beat.

Part One

Paris

January 1993

Caroline was dead. She had been dead for two years, two months, and twenty-seven days.

In any case, she would never have set foot in a place like this. Far less sat at the bar alone, a target for the eyes and minds of every casual male drinker in the place. Still it was odd how the girl at the bar was sitting in exactly the same way Caroline used to sit, with her hair falling round her face and her shoulders hunched protectively round her glass.

The girl looked up from her drink and he went rigid in his seat. It was Caroline. He could feel the blood draining from his face. It couldn't be Caroline. Caroline was dead. Or was she? After all, he had missed the funeral, he had never seen her dead. He took another swallow of whisky and got a grip on himself. Of course it wasn't Caroline. But the resemblance was extraordinary. He went on staring. The same olive skin, the same faintly Oriental features, the same air of fragility. The girl had seen his reaction. She was looking directly at him. Their eyes met. She picked up her drink and slid off the stool. Too late he realized what a girl like that was doing in a bar like this. She had misinterpreted his look and now she was coming to negotiate her terms.

She walked confidently across the room, followed by the eyes of all the lone male drinkers round the bar with their *demis de bière*. She was dressed entirely in black, unfamiliar layered garments, short sleeves over long sleeves, an odd kind of draped skirt over some kind of trousers, and heavy black laced-up boots. Clothes that contrived both to reveal and conceal her body at the same time. The English students sitting a couple of tables away with their backpacks and county accents looked up curiously as she went past. The man in the rumpled business suit across the aisle stopped gazing ardently at his much younger girlfriend and gave her an assessing glance.

She reached his table and looked down with a sudden air of diffidence. *'Je peux m'asseoir?'*

He had the impression that if he said no, she would simply retreat back to her stool.

'Si vous voulez.' He gestured vaguely at the seat opposite.

She put her glass down on the table and slid on to the banquette. Close up the resemblance was both more and less striking. Caroline had favoured white and pastels: he could not remember ever seeing her in black, let alone the exotic garments that this girl wore, but the skin, the hair, the features were all uncannily alike.

'Alors,' said the girl, in a tone that fell only a few degrees short of overt aggression, *'je vous plais?'*

He wasn't sure how to answer that. Instead he said, *'Vous êtes française?'*

'Non, anglaise.'

'Really?' That was the last thing he had been expecting. She certainly didn't sound *anglaise*.

'Yes, really. You too?' Her voice was nothing like Caroline's. Caroline's voice had been light and high-pitched, this girl's was low and grave.

'I'm sorry to stare, but you look exactly like someone I . . . I know.'

She nodded, apparently taking this in her stride. 'What's your name?'

He hesitated. 'Paul.'

'I'm delighted to meet you, Paul. My name's Claudia.'

No Scottish burr in her voice either. She spoke standard, middle-class English. She could have been from anywhere.

'What are you doing in Paris, Paul?' she went on. 'Do you live here, or are you over on business?'

'I'm just passing through.'

'Ah. Are you on your way back to England or have you just come from there?'

'I just left,' he said tersely. 'What about you? What are you doing here?'

'I'm on my way back. As soon as I get enough cash together, that is. Why that bloody country has to be an island, I don't know. I wish they'd hurry up and get their tunnel finished. If one could just hitchhike there like everywhere else, life would be so much simpler.'

'You've run out of money?'

'You got it.' She smiled ferociously. 'I don't actually plan to make a career out of what I'm doing now.'

'Don't you have parents or family in England who could send you the money for the fare?'

Her lips compressed into a thin line. 'No.'

'Then why not try the Consulate?'

'Oh I did,' she said airily. 'It didn't work out.'

Paul blinked. What was that supposed to mean? Repatriating stranded citizens was one of the routine functions of British consulates in foreign cities. But she was looking at him in a way that placed further questioning firmly off-limits. 'I . . . see. But isn't there some other way you could earn the money to get home?'

'Nope. There's nothing out there – nothing that pays serious money, that is. It's the recession. I did some waitressing last month and after that I got a few hours cleaning people's houses, which was okay for pocket money, but then the guy I was living with threw me out, I can't afford a hotel, the escort agencies won't have me ... It doesn't leave one much choice.'

The students had paid their bill and were heading off towards the Gare du Nord and the last train home. The portly middle-aged waiter, who had served Paul for the past three nights and was beginning to greet him as a regular, hovered at the edge of Paul's vision, his tray balanced on three fingers of his left hand and his right thumb hooked into the pocket of his striped waistcoat.

Paul looked at Claudia. The glass of red wine she had brought with her – probably the cheapest drink one could get in a French bar – was empty. 'Would you like another glass of wine?'

'Oh. Yes. No. No more wine, thank you. But, I think I—' She broke off and appeared to sift mentally through a series of alternatives. 'I'd like a *grand crème* please.'

Paul signalled to the waiter. 'Anything to eat?'

'Oh. Yes. Thank you, that would be very nice,' she said with unexpected demureness. 'It's late though, I don't know if they're still serving.'

'*Vous pouvez faire un sandwich pour Madame?*' suggested Paul, and the waiter gave Claudia an appraising look and said that no doubt they could, would that be ham, cheese, or rillettes? Ham *and* cheese, she said. When he came back with the sandwich she fell on it as if she hadn't eaten for a week.

'Sorry,' she said, when she had finished. 'That can't have been a very edifying spectacle. I guess I was hungrier than I thought.'

'Would you like another?'

'No. No, thanks. That was just fine.'

The waiter brought her coffee and she smiled up at him. Her smile was just like Caroline's too. Paul closed his eyes for a moment. When he opened them again, she was watching him gravely. The smile had disappeared.

'Who do I remind you of?'

'My sister. My half-sister actually. Forgive my asking, but are you part-Chinese too?'

'One-quarter. My mother's half-English, half-Chinese. She was born in Hong Kong.'

'And your father?'

'Italian, God rot him.'

Caroline had been half-Chinese, half-English. Her mother had been from Hong Kong too, but their father, as far as Paul knew, was pure English. He wondered what odd coincidence of genes had engineered this extraordinary likeness. The couple on the other side of the aisle got up to leave. The man, helping his companion with her coat, gave Paul a leer of connivance over her green wool shoulder.

Avoiding his eyes, Paul felt for his wallet and looked to see how much it contained.

'How much do you need to get across the Channel?'

Claudia opened her eyes wide in surprise. 'You mean you'd give me the money for my fare? Because I look like your sister?'

'How much is it?' he repeated.

'No.' She shook her head firmly. 'It's kind of you, but no. One, I don't take favours. Not from anyone. Two, I don't intend to go back on the bloody ferry, you know. It's too damn cold at this time of year. I'm going to wait till I can afford a plane ticket.'

Paul raised his eyebrows. 'First class or business class?'

'I'll settle for economy.'

'Plus of course a taxi from the airport to – where do your parents live?'

'My mother lives in Surrey,' she said, and then added, 'though it's none of your business. I don't know why I'm telling you all this. Do you treat your sister like this too?'

Paul thrust his wallet back into his pocket. 'My sister's dead.'

'Really? Oh my God. So that's why you looked as though you'd seen a ghost. Was she my age?'

'More or less.'

'Was it an accident?'

'Yes.'

'You don't want to talk about it. I'm sorry. Okay then, I guess ... Maybe I should ...' She drained her coffee cup. 'Look, it's been nice talking to you, and I really appreciate your offer, but—'

'You don't have to go.'

She looked at him and smiled briefly. 'I'm afraid I do.'

'Why? So you can pick up one of those guys over there and earn a hundred francs to put towards your plane ticket?'

'One hundred francs?' she said disdainfully. 'You must be joking!'

'If it's the big time you're after,' Paul retorted, 'you've got the wrong neighbourhood.'

'I know that. Last night I tried the Sixteenth arrondissement. Nice area, people use deodorant, hold open a door for you now and again. They even know what to do with the imperfect subjunctive. I earned a lot of money and a night in a hotel room, but, Jesus, I couldn't go through that again. Some of the things the guy wanted me to do I'd never even heard of. So tonight I thought I'd go a bit farther down-market. The hotel for the night's going to be a bit trickier to manage, but at least no one over there reminds me of my father.'

For a few moments they sat in silence. Claudia's face was turned away from him, looking past him towards the far end of the room, where the lights were turned low and the tables were empty. She wasn't Caroline, she was sharper and edgier and more streetwise than Caroline, but on appearances alone it could have been Caroline sitting across the table from him.

'Do you take drugs?' he demanded abruptly.

'No.' The tone was categorical. He believed her at once.

'What's your rate for the night?'

'What? You? Oh.' Calculation chased surprise across her face. 'I was going to ask five hundred, but for you I'll do four.'

'Five. I don't take favours either.'

'Okay.'

'Shall we go?'

Claudia's outdoor wear consisted of a vast but shabby cloak and a long knitted scarf. Standing beside her, he realized that she was about Caroline's height too. Small by Western standards: only an inch or two over five feet. As they left, one of the men at the bar made a crack and all the others laughed. Paul didn't understand the words, but the sense was easy enough to grasp. Claudia turned and spat something back at them. The laughter stopped abruptly.

'Enculés,' she said angrily when they were outside on the pavement. 'Sometimes I really hate men – oh, Jesus, I'm sorry.'

'That's all right. I admire your command of French.'

'Thank you.'

'How long have you been here?'

'Five months this trip. I've been working my way back up from Italy, actually.' She stopped and scowled, and then added, 'I was in Lille for a while last year though.'

'Have you any luggage?'

'It's in a locker at the Gare du Nord.'

'Do you want to collect it ?'

'Not for one night. I have some stuff in here.' She tapped her large black shoulder bag.

'We have to go there anyway to find a taxi.'

'Actually, it's so bloody cold, I've got most of my clothes on me already.'

Paul shrugged. 'As you like.'

They began to walk towards the Gare du Nord. The night

was black and bitter and an icy wind streamed down the boulevard. 'Why are you doing this, Paul?' she demanded. 'You aren't the type to pick up a girl in a bar. You're only doing it because I look like your sister, aren't you?'

'What does it matter why I'm doing it as long as you get paid?'

'That's true too. Where do you live?'

'Over in the Eighth, just off boulevard Haussmann.'

'Nice area. Not as nice as the Sixteenth, of course.'

'You said you were slumming tonight.'

'So I did.'

'Actually it's not mine. I'm just borrowing a friend's flat while he's out of town.'

The friend, Claudia decided, was a monk. Who else would live in a flat as bare and impersonal as a hotel room? A five-star hotel room, to be sure, with plenty of fake Louis Whosit chairs and machine-made Oriental carpets, but no sea shells marked A Present from Siena, or wherever Paul and his fancy friends went on their holidays, no back numbers of *The Guardian*, none of the cultural bric à brac of the consumer classes. She perched on a stiff brocade chair in the sitting room – no, that was the wrong word for something as grand as this, it was closer to what her father would call a *salotto* – sipping her whisky and taking in the scenery. There was something very odd about this flat. People who bought fake period furniture usually invested in the complete works of Shakespeare, Beethoven, Mozart and Tolstoy at the same time. And with all the galleries in this area, you'd think someone could have nipped out and picked up a couple of tasteful artworks to brighten up the acres of pale beige wallpaper. Yet there were no books in this room, no CDs, no videocassettes, not even a television set. Apparently the monk belonged to an order that had forsworn art, culture and information at one fell swoop.

But not technology. There was an answering machine in a small study leading off the hall, and Paul had shut himself up there to deal with his messages. First, however, he had apologised to Claudia for leaving her to her own devices and offered her a drink. Whisky or Perrier or both together? Noting the bareness of the monk's cellar, Claudia had chosen whisky on its own. It was her father's drink, it was even his brand, but that couldn't be helped. The two large glasses she had drunk the previous night had helped her maintain her equanimity throughout the evening. It might be wise to take the same precaution tonight, even though the proceedings promised to be considerably less of an ordeal. Paul, as far as she could judge, occupied the middle ground between the aristocratic perversity of last night and the wham-bam contempt of the Arabs, blue-overalled workers and late-night drinkers who had propositioned her so far today. The down side was that, having got her home with him, she had a strong suspicion he wouldn't have much idea what to do next. The initiative was going to have to come from her. Probably she should undress and get into bed like they did in the movies. Save everyone a lot of embarrassment. She got up and moved towards the door. First, however, she was going to case the joint. One, for clues to the monk's identity, and two, for food.

The flat was larger than she had expected. Besides the study and the *salotto* there were four bedrooms and two bathrooms. One of the rooms had a suitcase on the floor and a sweater on a chair, and was presumably Paul's. The other three were unused and empty: the monk, wherever he was, had taken his robes and alms bowl with him. She looked into Paul's wardrobe and was relieved to see that it contained the same kind of nondescript clothes he was wearing tonight. Not a Gucci loafer or Armani blazer in sight. Of course, Paul was nothing like her father or she wouldn't be here in the first place. To begin with, he was a good ten years younger. Early forties, at a guess, and blond. On first sight, he could pass for some kind of academic: spectacles, longish hair, faint air of aloofness. Claudia did not, however, believe that he was an academic. British academics in Paris stayed in crummy Left-Bank hotels and did not offer charity to indigent compatriots.

It was hard to say what he was. Living in a place like this, and lying to her about it, he was probably a serial murderer or a white slaver. She tried the suitcase, but it was locked. Looking around for possible clues, she spotted a book on the bedside table. Show me what you read, and I'll tell you who you are. The book was called *Pagan: The Glass Palace Chronicles of the Kings of Burma*. Burma? She focused on the one word that made sense. The picture on the front showed some kind of Eastern temple. Maybe Paul was a Buddhist. Or else his landlord was. She replaced the book and went to check the bathrooms. There was nothing to be seen in either of them but Paul's shaving tackle, sitting neatly in the bathroom adjoining his bedroom, along with a bottle of shampoo. The monk neither washed his hair nor got headaches.

The kitchen was right at the end of the passage, dazzling white plastic from floor to ceiling. Too clean by half. It didn't look as if much cooking went on in this flat. No eating either. There was no dining room, not even a dining table, which was odd for a fancy place like this. The fridge contained one litre of milk, one packet of butter, one bottle of mineral water. On the counter were a jar of Nescafé and a packet of *biscottes*. She made a beeline for the latter. Breakfast today had consisted of an apple she had swiped off a stall in the street, and lunch had been a packet of biscuits consumed in a discreet corner of the supermarket. Partly because she had stowed the aristocrat's money in her bra for safe-keeping, and partly because it would have been defeating the object of the exercise to spend it on food. She took a handful of *biscottes* and went back to the bedroom. Paul was still on the phone. She would take a look at his book on Burma and then get undressed.

★

Paul had found three messages on the answering machine: Rebecca wanting to know about arrival dates and hotel rooms, Adrian asking him to call when he got in, and finally Emma, umm-ing and ah-ing and plainly unsure what kind of message to leave. In the sudden hope that she might have changed her mind, he called Emma first, only to discover that she had merely been having an attack of guilt and needed reassuring. It took a good twenty minutes to convince her that yes he understood the situation, yes he was bound to find someone else, no it didn't really matter if he had to go on his own. None of which was the slightest bit true. Without all those years of professionally instilled patience, he doubted whether he could have stopped himself from suggesting very sharply that if she felt as bad as all that about her defection there was still time to change her mind, given that he was due to leave in three days' time and had practically no chance at all of replacing her between now and then.

By the time he had finally soothed her off the line, checked in with Adrian, whose ostensibly urgent need to communicate seemed to be focused mainly on finding out how Paul had spent his evening, and asked Rebecca to book him a room in Rangoon for Saturday night, it was half-past twelve. He was dead tired, and there was still this girl to be dealt with. The flat was silent. He went in search of her. A trail of crumbs led him into the bedroom. She had kicked off her shoes and was lying flat on her stomach, sprawled across the gold bedspread like a wild black bird, reading. She didn't look up when he went in, lost to the world in the book on Pagan that he had picked up in the Charing Cross Road the day he left London.

'Interesting?' he asked, sitting down on the chair nearest the bed, and she looked up startled.

'Oh, Jesus, yes, it's brilliant. The photos are superb, I've never seen anything like them, and the text is wonderful. Listen to this.' She flipped back a few pages and began to read.

' "*Honour to Him, the Holy, the Blessed, the Lord Buddha! Here begins the wonderful history of Anawratha and Kyanzittha: thus it is told in the Great Royal Chronicle which was written in the Sacred Chamber facing the Palace of Glass in the reign of King Bagyidaw, Master of the mines of gold, silver, rubies, amber and all gems, Lord of the sacred king of the white elephants, Prince of the Universe and Great Captain of the Law.*" Don't you just love the way it rolls off your tongue? "*Lord of the sacred king of the white elephants . . .*" Who are all these people?'

'They were medieval kings of Burma. Anawratha founded the First Burmese Empire in Pagan at about the time William the Conqueror was invading England, and Kyanzittha ruled the empire a little later. Between them, they built a fair amount of the temples you see in the photographs there.'

'You mean this is a Burmese equivalent of the Domesday Book?'

'No, because it wasn't written until 1829. King Bagyidaw, who ordered it to be written, reigned in the first part of the nineteenth century.'

'Mm. And where is Pagan? What is it?'

'It's a city in Upper Burma. It was the capital of the empire until the thirteenth century, and an important religious site. There used to be something like thirteen thousand temples at Pagan, and there are just over two thousand still standing today.'

'It looks amazing,' she said, turning back to the book again. 'Maybe I should get a decent job and save up some money to go and see for myself. Anyway.' She closed the book and pushed herself into a sitting position. 'You probably have better things to do than chat about temples all night.' The animation disappeared, her faced closed down into its earlier sullenness and she gave him a perfunctory smile. 'I meant to be all ready and waiting when you got off the phone, but I got sidetracked.' Her hands went to the knot at her waist which apparently held the whole mysterious structure of her clothes in place.

Paul said, 'There's no hurry. Would you really go all the way to Burma just to see Pagan?'

'Why not? It's about time I did something interesting with my life.'

'What have you been doing with it up to now?'

'Testing the waters,' she said gravely. 'If you're going to be doing something for the rest of your life, you have to choose carefully. I think I've narrowed the field down to four possible careers. Waitress, house-cleaner, grape-picker and typist. Now I just have to make the final decision.'

'But you speak French,' Paul objected.

'So I can clean houses in two languages.'

He looked at her in bafflement. 'I don't understand. You're intelligent, educated, you can get a better job than that.'

'I'm handicapped,' she said. 'I have what they call an attitude problem. I do not deliver cups of coffee to managing directors engaged in serious study of the sports news with the appropriate degree of respect. When customers shout at me, I shout right back. I think in the end I'm going to have to weed out anything that involves offices or restaurants. Or shops. Houses are better, except that they have owners. Best of all are grapes. They don't talk at all, and they only last about a month, which means one has time to catch up on one's reading during the other eleven months of the year.'

'It's going to take you a long while to get to Pagan,' said Paul drily.

'Yes,' she agreed. Her gaze wandered absently to the cover of the book. 'Never mind. Maybe I'll marry a rich husband like in the fairy stories. Some day my prince will come.'

'And whisk you off to Burma?'

'Right.' She yawned suddenly. 'Oh Jesus, I'm sorry. Look, are we going to do this or not?'

'No,' said Paul, listening to his own decisive tone with some surprise. 'I've got another idea.'

She looked at him warily. 'What kind of idea?'

'I'm leaving for Burma at the end of this week. I'll be there for about a fortnight. The girl who was supposed to go with me has dropped out. Why don't you come instead?'

A smile of pure glee crept over her face: the smile of a child being offered the inaccessible. The moon itself, no less. The first time he had seen that smile, he had been fifteen or sixteen. His first Christmas back in England. Caroline was three and they had decided she was old enough for her first tricycle. 'Bicycle for Caroline!' she had crowed triumphantly, and that smile of joy had burst out and lit up her whole face.

The smile faded and Claudia looked at him blankly. 'How can I? I've got no money.'

'I'm sorry, I didn't make myself clear. I'm inviting you to come with me as my guest. All expenses paid. Plus I would also pay you a . . . a salary for each day of your time.'

'I don't believe it,' she said slowly. 'Do you really mean that?'

'Yes I do.'

She stared at him with a mixture of perplexity and suspicion.

'Why?'

'I don't enjoy travelling alone,' said Paul blandly.

'I see. So how much are you going to pay for the pleasure of my company?'

'Let's see. You want five hundred a night, right? But there are the days too. So let's say a thousand francs per twenty-four-hour period starting tonight. Today's Monday, I want to leave Thursday. Fifteen days maximum in Burma, plus preparation time plus travel time. That makes about nineteen days. How about we round it off at twenty thousand francs?'

'Twenty thousand francs? Two thousand pounds? Jesus, I've never had that much money in my life!' The smile spread briefly over her face, and disappeared. 'Okay, Paul, what's the catch? What do I really have to do to earn two thousand pounds?'

'Nothing,' said Paul. 'Just be there. A man travelling on his own in Burma is too conspicuous. Tourists travel in pairs. Especially at my age. If I were twenty years younger, I could get away with it, but not any more. I need someone to pose as my wife.'

'To "pose" as your "wife"? Ah. So you're not going to Burma just to look at the temples then?'

'Not exclusively.'

'What else are you going to do?'

'That's the problem, Claudia. I can't tell you that. I realize that you may not be able to accept this, and that you may decide to turn me down because of it. I'm not going to answer any questions about who I am, why I'm going to Burma, what I'm doing there. All I'm going to tell you is that you won't be in danger, and I won't ask you to do anything illegal.'

Claudia's eyes narrowed. 'You're a drug dealer, aren't you? Burma's one of the countries in the Golden Triangle, isn't it? Sorry, Paul, it's not on.' She slid to the edge of the bed, and began groping round for her shoes. 'Not even for two thousand pounds and a trip to Pagan. Hard drugs aren't my scene. I've known too many people who got hooked. I've seen what it does to them.'

Paul put out his hand and stopped her. 'I give you my word I'm not a narcotics dealer.'

'What are you then?'

He shrugged and remained silent. After a moment, Claudia said, 'Why did your friend drop out?'

'The company where her fiancé works is undergoing restructuring. He's worried about his job, he's got chest pains and insomnia and a rash on his arms, and she thinks she should be there to hold his hand. The restructuring has been going on for weeks, and so have the symptoms, but she only decided two days ago that she wasn't going to come. Obviously it doesn't leave me much time to find someone else, or I wouldn't be making this proposal to a complete stranger.'

Claudia looked hard at him and then away again. She pulled her knees up to her chest and buried her head in her arms. The sensible thing would be to stand up, put on her cloak and bid this lunatic a polite goodnight. But it was cold out there, and besides she was seriously tempted to stay.

'Is it warm in Burma?' she demanded, without raising her head.

'Yes. Right now is the best time of year for travelling in that part of the world. The rains are finished and the hot season hasn't started yet.'

'What's the political deal? Wasn't there a big uprising a few years back?'

'Yes, in 1988, but the country is quiet now. If there was any danger of unrest, they wouldn't be allowing tourists in.'

Warm and repressive, then. Just like the rest of the Third World. Useless to query the morality of tourists spending their money to boost repressive economies: tourism was clearly not the point of the exercise. She pulled her arms tighter round her knees. So what was there to lose? Not a great deal, Claudia, let's face it. You're twenty-three years old, you have no money, no job, no profession, no qualifications. You're going nowhere, you have nowhere to go. So why not sign up for a trip to Pagan? It's the only way you'll get there, or anywhere else for that matter. The man's offering you a destination. Go for it.

She lifted her head and examined Paul again. He returned her stare impassively. There was something intimidating about him, but that on the whole reassured her. None of that smooth Mediterranean charm, skin-deep and unreliable. As far as it went, she was pretty sure he was making her a straight offer. He wasn't going to cut her up into little pieces and he wasn't going to sell her to some Burmese warlord to rejuvenate the harem. He'd have come up with a more plausible story if he had something like that in mind.

'All the same,' she announced flatly, 'I should tell you that my father is a regional director for Alitalia, and his wife is connected to the Agnelli family. My mother is secretary to a British Member of Parliament.'

'Meaning,' said Paul drily, 'that if my Burmese friends and I are planning to feed you to the crocodiles in the Irrawaddy river after our two weeks of orgies, we'll have the governments of two nations to answer to?'

Claudia reddened.

'Then you'd certainly better inform all of them exactly where you're going and when you expect to return. Meanwhile, I'm afraid I have to check on your bona fides as well. Would you roll up your sleeves, please?'

Silently Claudia did so. He inspected her arms without touching them. 'Thank you. Excuse me a minute.' He got up and left the room. Claudia rolled her sleeves back down. No, not a drug dealer. He reappeared with a pad and pencil.

'Now. I'd like you to tell me exactly what you've been doing since last summer.'

'She left Italy in August and hitched a lift into France. Worked in a hamburger joint in Nice for two days. Moved on to a bar in St Raphael. Met someone who was driving to Bordeaux, decided to go along and get a job picking grapes. That lasted till mid-October. Got a lift to Paris and moved in with the friend of someone's friend who has a *chambre de bonne* near République. Last week the guy threw her out. She has no job, nowhere to live, no money.'

'Really? And you picked her up in that bar you've been hanging out in? What a man.'

'Actually she picked me up.' Paul passed the sheet of paper across the desk. From the outer office, the muffled ringing of the phone filtered faintly through the sound-proofed walls. Adrian glanced swiftly down the page.

'Didn't breathe a word of this on the phone last night, you devious bastard.'

'That was before I had checked her out.'

A buzzer sounded on the desk. Adrian flicked the intercom switch. 'Yes, Mary? No, not now. Tell him half an hour.' He turned back to Paul. 'She sounds like a pretty desperate case to me.'

'She is,' said Paul. 'That's just the point. It makes her the perfect travelling companion for a trip like this.'

As soon as he said it, he could have bitten off his tongue.

'Is that right?' said Adrian innocently. 'So what kind of trip is this then, Philip?'

'I told you, a little unfinished business.' The less Adrian knew, the better it would be for him later on. 'And my name's Paul, remember?'

'If you say so. Got everything written down here, have you? Names, dates, addresses. Fine, I'll run a check on her.'

'One other thing. She's going to need a passport. Could you sort something out for me by tomorrow? Brand new, no visas, no dog-ears. London issuing number. Here's the information you'll need.' He passed over another sheet of paper.

'Let's see. Claudia Jane Miller. Date of birth, place of birth. No visible distinguishing marks, no children. Got a photo, have you? Thanks. Very nice, yes, can see why you— Wait, that's odd, could swear I've seen her somewhere before. My God, it's Caroline! At least, that is, awfully sorry, what I meant to say was—'

Paul cut brusquely through his apologies. 'That's right. They could be twins. When I saw her in that bar last night I thought I was dreaming.'

'That's an amazing resemblance. I would never have thought . . . And you want her to pose as your wife?'

'Why not?'

'Isn't that going to be a trifle ... ah ... awkward?'

'For God's sake, I'm not going to go to bed with her!'

'Of course not,' said Adrian, genuinely shocked. 'That's not what I meant at all. What I meant was, having a Caroline lookalike around twenty-four hours a day – are you sure you'll be able to cope with it?'

'It'll take a bit of getting used to,' Paul admitted.

'Well, I suppose you know what you're doing. When do you plan to leave, by the way? We might need the safe flat at the end of the week.'

'We'll fly out on Thursday, stop over for a day in Bangkok to get our visas, and aim to reach Rangoon on Saturday afternoon.'

'Bangkok.' Adrian's eyes lit up nostalgically. 'I still miss Thailand, you know. So does Jill. One of our best postings. Where do you plan to go from Rangoon, then?'

'Oh just the usual places,' said Paul vaguely. 'You've been to Burma, haven't you?'

'Absolutely. Jill and I went to check out the Golden Triangle, see what we could pick up cut rate.'

He laughed merrily, but he was watching Paul like a hawk.

'Well then, you know what it's like.' Deliberately avoiding his gaze, Paul got to his feet and pretended to inspect the view over the Embassy garden. If Adrian had got the idea that he was planning to slip off the tourist circuit into the rebel-held areas, so much the better. 'I'll drop in tomorrow afternoon to collect the passport. And the clothes too, if you're sure Jill won't mind.'

'Of course not, she'll be delighted. Right, I'll expect you tomorrow. What are you going to be doing in the meantime?'

'Briefing her,' said Paul. 'We've got a lot of ground to cover.'

Not a monk, but a spy. Holed up in a safe house in Paris, preparing a covert mission to Burma, recruiting low-level agents in bars to serve as cover. It all fitted so well, she couldn't think why she hadn't thought of it earlier. Of course, things had been moving so fast last night she hadn't had time to think. After he had finished writing down her long list of recent employers, he had worked out a biography for her forthcoming new passport, taken a photograph with some fancy camera he dug out of the study, made a list of vaccinations she was going to need, and noted down the details of her bank account. One half of her money was to be paid on the day they left Paris, the rest on the day they returned. By the time all that had been settled, it was three o'clock in the morning, she was in bed on her own in the room across the corridor from his, and the only thing she could think of was sleep.

So here she was, seven hours later, still tucked up in bed, alone and so far untouched, about to embark for two weeks in another life: the life of Paul's fictitious wife. What the real one was going to be doing during all this time was anybody's guess. He was already wearing a wedding ring, real gold by the look of it, not something he had picked up in Woolworths for the occasion, but in light of his 'no questions' stipulation she wasn't going to be able to ask. Still, it wasn't her problem, was it?

Her problem was that she had apparently gone completely crazy. Pick up a man in a bar, go home with him, get offered a free trip to Burma, two thousand pounds for the fortnight, on condition that you travel under a false name, on a false passport, and ask no questions about who he is and why he wants to spend a fortnight in Burma. She pulled the covers up to her chin and laughed softly to herself. *La nuit porte conseil*, as the French would say, but even with seven hours of good advice behind her, she hadn't changed her mind. What's more, she was looking forward to it. The money wasn't all that good when you thought about the risks involved, but who cared? Even if they shot her as a spy, it would be more distinguished than dying of hunger in the gutter.

Which brought her to the question of who Paul was spying for, and what he was looking for in Burma. The obvious candidate for the role of employer was the SIS, except that she was pretty sure he wasn't English. The language might be native, but the accent and intonation were not. At first she had thought he might be American, then she had considered South African. Towards the end of the evening, it had occurred to her that he could be an Englishman who had spent most of his life abroad. Never mind, she would figure it out in the end. The same with his non-drug-related business in Burma. If she was supposed to be his wife, he would have to haul her round with him most of the time. All she had to do was keep her eyes and ears open. What was there in Burma to spy on? Nuclear installations? Heroin fields? God knows. But she had two whole weeks to find out.

The restaurant where they went for dinner had red-checked tablecloths and traditional bistro food. *Boeuf bourguignon, blanquette de veau, lapin à la moutarde*. The *patronne* greeted Paul warmly and Claudia a lot more coolly. Some kind of territorial infringement was being committed.

'Do you come here a lot, Paul?'

He had seated himself with his back to the wall, she noticed with satisfaction, just like in the spy novels.

'Nearly every night, actually. Someone recommended it.'

'You're a creature of habit, aren't you? Same restaurant every night, same bar every night. Are we going there later too?'

They had spent nearly twenty-four hours in each other's company, but it was the first time she had managed to make him smile. 'I think maybe we'll give it a miss. Unless you want to show off your new shoes?'

'No, no.' Claudia glanced resentfully at the package on the seat beside her. 'I'm saving them for the jungle. It wouldn't do to wear them out beforehand.'

The package contained one pair of brand-new Reeboks. White, for God's sake. She didn't need them, she had protested, her Doc Martens were good enough for anything, including the jungle, but he had been adamant. When in Burma, do as the Burmese do. The Burmese wear Reeboks? she had said sceptically. No, they wear flip-flops, he had said, undeterred. You'll need those too, but we can pick them up in Rangoon.

They ordered *boeuf bourguigon* and a carafe of red wine from the dour-faced *patronne*, who defrosted slightly on hearing Claudia's fluent French. The wine arrived almost immediately: no doubt they looked as though they needed it. Paul was looking distinctly haggard and Claudia didn't feel too good herself. Tetanus and typhoid and polio and a few other things were chasing each other round under her skin and making her arm ache. The cold was making her teeth ache. Rushing round vaccination centres, the Gare du Nord and the *grands magasins* all afternoon had made her feet ache. Trying to remember the details of her new life and that of her alleged new husband was making her head ache.

She sipped her wine and looked covertly at Paul across the table. He really did look tired. And abstracted too. A million miles away.

'They do have jungle in Burma, I hope?' she said brightly, desperate for something to say, to bring him back from the graveside of his sister, or wherever else he was.

'Oh yes, lots of it.' He gave her a polite, acknowledging smile, but his eyes were as far away as ever. 'Most of the country is jungle, but unfortunately we won't actually be going there. That's where the fighting is, and foreigners aren't allowed to go there.'

'Fighting? What fighting?'

'The civil war.'

'Oh, right, the civil war. Silly me. So what civil war is this then? The government versus the democrats?'

'No, the government versus the minorities. The Karens, the Kachins, the Shans . . .'

'Oh I see,' said Claudia crossly. 'Now, let me guess. Is this one of those Yugoslavia-type situations where they've all been thirsting to slit each other's throats for the past five centuries? Or are they fighting for some other reason?'

'There are certain historic tensions,' agreed Paul delicately. 'But the main reason is that the minorities want an equal say in the government of the country and the Burmans don't want to give it to them.'

The *boeuf bourguignon* arrived and the conversation was interrupted while the *patronne* fussed around with bread and napkins, knives and forks, salt and pepper, none of which she seemed to consider worth putting on the table ahead of time. When she left them alone, with a cursory, *'Bon appetit'*, Paul said,

'But you don't have to worry. As I said, we won't be going anywhere near the fighting. Burma isn't dangerous for tourists.'

'Just for its own nationals?'

'You could say that.'

'How many times have you been to Burma before?'

'Me? I've never been to Burma before. How do you find the *bourguignon*?'

'Pretty good. I can see why you come here every night. Though I thought people like you weren't supposed to do things like that,' she added nastily.

'Things like what?'

'I thought you were meant to vary your routines. Leave the house at different times. Go to work by different routes. Never eat in the same place twice. Make it harder to track you down and so on.'

'I have no idea what you're talking about.'

'Of course not.'

'Claudia, I thought we agreed—'

'That wasn't a question, Paul. Merely an observation. I wouldn't want you to feel obligated to answer me in any way.'

They finished eating in silence.

'Well,' said Claudia, wiping her plate with a piece of bread. 'That was delicious.' Paul had left some of his stew: she wondered if she could offer to finish it up, and decided against it. 'What's for pudding?'

'Pudding?'

'Yes please. Dessert. I am entitled to dessert, I suppose?'

'Of course.'

'Good. Because that's the main reason I agreed to your little proposition last night. The trouble with being broke is that puddings are the first thing to go.'

'They're all on the counter over there. Why not go and have a look?'

'That's okay, I can see from here. The lemon tart looks good. What are you going to have?'

'I never eat dessert.'

'That's all right, it's never too late to start. *Deux tartes au citron, s'il vous plaît, Madame.*'

'*Mais non, je—*'

Claudia put her finger to her lips. 'Ssshh. Make the most of it. I bet they don't have lemon tart in Burma.'

'Of course they don't—'

'See, you have been there before.'

Paul stared at her in exasperation. 'Are you always like this?'

'Quite often, yes. Do I still remind you of your sister?'

'No you don't.'

'Good. It's bad enough knowing there's someone else out there who looks exactly like you, but if she behaves like you too then it's even worse.' She stopped and blushed. 'Sorry. Put all that in the past tense. You don't have a photograph of her by any chance, do you?'

There was a long pause and then his hand went slowly to the inside pocket of his jacket. The *patronne* arrived with the lemon tart and he let it fall by his side again. She set down the plates and went back to the kitchen. He took a picture out of his wallet and passed it across the table.

Claudia studied it in silence and passed it back.

'You're right. It's uncanny. How long ago was this picture taken?'

'Two and a half years.'

'And she died . . .?'

'Three months later.'

'What was her name?'

'Caroline.'

He began to demolish the lemon tart, shovelling it into his mouth as though he was anxious to stop up the holes and prevent any more words escaping. Claudia watched him for a moment or two, and then picked up her spoon. Judging by the way he was reacting he had been keeping it all bottled up for two and a half years. No wonder he behaved as if he was somewhere else half the time.

'Tell me about her,' she said, when they had finished. He was about to demur, so she added, 'It would be better, you know. Save me putting my foot in it more than necessary.'

A pause while he thought about it.

'We're going to be living in each other's pockets for the next two weeks, if I understand correctly. If I don't know where the pitfalls are, it's going to be difficult to avoid them.'

'Maybe you're right.' He sighed and prepared unwillingly to commence his revelations. 'Caroline was my half-sister. Twelve years younger than me. She would have been thirty this year. My father was quite old when she was born, and something went wrong at the birth which meant that Helen, his second wife, couldn't have any more children. Since I was living with my own mother at that time, Caroline was to all intents and purposes an only child. They lavished a good deal of affection on her, perhaps too much – in fact, they spoiled her to death. They gave her everything she wanted. Luckily, she was very sweet-natured, so it didn't have as bad an effect on her character as it could have, but it left her a bit directionless. She wasn't a very strong person, she always needed someone to look after her, tell her what to do, and she was very easily influenced.'

He stopped. Claudia waited. So what was it about this sweet nonentity that had left such a deep and painful scar in the mind of her much older half-brother?

'What happened to her?' He didn't answer. 'It was heroin, wasn't it?' she said.

His head jerked up sharply. 'How did you know?'

'Don't look so alarmed. You've asked me twice if I'm on drugs. It's not hard to work out.'

Paul looked at her with an odd expression in his eyes. 'Maybe not.'

'Definitely not. And you feel guilty because you weren't there to look after her, and send her off for a cure somewhere, and keep her away from the dealers and her junkie friends when she got out.'

'My God,' said Paul. 'You know all about it.'

'I've seen it happen once or twice. Not to anyone I really cared about. Just people I knew. But that was bad enough. I would never take hard drugs, myself, never. I'd be too scared of what it can do to you.'

'You're not like Caroline at all,' said Paul. He sounded faintly surprised by the discovery.

'Did you really expect me to be?'

'No. Of course not. But the physical resemblance is so strong, it's just ... strange that you aren't.' He shrugged, and gave her smile which for the first time implied that a human being might be lurking in there somewhere. 'Sorry, I guess that sounds ridiculous.'

'The things that sound ridiculous are usually the best. Why

don't you ask that harpy for the bill,' she went on, 'and let's go home. I think we both need an early night.'

The monk's hideout was only two streets away. They walked there in silence. When they got inside the flat, Paul double-locked the front door, wished her good night and headed towards his own bedroom.

Claudia stood indecisively in the hall. Did he think she was tired and was that why ...? Since he was paying her shouldn't she ...?

'It doesn't have to be an early night in separate beds,' she said.

Paul stopped dead. He turned round and studied her thoughtfully. Then he sighed and took a couple of steps back towards her.

'I think there may have been a slight misunderstanding.'

'You don't want to sleep with me?'

'You saw the photo of Caroline.'

'I'm sorry, I should have thought.'

'I'd feel as if I were committing incest.'

'I just wasn't sure. Last night, you didn't say that—'

'You're quite right. I should have made it clear from the start.'

'Yes,' said Claudia irritably, 'you should.' He was too old, too blond, and too serious. He was not her type. But did he have to turn her down quite so categorically?

'I assume you don't want to sleep with me any more than I want to sleep with you?'

'Of course not,' said Claudia, and turned on her heel. 'Why ever should I?'

'Wait,' said Paul. 'I haven't finished. We're going to be posing as husband and wife. This means there's going to have to be a certain amount of hugging and kissing at times. Physical contact,' he explained, as if it were the name of a particularly odious disease. 'For show, that is. Like actors in front of a camera. Switching on and off as the occasion demands. I suppose I should have spelled all that out too last night. Anyway, I need to know right now if you're going to be able to handle it or not.'

Handle it? What do you mean, handle it? Can a trainee prostitute and presumed nymphomaniac such as myself survive for two weeks in a totally asexual environment? Is that what you mean? Can I be trusted to refrain from threatening your virtue in private, however much you maul me around in public?

Claudia gave him the biggest, cheeriest smile that rage would allow. 'Don't worry, Paul. For a hundred pounds a day, I can handle anything.'

So that was Tuesday. Shoes, vaccinations and sexual guidelines. On Wednesday, they got down to the serious business of constructing their fictitious life together. What Claudia liked best was her new, untarnished past, in which she had failed to drop out of university two weeks before Finals, hadn't even been there, never met bloody Nick, but done a secretarial course after A-levels instead, and got a nice, straight nine-to-five job with the pharmaceutical company where Paul was a marketing manager. He was German, apparently, seconded from the German branch of the company in Frankfurt, special responsibility for shampoos and skin care. They had known each other for three years, gone out together for two, been married three weeks ago at a registry office somewhere, and lived chastely in adjoining rooms ever since.

Paul was a remote, humourless, but infinitely painstaking teacher. Ignoring her barbs, taunts and occasional lewd suggestions, he went over the ground until she was not just word perfect, but sure enough of her new persona to improvise as needed. Bit by bit, he moulded her into her new identity. When she forgot things he was patient, when she despaired he was encouraging. He kept her at it when she got bored and demanded a break, he refused to let up even when she knew it forwards and backwards and sideways too.

'What did you buy your fiancé, as I was then, for his fortieth birthday?'

'Oh come on, Paul, who the hell's going to ask me that?'

'What did you buy me? Think.'

'I took you out for a meal. I couldn't really afford it on my humble secretarial pittance, but forty is a big deal. So I took you to the Indian place in Twickenham, the one not far from the river, that we'd been to once or twice before. And I bought you a present too, nothing too opulent, just a little something to mark the occasion. Let's see, what did I buy you? You're German, so you probably like classical music, right? How about some Brahms? The violin concerto, say.'

'Not Mozart or Beethoven?'

'Mozart's too ordinary. Everyone has Mozart. As for Beethoven, I wouldn't buy him for anyone, simply because I don't like him much myself.'

'Fair enough.' He went back to his notes.

'So what about Brahms? Will he do, or not?'

'Brahms is one of my favourite composers. He's fine.' He looked up and grinned at her for the first time all day. 'Well done.'

'Maybe you can give me a degree in espionage to make up for the one I missed in French.'

Later that night, instead of going straight home from the harpy's red-and-white-checked restaurant, they made a detour down the rue de Miromesnil. Lights shone out of the windows of the art galleries on each side of the street, and their footsteps echoed in the cold. There was no one about. At Claudia's insistence, they were holding hands. The ghost of Caroline was hovering near and she could tell that Paul wasn't too happy with this arrangement, but he could hardly argue with her contention that their cover required it, though he did argue, and strenuously, with her use of the word 'cover'.

'I don't know what on earth you're imagining, but this isn't some kind of espionage mission we're engaged in. We're tourists, Claudia, nothing more. Please stop using that word or you'll find it slipping off your tongue in front of some Burmese official, and then we'll have some serious explaining to do.'

'I'm sorry, Paul. I don't know where that word came from.' She smiled at him demurely. 'As you said, it just slipped off my tongue. You know, it's really cold tonight. If we've only been married three weeks, don't you think you might have your arm round me at this point.'

'You should wear more clothes,' said Paul, which was unfair because she was wearing practically everything she possessed, and he knew it. It wasn't her fault if she only had the summer clothes she had taken to Italy last August, plus the cloak she had picked up for fifty francs at the flea market. When she was living with Olivier she had worn his sweaters, but he had made her leave them behind when he threw her out. Even wearing a skirt over leggings with three T-shirts wasn't enough to keep warm in this weather. She had evaluated Paul's sweaters, but rejected them on grounds of colour. One was light blue and the other was royal blue. Not quite her style. He had made her wear the light blue one to have her photo taken, announcing that black was not a suitable colour for her new persona, but she had decided to waive her claims on it thereafter.

They stopped in front of one of the art galleries that lined the street, as they had done several times already. Claudia studied the painting in the window resignedly. Daisies and sunshades and long floating dresses, some kind of pseudo-Renoir picnic. She had the feeling that Paul's mind was no more on art than hers was. Was this some kind of manoeuvre designed to reinforce their allegedly non-existent cover? As long as she wasn't going to be given a crash course in art history too. With all the facts about Burma he had been stuffing into her, she was beginning to feel like a walking history book. First the poor sods had been colonized by the British, adding sub-jewels to the crown, and then invaded by the Japanese, who were keen to get their hands on the Burma Road. In 1948, Independence gave everyone the chance to leap at each other's throats with no foreigners to get in the way. Civil war in the hinterland, inter-party squabbling in Rangoon, culminating in 1962 in the usual post-colonial lurch into totalitarianism. A general called Ne Win staged a military coup and re-directed the country on to what he called the Burmese Way to Socialism, an eccentric fusion of Buddhism and Marxism, with occasional input from the general's numerologist. In 1987 the numerologist recommended a demonetisation that wiped out most of the country's savings and led to a mass revolt against Marxist-Buddhist economic theory. Thousands of people were killed, Ne Win stepped down, and an entity called the State Law and Order Restoration Council took his place. Ne Win went on pulling the strings from behind the scenes. It was not known what happened to the numerologist.

Claudia would have preferred to hear more about Anawrahta and Kyanzittha, but it seemed the founding fathers were not essential to an understanding of present-day Burma. The new military government, which Paul referred to by the Tolkienesque acronym of SLORC, had placed the leader of the opposition under house arrest, declined to hand over power to the democratic winners of free elections, imprisoned hundreds of dissidents, and started to sell off the country's teak forests in an attempt to make ends meet. If nothing else, Burma sounded like an exciting place to go.

Paul tugged at her hand and they walked slowly onwards. After only a few steps, he stopped again. 'Look,' he said, and something in his voice told her that they had finally come to the reason for their little evening constitutional.

Hanging in the window was a tapestry worked on black velvet. Two figures fighting under a vast, spangled expanse of sky. One with his sword upraised ready to strike a final blow, the other on the ground, arm curved above his head, imploring mercy. The whole tapestry gleamed and shimmered with gold and silver thread, beads, spangles. The two figures seemed to leap out of the tapestry, and Claudia realized that they were padded with something to make them stand out. The colour and style told her immediately that it was of Eastern origin. She looked at the name of the gallery embossed in gold letters on the glass door. *Galérie Rajasthan. Paris, Londres, New York.*

'It's beautiful. Is it Indian?'

'No, it's Burmese.' He pointed to a label under the tapestry which she had failed to notice. Claudia leant forward and read, *Chroniques du Palais de Cristal des Rois de Birmanie.* The Glass Palace Chronicles of the Kings of Burma.

'Oh. It's the same as that book you have.'

'That's right. This is one of a series of tapestries based on the Glass Palace Chronicles. It was done by an artist called Min Saw. You haven't heard of him? He's quite famous these days. Well, it doesn't matter. This shows King Anawrahta duelling with his brother Sokkate. He killed his brother, took the throne in his place, and then started building pagodas to salve his conscience. It's to him that we owe Pagan.'

Claudia looked at him curiously. He was standing there, oblivious of the cold, hardly aware of her presence at his side, gaze intent on the tapestry. Clearly, there was some connection with their forthcoming trip. She waited expectantly for him to tell her what it was, but he said nothing, merely turned away with a little sigh and said, 'Let's go home.'

'Good idea. I'm freezing. Darling,' she added mischievously.

'What?'

'Darling. All the newly-weds I've ever known called each other darling.'

No answer.

'And I think you should kiss me from time to time too.'

'In the street?' The tone was detached, not even disapproving. How did one break through his mental armour, how did one get in there and find the place he lived?

'Why ever not? People do in these liberated days, haven't you noticed?'

'Not in Burma. The Burmese frown on public displays of affection.'

'They can't be much fun then,' she retorted and dropped his hand crossly. Her attempts to wean him from his sister's ghost were getting nowhere; she might as well give up. Maybe she had been wrong about him. Maybe he was a spy *and* a monk.

Back at the monastery, he handed her a plain manila envelope, which turned out to contain her passport. Here it was: tangible proof of her new identity. Not just words any more: she really was someone different. Claudia Jane Miller, rigged out in a grisly shade of blue, skulking between the unfamiliar dark-red pages of a European Community passport. Only the suspicious scowl on her face, the exact same expression she had worn for her old passport photo, reassured Claudia that it was still her.

When she had signed the passport, Paul announced that it was time to start packing. Tomorrow they were leaving for Bangkok. He had given her a canvas travelling bag to replace her old one which was splitting at the seams, and she was busy piling in her stock of leggings, T-shirts, and miscellaneous bits of cloth which always came in handy as belts or miniskirts or sarongs or something, when he came into the room and dumped another pile of clothes on the bed.

She straightened up, puzzled. 'What's all that?'

'Your clothes for the trip.'

'But I've got clothes. All my clothes are summer clothes. They'll be fine.'

'Claudia, I'm sorry, but everything you have is short, tight, backless and sleeveless. You can't dress like that in Burma.'

Too late she remembered the impassive face with which he had gone through her bag when they brought it back from the Gare du Nord, laying aside her stash of condoms with a quizzically raised eyebrow, taking out each garment and holding it up for a thoughtful, silent inspection. At the time, she had been amused. Monks didn't have to worry about things like AIDS, at least not hermits like him: was it possible that he didn't even know what they were? As for her wardrobe, she knew it was provocative. It was meant to be. If someone didn't like it, that was their problem, not hers. Only now, it slowly dawned on her, things were a little different.

'Why can't I dress like that?' she snapped. 'Are they going to put me in a pit and stone me?'

'No, but you're going to attract attention and give needless offence. Revealing, tight-fitting clothes simply have no place in their culture. I'm not trying to put you down, but I think you'll understand what I mean when we get there. Please take a look at these and see if you think they'll fit.'

Scowling, Claudia turned her attention to the pile of clothes. Two sweat-shirts, one grey, one dark green. One pair of jeans, two pairs of baggy beige trousers. One Indian cotton skirt in some kind of pink and purple pattern. A collection of T-shirts, blue, grey, pink, white, all with decorous round necks and short sleeves. One was apparently allowed to bare one's flesh from the elbow to the wrist and from the calf to the ankle. But where on earth had he come up with such a grisly assortment of colours? And then something else hit her, and she looked more closely.

'You didn't buy these clothes. They've been worn.'

'Of course they have. I borrowed them. You can't arrive in Burma with a bag full of brand new clothing. They'd think you'd come to sell it on the black market.'

'Whose are they?'

Paul hesitated. 'They belong to a friend of mine. She and her husband visited Burma a year or two ago, and this is what she took with her.'

He was watching her attentively, wondering no doubt if she was going to make a scene. Claudia took a deep breath, looked from one pile of clothes to the other, and decided to give in gracefully. As she had observed herself, for a hundred pounds a day, Paul was entitled to do what he wanted with her. She started to take her own clothes out of the bag again.

'Okay, I'll wear them. You're the boss. If you want to escort a total frump round the Far East for the next two weeks, who am I to stop you?' He was still looking uncomfortable, so on the spur of the moment she put her arms on his shoulders and kissed him on the cheek. 'Just remember, on the dot of midnight in two weeks' time, Cinderella is going to change back into a pumpkin, so just be sure you have me out of bloody Burma by then.'

On Thursday, in the plane, in the interludes between drinks and lunch and films and breakfast, the briefing continued.

'Name?'

'Claudia Miller.'

'Husband's name?'

'Paul Miller.'

'Husband's birthplace?'

'Hamburg.'

'How long have you been married?'

'Three weeks. December 15, Reigate registry office. The bride wore black,' she added before she could stop herself. It had been an old joke with Nick. They would both wear black and the organ would play the overture to The Flying Dutchman.

'Claudia!'

He was frowning at her, but she gave him the smile she always used on men when she was in a tight corner, and the frown began to melt. Today he seemed more susceptible to that kind of thing: it must be the cosseted atmosphere of business class travel, orchids and champagne and inscrutably smiling hostesses to wipe the crumbs off your table and supply endless mini-bottles of whatever you wanted to drink. So who was paying for all this, she wanted to ask him. No one travelled business class when it came out of their own pocket, so who was the sponsor for this little jaunt?

'I hope no one can hear this conversation. They might find it a little strange.'

'Aeroplanes are full of strange people.'

'That's true. You have to be weird to get into one in the first place.'

'You're not afraid of flying, are you?'

'No. You'd know about it by now if I were.'

'Mm. You don't believe in keeping your feelings to yourself, do you?'

'No, I like people to know about them. That way, if there's something they're doing wrong, they have a chance to correct it. That's fair, don't you think?'

'Of course, very fair.'

'My notions of fair play were instilled in me by my father. So if there's something not quite British about them, you know who's to blame.'

'I think you've drunk too much champagne.'

'Of course I have. And you haven't drunk enough. One should always take advantage of free champagne. There may not be any when you wake up the next morning.'

'They'll probably give you some for breakfast if you ask nicely.'

'Will they? Maybe we should take some to Burma with us too, in case they run out. I think I like you better when you've been drinking champagne. Even if it is only one glass. You're being much nicer to me than you ever were in Paris.'

'They ran out years ago,' he said, ignoring the second part

of her declaration. 'If they ever had any to begin with. You might get some Mandalay rum if you're lucky.'

'I don't know if I'm going to like Burma. I'm glad you'll be there to look after me.'

No reaction. Careful, Claudia, don't overstep the boundaries. Rule Number One, No Flirting. Right now your employer is in transit. He's finished preparing for his mission, and the mission itself hasn't yet begun. This is half-time, which is why he can afford to push his seat-back into reclining position and smile indulgently at your girlish nonsense. But let's not lose sight of the fact that, however charming and attentive he is right now, looking after you is not part of his ultimate plans. This is business, not sex, and with you rigged out in your English Lady's Tropical Kit, priorities are unlikely to change.

Claudia looked down at herself and grimaced. There was something brisk yet dainty about all those sagging jeans and ill-fitting T-shirts that was enough to make one feel quite queasy. Their owner was probably one of those trim, organized Englishwomen who went to bed in gloves and a hairnet and disapproved of emotions and loud voices. Show me what you wear and I'll tell you who you are. It was a relief that she'd been spared the underwear, which was undoubtedly sensible Marks and Spencers cotton. Idly she wondered if it was really the Burmese who didn't like to see too much flesh on view, or if it was Paul himself. Was he a monk by vocation or from circumstance? She wondered how he was going to manage when they found themselves sharing a bedroom, and grinned maliciously to herself.

'Right, let's get back to our interrogation. My turn now. Name?'

'Paul Miller.' That was the name on his passport. That meant nothing.

'Age?'

'Forty-two.' No hesitation. It sounded about right.

'Nationality?'

'German.'

'No, I mean really. Are you really German?' She still hadn't made up her mind about that. His English was word perfect, but there was that odd little intonation she had noticed when she first met him.

'Of course. That's what my passport says. Passports never lie.'

'Mine does,' Claudia pointed out.

'Well mine doesn't.'

'If you say so. Date of marriage.'

'Fifteenth December. The same as you.'

'No, not that one. The one before. The real one.'

'I'm not married, Claudia. Except to you.'

'You wear a wedding ring,' she insisted. 'A real one. Not a fake one like mine. You had it already the day you met me.'

He looked down at it and twisted it round his finger. 'I was married. She died of cancer. Six years ago.'

'I'm sorry.'

'That's all right.'

'What was her name?'

'Lucy.'

He was on the verge of retreating into his shell again. Stay with me, she wanted to cry. It gets lonely out here, all on my own. Real solitude she could handle, but not this semi-solitude, with a stranger sitting beside her coming between her and her peace of mind. It reminded her of the last days with Nick, when they had drifted so far apart that they literally had nothing left to say to each other, until finally it got so bad that one morning she packed her trunk, wrote a letter to the Dean, and went off to Lille to work as an au pair for That Awful Woman.

'Don't ask questions, Claudia,' he said softly. 'That was part of the bargain, remember?'

'I'm sorry. I'll try.'

'It's for your own safety. What you don't know, you can't tell anyone.'

'Oh? Am I going to be captured and interrogated?'

'Of course not,' said Paul irritably. 'I wish you'd stop pretending to be Mata Hari.'

'I brought my lipstick,' she informed him solemnly, but the charm was broken, he scowled exasperatedly, released her hand, and announced that he was going to get some sleep and if she had any sense she'd do the same.

'Go ahead, Adrian, the line's secure. What's the weather like in Paris?'

'Bloody cold. The forecast this weekend is for snow. Right now I wouldn't mind being where you are.'

'In Rangoon? Nonsense. No one in their right mind wants to be in Rangoon. So when's this chap of yours arriving?'

'Saturday afternoon. He's travelling on a German passport, she's got one of ours. Both in the name of Miller.'

'Miller? Don't be ridiculous, dear boy, that's an English name.'

'It's a German name too, apparently.'

'Oh is it? Well, what's his itinerary then?'

'Can't help you there, Tony, I'm afraid. Refused pointblank to tell me what he was going to do once he got there.'

'That's a bit of a pain, isn't it? If he's travelling on a tourist visa, he's not going to hang round in Rangoon. Armpit of the world, Rangoon. Everyone gets the hell out as soon as they can. Especially tourists. You ever come over while you were in Bangkok?'

'Absolutely. Jill and I spent a week there two years ago.'

'Then you know what it's like. The point is, dear boy, we're hellishly short-staffed. You should know that, for God's sake. Now as regards this chap of yours, I appreciate it could be a little tricky if we let him go racketing round on his own and the Burmese find out who he really is, but on the other hand I simply can't spare anyone to babysit him round the tourist circuit and keep him out of trouble.'

'That's what I wanted to tell you, Tony. It's all taken care of. Listen.'

Part Two

Rangoon

The flight from Bangkok to Rangoon took an hour and a half.
Three hundred and fifty miles north-west, and half a century
back in time. If not more. In some parts of the country, Paul
reflected, the peasants had probably been tilling the ground
and cultivating their crops in much the same way since the
time of Anawrahta.

The plane was full. Travellers curious for a glimpse of the
Golden Land, businessmen intent on buying up the teak
forests or the oil deposits, diplomats returning to their postings
after the Christmas holidays. Paul had kept a sharp eye open
as the passengers drifted into the departure lounge at Bangkok
airport, but he had seen no one he knew. As the plane took
off, he felt an exhilarating sense of weightlessness, of burdens
dropping away from him. For months his old life had been
hanging round his body like a cumbersome second skin: it was
a relief to shed it at last.

The plane continued to climb. From the window, Paul
could see a featureless amalgam of fields, lakes and European
style apartment buildings. Nothing he was going to regret. He
had cut himself free from the web of possessions, acquaintances and obligations that had made up his life, and there was
no going back. The plane rose higher, the ground dropped out

of sight. Something stirred in his memory, and he suddenly realized that it wasn't the first time this had happened to him. It wasn't the first time he had sat in a plane with a stranger beside him, looking down at the life he was leaving behind. Dear God, he hadn't thought of that for years. Amazing the tricks life played on one.

'What's the matter?' said Claudia.

Thirty years ago, on the flight from Hamburg to London, it had been his father sitting beside him, already immersed in Herodotus as the plane took off. This time it was a girl he had met in a bar five days earlier. A book lay open on her lap, but she wasn't reading.

'Nothing,' said Paul.

'You look weird. Are you all right?'

'I'm just tired.'

'Do we have a hotel booked in Rangoon?'

'Yes.'

'Good. I'm tired too. The honeymoon couple can retire early to bed.' She reached for his hand and closed her eyes.

Paul looked down at her with a mixture of amusement and annoyance. He had spent a great many hours wondering why he had invited Claudia along, and had reached no satisfactory conclusion. Her presence, though it would help avert suspicion, was not indispensable. As he had told her, he would be conspicuous travelling alone, but not that conspicuous. Not enough to outweigh the risk he was taking bringing her with him. He knew nothing about her, and what he was learning suggested that she would not be not easy to handle. When he told her why he had brought her to Burma, he had no idea how she would react. There was a chance that things might go very wrong indeed. Normally he was a cautious person: in a job like his you had to be. Then why take such an uncharacteristic risk?

There was no answer to that, or if there was, it was one he would not have wanted to voice out loud. Paul did not believe in fate, but this did not prevent him from harbouring the distinct impression that it was fate which had cast Claudia in his path. Adrian's check on her background had run up nothing untoward. Everything tallied, which ruled out the possibility that some third party had been giving fate a helping hand. Their meeting, in some way he couldn't explain, was meant to be.

The plane descended towards Mingaladon airport. Claudia craned curiously towards the window for her first glimpse of Burma. There was not a lot to see. Thick tufts of green foliage, half-shrouded rooftops, a complex of grey, military-looking buildings. From the air, the mystery remained intact, and the air was the only way to get into Burma. LAND ROUTE NOT PERMISSIBLE said the visa stamped in her passport, but in any case there was no land route. The famous Burma Road no longer existed, and no other roads or railway lines linked Burma with its neighbours. No legal ones, anyway. Apparently one could slash one's way through the jungle to Thailand or China, if necessary, taking one's chances with the bandits, insurgents and opium smugglers one was likely to encounter along the way. 'Enjoy your stay in this country,' said one of the Thai stewards to Claudia as she left the plane. There was a distinctly mocking undertone to his voice. Now what did that mean, she wondered.

The airport terminal was a low airless shed with a layout like an obstacle race. They checked first you, then your money, and finally your possessions. First prize for ideologically pure and financially solvent candidates: entry into the Union of Myanmar, period of stay restricted to fourteen days, single journey only. Myanmar? Claudia had demanded, when she saw the visa, what the hell's that? But it seemed they had changed the country's name from Burma to Myanmar in 1989. Hoping perhaps that if people couldn't find it, they would decide not to visit. Ne Win could have taught Joseph

Stalin a thing or two. With communications policies like that, who needed an Iron Curtain?

The immigration counter offered a choice of windows: Diplomats Only, Foreigners, Tourists, Myanmar Nationals, Myanmar Seamen. What were seamen doing at an airport? Paul headed straight for Diplomats Only, before changing course at the last minute and joining the queue for Tourists. Now that was interesting. Had he been a German diplomat in his last Burmese incarnation, or a British one? He glanced at her to see if she had noticed the slip. Claudia kept her eyes straight ahead. Ever since Bangkok, she had had the impression he was functioning on automatic pilot. What was he thinking about? The immigration officials, who seemed to outnumber the disembarking passengers, came and went and changed places and called to each other and compared every detail of the immigration form against each person's passport. Marxism-Buddhism bred suspicious minds. When it was Claudia's turn, she was seized with a sudden fit of panic. Neither the French nor the Thais in their streamlined bullet-proof boxes had worried her, but these little men buzzing round like nineteenth-century clerks scared her stiff. Her passport was too new, her name too improbable, they were going to know straightaway that she was a fake. The official went painstakingly through the crisp new pages, checking the visa they had given her in Bangkok, checking the form she had filled in on the plane, but paying little or no attention to Claudia herself. Papers were real, people less so. He stamped her passport and motioned Paul forward. Claudia watched nervously. Same performance, same uninterest, same stamp. She let out her breath in a long sigh of relief.

After that, it wasn't so bad. They changed two hundred dollars each into the local currency, which was called kyats, and Paul swore quietly to himself at the exchange rate. Another official stamped their currency forms, someone made a cursory chalk mark on their bags. They were free to leave.

Half Burma seemed to be clustered in the airport, waiting for their friends and relatives to emerge from the customs area. Paul pushed his way through the scrum towards a cluster of bright blue pick up trucks, which turned out to be taxis, and bargained authoritatively with one of the drivers over the fare into Rangoon. Oh yes, he had been here before. Claudia turned to stare at the pushing, shoving crowd that surrounded them. Men and women alike were wearing a kind of sarong-like garment that covered them from the waist to the feet. According to the guidebook, it was called a *longgyi*, and it was clearly the in thing. There wasn't a skirt or a pair of trousers in sight. Paul came to an agreement with the taxi-driver and gestured to her to get in. The pick up had two narrow bench seats facing each other. There was just enough room for them and their luggage.

The road into town led through a green, prosperous-looking suburb into an urban shopping area with incomprehensible advertising posters in the graceful, curving Burmese script. At first sight, Rangoon was leafy and open and less repressive than Claudia had expected. On this pleasant Saturday afternoon, there were no soldiers on street corners, no roadblocks, no anguished faces peering out of the backs of police vans. After the black January chill of Paris, the air was soft and warm and slightly damp. The taxi stopped three times for the driver to put water in the radiator. Other cars over-took, honking noisily, and the drivers yelled at each other, but whether in greeting or imprecation it was impossible to tell. A quiet, slightly run-down tropical city. And then suddenly at a busy intersection, she caught sight of a large sign, written in white letters on a dark red background. THE TATMADAW SHALL NEVER BETRAY THE NATIONAL CAUSE, it said, in both English and Burmese, because this was plainly something that foreigners needed to know about too.

'What's the Tatmadaw?' said Claudia.

'The army.'

'And what's the national cause?'

'Unity. The minorities want a federated state, not a union. This is a way of telling them that they aren't going to get it.'

'Subtle,' said Claudia.

The hotel was built on the edge of a lake and possessed a creaking colonial charm. A long terrace with low tables and cane chairs overlooked the lake, and green-roofed bungalows stood in well-kept grounds. Giant philodendrons drooped over the water and geese cawed in the distance. It used, said Paul, to be the premises of the Orient Boat Club. Their room, damp and vast, lay at the end of a long dark corridor. The clerk at the reception desk had described it as a suite, and sure enough there were four fake leather armchairs grouped round a rickety bamboo table and a fridge-freezer humming away in the corner. A damp patch the shape of South America decorated the ceiling. A lizard, disturbed by their arrival, ran down the wall and disappeared into the floor. Paul presented the boy who had shown them to their room with a disposable lighter. Claudia sat down on one of the twin beds and gazed around her, reassured, despite the lizard, by this semblance of Western comfort. After the airport, she wouldn't have been surprised to discover that she was expected to sleep on a mat on the floor.

'You look exhausted,' said Paul. There had been two messages waiting for him at the reception desk. He read them through and put them carefully in his pocket.

'Yes. I guess I am a bit.' She realized that the room was spinning slightly.

'Why don't you sleep for a while?'

'You don't want to go out or anything?'

'No. I'm going to take a shower.'

'Maybe I will, then, if you don't mind.' She swung her feet up on the bed and lay down. Her legs and arms felt as heavy as lead. When Paul came out of the bathroom fifteen minutes later, she was fast asleep. He put a couple of things into a small canvas backpack and tiptoed silently out of the room.

Rebecca was expecting him. She opened the door with a greeting on her lips, and then her smile died, she broke off in mid-sentence and started to apologize. Paul began to laugh. She stopped, hesitated, stared at him more closely.

'Philip! Paul, I mean. It is you! I don't believe it! What on earth have you done to yourself? Come upstairs and let me look at you.' She hustled him upstairs to the first-floor sitting room and stood him under the light and inspected him thoroughly and declared that she would never have believed it. Even though he knew from experience that Rebecca was not the most perspicacious of observers, Paul was gratified. Ninety percent of the world's population was not particularly perspicacious either. None of the immigration officials had looked twice at him. It seemed that his disguise had a good chance of holding up.

After the chaos of the airport and the run-down minimal-ism of the Kandawgi, Rebecca's house was an oasis. White walls, wooden floors, a lot of open space. Lacquer chests, wicker chairs, low tables. Tropical furniture to lounge away the heat of the day. White curtains of some thin, gauzy material separated the sitting room from the verandah that overlooked the garden. A cool night breeze blew in, making the curtains billow and the candles flutter. Paul sat down and looked around. Since he had left Rangoon ten months earlier, nothing had changed.

Or had it? Rebecca was fussing around plumping up cushions, turning on lights, making a great to-do with ice cubes in a lacquer bowl. Not her usual style at all. His attention sharpened. The room was full of doorways leading out to the rest of the flat, and the outer rooms were all in dark-ness. She poured them both a sizeable measure of scotch, sat down next to him, and put a hand possessively on his knee.

'So, darling, tell me all about it. Such a lovely surprise. What's going on? What are you doing here?'

It was the perfect opening. Now was the time to tell her why he had come, and request her help.

'I had some leave to take.' Paul watched her carefully. 'I thought it would be a good idea to come back here and travel round a bit. See things I never had time to see before.'

'You've come all this way disguised as a German tourist just for the pleasure of climbing up Mandalay Hill?' said Rebecca derisively. 'Come on, darling, tell me the truth!'

He smiled at her blandly. 'There's a nice view from up there.'

'So there is. I'll tell you what, I've got a bit of leave due, why don't I come with you for a few days? It might be fun, don't you think?' Paul shook his head. 'No? You don't want me finding out all your little secrets? Not even if I promise not to tell?'

'I'm afraid I already have a travelling companion.'

Rebecca's eyes opened wide. 'You do? Who?'

'A friend.'

'Really? Oh. Why on earth didn't you tell me? Did the Kandawgi have another room?'

'We're sleeping in the same room. I didn't mention her before because it wasn't clear till the last minute whether she was actually coming or not.'

'She? Oh.' Rebecca's eyes opened wider. 'How exciting. Anyone I know?'

'No.'

'Where is she? Why didn't you bring her with you?'

'She was tired from the trip. She went to bed as soon as we got in.'

Rebecca shook her head disapprovingly. 'She's going to wake up at three in the morning. You shouldn't have let her do it.'

'She insisted.'

'Well, never mind. I'll tell you what. Why don't you both come to lunch tomorrow instead? I'm having a few people over.'

Paul strained his ears, but there was no sound from any of the darkened inner rooms, only the low murmur of the wind in the trees outside. He screwed his face up doubtfully and pretended to hesitate.

'A stray German tourist going to lunch with the British ambassador's secretary? I don't know if that's a good idea.'

'Nonsense, darling,' said Rebecca briskly. 'How are you going to justify coming here tonight? Assuming that anyone cares enough to ask?'

Paul reached into the Bangkok airport carrier bag he had brought with him, took out a small package and handed it to her.

'What's this? Oh no! Lemon curd! Darling, how sweet of you to remember!'

She leaned over and kissed him on the cheek.

'That's not from me. That's from your brother in London. He's a colleague of mine, you see. We work together at Capa-Derrick Pharmaceuticals. He asked me to bring you this when he heard I was coming out here.'

For a moment or two Rebecca sat absolutely still. Then she gave a strained little laugh.

'My God, you certainly do your homework well. How did you know Jeremy had moved to Capa-Derrick? All right, don't answer. Anyway, it solves our little problem. You came over here to give me the present from my brother, and I, in gratitude, invite you and your girlfriend to come to lunch the following day. No, darling, don't argue. I absolutely insist.'

Paul eyed her reflectively. Maybe it would be as well to play along with them and find out what they thought they had in store for him.

'Who's going to be there?'

'No one you know. There's been a lot of movement this

past year. Julian left not long after you, and Sam got posted to Venezuela last month. It's all new people coming tomorrow. None of them will have any idea who you are.'

'You're sure of that?'

'Darling, I know who I've invited to lunch, for heaven's sake! That's settled then. I'll expect you at half-past twelve. And don't forget to bring your girlfriend this time.'

'Actually, Rebecca, she's not my girlfriend.'

'Oh she's not? What is she then?'

'My wife.'

Rebecca's eyes widened in incredulity. 'What? You've got married again? I don't believe it!'

Paul hesitated. The flat was silent. There was no point trying to hide it from Rebecca: she knew him too well. 'Not exactly,' he said reluctantly. 'Let me explain.'

Paul left half an hour later. Rebecca accompanied him as far as the path that led to the main road, kissed him goodnight in a way that was quite like old times, and walked rapidly back to the house. As soon as he heard the front door slam, Paul doubled back on his tracks. He stationed himself in the shadow of the verandah. Above him, the sitting room windows were wide open. He heard a soft ping and a series of clicks as Rebecca picked up the phone and dialled a number. Not what he had thought. The listener was not in one of the darkened rooms upstairs, but at the other end of a telephone line.

'Tony? Sorry to call so late. He only just left ... Yes, all arranged. Lunch tomorrow. There's just one problem. He's not here on his own ... Oh, you knew that already ... All right, yes, tomorrow morning ... No, darling, he wouldn't tell me a word about it. He claimed it was just a holiday. You'll just have to ask him yourself, won't you? ... Goodnight, Tony.'

Paul stole silently round the corner of the house back to the road. So he was right. Lunch was a set up. He didn't know who Tony was, but he could guess. He sighed in exasperation. Three hours in Burma, and things were already going wrong. He thought he had taken adequate precautions, choosing Paris rather than London as a base to prepare for the trip, telling no one of his destination but Adrian and Rebecca. Unfortunately, he seemed to have confided in the wrong people. If Tony knew he was not travelling alone, there was only one person who could have told him that. God damn all brothers-in-law.

When Claudia awoke, the sun was rising over the lake. She got out of bed, pulled back the curtains and watched for a while. Paul was still asleep. She wondered what time he had gone to bed. A flock of geese flew high into the faint pink sky. From the window she could see on to the terrace. There was no one about. The pink light faded, the sky clouded over, and it was almost cold. Claudia shivered and turned back into the room. What on earth had possessed her to come halfway round the world with this silent, sleeping stranger? Paul was lying with his back to her on the far side of his bed. There was room for her to slide in beside him: she wondered what would happen if she did. Probably he would wake up – he was too edgy to be anything other than a light sleeper – and it was unlikely that he would be pleased. Or even understanding. Human warmth was not part of their contract. She glanced at her watch. Twenty past six. She sighed and crawled back between her own chilly sheets.

Ten minutes later, she got up again. She had slept for thirteen hours and she was wide awake. What's more, she was starving. Paul appeared to be dead to the world. She would get dressed, take a look around and see if she could get something to eat.

Breakfast was served on the terrace overlooking the lake. Eggs, coffee, toast and weak fruit squash. At this early hour, only one other table was occupied: by a middle-aged

Westerner with a substantial stomach and a bushy beard. He gave her a brief nod, and concentrated on his breakfast. Claudia did the same. Not until they were both on their second cups of coffee, did their eyes meet again.

'Hi, there,' said the man expansively.

'Hi,' said Claudia.

'Haven't seen you before, have I? You just get in yesterday?' American, judging by the accent. Claudia eyed him more carefully. Something about him suggested that he wasn't a tourist, but with his rumpled khaki trousers and washed-out blue T-shirt, he didn't look like a businessman either.

'Last night. And you?'

'Oh, I've been here a while,' said the American obliquely. 'You travelling alone?'

'No, I'm with my husband, but he's still asleep.'

'Uh huh. First time in Burma?'

'Yes. I gather it's called Myanmar, though, these days.'

The American snorted derisively. 'You don't want to take any notice of that,' he advised her, though he looked around to make sure none of the waiters were in earshot, before continuing in a lower tone. 'That's for internal consumption only. A shot across the bows of the ethnic minorities.' He broke off and gave her a dubious look. 'You know about the ethnic minorities, do you?'

'Of course,' said Claudia. 'The Karens, the Kachins and the Shans.'

'That's right. You know where the word Myanmar comes from? It's the ethnic Burman name for Burma. Minorities don't like it. Can't blame 'em, can you? As for the rest of the world, they've hardly heard of Burma to begin with, how can you expect them to remember the place is now called Myanmar? They know that,' he added, referring presumably to the instigators of the name change.

'Oh I see.'

'Anyway,' he glanced at his watch and rose to his feet, 'gotta go. Time and tide wait for no man. Nice talking to you.'

He picked up his room key and left the restaurant with a long, lithe stride. So what, Claudia wondered, was so urgent at half past seven on a Sunday morning in Rangoon?

She finished her coffee and wandered back to the bedroom. Paul was shaved and dressed and rearranging the contents of his travelling bag. Doing complicated things with string and paper clips, no doubt, as laid down in the Spies' Manual, to make sure no one could search his stuff without his noticing. He glanced up as she came in, and she noticed that he wasn't wearing his spectacles.

'Where've you been?'

'I went to get breakfast. I hope you don't mind. I was starving.'

'It might be better if we had breakfast together in future. If you remember, we haven't been married very long.'

He sounded like a businessman reminding his secretary to put copies of correspondence in the chrono file. Claudia didn't answer. The spectacles were lying on the bedside table, and he didn't seem to have any problems seeing without them.

'Did you sleep all right?' he inquired, working down his checklist.

'Yes thank you.' And where were you when I woke up all on my own in the dark at ten o'clock? Mightn't it be better if the newly-weds went night-clubbing together?

'Good.' He ran his eyes over her thoughtfully. She was wearing baggy trousers and a grey sweatshirt. 'There was a skirt with the clothes I gave you, wasn't there? It might be better if you wore that today.'

'Why? Are we going to church?'

'No. Today we're going to lunch with an old friend of mine.'

The man was there again today. Jürgen could see him from the window of his room, squatting in the dust on the other side of the road. It was the same man who had followed him from the station to the hotel. He wore the same red and green checked longgyi as yesterday and his face was set in the same patient stare. He hadn't moved for an hour. Oblivious of the noise and shoving of the crowds around him, his jaw revolved in a rhythmic chewing motion and his gaze stayed fixed on the entrance to the hotel. As Jürgen watched, he spat a stream of betel juice into the dust.

How had they found out about him? Had they been asking questions at the monastery? Had someone been with him in the train all the way from Mandalay?

He glanced at his watch for the third time in ten minutes. Quarter to twelve. He was due to meet Philip at the Shwedagon at five. He had planned to stay here in the comparative safety of the hotel all day, but the dingy little room was getting on his nerves, with the noise of the traffic outside and the man in the red and green longgyi never moving from his post by the opposite kerb. He had tried to pray, tried to meditate, tried reciting the Triratna, but to no avail. *I take refuge in the Buddha. I take refuge in the Dharma. I take refuge in the Sangha.* Everything he had learned in the monastery had vanished and all his Western fears and uncertainties had come flooding back.

Abruptly he got to his feet. He would go to the Shwedagon now and spend the afternoon praying. A monk, a holy man, absorbed in his devotions at one of the shrines of the pagoda – they wouldn't dare to touch him. He considered leaving the package for Philip hidden somewhere in the room, but decided that there was nothing to stop them getting in and searching the place as soon as he had left. He thrust the parcel carefully into the concealing folds of his robe and opened the door to the corridor.

Lunch was not a meal, but a full-scale ambush. Mind you, thought Claudia grimly, she should have expected it. Who but the British would invite one to Sunday lunch? While the Burmese took their children to the Zoo and the Aquarium and the Shwedagon, and rode across the lake in front of the hotel in curious yellow excursion boats with carved roofs, the British congregated in each other's houses and drank duty-free scotch and waited for a slave to appear with roast beef and Yorkshire pudding. Burma had been independent for over forty years, but the colonial ghetto endured.

They were sitting on wicker chairs in Rebecca's airy first-floor sitting room: Paul, Claudia, Rebecca, Franco, Veronica and Tony. It was the first time Claudia had found herself in the company of so many English people for months, and it was giving her claustrophobia. On the Moroccan brass tray that served as a coffee table stood a bottle of Johnnie Walker – the very one, she was prepared to swear, that Paul had purchased in Bangkok airport yesterday. But he hadn't had it with him when they left the hotel. He had put his sweater and his camera and a few other odds and ends in a small backpack, but no bottle. *Ergo*, he must have given it to Rebecca beforehand. *Ergo*, this was where he had been last night. No wonder he had been so anxious for her to go to sleep. When Rebecca opened the door to them, there had been none of the exclamations and questions one might expect from old friends meeting after a long separation, merely a self-assured kiss on the cheek from him and a perfumed murmur of Darling from her. Rebecca had shoulder-length dark hair and green eyes. Her yellow linen dress curved in a perfect line from shoulder to hem. So Paul wasn't a monk after all. On the whole, Claudia found this reassuring.

She took a gulp of whisky and surveyed the illicit couple covertly. It was an interesting situation. Rebecca trying rather unsuccessfully to keep her hands off her alleged old friend. Paul trying to play the enamoured bridegroom with his fictitious wife while maintaining an air of affectionate discretion towards the long-lost lover he was creeping out to fuck in the middle of the night. Claudia herself trying to look the picture of honeymoon bliss and being fucked by nobody. She felt a faint flicker of resentment, and immediately quelled it. If her employer preferred to keep business separate from pleasure, that was entirely his privilege. For God's sake, he wasn't even her type.

Nor, unfortunately, were either of the other male guests present. Tony, Rebecca's colleague from the Embassy, was tall and pale with the idle, superior look of the professional diplomat, and Franco was an archaeologist doing something or other to the temples at Pagan. He was Italian, which, as far as Claudia was concerned, placed him sexually off-limits. His hooded, hungry eyes kept wandering in her direction and roving thoughtfully over her body. Plainly he didn't share her scruples. His English wife, Veronica, was one of those determined, dowdy-blonde Englishwomen who had beaten life into submission. She smoothed her skirt over her knees and feigned not to notice her husband's interest in Claudia.

'So which part of Germany are you from, Paul?' inquired Tony.

'Hamburg, originally, but since ten years I have been living in England.'

'Ah, then that's where you met Claudia,' said Tony, and Paul agreed, and trotted out their marital legend in fluent but accented English, using just the right amount of Germanic syntax. Claudia listened admiringly. Clearly he had played this game before. He reached the culminating point of their storybook romance and shot her a tender, exclusive, totally unexpected smile across the table. Rebecca's lips pursed thoughtfully. Claudia did her best to stop her jaw dropping. She hadn't realized he knew how to smile at people like that. Maybe he had practised on his wife in days gone by.

Someone asked where they were planning to go during their stay in Burma.

'Claudia wants to go to Pagan,' said Paul, giving her that

besotted smile again. 'Perhaps we shall go there first.' He had put his spectacles back on before they left: it was amazing how they changed his face. She wondered idly if his hair was normally as blond as that.

'Good,' said Franco, speaking directly to Claudia, 'then we see you there. I show you round the most interesting temples myself. We drive back tomorrow. If you like, we give you a lift.'

'Gosh,' said Rebecca, 'now there's an offer you can't refuse. Better than waiting three days to get a seat on the plane.'

'Safer too,' said Tony. 'The lads at Myanmar Airways get their security training from Aeroflot, I've heard.'

They all looked expectantly at Paul. He smiled and shook his head. 'That's very kind, but for us tomorrow is a bit early. We haven't yet had the chance to visit Rangoon. But thank you all the same.'

'Well,' said Tony, 'if you change your mind, all you have to do is let Franco know. Right, Franco?'

'I hope you will,' said Franco, staring straight at Claudia.

There was a pause, Rebecca and Tony exchanged glances, and then Tony launched into a disquisition on the state of the Burmese economy, which had, he explained, been going from bad to worse since 1988. The country was in desperate need of hard currency—

'To buy arms from China to shoot more demonstrators?' said Franco, smiling at Claudia. 'But, Tony, if they need money, surely all they must do is produce a little more heroin? I hear you get extremely good rate on the world market. Even the Colombians plant opium these days.'

There was a strained silence.

'Well it could be a handy little solution,' said Tony languidly. 'Trouble is, of course, that it's not the government which controls opium production, it's the insurgents. The MTA. Khun Sa and his merry men.'

'Khun Sa?' said Franco incredulously. 'Khun *Sa*? My

goodness, Tony, is not surprising you British lose your empire with information like that.'

'Oh, shut up, Franco, do,' said Veronica, but her husband's eyes were riveted on Claudia.

'Don't you know that Khun Sa visit Rangoon himself in person just a year or two ago? And of course Burmese military officers are dropping in at his headquarters in the jungle for years.'

'Nonsense, dear boy,' said Tony irritably. 'Where on earth did you hear that?'

'But is nothing to worry about. If SLORC working hand-in-glove with Khun Sa, is only because they trying to enrich their country. They have their people's welfare at heart. They are good Buddhists, and they know that if they don't do something nice for the people, they all come back as cockroaches in the next life.'

Claudia was the only one to laugh. Downstairs the bell rang and Rebecca got up to answer it.

'Who else is coming?' said Veronica, glaring at her husband.

'Don't quite know,' said Tony. 'All kinds of people, by the sound of it. Charles and Andrea. Ralph and Jennifer. Rebecca's American chap from the DEA, I suppose. And that Burmese artist, the one who does the tapestries, I gather he's coming too. Quite a heterogeneous little gathering, really.'

The hotel had only one exit, and it was impossible to slip out unnoticed. As soon as Jürgen appeared, the man across the street stood up, spat out his betel, and retied his *longgyi* with a businesslike air. *I take refuge in the Buddha. I take refuge in the Dharma.* Jürgen glanced down the street with what he hoped was a casual air. Twenty yards away, another man was getting to his feet. There were two of them now. His heart gave a sudden leap of fear. All Philip had asked for was information. What on earth had possessed him to lumber himself with the package? He should never have got himself mixed up in this.

He forced himself to be calm. They were watching him, that was all. If they had anything else in mind, they would have confronted him hours ago. The regime was trying to clean up its image. They were building hotels for foreign tourists, signing ceasefires with the insurgents, releasing a few of the more harmless political prisoners. They wanted to get themselves re-admitted into the community of nations and earn some hard cash. They wouldn't risk a scene with a foreign monk in the middle of Rangoon. Jürgen shut them out of his mind. *I take refuge in the Sangha.* Muttering the words aloud, over and over, he began to walk with long strides in the direction of the Shwedagon.

Lunch was in buffet form: a rather eclectic mixture of Chinese, European and Indian cuisine. Claudia was relieved: at least she wouldn't have to sit between two of Her Majesty's creeps and make polite conversation. She helped herself to tandoori chicken and sausage rolls, and stationed herself in a corner with her back to the wall. More guests had arrived, Cultural Secretaries, Second Secretaries, Fifteenth Secretaries, and the like, and the group around the coffee table had split up and re-formed on gender lines, the better to get to grips with serious conversational issues. The men were discussing the Test match and the women were focusing on lacquer cabinets. Paul had joined the Test match discussion, though it was unclear what a German could contribute to that without engaging in a serious breach of cover. Rebecca, dark and glamorous in her yellow dress, was going from group to group, fussing with the food and looking at her watch.

'Well, Claudia, how do you like Burma?'

She turned to find Franco standing beside her. Surprise, surprise.

'I don't know yet. We only got here last night. So far it's not what I expected.'

'What you expect?' His English was good, but the lazy syntax reminded Claudia of her father.

'Much more of a state of emergency. Curfews, tanks, machine-guns. But it all seems very quiet.'

'That's because it Marxist-Buddhist state of emergency. Curfew in Burma is not necessary. There's nothing to do at night, so people go to bed. Tourists, dissidents, democrats and Tatmadaw, all in bed at nine o'clock. No problem.'

'What about the civil war?' said Claudia, catching the tone of the conversation. 'Do they stop fighting at nine o'clock every evening too?'

'Oh no, much earlier than that. It gets dark at six here. You can't fight in the dark, you know.' He leaned closer towards her and sank his voice to a stage whisper. 'I hear a rumour they going to use floodlights, like football pitches, you know, but I don't believe this myself. Already in Mandalay, the power go off for most of the day, so . . . I think this is just government propaganda to frighten the insurgents and cheer up the foreign investors.'

He shrugged. Claudia laughed. Rebecca, on her way to answer the doorbell, gave them a speculative look.

'They're looking for foreign investors, are they? Well I hope they start by investing in the hotels. We shared a room with a lizard last night.'

'This normal. The lizards put there on purpose to please the tourists. Local colour, you know. Some of high-class establishments use scorpions too. In the shower mainly.'

Claudia shuddered. 'As long as they aren't in the beds.'

Rebecca reappeared with a plump little Burmese man in a checked *longgyi* and a Lacoste polo shirt. 'So glad you were able to come,' she was saying. 'Let me see, you know Franco already, don't you? And this is Claudia . . . er . . . Miller who's just here on a visit. You've heard of U Min Saw, of course,

Claudia? Tony Mansell from the Embassy . . .' The presentation line moved on. Claudia and Franco were left alone. Franco moved a little closer. Claudia glanced nervously round, just in time to see Paul abandon the cricketers and disappear through one of the doorways leading out of the room.

'What about the political repression?' she asked brightly. 'Won't that deter the foreign investors?'

'No, because political repression in Burma is finished. Tatmadaw has converted to capitalism. They stop using military trucks to take dissidents to prison, instead they use them to transport heroin. Is more profitable, you see. Tatmadaw is very pragmatic organization.'

'I see.'

'The country very poor, and they anxious that their people have a nice life. Is that not magnificent? Tell me, Claudia, where else you find such a humanitarian, democratic and caring regime? Give me one example!'

He put a hand beseechingly on her arm. Claudia took a step back, and found herself trapped between the wall and the table.

'Colombia?' she suggested, but Franco wasn't listening any more.

'Where you staying in Rangoon?'

Claudia eyed him cautiously. 'I can't remember.'

'You don't know?'

'I'm finding all these Burmese names a bit hard to handle.'

'You're not German, are you? You don't have any German accent.'

'No, I'm English.'

'Really? You don't look it. It's rare to see an English person as dark as you. You're so dark you could almost be Italian. Such beautiful dark hair.' He reached out and picked up a few strands and let them slide slowly between his fingers.

'Franco!' came his wife's voice from across the room. 'Got a minute?'

'Coming,' he called over his shoulder, and turned back to Claudia. 'Don't go away. I come right back.'

But it was clear from the proprietorial way that Veronica took his arm and drew him into the discussion that he was going to find himself under marital custody for some time to come. Claudia turned her attention to the food cooling on her plate. Paul had not reappeared. Rebecca had finished her introductions and was leading Min Saw over to the buffet. His name sounded vaguely familiar, but Claudia couldn't think where she had heard it before. Tony had posted himself on the far side of the room. Although he was ostensibly observing the festive throng, his eyes kept wandering in Claudia's direction in a distinctly predatory fashion. Jesus, not another one! Where was her bloody bridegroom? If he was as concerned about his cover as he claimed to be, he would be by her side keeping all these sex-starved colonizers at bay. Claudia finished her plate and headed cautiously back to the buffet for a second helping, keeping well away from Tony and giving a wide berth to the group of wives in their flower-print dresses and white sandals.

'. . . of course, as a diplomatic wife, one has to learn to put up with anything . . .'

'. . . but Burma does rather take the biscuit . . .'

'. . . pity because the people are charming . . .'

'Thank God for the diplomatic bag! We take turns, you know, Veronica, every week someone has to go to Bangkok with the bag . . .'

'. . . I can tell you there's a lot of competition . . .'

'. . . not always very dignified, unfortunately . . .'

'. . . after three months in Rangoon, Bangkok feels like the Promised Land. A hotel with air conditioning and a shower that works . . .'

Claudia refilled her plate and drifted back to her corner. On the way, her eye was caught by a large tapestry hanging on the wall, and she paused to examine it. The style was similar to the one Paul had showed her in Paris: Rebecca must have bought it here.

'That is Death of Anawrahta, madam,' said a voice behind her, and she turned to find Min Saw looking at the tapestry too. Most of the Burmese she had seen so far were short and skinny: this man was short too, but far from thin. His *longgyi* strained over a capacious stomach, and his elegant Lacoste shirt seemed in imminent danger of bursting.

'Yes? So it is Burmese?'

'Of course.' He looked slightly offended. 'It is my *kalaga*.'

'Yours?' said Claudia, baffled. 'It was you who did this?' He was looking more and more put out. Suddenly remembering where she had heard his name before, she pulled herself together. 'I'm sorry, Rebecca didn't explain properly, I didn't realize who you were.' She had a stroke of inspiration. 'Is this from the Glass Palace Chronicles too?'

'*In the time of his death,*' recited Min Saw, '*bees clustered at the door of the throne, an ogre sneered on the threshhold of the Tharaba gate, the royal sabre lost its shine, a vulture alighted on the palace.*'

Claudia looked at the tapestry more closely: the details were all there. The prostrate figure of the dead king, the bees, the ogre, the sabre and the vulture.

'I saw one of your tapestries in Paris,' she told him. 'In the Rajasthan Gallery. I must say, I think they're absolutely wonderful. It's so exciting to meet you in person. I wish I'd realized who you were before.'

There was nothing like a little social gushing to get one out of a tight corner: he perked up at once, asked which of the *kalagas*, as he called them, she had seen in Paris, and informed her that his tapestries were exhibited all over the world.

'I have exclusive contract with Rajasthan Gallery. In Paris, London and New York, and I travel very often to these beautiful cities. Besides also to Geneva, Madrid, Chicago and Boston.'

Claudia blinked. 'I didn't realize it was so easy for Burmese to travel abroad.'

'Indeed, for ordinary people, not easy. That is so. But me, I earn very much money, and my tapestries are very well known. Because of me, Burma is very well known too. So to me, government gives passport. It is no problem. Look.' He groped round the side of the sofa, picked up an expensive-looking attaché case, and produced a wad of photos. 'Here is picture of me in New York. You know Statue of Liberty?'

'I've heard of it,' said Claudia.

'These are American persons, husband and wife, very excellent friends of mine. They own Rajasthan Gallery on East Seventy-second Street.'

'Gosh,' said Claudia. 'So they took you to see the Statue of Liberty?' A flash of yellow swung through the edge of her vision. Rebecca had gone to join Paul in the kitchen. Shit. Min Saw worked his way through the Eiffel Tower, London Bridge and Lake Geneva. Outside Burma, he wore a Western business suit and an air of complacency. Claudia began to run out of appreciative remarks. To her relief, one of the wives drifted up to stand on Min Saw's other side. The one called Andrea, as far as she could remember. Claudia kept a vigilant eye on the kitchen door. No one went in or out: no movements were discernible from within.

'No two tapestries are the same,' Min Saw was saying. 'I obey always my creative impulses. Maybe I do four, five times death scene of Anawrahta, but always different. This is firm principle with me.'

'Is all your work based on the Glass Palace Chronicles?' said Claudia.

'Yes, all. I am Burmese patriot, madam. My country is very dear to me. My tapestries based on Chronicles are national treasure.'

'It's so important for the artist to have a personal cultural tradition on which to draw, isn't it?' said Andrea. 'One might even say that it's essential for a creative artist to be able to live and work in their own country.'

'Many fine people offer me to go and live abroad. London, New York, Geneva, every people there implores me to stay. But always I return to our Burma. In London and New York I can make much money, very great deal of money, but roots of my art are here. Here in our Burma is where I must work.'

'I know exactly how you feel,' said Andrea. 'I'm writing a novel, you know, and it's frightfully hard sitting here in Burma trying to write about Putney. One's artistic inspiration just doesn't function the same way in a foreign country.'

She tilted her face expectantly towards Min Saw with a complicitous artist-to-artist smile. For several seconds, Min Saw said nothing. Andrea's smile began to acquire a desperate edge. A small frown of puzzlement crossed Min Saw's brow, and then he said,

'I also am writer, madam. I write five articles. One of them I write even in English. Unfortunately I do not have them here today, or I am pleased to show you. If you come one day to my workshop in Mandalay, then I show you. Today, unfortunately, is not possible. I am so very sorry.'

The crowds ebbed and swirled round the wide marble terrace of the Shwedagon, and the immense golden dome of Burma's most sacred pagoda soared majestically into the sky. Jürgen knelt before one of the shrines and pretended to pray. It had been a mistake to leave the hotel. Out here, on the open terrace, he felt unbearably exposed. According to his teacher in the monastery, the best way to cope with the trials of daily life was to cultivate a calm and balanced mind. But how could he be calm when the men were right behind him, watching him? He tried to get a grip on himself. When meditation failed, it was because of mental impurities. He had to be patient, he had to persevere ... There were even more of them now. He could sense their presence, and he had caught glimpses of them out of the corner of his eye. There were at least four of them waiting a few yards away to move in and seize him.

What were they waiting for? For him to finish praying? For some kind of official signal? For the night to fall and the shrine to empty of people?

A group of monks in robes identical to his own approached, moving through the idle throngs on the terrace with a purposeful gait. Abruptly, Jürgen reached a decision.

He got to his feet and merged into the group as it went past. They made for the South Staircase and descended the steps to the street at a brisk pace. Behind him, he sensed that the watchers had been thrown into confusion. From the front, his European features gave him away, but from the back he knew it was impossible to tell him apart from the other monks. He heard shouting at the top of the staircase, but there were too many people on the steps for the policemen to push their way through the mob and catch up with the monks before they reached the bottom. At the foot of the staircase, the group split up and the monks went their separate ways. Jürgen felt a sudden surge of confidence. God was with him. With luck, he would have gained the few precious minutes he needed to get back to the hotel and dispose of the sachets before they came to arrest him.

When he reached the door of the hotel, there was no one in sight. He went straight up to the first floor and down the corridor to the evil-smelling toilet at the far end. But the door was locked. He shook it desperately and an angry mumbling emerged from inside. What was he going to do now? He looked nervously down the corridor. Still empty. He had to get out of sight. He went inside his room, relocked the door and walked over to the window. They were just arriving in front of the hotel. As he had thought, there were four of them now. Two remained on the pavement and the other two marched purposefully inside.

They would have to talk to the desk clerk and find out the number of his room. He had two minutes at most before they came to find him. He looked desperately around. The room had no washbasin and no toilet. There was no possible place to hide the sachets. That left only one solution. He pulled the sachets out of their newspaper wrapping and put them in a pile on the bed. Then he picked up the bottle of mineral water on the bedside table.

When the policemen knocked on the door of his room two and a half minutes later, Jürgen was sitting calmly on the bed waiting for them.

Paul leant against Rebecca's kitchen counter and stared irritably at the wall. Why had he been stupid enough to accept her invitation to lunch? He had known he was being set up, and he had walked right into it. And now he was trapped. The Embassy babysitters were out in force. A whole army of chauffeurs and bodyguards had been mobilized to keep him out of trouble. If he stayed in Rangoon, they would summon up someone to show him the sights, if he said he was going to Mandalay they would wave their wands and produce someone who just happened to be going to Mandalay too. Why couldn't Adrian have kept his goddamned mouth shut?

The voices from the other room rose in a crescendo. What on earth was he doing here? For months, people had bored him to the extent that it had been an effort to talk to them. What had possessed him to come to a party, of all things? He opened the door a crack and looked out. His fellow guests were having the time of their lives. The buffet had been demolished, most of the bottles were empty, and they were well into the usual conversational staples: Embassy routine, Ministry directives, news from England. Exactly what he had wanted to get away from. And there was Min Saw too, still standing in front of the *kalaga* he had sold Rebecca two years ago, talking to Claudia and another woman. From time to time, he stole a thoughtful sideways glance at his own creation. Paul shuddered. He should have known Rebecca would manage to overlook some undesirable on the guest list. Thank God he had resisted the temptation to confide in her last night.

Shifting position, he caught sight of Tony, standing slightly apart from the rest, eyes darting back and forth over the merry throng in a way Paul recognized immediately. The professional's look. Even without last night's telephone call, he would have known at once who this was. The odd thing was that Tony had made no attempt to approach him. Judging by what he had heard last night, this lunch party had been set up for the express purpose of bringing him and Tony together. But if Tony was so interested in his movements, why wasn't he trying to find out more about them? Tony's gaze had stopped roving and fixed on something on the other side of the room. His eyes narrowed: the hunter intent on his prey. Paul craned to see what had attracted his attention. With a slight shock, he realized that Tony was staring straight at Claudia.

Rebecca came in and shut the door behind her.

'Darling, there are so many people drinking in the master's pearls of artistic wisdom that he really isn't going to notice one defaulting client at the other end of the room.'

'Can't be sure of that,' said Paul.

'Nonsense. He's so wrapped up in himself, he never recognizes anybody. I've introduced Tony to him three times already. And even if he does, what does it matter? So you ordered a *kalaga* and you didn't collect it and you didn't pay for it, so what? Probably happens all the time. He'll have sold it to someone else by now, don't worry.'

'It's embarrassing, that's all.'

'Don't be silly, darling. You can't lurk in here all afternoon. People are going to wonder what's going on.'

Paul restrained a wry smile. One thing he was sure of: the people out there were not taking the slightest interest in him and his activities. His new identity made certain of that. As far as they knew, he was a German businessman who had lived for ten years in London and married an English girl. Not a complete social castaway, not beyond the reach of second-order conversational topics like European union and the American elections, but shut out definitively from matters of burning concern such as the batting order for the Third Test. Of course, you Germans don't play cricket, someone had said. Although not ill-meaning, the phrase had stayed with him. You Germans. He was on the outside now, looking in. It was what he had wanted and it was what he had got.

But it was no use trying to tell any of this to Rebecca. Instead he said, 'I don't want to risk him recognizing me.'

'He can't possibly recognize you with your hair like that. And those spectacles you've got. Even I didn't know who you were.'

'What's he doing in Rangoon, anyway?'

'He brought a consignment of tapestries to ship to London. They're going to Bangkok in the pouch on Tuesday.'

'In the pouch? What on earth . . .?'

'Yes, that's new since you left. It's a special arrangement with the Burmese. The Ambassador hates it, but there's nothing he can do about it. Whenever we try to broach the subject with the Ministry, they start insisting that the tapestries are national treasures and refuse to budge.'

'Yes, but the pouch, I mean—'

'Darling, you've been in Germany too long,' said Rebecca impatiently. 'You don't remember the expedients one gets driven to in places like this. This is the Third World. We make it up as we go along.'

'Well I know that, but even so—'

'More to the point, since they've expelled three British diplomats in the past two years for no particular reason, the Ambassador doesn't want to risk losing anyone else.'

'Min Saw must have powerful protectors,' said Paul thoughtfully.

'He certainly does. I've heard he's in cahoots with the Deputy Commander of Mandalay Military Division. And he knows people in Rangoon too.'

'Why doesn't he use the Burmese diplomatic pouch then?'

'I'm not sure. He used to, but one gathers there was some kind of distribution problem when the things got to the other end. They never got to where they were supposed to be going. Since Burmese embassies in the West usually have about one and a half employees, it's not surprising really. They probably just didn't have time.'

'Probably not,' said Paul, though he doubted that was the real reason the tapestries had gone missing. 'So where's this consignment now?'

'In the Embassy, waiting to be packed. Stacked in a heap on the floor of my office, if you must know.'

'Min Saw doesn't pack them himself?'

'The Ambassador won't let him. He insists on having it done in the Embassy.'

'Don't blame him,' said Paul. 'I'd do the same myself.' He turned away and took another spring roll. 'By the way, talking of the Embassy, I was wondering if I could send a signal to Berlin?'

'Of course, darling, any time you want. Why don't you come over tomorrow?'

'Rebecca, I'm supposed to be a German tourist, remember.'

'Ooops, so you are. You shouldn't switch your accent on and off like that, it confuses me. You can't give the message to me, I suppose? Too confidential? Then I suppose the best thing would be to sneak you in after hours, and let you send it yourself. You know how all that stuff works, don't you?'

'That might be the best idea, yes. Later on tonight?' He drained his glass and set it down on the counter. 'How about nine o'clock outside the Embassy?' He opened the door and glanced out. 'Make sure you don't mention it to anyone.'

'Of course I won't. Darling, you're not leaving, are you?'

'I think it would be better.'

'But he's never going to notice you, not in this mob. In fact, he seems to be positively riveted on your little friend. Mind you, with her looks she could almost pass for Burmese. No doubt that's the source of the attraction.'

'No doubt.'

'She was getting on rather well with Franco too earlier on. Quite a hot little number. Wherever did you find her, darling?'

'Growing on a tree,' said Paul.

'As long as it wasn't on a street corner.'

'Hadn't you better get back to your guests, Rebecca?'

'Sorry, darling, I shouldn't have said that. You really aren't coming?'

'No, I'm going to slip out when he has his back turned. Would you mind asking Claudia to meet me outside?'

'Sometimes,' said Rebecca crossly, 'I really think men do the best they can to ruin one's parties. What with Franco making all those awful remarks about SLORC, you sneaking out early, and Marty closeted with his visiting hotshot from Washington and not coming at all—'

Paul leaned over and kissed her cheek affectionately. Whatever her faults, he had a soft spot for Rebecca. 'Next time, darling, you can just invite the wives. If you ask me nicely, I might give Claudia permission to attend.'

What a way to spend one's first day in Burma. Had she really come halfway round the world to wind up with a collection of English bores, a Burmese monomaniac and an Italian? Min Saw had been drawn into the circle of wives (excluding Andrea, who had gone off to sulk in the garden), Franco was talking to Tony in a corner of the verandah, Paul and Rebecca were closeted in the kitchen with the door shut. There was no one else Claudia felt like talking to. Normally, in a situation like this, she would clear out. Unfortunately, she was being paid to stay. Noticing a bookcase in an adjoining room, she set off to examine it. Maybe she could find a quiet corner to read in till her fake husband had finished his mid-afternoon quickie and was ready to leave. Rebecca's books were disappointing. Dick Francis, Sidney Sheldon, Danielle Steel. A few books on Burma, the Oxford Concise English Dictionary, a pile of old Vogues. Claudia pulled out one of the books on Burma and began to leaf through it.

'Ah, there you are, Claudia.' Rebecca glided elegantly across the room towards her. 'Enjoying yourself?'

'Yes thank you.'

'I suppose you've been looking for Philip?'

Claudia looked at her. So his real name was Philip, was it? And the silly cow had let it right out of the bag.

'If you mean Paul, no I haven't. Not actively.'

Rebecca didn't miss a beat.

'That's a pity, because he was looking for you.'

'You surprise me.'

'You know, Claudia, Paul and I are old friends. We have a lot to talk about. You mustn't let it upset you.'

'I'm not upset, Rebecca.'

'When you're ready, Paul's waiting outside for you.'

'Not leaving already, are you?' Tony appeared in the doorway. He had a book in his hand: Claudia recognized the orange spine of a Penguin paperback. 'I'd been hoping for a little chat. So seldom we see a new face round here.'

'Don't keep her too long, Tony. Her husband's waiting to leave.'

'Oh he won't mind,' said Tony confidently. 'Just a few minutes. Why don't we go out on the verandah where we won't be interrupted?'

*

The great golden dome of the Shwedagon gleamed in the gathering dusk, rising stately and serene out of the jumble of shrines, pavilions, temples and stupas that clung to its base. At this hour, the broad marble terrace that ran all the way round the pagoda was thronged with people: family groups, courting couples, giggling young girls, monks in their brown and ochre and saffron robes. Paul touched Claudia's arm and they stepped on to the terrace, shoes in hand. Neither of them spoke. The spell enveloped them. The marble flags were warm beneath their feet from the heat of the day, and the air smelt of incense and jasmine. Gradually, Paul felt his tension easing away.

The crowd was in a cheerful, festive mood. The men sported their best *longgyis*, and the women wore flowers in their hair. They promenaded round the terrace, arm in arm, hand in hand, stopping to greet friends, exchange gossip, light candles, place flowers at a favourite shrine. Some people bent their foreheads to the ground in prayer, others picnicked in corners of the vast terrace. Children darted in and out of the pavilions and round the statues. Others walked solemnly beside their parents with their eyes on the ground. Paul kept an eye open for Jürgen, but there was no sign of him. With this crowd, it might take them a while to find each other. In any case, Jürgen had never had any notion of time. Paul wasn't worried. In a place like this time was infinite. He was content to wait. A row of wrinkled old ladies smoking cheroots fell silent as they walked past. A monk with a thin curious face called out, 'What nationality?' 'Italian,' said Claudia, and he nodded contentedly to himself.

'Italian?' said Paul, startled. She didn't answer. 'You're very quiet tonight.'

She shot him a quick look. Her face was closed and set, and he suddenly realized that she was furious. But before he could ask her what the matter was, she observed quite calmly, 'We should have come here for lunch instead of going back to

England. Everyone here seems to have had a pretty good time.'

'I take it you didn't.'

'Not my kind of thing, I'm afraid.'

'I'm sorry I wasn't able to spend more time with you.'

'Please don't apologise. I quite understand that you had other . . . duties to attend to.'

He wasn't sure what she meant. After a moment's hesitation, he asked, 'Did you find anyone interesting to talk to?'

'Yes, thank you.'

'Franco?'

'He was quite amusing, yes. I talked to Min Saw for a while too. Very full of himself and his Creative Processes.'

'Anyone else?'

'Not really. The consular classes aren't exactly my scene, I'm afraid.'

'Nor mine,' said Paul without thinking, and she turned a wide cool stare on him.

'Now that's a very odd remark.'

'Why is it odd?'

'Well, aren't you one yourself?'

Paul hesitated. She saw him wondering whether to deny it or not and smiled mockingly.

'I'm sorry, we're supposed to be pretending you've never been here before, aren't we? Okay, forget I said that.'

Paul gestured in the direction of a large, open platform. 'Let's go and sit down for a bit.'

They sat on the edge of the platform, legs dangling over the sides. Paul swung his backpack off his shoulder and glanced casually round. There was no one within earshot. On the other side of the terrace, a monk with a long stick stood in front of a pink and white shrine that looked rather like an outsize birthday cake and tapped a bell gently at intervals.

'So what makes you think I'm a diplomat, Claudia?'

She answered without hesitation. 'One, you're used to

entering the country on a diplomatic passport. Two, the British Embassy made our hotel reservation. Three, you have a close and cordial relationship with Rebecca and an intimate knowledge of the layout of her house. Four, you know the ropes. You know the price of a taxi from the airport into Rangoon, you tip the bellboy with a lighter instead of money.'

She paused. The monk went on tapping his bell. Paul waited uneasily for the *coup de grâce*.

'Five, you know the best place to come to recover from a trying day.' She smiled at him: a real smile this time. 'We can go to as many diplomatic receptions as you want if you promise to bring me back here every night.'

Paul smiled back reluctantly, conceding defeat. She was sharper than he had realized: he was going to have to be careful. 'This is the best time. Early in the morning is nice too. But I like the evening best.'

A bevy of teenage girls wandered past, giggling behind their hands at some private joke. A few paces behind came two men, heads together, deep in conversation, totally unaware of the seething, swirling mass around them.

'It's odd,' said Claudia dreamily, 'this is my first day in a country I've never set foot in before, it should all be weird and strange, and yet it isn't. I feel as if I'd been coming here all my life.'

'I know. It gives me that feeling too. I used to come here a lot.'

'How long were you stationed here?'

'Thirteen months.'

He hoped this wasn't going to develop into an interrogation, but she didn't ask any more questions. Night was falling, merging with the dark green fronds of the hillside, and the pagoda swelled in the darkness like a great golden ship, afloat in the ocean of eternity.

'Would you mind if I didn't go back to England with you

at the end of the trip?' said Claudia. 'I may just buy a *longgyi* and stay here forever.'

'What happened at Rebecca's? Did someone say something to offend you?'

She shook her head.

'Was it Rebecca? Did she upset you? My relationship with her isn't as close and cordial as you seem to think, by the way.'

'Listen Paul, you don't have to give an account of yourself to me. You can fuck Rebecca if you want to. It's none of my business. No it wasn't her.'

'Who then?'

'It doesn't matter.'

There was a pause. Two children scurried past and dived for cover under a large bell. Franco? Min Saw? And then he remembered Tony and the way he had been watching her across the room.

'Claudia?'

'Yes?'

'Did you talk to Tony this afternoon?' He could see by the sudden glint in her eyes that he had guessed right. 'Did he make a pass at you? Is that it?'

Claudia didn't answer. She had turned her face away. A man in a blue-checked *longgyi* walked slowly past, surveying the crowd. His eyes slid over Paul and Claudia, moved on, returned. Paul's attention sharpened. He had seen that face before. He turned back to Claudia. Before he could formulate a question, she said, 'Please don't ask. I don't want to talk about it.'

'I'm sorry. It won't happen again. No more diplomatic receptions.' The man was leaning idly against a column with his back half-turned to them. So Tony had taken advantage of the party to put a watcher on him. Paul looked at the time. Six o'clock, and still no sign of Jürgen. In the circumstances, that was just as well. This was one meeting he wouldn't want Tony to find out about.

He slid down off the platform and held out a hand to Claudia. 'Come on, it's time to go.'

They started walking back the way they had come.

'Aren't we going the wrong way?' she asked. 'Everyone else is going in the other direction.'

'That's right. Clockwise round the pagoda is the best way to salvation. I just wanted to check something. Now, let's stop here and make a little contribution to temple maintenance.'

He stopped by a large glass case stuffed with banknotes, took a wad of notes out of his pocket and pretended to sort through them, shifting round towards the light, glancing casually back the way they had come. The man in the blue longgyi had followed them anticlockwise round the pagoda and was standing a few paces away. Alone. Good. Claudia was examining the inscription on the side of the glass case.

'How do you know this is temple maintenance? You don't speak Burmese, do you? For all we know it might be the military pension fund.'

'Then maybe we'll come back as cockroaches too.'

'Is it true they use military trucks to cart heroin round the country?'

'It wouldn't surprise me.' Paul stuffed a couple of one-kyat notes through the slit in the case and took her hand, leading her onwards. 'SLORC's up to the eyes in the heroin trade. It's the only way they can stave off bankruptcy. Claudia, listen. There's someone following us.'

She shot him a quick, startled look. 'Are you sure? How on earth can you tell in this crowd?'

'Because I saw him earlier, outside Rebecca's, while I was waiting for you. He must have followed us here.'

'What are we going to do?'

'The best thing is to split up. He's on his own; if we separate he'll follow me, not you. Now listen carefully. I want you to do exactly as I say. We don't want him to know he's been noticed. When we get to the next staircase, we're going to separate, and you're going to go straight down the stairs to the bottom. Don't hang about looking at the stalls, just go straight down. When you get to the road take a taxi, go back to the hotel and stay there. Is that clear?'

'Yes. What are you going to do?'

'Leave by a different staircase, take a taxi somewhere, and try to lose him.'

'Will you be all right?'

'Of course I will.'

'Yes, I suppose you will. That figures.' She slid him a sly sideways look. 'I'll see you back at the hotel then.'

'Yes. I won't be back for a while though. I'm meeting Rebecca later.'

Another malicious little smile. 'You can stay out as late as you like. Just remember we have to have breakfast together.'

'I'll be back long before breakfast,' said Paul. 'Right, here's your staircase. Remember, straight down, no stopping, straight into the taxi.'

He raised a hand in farewell and continued at a steady pace towards the Southern Stairway, which was the main exit from the pagoda. The long flight of stairs was lined with stalls selling various kinds of Buddhist paraphernalia: incense, flowers, temple bells, statues of the Buddha, papier mâché owls covered in gold paper, ancient religious texts ... Paul dawdled, stopping to examine a Pali text, retracing his footsteps to ask the price of a statue. The man in the blue *longgyi* overtook him and started a discussion with an owl seller a few steps further down. Reassured, Paul descended the remaining steps to the street, put his shoes back on, approached the nearest taxi and announced, loudly enough to be overheard, that he wanted to go to thirty-eight Carradine Road.

The taxi moved off. The man in the blue *longgyi*, who had made himself inconspicuous behind one of the *chinthes* at the foot of the stairway, got into the cab behind. The procession moved off in the usual erratic Burmese fashion, with a lot of fuss and hooting.

Carradine Road was in a wealthy residential suburb in the hills behind the Shwedagon, at the far end of a long winding street of hidden villas and obscure embassies, numbered sporadically, illogically, or not at all. Street lighting was rare or non-existent out here, and there was practically no traffic. As Paul had expected, the second cab fell back out of sight almost immediately. Since the man in the blue longgyi already knew where he was going, there was no need to alert the quarry by arriving on the doorstep immediately behind him. Paul's taxi drew level with house number thirty-four. Number thirty-eight, he knew from experience, did not exist. The follower was nowhere in sight. Paul banged on the roof of the cab to attract the driver's attention, announced that he had changed his mind and gave him another address a few streets away. They drew up at a square white house, with a large garden. The gates were closed, but lights shone out of the upper windows. Paul examined the house critically. They had fixed the roof since he moved out. About time too. When the cab had pulled away into the darkness, he walked a few yards down the road and stationed himself in the shadows where he could see without being seen.

He had been waiting nearly half an hour when he finally heard the noise of a car engine approaching. The cab pulled up outside the house, and the man in the blue checked *longgyi* climbed out, paid the driver, and opened the gate. Paul smiled grimly to himself in the darkness. Just as he thought. The watcher had returned to make his report.

The police had gone through Jürgen's hotel room with a fine-tooth comb. They had taken him to the police station, searched him, questioned him, threatened him. Finally, they had let him go.

It was five hours since he had swallowed the sachets. For

the time being, he was in no danger. It would be another seven hours at least before the stomach acids began to dissolve the plastic sheathing.

He considered going to the Shwedagon in case Philip had waited for him, but then realized that it was nearly eight o'clock, and decided to go straight back to the hotel. Philip knew where he was staying. They would find each other sooner or later.

He reached the hotel and went straight to his room, ignoring the curious stare of the desk clerk. Out of habit, he cast a cautious glance out of the window, and then shrank back immediately in fright. They were back again. They were still watching him. The man in the red and green checked *longgyi* and another one. They squatted on their haunches across the street, making no move to approach.

Jürgen felt despair closing in on him again. He had thought he was out of their nets, but by the look of it the game was only just beginning. Thank God he hadn't gone to the Shwedagon. He would have to contact the Kandawgi and somehow warn Philip, prevent him from coming here. But first, he had to rid his stomach of its dangerous contents.

He opened the package containing a mild laxative which he had obtained on his way back to the hotel and began to swallow the contents.

On Sule Pagoda Road, the traffic was beginning to thin out, though the crowds swirling over the pavement under the bright, uncomplicated gaze of the cinema posters were as dense as ever. In front of the fire station, a group of recruits were engaged in some kind of drill. The Rangoonese went about their nocturnal business: buying snacks from the road-side vendors, smoking cheroots, drinking tea on low stools in the pavement cafés, arguing, chattering, loafing, watching. Paul had changed taxis several times on his way back into the city centre. As far as he could tell, there was nothing to worry about. There was no sign of the man he had seen in the Shwedagon. No one was watching him with anything more than normal curiosity.

He turned off the main thoroughfare on to a side road, noting the presence of several stretched-out sleeping bodies. It was new to see people sleeping in the street, but it was hardly unexpected. Over the past thirty years, Burma had declined from one of the richest and most fertile countries in Asia to one of the ten poorest nations in the world. Small wonder that the government had turned to drugs to keep the economy afloat.

Away from the town centre, the streets were silent and for the most part empty. The darkness hid the dilapidation of the broad colonial avenues and the once-stately buildings fallen on hard times. He picked his way cautiously over the uneven pavements, keeping an eye out for open drains and potholes. This was not a good time to fall and twist his ankle. A group of Burmese chattering in a doorway cast him cursory glances and carried on with their conversation. He turned left on to Strand Road, and ambled with apparent nonchalance towards the Strand Hotel, turning round occasionally as if to inspect the shaggy buildings, alert for suspicious movements either behind or in front of him. In general it was a waste of time for Europeans to practise classic surveillance-detection techniques in Asia. There were always too many people sitting patiently in doorways, squatting under trees, communicating by unseen signals. Here it was the prey who stood out, not the hunter. It was sheer good luck that he had noticed the man at the Shwedagon. But tonight the streets were deserted and there was no one to be seen, only a rat that climbed silently out of an open drain and skittered across the pavement ahead of him. The restaurants were closing, the tiny shops with their miscellaneous arrays of biscuits, medicines, cigarettes, and spices were putting up their shutters for the night. In the distance came the melancholy hooting of a boat on the river. Rangoon was preparing for bed. Not far away, in the darkness, the jungle waited, imperceptibly encroaching, putting out growths through the façades of the buildings and the cracks in the pavements, preparing slowly to engulf the city and drag it back into the swamps.

He stopped on the corner in front of the recently renovated Strand Hotel, pretending to admire the restored façade, went a few steps back and took another look, went round the corner, came back again. From across the road towards the port came the glow of a brazier and the spicy smell of cooking, a low murmur of voices, and from somewhere farther off a rich, fetid smell of decomposition. No one was taking an interest in his movements. He glanced at his watch: ten to nine. He walked slowly on, past Myanma Airways, past the British Embassy, past the Post Office with its red British-Empire mailboxes. Everything was quiet. A Japanese-made saloon car approached from the other direction and glided to a stop in front of the Embassy. Rebecca. Right on time.

He hunched into the shadow of a doorway out of sight. Rebecca glanced impatiently up and down the street. Paul stayed where he was for three more minutes. Since it was forbidden to allow unauthorized persons into the Embassy out of hours, he doubted she would have mentioned their little nocturnal tryst to Tony, but there was no harm in making sure. When it was clear that no one had followed her, he emerged from his hiding place and began to walk towards her.

Adrian had been uneasy ever since Philip had paid his final visit to the Embassy to pick up the passport and clothes for his new travelling companion. It was the end of the day and Adrian was getting ready to lock up his office and drive home. 'See you in two weeks,' he had said casually, and it was then that Philip had surprised him by holding out his hand. It was something he had never done before. Even when he married Lucy, they hadn't shaken hands at the wedding.

'Thank you, Adrian.'

'My pleasure. Have a good trip.'

'For everything. I really appreciate it.'

So they had shaken hands for the first time since they had met over twenty years earlier, and there had been an odd look in Philip's eyes that had been nagging at Adrian ever since. Even though he had known Philip for a long time, he would not claim to know him well: Philip wasn't the type to let anyone too close. But he was still, technically speaking, part of the family, and Adrian knew enough to sense that there was something very strange about this trip to Burma. Unfinished business: what did that mean, anyway?

The look in Philip's eyes stayed with Adrian all the way out to the suburbs in the evening rush hour, and four days later it was still there. Don't worry about him, he knows what he's doing, Jill had said briskly, but it wasn't as simple as that. The trouble was that he had always felt vaguely responsible for Philip, ever since they had had rooms on the same corridor in their first year at Cambridge. As a foreigner, or at least a semi-foreigner, there were things Philip simply didn't know. Adrian had taken on the role of mentor, and to a certain extent, he had kept it ever since. Jill was right, Philip knew what he was doing, but Adrian still felt this ridiculous need to make sure he was all right. Philip was aware of it, Adrian knew, and was not above exploiting it at times. Where else would he have got himself a safe flat and a false passport, no questions asked?

Finally, on Sunday afternoon, for no reason he could think of, he took out his address book and turned the pages until he came to the letter H. There it was. Philip Hamilton, and an address in Camberwell. The house was quiet. Jill was busy in the kitchen, the kids were in their rooms. Outside, as promised, it was snowing. It was pointless to ring London, perfectly pointless. Philip had been in Rangoon since yesterday. Adrian picked up the phone, dialled the number, and listened to it ringing. So who did he expect to answer?

What was he wasting his time for? Didn't he have anything better to do than listen to a phone ring in an empty flat?

The ringing ceased abruptly and a harassed female voice said, 'Hello.'

Adrian had a good memory for voices. This one was completely unfamiliar.

'Yes, hello, I'm looking for Philip Hamilton.'

'He doesn't live here any more,' said the voice. 'He sold us the flat. We just moved in yesterday. No, darling, not there, for God's sake, the other corner. Sorry,' she added, turning her attention back to Adrian, 'can't help you.'

Sold his flat? And never said a word?

'Gosh, I didn't realize he'd moved out already. You wouldn't happen to have his new address by any chance?'

'No, I only wish I did. There's a pile of mail for him and the wretched man doesn't seem to have left any forwarding address.'

'Well, I suppose you could send that to me,' said Adrian casually. 'I'm his brother-in-law. I'll pass it on when I catch up with him.'

An icy chill was creeping down his spine. Philip was much too methodical to take off without leaving a forwarding address. Something was wrong.

'Actually I think he's abroad at the moment. He said he was going away for a while.'

'Let me give you my address,' said Adrian. 'If you could pop it all in the post tomorrow, that would be awfully helpful.'

The tapestries lay in a tidy pile in a corner of Rebecca's office. Nineteen in all, with the name of the recipient pinned carefully to each. Paul went through them carefully, picking each one up and laying it aside, assessing its weight and bulk as unobtrusively as possible. Rebecca was immersed in *The New Light of Myanmar*, the local English-language propaganda sheet, and paid no attention to either him or the *kalagas*. She had been forced, she said, to inspect each one at length the previous day, and she was thoroughly sick of them.

The biggest tapestry was intended for the Burmese Embassy in London. Another was destined for some Foreign Office official, who had presumably visited Rangoon and met the great artist. There were two other English names Paul didn't recognize, and three Burmese names. The other twelve were routed to the Rajasthan Gallery in Bond Street. None of them was padded in the traditional Burmese style. None of them appeared to be in any way abnormal.

God damn it. He sat back on his heels and sighed.

'What's the matter?' said Rebecca, looking up.

'Nothing. I was just admiring them.'

He began to replace the tapestries in their pile, and Rebecca returned to the newspaper. *Khanti ca, patience; this is the way to auspiciousness*, said the dictum printed across the top of the page in bold black letters. Patience, yes, patience. Paul knew a thing or two about that.

'Make sure you put them back the way you found them,' said Rebecca. 'He crossed them all off in order on a list he had.'

'He's not going to check them again, is he?'

'No, but he will if he sees they've been moved.'

The smallest tapestry was called 'Portrait of Anawrahta' and was consigned to the Rajasthan Gallery. Paul glanced up. Rebecca was invisible behind the newspaper. He put the tapestry discreetly on one side.

'Beautiful work. What happens when he sends his stuff to Paris or New York? Does that go through London as well?'

'No, he drops them off at the French Embassy or the American Embassy and they go direct to France and the States.'

'Through the pouch?'

'Mmm.'

Paul put the 'Portrait of Anawrahta' back on the pile.

Second from the top where he could get at it easily. 'Sounds like he's got the whole of Rangoon sewn up,' he observed casually.

'He should have,' said Rebecca. 'He spends enough time going back and forth. He's driving up to Mandalay tomorrow, flying back here a week on Wednesday to see some Minister or other, and driving down again the week after that with a consignment for the U.S.'

'You know all about it, don't you?' said Paul admiringly. 'No wonder you were jealous when he spent all that time talking to Claudia this afternoon.'

Rebecca lowered her newspaper and glared at him.

'Darling, he confides in anyone who doesn't actually get up and walk away while he's talking to them. He tells everyone, just to show how important he is. I know his entire schedule for the next six months. He's told it me three times. I asked him why he didn't just move his workshop down here, to save all this coming and going, and do you know what he said? He said the light of his creative genius shone more strongly in Mandalay than anywhere else on the planet.'

Paul laughed. 'It's also the best place to get skilled embroiderers. They don't know how to do it down here.'

'That's what I told him. But by then he'd stopped listening, of course.'

Paul straightened up. 'How's the pile? Neat enough? I'd hate you to have to admire them all over again. Good, then I'll get on with the signal.' He left his backpack lying next to the pile of tapestries. 'Did you get the keys out of the safe?'

The signals room was just across the corridor. Knowing that Rebecca could hear the clicking of the keys from her office, Paul typed a few lines from a poem by Goethe and put them into code. He would abort the procedure once he had got what he wanted. Ignoring the red Transmission key, he pressed the key marked Call. As he had expected there was a low ringing sound. He waited thirty seconds, and went in search of Rebecca.

'I think there's something wrong. There should be an incoming message, but nothing seems to be arriving. You know anything about this machinery?'

'Me?' said Rebecca, raising her eyebrows, but he knew perfectly well that in a small embassy like this everyone knew things that they would normally not be allowed to know, and she got up obediently and went across the corridor to look at the transmitter. It took Paul just over thirty seconds to pull the 'Portrait of Anawrahta' out of the pile, fold it up and put it in his backpack. Leaving the backpack where it was, he followed her back into the signals room.

'Are you sure you didn't press the wrong button?' said Rebecca.

'I pressed Call.'

'Then no wonder it's ringing. That's the one for incoming signals. You need Transmission. Look, down here.'

Rebecca had arranged to go directly from the Embassy to visit her friend Marty. He had had a rough day, poor lamb, and he needed her to go and cheer him up. Would Paul mind terribly if she didn't drive him back to the hotel? Paul acquiesced promptly. No problem at all, he would pick up a taxi. He left her in front of the Embassy and strode off in the direction of Sule Pagoda. When the taillights of her car had disappeared round the corner, he retraced his footsteps. He had no intention of going back to the Kandawgi just yet. First, he had another call to make.

Jürgen's hotel was a nondescript concrete cube sandwiched between two overgrown colonial buildings near the train station. During the day, the street where it stood was crowded, but at this hour the shops were closed, the tea houses had put away their tables and stools, and the only sign of life was two men talking quietly together under a tree. Paul walked past them into the hotel.

The lobby was dark and none too clean. The desk clerk gave him Jürgen's room number and confirmed that Jürgen was in. Paul climbed the dingy staircase to the first floor. There was a line of light under Jürgen's door. He knocked, but there was no answer. He tried again. Still no reaction. Maybe Jürgen had fallen asleep with the light on. He pushed the handle gently downwards. The door opened. Paul put his head through the crack and stood transfixed in the doorway.

Jürgen was lying flat on his back on the floor with his arms thrown out on either side of his body. His face was contorted in an expression that Paul could not identify. Shock? Pain? Terror? It was clear that he was dead. Paul glanced rapidly up and down the corridor. There was no one in sight. No sound could be heard from the lobby. The sensible thing to do was to leave again immediately. But first he had to search the room. He went softly inside and closed the door.

The curtains were drawn, and there was no risk of anyone seeing him from the street. He crossed to the body and felt for a pulse. As he expected, there was none. The skin was warm to the touch. Jürgen hadn't been dead very long. Paul stared down at him, perplexed. What had happened to him? There was no sign of violence on his body, no contusions, no bleeding. The room was tidy, it didn't look as though a struggle had taken place. Could it have been a heart attack? Jürgen couldn't have been more than thirty-five, but these things happened.

Paul got up and began to search the room, working methodically from the bed to the chair, the table and the wardrobe, making sure that no traces of his investigations remained. There was nothing much to see. Jürgen had been a Buddhist monk, and Buddhist monks were allowed only eight personal possessions: three robes, a razor, a needle, a strainer, a belt and an alms bowl. The alms bowl and the razor were there, as were a small canvas bag, and a packet half full of a proprietary brand of laxative. But that was all. There was nothing under the mattress, nothing hidden on top of the wardrobe, nothing in the bottom of the canvas bag. So where was it? Jürgen had said in his note that he had information to give him. What had he done with it?

Baffled, Paul cast a last glance round the room. His eye fell on something shiny on the floor near the bed. He picked it up. A small silver spangle. He knew immediately where it had come from. His stomach tightened. Was this it? Was this the information? But where was the rest of it? He looked round the room again, searching for hiding places, and his eyes fell on the box of laxatives. And then he remembered the two men who had been standing in the street when he entered the hotel. His gaze went from the spangle to the laxatives to the silent scream on Jürgen's face and he nearly cried out loud. Dear God, what a way to die.

Paul got a grip on himself. He had to get out of here before the two guys in the street decided to come up and investigate. Presumably they didn't yet know that Jürgen was dead. The last thing he needed was for them to find him here. He took a final look at the body on the floor, and opened the door. The corridor was deserted. Through an open door at the far end, he could see the outline of a sink. That would be the communal washroom. He walked silently down the corridor. There was no point letting the desk clerk and the men in the street get another look at him. As he had hoped, the window of the washroom overlooked the alley that ran down the side of the hotel. He raised the sash and looked cautiously out. No one in sight. He climbed through the window and lowered himself slowly until he was hanging by his arms. Then he let himself drop. He landed with what seemed like a lot of noise. Without waiting to see if anyone had heard him, he walked swiftly away down the alley.

Franco was on the point of drifting off to sleep when the phone rang. Sighing, he picked it up. 'Yes ... Yes, I

remember. Oh . . . Oh . . . Really? . . . Oh . . . Yes, no problem
. . . Tomorrow morning, yes, we leave early. Where you
staying? . . . All right, we pick you up at five.'

'Who on earth was that?' said Veronica, propping herself up
on one elbow.

'The German from Rebecca's. The one they want us to
take to Pagan. He change his mind. They going up to Pagan
with us tomorrow.'

'Really?' said Veronica. 'Well, how odd. What made him
change his mind? He seemed dead set against the idea at
lunchtime.'

'I don't know. He don't say.'

'Maybe you should call Tony to let him know.'

'Yes,' said Franco. 'I do that right now. He going to be very
pleased.'

When Paul got back to the hotel, Claudia was sitting in bed
reading. Before they left Paris, she had made him buy her a
supply of books. *The Unbearable Lightness of Being, An Instant
in the Wind, The French Lieutenant's Woman, L'Etranger*. A
curious collection. It seemed to him that they all had something in common, but he had not yet worked out what it was.
She closed her book as he came in, and her face lit up with
unconcealed relief.

'Did you get rid of him?' she demanded.

Paul had to make an effort to remember who she was
talking about.

'Yes I did. What about you? Did you get back here all
right?'

'No problem.' She held her arms open to him. 'Come here.
Please.' He went and sat on the edge of her bed, avoiding the
reach of her outstretched arms, taking her hand instead. 'I was
worried about you,' Claudia said.

'There was no need. He wasn't very good. I didn't have any
trouble losing him.'

'Who was he? What did he want?'

Paul hesitated and then said, 'He was from the Embassy.' There wasn't much point trying to conceal it: she had probably figured it out already.

But it seemed the possibility hadn't occurred to her. 'The Embassy? Why?'

'They know who I really am. He was sent to see what I was up to.'

'But who sent him?' The tone, he noted with amusement, was one of outrage. Despite her professedly low opinion of her country and its embassy, she clearly felt she was entitled to more respectful treatment than this.

'Tony.'

'Tony? But—'

'This has nothing to do with what happened between you and him this afternoon. When the Burmese guy lost me, he went straight to Tony's house to report.'

'Oh, I see.' A sly little smile. 'Well, I'd better not ask why it was Tony he reported to, had I? So what happens next? Are you going to talk to Tony?'

'Certainly not. Why let him know that we know he's having us followed?'

'We know that you know that we know—' She let out a derisive hoot of laughter. 'I don't believe it.'

'In any case,' Paul went on, 'we don't have time to talk to Tony. We're leaving for Pagan tomorrow morning.'

'We are?' She stared at him. 'Not with Franco, surely?'

'Yes. He's picking us up at five.'

'I don't understand. Why are you accepting a lift from another of Tony's spies?'

Paul eyed her sharply. She caught his look and smiled.

'Come on, darling, it was obvious. They were all so eager for you to drive up to Pagan with Franco, it stood out a mile.'

'Something's come up. We have to leave Rangoon as soon as possible.'

'I thought you were looking a little white around the gills. Are you all right? Is it something serious?'

'No, I don't think so. I don't think it's going to be a problem. But we really shouldn't stay here any longer than necessary.' He picked up the book she had been reading. '*Pride and Prejudice*? This isn't one of the books I bought you, is it?'

'No, I had it already.'

'I wouldn't have thought it was your kind of thing.'

'Oh I'm always open to interesting new experiences. Are you sure you're all right? You don't look well at all.'

For a moment, Paul was tempted to confide in her. No, I'm not all right. I've just suffered a bereavement. Someone I've known since he was a baby. I didn't know him all that well and I didn't like him very much, but he was part of my life, and it's a shock, and it's just beginning to hit me, and I feel terrible.

He bit back the temptation. It wasn't going to do any good.

'I'm fine,' he assured her. 'Just jet lag catching up with me I guess.'

Part Three

Pagan

Jet lag indeed. A likely story. People like him didn't know what jet lag was. He didn't eat, he didn't drink, he didn't smoke, and she would be very surprised if his friend Rebecca let him fuck her more than once every three weeks when the stars were in the right conjunction and it wasn't her day for the hairdresser. With flesh as mortified as that, he had never had jet lag in his life.

The truth was that something nasty had blown up, either when he was with Rebecca or, more likely, immediately afterwards, as a result of which they were now on the run. Why else would they go slinking out of Rangoon like thieves in the middle of the night? Claudia tried to work out what might have happened, but had to give up almost at once. The only thing she was sure of was that it had nothing to do with the man at the Shwedagon – when she raised the topic, he had been hard put to remember what she was talking about. For the time being, ignorance didn't bother her. He had found the best place on earth to hide out, and she was too busy being grateful for that to worry about what they were running from.

Pagan was magic. It was everything Claudia had hoped for and more. She had expected to find herself in another town, hot and humid like Rangoon, but this was the country. The air was cooler and drier, and the landscape purer and emptier. Nothing but red soil, scrubby vegetation and occasional clumps of brightly coloured flowers. No houses, no factories, no streets, no cars. Nothing but bicycles, horse-drawn carriages and ox-carts. It was an entirely different universe from the bustling Victorian metropolis of Rangoon. They had gone even farther back in time, to an older, quieter, slower civilization. It felt like the beginning of the world.

Of Pagan the former imperial capital, nothing remained. The city had been conquered in 1287 by Kublai Khan, the wood-built palaces of the emperor and his court had long since crumbled into dust, and the capital had moved northwards, through the vicissitudes of history, to Ava, Amarapura, and finally Mandalay. Only the temples remained, over two thousand of them, built in brick, rising out of every corner of the plain. Every way you turned, there was a temple, and when you climbed up the terraces and looked out towards the Irrawaddy River, there were temples stretching for miles into the distance on every side. It was amazing. If Pagan had been anywhere but an obscure corner of central Burma, cut off from the outside world by mountains and jungle and megalomania, there would have been charters landing every half hour, tourists swarming everywhere, T-shirts proclaiming I Love Pagan, and a hot dog stand next to the sign at the old city gate that said LOVE YOUR MOTHERLAND, OBEY THE LAW. Instead of renting rickety bicycles from the hotel and idling along the dirt roads from one temple to another, she and Paul would be driving round in an air-conditioned bus listening to a commentary in four languages. The charm of the place, the spell woven of silence, emptiness and abandon, would be gone forever.

The peace of Pagan was so thick you could practically cut it with a knife. A little paradoxical when you considered the history of the site, and the circumstances in which it had been built. The temples here were some three centuries older than the Shwedagon, and they were the product of a darker, more warlike age. To Claudia's eye, there was something of the fortress about them. The red brick had a fierceness that spoke of archaic bloodshed and barbarity, and the immense plaster statues of the Buddha brooded grim-faced in their peeling paint. This was not Buddha the comforter, and the temples possessed nothing of the serene golden familiarity of the Shwedagon. This was Buddha the warrior, austere, sacrificial and demanding, and his temples had been built on blood. The Ananda, whose architect had been executed to ensure that the temple could never be duplicated. The Shwegugyi, where King Alaungsithu had been smothered in his bedclothes by a son intent on seizing the throne. The Dhammayangyi, founded by Narathu the regicide to expiate his crime.

It was Franco who had told them about Narathu and his relatives on the drive up from Rangoon. The journey had been less trying than Claudia had feared. Franco had kept his hands on the wheel, his eyes on the road, and his conversation free of innuendo. Claudia had sat in the back with Paul, and Franco and Veronica had shared the driving. At intervals, Franco attempted to find out why they had changed their minds about travelling to Pagan, but Paul remained unforthcoming. Claudia had already tried some probing of her own, with a similar lack of success. Remembering the look on his face when he had arrived back at the Kandawgi, she surmised that he wasn't playing need-to-know, he genuinely didn't want to talk about it. Not just dangerous, but painful too. After assuring Franco several times that they had decided to leave Rangoon because there wasn't an awful lot to see, he turned the conversation firmly towards Pagan, and asked endless questions about the temples, their architecture, their history, the effects of the 1975 earthquake, the progress of restoration, the volume of tourists ... Franco, if he realized that the change of subject was deliberate, did not appear to mind. The temples, it was clear, were his favourite topic of conversation. He knew a lot about them and discussed them with genuine enthusiasm. Claudia's reserve began to melt: she decided he was more likeable than she had thought. Someone who talked about Pagan like that couldn't be all bad, even if he was Italian and a spy.

The drive from Rangoon took nearly eleven hours. Towards the end of the afternoon, everyone fell silent. The dust blew through the open windows of the car. Everyone was hot and sticky and tired. Veronica was driving, and Franco seemed to have dropped off to sleep. Claudia glanced at Paul to see if he was asleep too. But he was staring straight ahead with such a look of desolation on his face that she reached out without thinking and put her hand over his. To her surprise, he grasped her hand and held on to it ferociously. After a while, he turned his head and gave her a rueful little smile. Yes, you see, I'm human after all. Claudia smiled back encouragingly. Of course you are, don't worry about it. Keep on going. You'll be just fine.

On Tuesday morning, Adrian received Philip's accumulated mail from London. Four letters. The Midland Bank, the Gas Board, British Telecom and a firm of solicitors. He steamed open the envelopes and read the contents.

Philip had settled all his outstanding debts. He had paid his gas, electricity, and phone bills, and he had paid his solicitor's fees. He had authorized two separate transfers to a bank in Kingston, Surrey, in the name of Claudia Reynolds. One had already gone through: the other was scheduled to be made on February 1st. He had sold not just his flat, but all his stocks and shares. The money from the shares had gone to pay Claudia Reynolds. The money from the flat was to be transferred to the account of Mr and Mrs James Ferguson at a branch of the NatWest in Oxford. Also on February 1st.

On February 2nd, the bank was instructed to close Philip's

account and send the balance, if any, to Mr and Mrs Ferguson.

Adrian felt his blood beginning to freeze. Before leaving for Burma, Philip had effectively closed down his life. By the look of it, he had no intention of ever coming back.

Two days after Jürgen's death, Paul's initial shock and grief were beginning to subside and he was able to contemplate the event with a degree of equanimity. There was, he realized, a certain inevitability about it. Jürgen had been courting death on and off for years. When you thought about it, it was a miracle he had been spared so long. Even though he claimed the monastery had changed his understanding of himself and the world for the better, Paul doubted that it had honed his instincts for self-preservation. The fact that he had been planning to present Paul with concrete rather than verbal evidence, in defiance of Paul's explicit instructions, testified to that. Jürgen might have developed what he called mindfulness, but he did not seem to have acquired the capacity for survival.

Showering and shaving in cold water on his first morning in Pagan, Paul resolved not to dwell on Jürgen's fate any longer. There were other, more pressing problems to be dealt with.

As he expected, Franco and Veronica were waiting in the restaurant when he and Claudia went downstairs for breakfast. Franco was reading the newspaper and Veronica was poking listlessly at a fried egg. Franco looked up as they entered the restaurant and made energetic signs of greeting across the room. There was no alternative but to go and join them. They ordered breakfast and poured themselves coffee. Paul waited resignedly to see who was going to volunteer to drive them round the temples. Today there was nothing he could do about it, but tomorrow they would get out of here. He would line up a taxi when Franco wasn't looking and arrange to leave town first thing in the morning.

'Excuse me.' Veronica abandoned her egg and got to her feet. 'I must run. I'll see you at the museum, Franco. Enjoy your day,' she added to Paul and Claudia.

'What are your plans for today?' said Franco, folding up the newspaper.

'We thought we'd hire bicycles,' said Paul, watching his reaction, 'to ride round and look at the temples.'

'Yes, good idea.' Franco drained his coffee cup. 'I think you must go first to the Dhammayangyi. Look carefully at the masonry there. Is unequalled in Pagan. Narathu had the masons executed if a needle could be pushed between the bricks they laid. Then after that you can go to the Ananda. Maybe you enjoy the temple festival too. Is right in front of the Ananda, you can't miss it.'

A young man in baggy shorts and a grubby white T-shirt appeared in the doorway and waved urgently at him. Franco waved back and stood up.

'Forgive me, I leave you, they are waiting for me. We fall behind on our work here, and we must leave in three weeks' time. I see you in the bar this evening, and you tell me what you've seen. For lunch, try the Nation. Opposite the Shwezigon Pagoda. It's the best restaurant in Pagan. Here, I leave you the newspaper if you want.'

He strode briskly across the restaurant and disappeared.

'Goodness,' said Claudia, 'is he letting us out on our own?'

'It looks like it.'

'Does Tony know?'

'I doubt it. More coffee?'

'Please.' Claudia picked up the newspaper. 'What on earth's this thing?'

'The local English-language propaganda sheet. If you want real news, we can try tuning in the BBC World Service. Franco has a shortwave radio, I believe.'

'Real news? From the real world?' Claudia made a face. 'I don't think so. I'm sure I can find everything I need to know right here. *National Convention Convening Commission Chairman Hosts Dinner for Members of Panel of Chairmen.* Sounds exciting. *Industry-1 Minister Tours Mandalay Division, Inspects Mills under Ministry.* My God. Wait, this is more like it. *Dead Foreign Monk Yields Heroin.* That's a nice turn of phrase. Like the harvest or something.'

Paul put the coffee pot down abruptly. 'What?'

'A monk who died when a heroin sachet burst in his intestines. How perfectly ghastly.'

'Let me see.' Paul kept his voice steady.

Claudia passed over the paper and ate her eggs. She didn't seem to have noticed anything. Paul read the article and looked carefully over the photographs that accompanied it. Jürgen Barzel after postmortem. Packets of heroin retrieved from Jürgen Barzel's intestines. Jürgen Barzel's passport. Christ, what a mess. Death might have been inevitable, but Jürgen had managed to get himself killed in a peculiarly horrible way.

> *The cause of the death of Jürgen Barzel, a German, became clear when Rangoon General Hospital, after performing a postmortem, informed the Narcotics Division of the People's Police Force of his death from overdose of a narcotic drug. Jürgen Barzel had been living at the Atumashi Kyaung monastery in Mandalay for the past eighteen months. Altogether thirteen plastic packets of heroin were found in his stomach and intestines. One of these packets had burst in his stomach when the plastic had become worn out, thereby causing his death. Police are trying to trace a Western man who visited Jürgen Barzel in his hotel room on Sunday night close to the estimated time of death.*

'Gruesome,' said Paul, returning the paper.

'What was he doing with all that heroin in his stomach? Trying to smuggle it out?'

'I suppose so.'

'Aren't you going to eat your eggs?'

'No, I'm not very hungry this morning. You can have them if you like.'

'Well, if you don't want them . . .' Claudia attacked the eggs with enthusiasm. Paul drank his coffee and tried not to look at the photo of Jürgen, face up on the table.

'Aren't you going to have any toast either?'

'No, you can have that too.'

She buttered a slice and held it out to him. 'Here. You can't last out all morning on just one cup of coffee. There are over two thousand temples out there.'

'No thanks, I really don't—'

'Eat it,' said Claudia. 'Do as you're told. And then we'll go and see if we can get a needle through the cracks in the Dhammayangyi.'

The Dhammayangyi was a square red-brick pyramid, rising high above the plain, surrounded by a walled courtyard. The interior of the temple was musty and ill-lit and faintly oppressive. Narathu the parricide had been assassinated in his turn while work was still in progress, and the temple had never been finished. Blood for blood. The masonry was all that Franco had promised. Passages led off the central sanctuary in all directions, some into tiny chambers, others into dead ends. In some places, openings in the walls had been closed up. They found a stairway half concealed inside one of the massive walls and climbed up to the outside terrace.

Paul cast a brief glance round and went on climbing. Franco's apparent nonchalance might not be all it seemed. He could easily have lined up a Burmese on a bicycle to trail them from temple to temple, or maybe one or two of his young archaeologists. He walked slowly round the upper terrace, pausing every few steps to scan the courtyard and the plain beyond. But there was no one to be seen. Paul began to relax. If Tony thought Franco was a suitable successor to the man in the Shwedagon, he had made a mistake.

He found Claudia sitting on the flags of the lower terrace with her back to the wall. Hearing his step, she looked up.

'What's the view like from up there? See any spies lurking in the bushes?'

'Nope.' Paul sat down beside her. 'All quiet so far.'

'This place is wonderful. I want to thank you for bringing me here.'

'Oh, well, er . . . good. I'm glad you like it.' He deliberately didn't look at her. For all the promises he had made in Paris, he had never intended to set foot in Pagan. His business in Burma lay elsewhere. If it hadn't been for Jürgen's death and the need to slip out of Rangoon as fast and unobtrusively as possible, he would never have come near the place. Especially not with an Embassy escort. Though if Franco's notions of surveillance began and ended in the bar, there wasn't much to worry about.

'How long are we staying?' she went on.

'I don't know,' said Paul slowly. 'I'm not sure yet.'

He tipped his head back and turned his face up to the sun. Pagan was beginning to look like a good place to lie low for a few days. Even if the Burmese police managed to work out the connection between the dead German monk and the man who had stayed two nights in the Kandawgi, they had no idea where he was now. If they were looking for him in connection with a narcotics-related death, this was the last place they would come. No one but Tony knew he was here. Tony, of course, would certainly give him away if it suited him, but why would the police discuss his whereabouts with Tony?

The sun was warm on his face. All around, as far as the eye could see, were temples, pagodas, stupas, overgrown lumps of brick rising out of the dust. An ox-cart trundled past along the red earth road and the driver called out a greeting to the workers tilling a nearby field. It was very peaceful. The kings and the parricides were returned to dust, the blood they had spilled had dried, and Pagan had slipped off the map of the world. Yes, they could stay here for a while. It would probably be wiser to keep away from Mandalay for a few days in case the Rangoon police sent detectives up there to investigate Jürgen's death. In any case, judging by what Rebecca had said, he had no need to be in Mandalay until next week.

'I'm hungry,' said Claudia's voice beside him. 'Is it lunchtime yet?'

'Already? We only just had breakfast.'

'That was three hours ago. Aren't you hungry too? All you had for breakfast was that little piece of toast.'

'Not really.'

'I can't believe it. You should cultivate the sins of the flesh a little more, darling. Do you good.'

Paul smiled. He was beginning to get used to Claudia's operating methods. 'Any particular ones you had in mind? Gluttony? Sloth?'

'Both. Sitting in the sun and eating, that's just what you need. A spot of lust wouldn't do you any harm either, but I suppose that had better wait till you get back to Rebecca.'

Paul sighed. 'Claudia, I think you should know that Rebecca has a new man called Marty. An American.'

Claudia eyed him disbelievingly.

'Does she really? What a good job he wasn't there on Sunday. I don't know if he'd have appreciated the way she was behaving to you.'

'Oh, she was just doing that for your benefit. You put her nose out of joint, I'm afraid.'

'I did? What on earth makes you think that?' Paul smiled and didn't answer. After a moment, Claudia said, 'So where was Marty on Sunday?'

'Attending meetings with a big wheel from Washington. My affair with Rebecca ended when I left Rangoon.' He got to his feet and looked down at her. 'Satisfied?'

Claudia sniffed, only partly convinced. Paul took a couple

of steps towards the stairs. 'Come on then. I thought you were hungry.'

'Oh I am,' said Claudia, scrambling hastily to her feet. 'What about you? Have you got a new woman somewhere?'

'No,' said Paul. 'I love you and only you and for the past two years I have been entirely faithful to you.'

'My goodness,' said Claudia, 'that's pretty rare these days. Maybe I should snap you up. Tell me, darling, have you ever thought of getting married?'

The best place to look for Westerners was in the hotels, and it was there that the Narcotics Division of the People's Police Force began their investigations. The officer in charge of the inquiry was not optimistic. Information on the man who had visited Jürgen Barzel's hotel room on Sunday night was distinctly sketchy. The two plain-clothes men who had been posted in front of the hotel had caught only a brief glimpse of him in the dark. The reception clerk had seen him more clearly but proved incapable of providing a detailed description. All they knew for sure was that the man was tall, and had been wearing a blue shirt. For the time being, it was decided to assume that he was of the same nationality as the dead man. If this line of inquiry failed, they would widen the scope of the investigation later.

Two policemen, armed with a description of the visitor and a photograph of the deceased, were detailed to go round every hotel and guest house in Rangoon. At the first two hotels they tried, there was nothing useful to be learned. One had had no German visitors for two months. The other turned up a German couple who had stayed for two nights and left for Mandalay the previous Friday. The third hotel was the Kandawgi. The desk clerk knew perfectly well why the policemen were there, and so did the manager. The two of them conferred in low voices, consulted the register and produced a party of four

Germans, all members of a big German industrial concern which was thinking of investing in Myanmar, who were eating lunch at that very moment on the terrace. The manager ushered the policemen down to the terrace for a look. Four large red-faced Germans, none of them wearing a blue shirt, sitting round a table laden with food in the company of three Burmese, one of whom was instantly recognizable as the Minister of Industry. They began to withdraw. It was not the moment to intrude.

'We had another German staying over the weekend,' offered the manager, as they climbed the steps to the lobby. 'But he left on Monday morning.'

The policemen exchanged glances. They could tell there was more to come.

'He arrived on Saturday. Two days before he came, a monk came to leave a message for him at the desk.'

One of them felt in his pocket for a photograph of the dead monk. 'Was this the man?'

The manager scarcely glanced at it. 'Oh yes, the very same.'

'What did the message say?'

'Unfortunately we cannot tell you that,' said the manager primly. He waited for the policeman to open his mouth to unleash a torrent of threats and added, 'It was written in German.'

The policeman closed his mouth again.

'What was this man's name?' asked his colleague.

'Paul Miller.'

'Where is he now?'

'I have no idea. A private car came early in the morning to pick up him and his wife. He didn't say where he was going.'

'He was with his wife? What was her name?'

'Claudia Miller.'

'Was she German too?'

'No, she had a British passport.' The manager waited for this to sink in, and moved smoothly on to the *coup de grâce*.

'Actually, their reservation was made by the British Embassy. Maybe they could give you more information.'

The best restaurant in Pagan was almost completely deserted. The gourmet lunchers had gone elsewhere, and the only other clients were a couple in their early forties. Paul had noticed them at the hotel the night before. Most people dressed down for Burma, in acknowledgement of the heat and dust and generally arduous conditions. These two, in contrast, looked like models posing for a magazine feature on casual chic. When they raised their voices to give their order to the waitress, their accents revealed them as American.

'What's "Burmese dish",' said Claudia, scanning the menu.

'It's the stuff they give you to eat in all the other restaurants in Burma.'

'Chicken curry and/or beef curry, you mean? Why is there only one dish in the whole of Burma?'

'A side effect of colonization. They were only allowed one dish. For their own good, of course.'

'So that sooner or later they'd get bored and start eating lamb with mint sauce like normal human beings?'

'Exactly.'

Claudia laughed. Paul leaned back in his chair and drank his beer. The sun had smoothed out his nerves and blunted his reserve. He felt relaxed and lazy. It didn't matter what he said to this girl. He could tell her anything, whatever came into his head, it was of no consequence at all.

'You're improving, Herr Miller. The further you go from civilization, the better you get. We may make something of you yet.'

'You really think so?'

'A couple of weeks round the pagodas and we'll have shaken you out of all your nasty strait-laced English habits.'

He took another swallow of beer. 'Some of it's pretty ingrained. It may take longer than that.'

'You're forgetting you're with me. I guarantee to get rid of your unhealthy allegiance to Queen and Country.'

Paul laughed out loud at that, and the American couple looked up curiously.

'Talking of Queen and Country, what happened to you at the consulate in Paris? Why wouldn't they send you home?'

Claudia gave him a wintry smile. 'I didn't ask them to. After sitting in their waiting room for an hour, I decided I didn't want to go back.'

'Why not?'

She sighed and fiddled with her cutlery. 'Because I don't belong there. I never have. I've always felt like an impostor in England. Trying to pass myself off as something I'm not. I was already beginning to feel like an intruder just sitting in that waiting room, listening to all these paid-up citizens demanding passports by Tuesday for their trips to Tokyo and putting the kids on their wives' passports ready to go skiing. I'm not like that, and I never will be. People like that come from a different planet as far as I'm concerned.'

'Yes but Claudia, English people sent by their companies to Paris aren't exactly—'

'I know, but I have nothing in common with the ones who stay at home either.'

He stared at her, perplexed. 'So what about the bar? I thought you were trying to earn your fare home?'

She sighed again. 'I was, yes, of course I was. I had to, I had nowhere else to go. I just didn't want to ask for help from those people at the consulate. I'm sorry,' she added, 'I shouldn't be telling you all this. You probably don't have the faintest idea what I'm talking about.'

You Germans don't play cricket. 'On the contrary, I think I do.' Claudia smiled sceptically. 'So tell me. Who does one owe allegiance to, if not Queen and Country?'

'Oneself, of course. Who else? No one else is going to pull you out of the shit when it comes to the crunch.'

'Is that really what you think?'

'Nothing has ever happened to make me doubt it.'

The Americans were still watching them. The man said something to the woman in a low voice. Paul reached across the table for Claudia's hand. The cameras were turning.

'Well then, welcome to married life. For the next two weeks you have a husband to haul you out of the shit and fight off the wild beasts. Take a holiday from the jungle. Be my guest.'

'Oh yeah?' said Claudia. 'Come on, we didn't come here for a holiday. You didn't bring me all the way to Burma just to ride round and look at temples. We're waiting for something, aren't we, Paul? What are we waiting for?'

He smiled and said nothing. She tried again.

'Come on, darling, you can do better than this. It's too quiet here. There isn't even anyone watching us any more. What happened to the little man from the Shwedagon?'

'He stayed at home. Tony doesn't have the resources to mount a proper surveillance operation outside Rangoon.'

'How do you know?' said Claudia. 'No, on second thoughts, don't answer that. You know that I know that they know ... What about the CIA and the KGB? Are they anywhere around?'

'Not that I've seen. Not even the DDSI.'

'What? Who are they?'

'The Burmese security police.'

'Not even them? Well, it's not enough. I need bandits, spies, assassins. At the very least, a heroin smuggler or two. I came here to risk my life, remember.'

Paul's smile broadened. 'What can I say? I'm sorry to hear you're not getting your money's worth. Maybe—'

He broke off as two men entered the restaurant. Neat shirts, close shaves, unsmiling faces, and a discreet but unmistakable sub-Rambo swagger. They gave the Nation and its clients an appraising stare and chose a table in the corner nearest to the door.

'My God,' muttered Claudia as they sat down, 'look at that. Who do they work for?'

Paul glanced across at them. 'The French Foreign Legion, I should think. Is that the kind of thing you had in mind? Stick with them, Liebling, and maybe the trip will be worthwhile after all.'

Tony was not having a good week.

On Sunday, a lot of time and trouble had gone to waste when Paul Miller spotted the watcher assigned to him and gave him the slip. It was clear from the way this had been done that the action was deliberate. Plainly Miller had had plans for the evening that he didn't want anyone to know about. Tony had no idea what they could have been, and it made him nervous.

On Monday, one of Min Saw's tapestries went missing. The tapestries were due to be crated and sent to London, the artist had turned up to oversee the proceedings, taken it into his head to do a recount, and found one tapestry missing. The whole day had been lost in a deluge of counting and recounting, verification and counter-verification. Everyone had assured Min Saw that it was impossible for a tapestry to disappear, but after half the Embassy had checked the pile against the list, it was evident that he was right. After another hour or so of verification, it was established that the missing work was called 'Portrait of Anawrahta'. The artist, hysterical with rage, threatened to have the entire Embassy staff simultaneously thrown into prison and expelled from the country. Diplomatic relations with Great Britain would instantly be severed. Didn't they know who he was? Didn't they know he had friends in high places?

On Tuesday, a flunkey from the Interior Ministry telephoned to complain about lack of respect for national treasures, and The New Light of Myanmar ran a front-page piece on the German monk who ate heroin sachets for dinner. Tony guessed immediately that the foreigner who had visited Jürgen Barzel's hotel room was Paul Miller. At least now he knew what Miller had been doing Sunday evening. But someone like Miller wasn't going to be involved in drug-running. What else was going on? His guess was confirmed when two officers of the People's Police Force rolled up at the Embassy in the middle of the afternoon. Neatly pressed *longgyis* and respectful smiles. The dead monk Jürgen Barzel had been in contact with Mr Paul Miller, whose reservation at the Kandawgi had been made by the British Embassy. Was anyone in the Embassy aware of Mr Miller's movements on Sunday night, and did anyone know where he was now?

Tony showed them into his office and went in search of Rebecca. The Ambassador's secretary, in his opinion, had a pea instead of a brain, but she was going to have to handle this, not him. He gave her a curt, two-sentence briefing in the corridor, and to his surprise she did an excellent job. Yes, of course she knew Paul Miller. Yes, of course she'd made his hotel reservation. He was a friend of her brother in London, he'd brought her a pot of lemon curd as a present on Saturday night and so she'd invited him and his wife to lunch on Sunday. Had anyone offered them some tea? No? Were they quite sure? So anyway Miller and his wife had stayed at her house until three or four o'clock, and she thought they had gone from there to the Shwedagon. No, she was terribly sorry, she had no idea where he was now. He wasn't a close friend and they hadn't discussed his movements in detail. He and his wife were planning to travel round Burma, but that was all she knew. Yes, of course, she'd let the police know if the Millers happened to get in touch with her again.

As far as Tony could see, they believed her. She'd been pretty convincing, he had to grant her that, though why the silly bitch had been stupid enough to make the hotel reservation through the Embassy was beyond him. Without that, the police would never have found them in the first place. At least the Ambassador was out when they appeared. One had to be thankful for small mercies.

In the afternoon, at Claudia's insistence, they went to the temple festival. It was a sort of Burmese equivalent of Blackpool, which went on all day and half the night for the whole month of January. It was crammed with stalls selling baskets and *longgyis* and Chinese tin mugs and God knows what other rubbish, and boasted a soccer match and a bullock competition and a beer tent and booths where announcers with microphones solicited contributions to the temple fund at a decibel-level calculated to raise the temple ghosts for miles around.

Claudia made Paul watch part of the soccer match and buy her a basket and contribute ten kyats to the temple fund on the grounds that it would balance out the money he had given to the military pension fund in Rangoon and save them from being reincarnated as cockroaches. Contrary to his expectations, Paul had a good time. He had, it occurred to him, been having a good time all day. He contemplated the discovery with mild surprise. It had been so long since he had enjoyed anything, he had assumed it was no longer within his power to do so. Walking back to the hotel after they had eaten dinner (Burmese dish) in a grimy café on the river bank, past bamboo houses and overgrown stupas, he decided it was fortunate Emma had opted out when she did. As Caroline's friend and flatmate, she had seemed the obvious choice of companion, but he could see now that she wouldn't have done at all. She wasn't as sharp as Claudia, she wouldn't have noticed as much, but she was too prim and serious for a place like this. She would have spent the whole time worrying about the dust and the food and driving him crazy.

Claudia stumbled in the dark and he reached out to grab her arm. The city fathers of Pagan had not yet discovered street lighting.

'Thanks,' she said, and took hold of his hand. 'I'll just hold on to you for a while, I think. Before I break my leg or something. Not to mention the fact that our cover is slipping. If we were really on our honeymoon, we'd be having it off right behind that stupa over there. Moonlight in Pagan. Yielding to our uncontrollable frenzy in the dark, with everyone safely out of the way at the temple festival—'

'And all the snakes and scorpions crawling over us?'

'Snakes and scorpions?'

'I'm afraid so.' Paul strained his ears. Was that a footfall he had heard behind them?

'Oh. That is a bit of a problem. I suppose one would just have to lie back and think of England.'

'Deutschland, if you don't mind.'

'Deutschland? Ah, yes, of course. I've never tried that actually. You'll have to show me what to do.'

'My pleasure,' said Paul. He steered her off the path into the shadow of a tree and put his arms round her. 'Let's just stand like this a minute. I think I heard footsteps behind us. Can you put your arms round my neck, please.'

Claudia, after a moment's hesitation, complied. They waited in silence. Paul strained his ears, but couldn't hear anything. The footsteps, if that was really what he had heard, had stopped. Claudia's hair smelt of dust and sweat. He could feel her heart beating against his chest. He watched the path over her shoulder, but nothing moved. There was no one in sight, and no sound but the distant blare of the loudspeaker from the temple festival. No, he was imagining things. The danger had been left behind in Rangoon. There was nothing to worry about.

'You're not still thinking about that guy we saw at lunchtime, are you?' said Barbara.

'I just wish I could remember where I've seen him before.'

'Maybe you saw him in Rangoon. At the hotel or

something. Or maybe on the plane from Bangkok.'

'It wasn't here. It was before that. Somewhere else, but I can't remember where.'

'At home, then? But, Michael, it could have been anywhere. In the supermarket, or something.'

'I wouldn't have remembered him if I'd seen him in the supermarket.'

'Ah.' Barbara spread cleanser over her face and wiped it off carefully with a tissue. What the dust in this place was doing to her pores, she hated to think. This was their first trip to Burma and, she devoutly hoped, their last. Or at least, her last. Michael could come here as often as he wanted, but she really didn't see why she had to come along. She stared at the dirty tissue with distaste. He didn't care about things like crummy hotels and non-existent air-conditioning, he never had, but she didn't see why she had to put up with them.

She peered at Michael's reflection in the dusty glass of the bedroom mirror. 'What about the girl? Have you seen her too?'

'No. If I'd seen her before, I'd know exactly where it was.'

'Oh you would?'

'Come on, honey, she's very striking.'

'I guess,' said Barbara grudgingly. 'What I don't understand is why you're so upset about all this? What does it matter if you've seen this guy somewhere before? So maybe you ran into him at an opening one time, and now he's taking a trip to Burma at the same time as we are. So what?'

'Why Burma?' said Michael pointedly.

'Well, I don't know. You certainly got to want it to come here. I've never seen anything like this place, that's for sure.'

She cast a disparaging glance round the room. It had blue walls, battered furniture and a view over some scrubby under-growth and a ruined stupa. The bathroom was the worst she'd ever seen, worse even than the one in Rangoon. The water from the shower ran all over the floor and there wasn't so much as a hook for your robe or a shelf for your make-up.

'I really hope this trip is going to be worth our while. When I think that if we'd only waited a few months – '

'Look, Barbara, we've been over all this already. If we hadn't come here, Curtis and I would have been sitting around twiddling our thumbs for six months, and during that time there'd have been no extra income coming in. You're the one who wanted a kitchen extension, not me.'

'Well, sure, but—'

'It's much better to come here, talk it all over, and get the ball rolling. That way, with luck, you should be able to get the work done over the summer.'

'Well, okay, if you say so. Anyway, like I was saying, what if it were just a coincidence?'

'With everything that's at stake on this trip, we'd better not believe in coincidences.'

'Then what—'

'Just give me time,' said Michael. 'It'll come back to me. I'll figure it out in the end.'

Franco was waiting for them again at breakfast the next morning. Alone. Veronica, it seemed, was feeling a little under the weather. He devoured his eggs and inquired after their plans for the day. Paul told him. The Shwegugyi, the Sulamani, one or two lacquer shops. Franco drank his coffee, eyed Claudia with a distinct resurgence of lust and recommended the sunset at the Dhammayangyi. Paul felt a sudden surge of irritation. Was he going to offer her a guided tour? With Veronica out of the way, did he think this was his big chance? With a final hungry look, Franco wished them a nice day and went off to join his acolytes.

'Is he really phoning all this back to Tony every day?' said Claudia.

'Given the phone system here, I hope not, for his sake.'

'What's going to happen when we leave? Franco's going to

tell Tony where we're going. Won't Tony just line up someone else to take over?'

'To tell you the truth, I haven't figured that one out yet. We may have to sneak out the back door in the middle of the night.'

'Great,' said Claudia. 'A little excitement at last. Have you finished your coffee, darling? Are we ready to head out and do a little work on our tourist cover?'

'Watch your vocabulary, someone's going to hear.'

Paul glanced round automatically, but the restaurant was nearly empty. Only two other tables were still occupied, one by two middle-aged couples discussing in various kinds of broken English the logistics of sharing a taxi to Mandalay, and the other by a young couple with a pile of postcards in front of them. They were deep in an intense conversation in German about somebody's new address, and barely looked up as he and Claudia got up to leave.

Mindful of the footsteps he had heard the previous night, Paul kept a sharp eye open as they left the hotel and cycled across the plain. But the only people around were other tourists. At the Shwegugyi they spotted the Americans; on the dirt road leading out of Pagan, they rode past the postcard writers. The sun was warm and the sky was a clear, pure blue. There was no one here except a few people on holiday enjoying themselves. Just to make sure, he stopped halfway to the Sulamani and led Claudia off the path to explore some nameless temple where no one had been for years, and the only signs of life were a colony of ants on the outside terrace and the trace of a snake in the dust on the floor of the sanctuary. No one followed them. Everyone had better things to do.

By the time they got to the Sulamani, it was midday and the sun was high in the sky. The fields were quiet, and they had the temple to themselves. They walked round the sanctuary, which was enlivened by a gaudy fresco of red and orange Buddhas, and climbed up to the terrace to admire the view. Green fields, red brick, a lone white stupa in the distance. On the horizon, the faint grey smudge of the Irrawaddy. Paul felt his fears draining away. Up here in the heart of Burma, where the temples drowsed in their thousand-year quietude, Rangoon and everything that had happened there was beginning to seem increasingly unreal. A dusty breeze blew in his face. Jürgen was at peace. Whatever the anguish he had known in the hours before his death, it was over now. He had attained the most blessed of earthly states. Nothing could touch him any more. He was at rest. The ox-carts plodded through the empty landscape and the stupas crumbled silently into the earth. Dust to dust.

Down in the courtyard, something caught Paul's attention. A movement, a shadow, some change in the quality of the light. He put an arm loosely round Claudia's shoulders. They were not alone.

'Have you seen enough, Liebling? Shall we go down again?'

On the lower floor, he took her hand and they lingered in the sanctuary, ostensibly inspecting the paintings. The sun swirled into all the corners, driving out the shadows, laying bare the secrets. Paul scanned the passages leading out of the sanctuary, but could see nothing. The voice made them both jump.

'These are new paintings. They are not from time of Pagan. Monks do them.'

The girl had come up behind them without making a sound. She had delicate features and a solemn, exquisite smile. Paul judged that she must be about sixteen. One of the self-appointed guides who hung out in certain temples in the hope of earning a few kyats from the tourists. He let go of Claudia's hand and they listened respectfully while she told them about the monks in surprisingly good English.

'Where did you learn English?' Claudia asked when she had finished. 'Do you learn it at school?'

'No, I do not go to school. I learn only from tourists. My sister goes to school. I must earn money to buy school uniform. It is very expensive.'

'School uniform?' said Claudia incredulously. 'You have to wear school uniform here?'

She went on asking questions, and Paul wandered off, grinning to himself. The colonists still screwing the masses forty-five years after they had officially left – he was beginning to know the way Claudia's mind worked. He reached the hall leading out into the courtyard and leant against the wall to wait for her. Two cyclists turned in through the gate and rode towards him. The two men they had seen in the restaurant yesterday. He watched them approach. Definitely military men of some description: there was no mistaking the way they held themselves. Claudia and the Burmese girl came out of the sanctuary, deep in discussion. It was lighter out here, the sun was flooding in, the girl stopped talking and stared hard at Claudia. Something suddenly clicked into place in Paul's mind. He had been here before, he had seen this girl before—

'I know you,' said the girl to Claudia and broke into a sudden beaming smile. 'You come before. You take photo with me, you send me photo, I have at home.'

Claudia stared at her blankly. 'But I've never been here before. It's my first time in Burma. You must be confusing me—' She broke off abruptly. Her eyes, wide and alarmed, met Paul's over the Burmese girl's shoulder.

Yes, he remembered clearly now. They had met the girl and her sister too. Two little girls, grave and beautiful, aged about ten and eight. Caroline had given him her camera so he could take a photo of the three of them together, and asked for their address to send them a copy. How was he to know she had kept the address and sent the photo? He dug blindly in his pocket and produced a perfume sample and two more key-rings.

'For you and your sister. Come, Liebling, please. We have to go.'

Miller was not in Rangoon. He was not in Pegu or Syriam or any of the other southern towns easily accessible from the capital by car. He had not left Rangoon by plane, train or bus for any of the destinations normally permitted to foreigners. Nor had he left the country. The police had combed the hotels, the guest houses and, mindful of his connection with Jürgen Barzel, the monasteries. There was no trace of him anywhere.

The investigating officer considered widening the search to the rest of the country, but after due reflection, decided against it. The lady at the British Embassy had said Miller was going to be travelling, but she had no idea where he planned to go. Why waste valuable resources hunting for someone who wasn't even suspected of murder when there was a much simpler way to catch him?

Miller's two-week tourist visa was due to expire on Saturday of the following week. Some time before then, he would have to leave the Union of Myanmar, and the only way he could do that was by air from Rangoon. A directive was dispatched to the airport immigration offices ordering them to detain the German national Paul Miller when he tried to leave the country.

Paul went off on his own that afternoon. 'I'm going to take a look round some of the lacquer shops,' he announced after a mostly silent lunch. 'You don't have to come with me, Liebling.' Claudia didn't argue. When he called her Liebling, he was issuing instructions, not making suggestions. She settled herself on the balcony with *Pride and Prejudice*, and waited while he rummaged through his bag for a pair of clean socks. The balcony overlooked the rickety bridge that formed the main entrance to the hotel. Paul pedalled rapidly across the bridge and disappeared round the bend in the road. For another ten minutes, Claudia stayed where she was, watching the road. Then she put down her book, went back inside, and locked the door leading to the corridor. This was the chance she had been waiting for.

Paul's travelling bag stood open on the floor beside his bed. Its contents, she was pleased to see, were thoroughly jumbled up. Not a string or a hair or a right angle in sight. Judging by the trouble he had had finding his socks, the days they had been on the road had taken their toll on his safety system. She memorized the things that lay on top – she had always been good at Kim's Game – and began to empty the bag, inspecting each article for secret compartments and other amenities, before laying it carefully on the bed. T-shirts, underwear, sun lotion, malaria pills. No mysterious bits of metal that might slot together to form a telescopic rifle. No large lumps of chewing gum that might turn out to be Semtex. So where were his little secrets, then?

She opened the plastic bag where he kept his stock of ballpoint pens and perfume samples. Eureka. Along with the junk he handed out to bellboys and taxi drivers were a Sony clock radio, a Swiss watch, a bottle of Chanel No. 5, and a Philips Walkman. By the look of it, he was expecting to engage in some large-scale bribery at some point. She put the bag on the bed with the rest and went on delving. Two paperbacks in German. A nice touch, that. She was nearly at the bottom. Just one last plastic bag. An ordinary green Marks and Spencer's bag. Probably his dirty washing. She opened it anyway, hesitated for a moment and then drew out the contents. 'Portrait of Anawrahta. U Min Saw. Rajasthan Gallery, London.' Even without the label stapled to the top of the tapestry, she would have recognized it immediately.

'Got it!' said Michael.

'Got what?' said Barbara.

'The guy in the restaurant. I just remembered where I saw him before.'

'Did you? That's great,' said Barbara, casting a critical eye over the shelves of lacquer bowls in front of her. 'Listen, honey, what do you think of these?' She took a bowl off the shelf and held it out to him. 'If we bought half a dozen and put them in a row on the shelf at the top of the stairs . . .'

Her voice trailed off as she saw Michael's face.

'What's the matter? Where did you see him?'

'In the gallery.'

'Oh really? We should have thought of that before. Did he buy anything?'

'No. He stayed for an hour and a half, looked at every piece we had on display, wanted to know where it came from, how it got there, who bought it. He wasn't there to buy, he was there to ask questions. It wasn't just casual interest, either. He was after something.'

Barbara put down the bowls abruptly. The shopping would have to wait. This sounded serious.

'But, Michael, if he asked you questions for an hour and a half, how come he hasn't recognized you too?'

'He didn't see me,' said Michael with grim satisfaction. 'Curtis signalled to me what was going on, and I stayed out of sight and watched through the one-way mirror. No sense in us both getting burned.'

'But if he doesn't know you have any connection with the gallery, why would he be following us?'

'I don't know, Barbara, but I don't like it. You know why it took me so long to figure out where I'd seen him before? He's changed the way he looks. His hair's different, he's lost weight, and I bet those eyeglasses aren't real either.'

'Are you absolutely sure it's the same guy, then?'

'Absolutely. And he's changed his accent too. This fellow sounds Scandinavian or something, German maybe, but Curtis swore the other one was a Brit. He's a professional, Barbara, there's no doubt about it.'

'Oh my lord. What about the girl? You think she's a professional too?'

'Doesn't look like one. My guess is she's just there to keep him warm at night.' Michael pulled indecisively at his lower lip. A muscle was twitching in his cheek. Barbara eyed him shrewdly. In times of stress, Michael needed action. She had to head him off before he did something they would both regret.

'You know what, Michael, I think we should find out more about them.' She moved briskly towards the door of the shop. 'Let's get back to the hotel. What we need to do is get talking to them. Find out if they're regular tourists or if there's something else going on. And then we'll decide what to do next.'

The idea that anyone would remember Caroline had never once occurred to him. It had been so long ago, how could anyone recall one stray tourist among so many? How could he have known that she had sent a photo to someone she had met; that it had, against all odds, got through, and that the recipient had kept it?

From where he was sitting, on the upper terrace of the Dhammayangyi, Paul could see across the fields to the Sulamani. When he had left the hotel, he had no very clear idea where he was going, but he knew perfectly well why he had come here.

The girl in the temple was his last link with Caroline. He had burned all the photos but one when he moved out of his flat, and destroyed that last one before leaving Paris. And now her image was beginning to blur in his mind, her face was dissolving. He could no longer hear her voice or remember her soft Scottish accent. When he thought of Caroline, it was Claudia's face he saw and Claudia's voice he heard. Claudia was taking Caroline's place, she was driving Caroline back into the shadows. The resemblance which had seemed so strong in that bar in Paris was becoming progressively fainter. He was beginning to wonder if it had ever existed, except in his own mind. Maybe he had wanted so deeply to see Caroline again that he had projected on to this other girl a likeness which had never really been there.

He shifted restlessly on the stone ledge. He had come here for Caroline. He couldn't allow himself to forget her. All he had to do was ride across the fields to the Sulamani and ask the girl to show him the photo of Caroline.

No, it was impossible. That was the last thing he could do.

The sound of voices came from further down the terrace. He sat up, relieved by the interruption. He needed to get away from Claudia for a few hours, but he couldn't stay here brooding all afternoon either. It was time to pull himself together. He would ride back to Pagan and look at the lacquer shops as he had said he planned to do.

The voices were coming nearer. Someone said something loudly in Italian. Paul looked up, startled, and found himself face to face with Franco.

Claudia repacked Paul's bag, collected her book and went purposefully down to the garden. If he noticed his things had been touched, she would claim someone had been to the room during her absence.

The garden of the Irra Inn was considerably better tended than the hotel: perhaps because the dust didn't show up as much. She found a seat overlooking the river, and flicked through the pages looking for her place. She still didn't know what they were doing in Burma, but one thing was sure, it was something to do with Min Saw. His name, his person, and his works kept reappearing like a leitmotiv. The tapestry in the gallery in Paris, the tapestry in Rebecca's house, the tapestry Paul was carrying round with him.

She gazed down at the pages unseeingly. Mr Collins had just proposed to Miss Lucas. Paul was right: it wasn't her kind of book. But then why had Paul gone to such pains to avoid Min Saw at Rebecca's party? It didn't make sense. Someone sat down on the next bench. It was the American woman they had seen with her husband in the restaurant yesterday.

'Hi,' she said, and Claudia smiled vaguely. The woman was older than Claudia: she and her husband were about Paul's age. They were both thin and blond and chic and, to Claudia, vaguely intimidating. Rich American yuppies taking a look at how the rest of the world lived: she had no idea what to say to people like that.

'Great view, isn't it? How long have you been here? Did you come here straight from Rangoon? Yeah, so did we.'

Fortunately, it wasn't the kind of conversation where one was required to say much.

'We were planning to go straight to Mandalay, but someone told us we ought to come here, so we did. It's quite something, isn't it? All those temples. I've never seen anything like it before.'

Claudia wasn't surprised. This woman looked as though she had never in her life set foot outside the principal shopping streets of a few carefully selected Western capitals. Although she wore the same trousers and T-shirts as Claudia and Mrs Gloves-and-Hairnet and all the other Westerners in Burma (Claudia had long stopped resenting her borrowed wardrobe), she actually managed to look elegant in them. Mind you, the T-shirt was Ralph Lauren and the jeans were Calvin Klein. That probably helped.

'I'd just love to have seen Pagan in its heyday, wouldn't you? Did you know Marco Polo came here?'

Claudia's interest was awakened. 'No, I didn't know that. When?'

'Hey, I don't know exactly. There's something about it in the guidebook.' She scooped a lock of hair off her face with a carefully manicured fingernail. Even the dust looked as though it was meant to be there. 'You're English, aren't you?'

'Half-English,' said Claudia, remembering the school uniforms. 'And half-Italian.'

'Oh, right, Italian. You don't look English. Your husband yes, but not you.'

'Actually, my husband's German.'

'Is he really? Well, how interesting. And do you live in England, or the States?'

Why on earth would they live in the States? Claudia wondered, but she answered in a carefully neutral tone that they lived in London. The yuppie lady thought that was fascinating. So cosmopolitan. And how did they like Burma? Were they going to Mandalay next? How were they getting there? When were they leaving? How long did they plan to spend there?

Claudia hedged and mumbled. None of this was information that Paul had seen fit to part with. 'We haven't decided yet,' she explained. It sounded unconvincing even to her own ears. Why couldn't the wretched woman find someone else to talk to?

'You are going there, aren't you? The guidebook says there's a great view from the top of Mandalay Hill. And some really interesting pagodas.'

'Oh yes, we're going there,' said Claudia. If she remembered correctly, Min Saw's workshop was in Mandalay. That was probably as good a reason to visit as any.

So when were they leaving for Mandalay? the woman repeated. Were they going there direct from Pagan, or were they going somewhere else first? Her oddly insistent tone was beginning to get on Claudia's nerves. What did she care if they went to Mandalay or not? If she wanted someone to share a taxi, why didn't she come out and say so?

'We really like it here,' she explained. 'We aren't sure how much longer we're going to stay.' Why on earth was the woman so interested? A sudden wild suspicion entered her mind, and she added casually, 'But I'd like to buy one of those tapestries they make, and apparently Mandalay is the best place to find them.'

The woman looked at her oddly. 'Tapestries?'

'Yes, you know. Padded elephants on a black background, that kind of thing. Scenes from the Glass Palace Chronicles.'

'Excuse me?'

'Burmese history, that is.'

'Oh right. Elephants. We've gone mad on those little lacquer boxes ourselves. Don't you think they're cute?'

'Very.' Claudia dismissed her suspicions. It seemed unlikely this woman would ever have heard of Min Saw. Without the guidebook, she would probably never have heard of Mandalay either. To her relief, Paul rode round the corner of the hotel and got off his bike.

'There's my husband. I'd better go.'

The woman nodded amiably. 'Enjoy your stay,' she said, as Claudia walked away.

The call from Paris came through just as Tony was leaving the office for the day. He listened to what Adrian had to say with growing incredulity.

'Closed down his life? His bank account too? Who are these people he's transferred his money to?'

'His parents-in-law.'

'What d'you mean? I thought his wife was dead.'

'Former parents-in-law,' Adrian amended.

'So what does that mean? Aren't they your parents too?'

'Yes.'

'Why didn't you say so?' said Tony crossly. 'Never heard such a muddle. What do the parents think about all this then? They got any idea what he's up to?'

'He hasn't been in touch with them recently. They didn't know he'd gone.'

'Really? And you think he doesn't intend to come back?'

'Well, it does rather look that way. I got someone in Berlin to go and check out his flat there. He's left his clothes, a few books and so on, but there are no personal papers.'

'Bank account?'

'Still open, but he made a big withdrawal the day before he left.'

'So what does this all mean?' demanded Tony aggrievedly. 'He's not going to defect to the bloody Burmese, is he? Has he taken any files with him, anything like that?'

'Good God, no. That's not the point at all. My idea is that he might be intending to head into one of the, well, rebel-held areas.'

'And what's he going to do when he gets there? Sign up with Khun Sa to fight the Tatmadaw?'

'Well, that's the problem, you see. I just don't really—'

'You've got this far,' said Tony accusingly, 'you must have some idea. How long did you say you'd known him?'

'The only thing I can think of is that he's been a bit depressed for some time. He's lost both his wife and his sister in the past few years.'

'Oh he has?'

'I know he liked Burma. He was really pretty taken with the place, in fact.'

'Was he really?'

'I was wondering whether he might not have been thinking of spending some time in, well, a monastery.'

'A monastery?' said Tony disbelievingly. 'My God, that's all we need! What makes you think he's intending to do that?'

'He has a friend, well, an acquaintance really, who's been living in a monastery in Mandalay for several months. He told me recently that this person has gained peace within himself thanks to meditation.'

'Is that right? May one ask who this person is?'

'Philip knew him when he was young. They lived next door to each other.'

'Where?' demanded Tony.

'In Hamburg.' Adrian sounded mildly surprised by the peremptory tone.

'In which case, one may assume that this person was a German?'

'That's right.'

'I see,' said Tony. Well, that was looking a lot clearer, anyway. Miller must have arranged a reunion with his boyhood friend, found him dead on arrival, and decided to take the back exit, either because he suspected the man's drug-trafficking activities or simply out of a desire not to get involved with the police inquiry. One mystery solved. His spirits lifted abruptly.

'So you think he may be intending to sign up with a monastery. Well, Adrian, that's all well and good, but you can't just come to Burma and enter a monastery. Got to have a special visa for that.'

'Not in the insurgent areas.'

'Well, that's true, I suppose. Don't know if they give out life membership even there, mind you.'

'Life membership? Oh well, I—'

'That's what we're talking about, aren't we, if I understand you correctly?'

'Well, that's just it, I . . . well, I suppose . . . maybe . . .'

'My God, what a confounded nuisance. So what do you suggest we do now? Can't just let him wander off and shave his head and disappear into the jungle, I suppose?'

'No,' said Adrian, 'I don't think we can. The problem is the girl, you see.'

'Yes,' said Tony thoughtfully, 'she's not going to be much use to him in a monastery? So what's he need her for, d'you think?'

★

Paul had come to fetch her to see the sunset at the Dhammayangyi. Apparently, he had run into Franco, who insisted it was a sight not to be missed. Certainly half Pagan was queuing up for seats when they got there. Two horse-drawn carriages were standing in the courtyard and several bicycles were propped against the wall. A small group of people was visible on the upper terrace, and one or two others were wandering round the sanctuary. To Claudia's relief, there was no sign of Franco, however. She doubted Paul's presence would stop him trying to make a pass at her if he got the chance.

In the gathering gloom, the interior of the temple was even heavier and more oppressive than it had seemed on their first visit. They climbed up the steps to the outside terrace. The sun was already sliding gently into the mists above the Irrawaddy. Claudia sat down to watch while Paul wandered off down the terrace. So much for their romantic sunset together, Liebling. She suspected it was Caroline he wanted to see the sunset with, not her. Why hadn't he told her the two of them had been here before?

The horse carriages left, one by one, and the bicycles followed. The silence fell softly like a shroud and the abandoned temples faded into the dusk. Claudia glanced round. Everyone had gone. There was no sign of Paul. She was alone, for the first time in months. Even Nick, who had been with her all summer, marching invisibly by her side on the long trek through Italy and France, had finally evaporated. At this very moment, he was probably shooting sultry looks across his office at another entranced female student, and making suggestive remarks about Racinian tragedy.

The sound of footsteps came from the inner staircase. A late tourist. They were cutting it a bit fine: the sun had nearly set and in a few minutes it would be dark. Unless it was Paul who had found his way down by another staircase and come back to look for her. Claudia got up and moved towards the steps. They had spent enough time communing with their respective ghosts, and tonight, Paul had informed her, they were having dinner with Franco and the archaeologists. It was time to leave.

She reached the ground floor without seeing anyone. The footsteps had stopped. The sound must have been coming from somewhere else. Inside the temple, the light was nearly all gone. She felt her way cautiously along the massive stone passage towards the inner sanctuary. As she emerged opposite one of the great statues, a shadow vanished round the far corner of the shrine. Claudia stopped dead. What was that? The movement had been fast and furtive. Not the idle gait of a tourist taking in ancient Buddhist culture. Someone with completely different motives. Someone lying in wait in the darkness, waiting for her to come down from the terrace. Why? What did they want? And who did they think she was? Claudia? Or Caroline?

'Paul?' she called tentatively, and was annoyed to notice that her voice was shaking.

There was no answer. The silence enclosed her.

The Buddha statue seemed huge and menacing in the dim light. The musty smell she had noticed before was stronger now, and thicker, almost tangible. Claudia breathed deeply. Her heart was pounding. Where was Paul? Why had he insisted on coming here? She tried to fight a sudden wave of panic. The sanctuary was built in the shape of a square. The entrance, if she remembered rightly, was opposite to where she was standing now. She had to walk round half of this side, the whole of the next side, and then she would be able to see the broad entrance hall leading up from the courtyard. She couldn't move, she was frozen to the spot. What had he been doing this afternoon? Why had he made her stay behind? Come on, walk! The longer you wait, the darker it's going to be. She listened. The silence was absolute. Maybe there was no one there at all, she told herself firmly. Maybe she had imagined the whole thing.

She began to walk, keeping her eyes resolutely averted from the glowering Buddha. First corner. She had chosen the opposite direction to the one where the shadow had gone. Maybe it was just a local kid, hanging round in the hope of a biro. She kept on walking. One foot in front of the other. Nearly at the second corner. Why hadn't he told her he'd been here with Caroline? What was he using her for? Suddenly she heard a kind of shuffling sound behind her. Her nerve broke. She ran for it. Round the second corner it was lighter. Another few yards and there was the entrance. Right where it was supposed to be. She tore round the corner into the entrance hall and cannoned into someone coming out of another passage. Jesus, there were two of them. It was a trap. She screamed.

'Claudia, for heaven's sake!' said Paul. 'What's the matter?'

'What do you think you're playing at? Who is that in there? What's going on? Why did you bring me here?'

He cast a startled glance over her shoulder towards the sanctuary. 'What?'

'Who am I supposed to be? Claudia or Caroline? Who do you want people to think I am? Answer me, Paul, damn you!'

'What are you talking about?'

'You know exactly what I'm talking about. You offer me a trip to Burma, all expenses—'

The next minute, his arms had gone round her and his mouth was on hers, silencing her. Claudia tried to push him away but he was holding her too tight. She let herself go limp instead. His arms slackened, but he went on kissing her. Not just to shut her up, not any more, but because he wanted to. His mouth pushed hers open, his tongue sought hers. Instinctively, Claudia found herself responding.

He let her go and they stood staring at each other in the half light. 'Come, Liebling,' said Paul, 'you have had a bad fright.

We will go back to the hotel and you will tell me what you saw.' There was a steely note she had never heard before mixed in with his German accent. He put an arm round her shoulders and propelled her down the steps. 'I don't think there's anyone left here but us, actually. Maybe you met the ghost of Narathu.'

Their bicycles were standing where they had left them. 'Get on, Liebling, let's not waste time. We must arrive home before it gets completely dark.'

Dumbly, Claudia mounted. They rode across the court-yard. As they reached the entrance, she braked sharply. Two other bicycles were leaning against the wall by the gateway. 'Don't stop,' said Paul urgently from behind her shoulder. She hesitated, wobbled, and obeyed. They rode out of the courtyard and turned towards Pagan. Behind them the Dhammayangyi reared skywards, a sinister, Inca-like pyramid in the dusk. Claudia risked a swift glance over her shoulder. It seemed to her that two forms were standing on the temple steps, but it was too dark to distinguish whether they were Burmese or Westerners, men or women, ghosts or tourists.

As soon as they were out of sight of the temple, Paul swerved off the road behind a clump of bushes and gestured to her to do the same.

'Franco? Thank God for that. Bloody telephone gets worse every day. What did he do today? Still boning up on medieval Burmese culture?'

'I don't see him yet. We have dinner together. I find out then.'

'You're not relying on what he tells you he's been doing all day, are you?' said Tony. 'Oh dear, that won't do at all. You see, we're not—'

The line crackled and faded. Franco sighed. He had just received an article on new discoveries at Angkor Wat, and had been hoping to read it before dinner. When he could hear again, Tony was saying, '—got to get closer to him, follow him, see exactly where he goes.'

Franco raised his eyes to the ceiling. 'Look, Tony, is not that easy for me to follow them. I have work to do, I can't—' He stopped. The line had gone again.

'Call me tomorrow at the same time,' said Tony when communications were re-established. 'Stick with him and see if you can't get something a little more concrete. Something's come up, you see, and this is really top priority now. Oh, and if they say anything about leaving, be sure to find out exactly where they're going and when. All right, dear boy?'

'No,' said Franco, his patience snapping, 'is not all right. I cancel my meeting with the Ministry, I come back here four days early just to do you a favour, and I don't appreciate that you treat me like a fucking errand boy.'

'What? Look, dear boy, don't take it—'

'I have a job to do here, I don't have time to fuck around following a pair of tourists.'

'Look, Franco, sorry if I was a bit short with you. Been a bad day, quite frankly. I hope you're not going to, well . . . I was actually rather relying on you, if you want to know the truth, and I—'

'Bullshit,' said Franco. 'You already have someone keeping an eye on him – you said so yourself. He can't be as important as that.'

'Well, actually, dear boy, that's not for you to judge, if you don't mind me saying so. I know I didn't tell you much about him before, and I really shouldn't be telling you now, but—'

'Then don't tell me,' said Franco. 'Goodnight, Tony.'

Back at the hotel, Paul frogmarched her through the lobby and up the stairs, practically trampling on the postcard writers, who were on their way down. He locked the door of their room, and turned to confront her.

'Now. Will you please tell me what's got into you? What was all that about?'

Claudia swallowed. Contrary to what she had thought in Paris, he looked as though he was eminently capable of cutting her up in little pieces and feeding her to the crocodiles in the Irrawaddy after all.

'Well?'

'I . . . that is . . .'

'All right. Let's start at the beginning. What did you see in the temple?'

'I saw a shadow dodging out of sight, and I heard footsteps.'

'You've no idea who it was?'

'No.'

'But you think it was me who set it up?'

She didn't answer.

'Why?' He was getting more and more exasperated. 'Do you think I was trying to scare you on purpose?'

'I don't know. That's what I'm asking myself.'

'And you still think it was all my doing even though we've just spent half an hour hiding behind a bush trying to get a look at whoever it was?'

'That could have been for my benefit. To make me think you don't know who they are.'

'To lull your suspicions so we can try again in another temple tomorrow?'

'I don't know.'

'Oh, for God's sake!'

Claudia took a deep breath. 'Paul, you bring me here, you don't tell me why. This morning I find out quite by chance that you came here with Caroline. My identical twin. Since then, you—'

'Ah yes. What did you say to me back there? Did I want people to think you were Caroline? Why the hell would I want them to think that? What do you take me for? Some kind of ritual murderer or something?'

There was a sudden loud knocking on the door. Claudia started violently.

'Shit,' said Paul. 'That must be Franco coming to fetch us for dinner. Go and wash your face.'

'I can't go out to dinner. I can't face it.'

'You have to go out to dinner,' said Paul in the same Prussian-tempered steel accents she had heard in the temple. 'We have no choice. Hurry up, please.' She met his eyes and moved docilely towards the bathroom.

'And for God's sake don't tell him anything. Remember it's all getting back to Tony. We'll finish this discussion later.'

Whoever had been in the Dhammayangyi tonight, it wasn't Franco. He was waiting for them in the lobby looking calm and unruffled, talking to one of his colleagues about Cambodia, inquiring after the sunset with no trace of unease. In any case, from what Paul had seen of him, covert operations were not his style. Why would he bother to hide in the sanctuary when he could get all the information he needed from Claudia in comfort over a glass of Chinese beer? Why would he use a bicycle when he had his jeep?

Someone other than Tony was watching them. But who?

It was a great pity he hadn't managed to get a look at the two cyclists who rode away from the temple ten minutes after they had left. They had taken the road that led away from Pagan, instead of making for the centre of the village. Maybe they were Burmese villagers returning to their homes in the countryside. Or maybe that was just what someone wanted him to think.

'You're looking very thoughtful tonight,' said Veronica. She was sitting opposite him at one end of the long table. Franco was next to Claudia at the other end, and the middle ground was occupied by various members of Franco's archaeological team, chattering noisily in a mixture of French, English and Italian.

'I'm a bit tired. There is so much to see here. It is quite overwhelming. How are you feeling? Franco said this morning that you weren't well.'

'Oh, I get these little stomach problems from time to time. The food, you know. Nothing serious. How much longer are you going to be in Pagan?'

'Not more than a day or so.'

'Ah.' He followed her gaze to the other end of the table, where Franco and Claudia were sitting, heads together, engrossed in a serious, low-voiced conversation. Paul was too far away to hear what they were saying.

'Where are you going from here?' asked Veronica.

'We're not quite sure yet. There are so many interesting places to visit.'

To his relief, the woman next to Veronica made some comment in Italian, and Veronica turned away to answer her. Paul picked at his food and looked thoughtfully round the room. Franco had taken them to the Nation, and half the population of the Irra Inn seemed to have tagged along too. The Americans were there, so were the legionnaires, and so were two or three other familiar-looking couples. Pagan was a small place: you bumped into the same people everywhere you went. So which of these harmless-looking tourists had been hiding in the Dhammayangyi earlier that evening?

Not the postcard-writers, who had already been in the hotel when they got back. Not, he didn't think, the Americans. There was something glossy and confident about those two that was in direct contradiction with the behaviour of the watchers in the temple. It wouldn't occur to them to skulk furtively in the dark. Whatever they wanted, they would take openly. The same went for the legionnaires. So far, they had made no attempt to conceal themselves – why would they have stayed out of sight in the Dhammayangyi? He caught part of their exchange through a sudden lull in the conversation, but they were speaking a language he didn't recognize.

Flemish, maybe, or one of the Scandinavian languages. He listened harder, straining to identify the language, but there was too much noise, the archaeologists had begun to discuss the likelihood of Pagan becoming a major tourist destination and it was impossible to overhear them.

'Think of it, they might even get hot water in the Irra Inn,' said someone mockingly, and there was a raucous shout of laughter.

'Hairdryers in the bathrooms!'

'Mints on the pillow when you go to bed at night!'

Franco said something in Claudia's ear, and she burst out laughing. Paul thought irritably that they would do better just to build another bloody hotel. It was perfectly clear where those two were going to end up tonight. Franco had been coming to Pagan and staying at the Irra Inn for years: it would be a simple matter for him to bribe the receptionist into letting him have the use of an empty room for a couple of hours. Paul was submerged by a wave of annoyance whose strength surprised him. He should have realized from the circumstances of their first meeting – for God's sake, he should have realized just by looking at her! – that this was a girl who wasn't going to pass up any chance of sex that came her way. And if it meant breaking cover and jeopardizing security, did he seriously think that was going to make any difference at all to her?

Claudia was turning into a liability. If she was going to sleep with every man in sight, she was no use as cover, and if she was going to throw hysterical scenes like the one in the temple, she was more than useless, she was dangerous. Abruptly Paul reached a decision. He had made a mistake: he had to get rid of her. Tomorrow he would go to Tourist Burma and book her on the next plane back to Rangoon.

Paul had been looking as black as a thundercloud all evening, and Claudia could understand why. She was beginning to feel

– 137 –

distinctly ashamed of her outburst in the temple. She wasn't sure how she was ever going to look him in the face again, which was the main reason she had spent the whole evening talking to Franco. Well, all right, flirting with Franco. Italian or not, he talked nonsense and made her laugh. What was more, he knew a lot of interesting things about the history of Pagan. He even knew about Marco Polo. It was a relief to sit in a bright, well-lit restaurant and pretend that everything was normal, that no one was lurking in the temples lying in wait for her, that she was here on holiday having fun. Jesus, what a trip. She would be better off in Paris, selling her body, freezing to death, and thinking about Nick.

'Your husband looks very bored this evening.' Franco put a hand over hers.

'He's just tired.' Claudia withdrew her hand. 'We haven't been sleeping much,' she added pointedly.

'Then send him to bed early tonight. We drop the others at the hotel and I take you to see the temples by moonlight.'

'The temples by moonlight?' said Claudia disbelievingly. How corny could you get?

'Is an unforgettable sight.'

'How kind. But I am on my honeymoon, you know.'

Franco looked at her. 'Are you really? One wouldn't think so.'

Claudia met his gaze levelly. 'Appearances can be deceptive.'

'That exactly what I've been thinking.'

'Franco,' said one of the archaeologists, 'it's getting late.'

Without taking his eyes off Claudia, Franco raised his voice above the hubbub. 'Aye May, give us the bill please!'

Claudia decided it was better not to alienate him. Franco was a troublemaker: it was wiser to keep him sweet. 'I'm sorry, Franco. Wrong place, wrong time.' She organized a regretful smile. 'Maybe in our next incarnation things will work out better.'

To her relief, he laughed. 'When we both come back as cockroaches, you mean? Maybe they will. Thank you, Aye May. Here, this should cover everything. Come on then, girls and boys, we got an early start tomorrow. Veronica, please get them all into the cars. Goodnight, Aye May.'

They were all on their feet, collecting their bags and sweaters, moving slowly towards the door. Taking advantage of the general confusion, Franco threaded his way nimbly down to the far end of the table.

'Paul, if you don't mind. A word in your ear.'

They drove back to the Irra Inn in silence. Even the archaeologists were suddenly exhausted. When they got back to the hotel, everyone separated with the briefest of goodnights. Paul and Franco had kept them waiting for fifteen minutes, conferring mysteriously round the back of the restaurant, and they were all restless and irritable. No one suggested a nightcap. Claudia followed Paul up the stairs to their room with a distinct feeling of trepidation. It hadn't been clear to her in the confusion of departure just who had drawn whom aside: What had he and Franco been saying to each other?

Paul shut and locked the door. She sat on her bed and waited.

He sat down opposite her on his own bed and kicked his shoes off. 'So, Claudia. Do you want to go home?'

'Home?' Oh God, he really was pissed off with her. 'You mean back to Europe?'

'Yes.'

'Why?'

The question wasn't necessary, she knew perfectly well why, but he gave her a patient smile and a calm answer.

'I think it might be better. For both of us.'

Claudia sat up straight. Bite the bullet. Get it over with. 'Paul, I want to apologise about that business in the temple this evening. I'm afraid I let my imagination get the better of me. It was just so creepy in there, and there've been weird things happening all day. I guess I just . . .' Oh God, she was getting totally bogged down. 'I don't how how to say I'm sorry to someone for suspecting them of . . . well, I don't even know what I thought exactly—'

'Ritual murder, wasn't it?' said Paul drily, and she felt herself flush.

'—it's a little inadequate, to say the least. But I . . . well . . . I know you wouldn't really . . . I trust you,' she announced firmly. 'I always have. Otherwise I wouldn't be here.'

Pathetic, Claudia, pathetic. Next plane back to Rangoon.

He looked at her with an odd little smile. 'Thank you, Claudia. I accept your apology. Now, how do you feel about going home?'

'Are you throwing me out?'

'No, I'm offering you the chance to opt out.'

'You're pissed off with me. Aren't you?'

'Why should I be?'

'Oh, come on! You know perfectly well why.' Paul said nothing. Again Claudia felt herself floundering. 'Darling, there's nothing to be nervous about. I don't sleep with Italians!' His eyes had dropped to the bedspread; he remained silent. 'I'm not going to sleep with Franco. I'm not going to sleep with anyone this trip,' she asserted valiantly, and then added, for some reason she wasn't quite sure of, 'Except maybe you, if you decide to change your mind.'

He looked up from the bedspread at that and gave her a real consular-class, grade-one, keep-your-distance scowl. 'What would you want to sleep with me for? We're getting along fine like this. Why complicate matters?'

'Just a thought,' said Claudia brightly. 'Probably not a good idea though. You're quite right.' She couldn't take any more of this conversation. She stood up, mumbled something about her teeth, and slammed the bathroom door behind her.

What would I want to sleep with you for, Paul? She brushed her teeth with unnecessary venom. For a whole bunch of reasons you wouldn't know anything about. Recreational sex, friendly sex, ever heard of those? Sex because I'm frightened and you won't tell me what's going on, and if you won't share your mind with me then it would at least be considerate to share your body. Human warmth, Paul, human bloody warmth, it always comes back to the same thing, and if by your standards that makes me a nymphomaniac then that's just too bloody bad.

Paul listened to the sounds of water splashing. It was true that several things had happened today that he hadn't expected either. They were running up against all kinds of obstacles that he hadn't foreseen. He walked across to the window. Outside, all was still. The moon shone on a ruined stupa. The food stall opposite the hotel was closed, the children who played in the dust all day were asleep. Paul drew the curtains. The talk with Franco had calmed him down, and he was beginning to recognize that the scene in the temple tonight had been partly his fault.

The bathroom door opened and Claudia came out. She eyed him warily across the room. Paul sat down again.

'I'm sorry about this afternoon. I should have explained. That girl in the Sulamani . . . It shook me. I needed to be alone for a while.'

'I know.' She stayed where she was. 'I understand. I wasn't thinking straight.'

'I should have told you I'd been here before with Caroline. It was stupid of me not to say anything. It's not surprising you jumped to all kinds of strange conclusions.'

'No, it isn't,' said Claudia. 'And while we're on the subject there's something else I've been wondering about.'

He looked at her cautiously. 'Oh yes?'

'Why did we leave Rangoon in such a hurry? Was it

something to do with that report on the German monk in the newspaper?'

'My God,' said Paul, 'you don't miss much, do you?'

'Was that it?' she repeated.

There didn't seem much point denying it. 'Yes. I'm the Western visitor the police are looking for. When I got to his room he was already dead. I didn't want to get tangled up in a police inquiry, so I left the back way.'

'What about the heroin? Did you know he was a heroin smuggler?'

'Jürgen was no smuggler,' said Paul, surprising himself with his own vehemence. 'I've known him for a long time, and that's one thing I'm sure of. And I'm not a smuggler either,' he added pointedly.

'Good,' said Claudia, 'I'm glad we've got that straight. Then I suppose you have no idea why he happened to have all that heroin in his stomach?'

'None at all.'

'I . . . see. Well, I expect he was just hungry and mistook them for ravioli. Right, so if it wasn't heroin smugglers in the temple tonight, and it wasn't ritual murderers, then who was it?'

'I don't know,' said Paul. 'But tomorrow, believe me, we're going to find out.'

On the other side of the hotel, the side closest to the Ananda, Michael Buckley lay wakefully in the dark. The temple festival had kept him awake during the whole of their stay in Pagan. Barbara had resorted to ear plugs and sleeping pills. Michael, who usually slept like a log, was beginning to think he would have to do the same. The alternative was to lie here all night worrying about Barbara's conversation with the girl in the garden. God, what a rigmarole. She thought they were going to Mandalay, though she didn't know when, because she wanted to buy a tapestry with an elephant on it. What was he supposed to make of all that? Did it mean anything or not?

One of the bands rose in a crescendo, and the loudspeaker announced a mega-donation to the temple in the hysterical tones of a television quizmaster. Michael sighed. The only thing to do in a situation like this was to create one's own entertainment, but it had been a good twenty minutes since Barbara took her sleeping pill and he didn't think he was going to get much help from her. His thoughts drifted enviously to the guy from the gallery with his trophy girlfriend and their cute line in sexual games. Why did you bring me here? Who am I supposed to be? Remembering the way she had been flirting with the fellow in the restaurant later, Michael grinned to himself in the dark. He didn't know the rules of their game but he was ready to bet the two of them were having a high old time right now.

'Ought to take one of my tablets,' said a slurred voice from the next bed. 'Only way to get some rest.'

'Yeah, I know. Listen, honey. She said they were going to Mandalay because she wanted to buy a tapestry? That's all she said?'

There was a pause before Barbara answered. Michael repeated his question.

'Yeah. Tapestry with elephants on it. Or else a glass palace. Whatever that is.'

Michael sat up in bed and switched on the light.

'She said what?'

'Something about a glass palace.' Barbara blinked sleepily. 'Sweetheart, what on earth's the matter?'

'Why the hell didn't you tell me this before?'

'Only just remembered. Didn't know what she was talking about. Does it mean something to you?'

'Damn right it does. The Glass Palace Chronicles are a compendium of ancient Burmese legends. Historical events. Whatever.'

'Yeah, that's right. Burmese history. That's what she said. But why is that a problem?'

Michael told her.

Barbara sat up in bed, her sleepiness evaporating. 'Oh my lord. It sounds as though she knows all about it.'

'We can't handle this on our own any longer. We're going to need some help from the boys.'

A spy in action was an impressive sight. All morning, Claudia watched, fascinated, as Paul worked out his plans, briefed his collaborators and laid his trap. She had glimpsed his world of make-believe and illusion briefly in Paris, but this time it was more than just inventing birthday presents and remembering wedding dates. This time, it was the real thing. During lunch they went over the details one more time, and then everyone dispersed to establish their bona fides and lull the enemy into a false sense of security: Franco to the museum, Paul to the lacquer shops, and Claudia to her room, ostensibly for a siesta.

Sleep was obviously out of the question. The afternoon dragged on for ever. The tourists came and went across the bridge, the children played in the bushes, the stupas crumbled into the earth. At half-past five, Claudia went thankfully downstairs, collected her bicycle, and rode at a leisurely pace towards the Dhammayangyi.

Fewer people were watching the sunset than the previous night. The tourist population was shifting: there were a lot of unfamiliar faces in the hotel. People were moving on: Pagan was in flux. The legionnaires seemed to have broken camp, which was something of a relief, but the postcard writers were still there, and so were the Americans. The latter seemed to have devoted the day to serious shopping: Claudia had seen them returning to the hotel in the middle of the afternoon with a pile of newspaper-wrapped packages, and overheard the wife talking earnestly about a couple of shops they hadn't yet visited.

The dusk was drawing in and the temple was emptying. Time to see if she could raise the ghost of Narathu. Claudia walked to the edge of the terrace, glanced at her watch and mimed exasperation. Bloody husbands, what does he think he's doing, where the hell is he? She had no idea whether anyone was watching her or not. As far as she could see, there were no bicycles except her own in the courtyard, but that didn't mean anything. The Dhammayangyi was within walking distance of the centre of Pagan.

Night was falling fast. She took a deep breath and began to walk towards the stairs. There was no noise from inside the temple, no shuffling feet, no sound of breathing. Perhaps there was no one there. Perhaps they really had all gone home. Making a conscious effort to move at her normal pace, she descended the stone steps to the sanctuary. The darkness was opaque. There were no shadows. Nothing moved.

'Damn,' said Claudia aloud. 'Always bloody late.'

She began to walk round the Buddha statue towards the entrance. She had taken only a few steps when a form heaved itself forward off the wall and she was caught in a vice-like grip. Narathu himself. The ghost had risen. The right arm went round her waist, the left hand was clamped over her mouth. She tried to scream, but his fingers were like rocks and no sound got through.

'Keep quiet and you won't get hurt.'

He spoke in a hoarse whisper. She could feel his breath against her ear.

'I've got a knife. Here.'

For a minute she felt the touch of cold steel against her neck. Again she tried to scream, again he kept his hand against her mouth.

'If I need to, I'll use it. Do you believe that? Do you?'

Again the steel against her throat. He seemed to expect an answer. She nodded, a slight downward motion of her head.

No point impaling herself on the point of the knife. His grip relaxed slightly.

'Quiet then. Not a sound. Just answer my questions. All right?'

She nodded again. The hand moved fractionally away from her mouth.

'What's your name?'

She swallowed. 'Claudia Miller.'

'Your real name.'

'Claudia Miller.'

'What's your husband's name?'

'Paul. Paul Miller.'

'Are you sure of that?'

'Of course I'm sure. What do you want? What's the point—?'

'Keep quiet. I'm the one asking the questions. Why have you come to Burma?'

'To travel. To visit. It's our honeymoon.'

'Your honeymoon?' Despite the whisper, she could sense his bafflement. He hadn't been expecting that.

'Yes.'

'Tell me the truth. Why have you come to Burma?'

'I just told you. We—'

The silence was shattered by the noise of a car. Entering the gate, crossing the courtyard, drawing up by the entrance to the sanctuary. Narathu tensed. His grip tightened. The engine was shut off and a ripple of loud Italian voices broke the silence. What were they doing here, it was far too dark, the sunset was over, there was nothing left to see. Claudia wondered if Narathu spoke Italian, if he understood what they were saying. Was he going to hold her here in the dark and hope no one would see them? Was he going to finish her off with his knife before they came into the sanctuary? With a muttered curse, he let her go and vanished into the shadows. Sweet Jesus Christ. Claudia's legs gave way and she collapsed in a heap on the floor. The Italians erupted noisily into the sanctuary. Another voice came out of the darkness closer at hand, low and urgent:

'Claudia! Are you all right?'

'Yes.' It came out as a croak. She swallowed and tried again. 'Yes. He went up there somewhere.'

'Franco!' yelled Paul. 'Over here! Did you bring a torch?'

Immediately the darkness was pierced by four or five beams of light. Several people pounded past her. Claudia stayed limply on the floor as they shone their torches into the doorways, investigated the passages and climbed up the stairs to the terrace. By the sound of it, Narathu had either got away or gone to ground. The Dhammayangyi, she realized belatedly, was not a good place to set a trap. There were too many places for people to hide. Unfortunately, no one had thought of this beforehand, not even Franco. They had all been bent on re-enacting the scene of the night before.

Paul returned to her side. She could tell it was him by his voice. The sanctuary was so dark that she couldn't see anything any more.

'Are you all right?' He helped her to her feet. 'It never occurred to me that he could be armed.'

Claudia was unable to answer. Paul put his arms round her and she leaned thankfully against his shoulder.

The Italians came drifting over to join them, exclaiming disgustedly.

'Are you all right, *bellissima*?' said Franco.

'She's fine,' said Paul. 'He just roughed her up a bit, that's all. Can you take her back to the hotel in the jeep?'

'Is my pleasure.'

'What about you?' said Claudia. She was starting to shake. Delayed shock or something. She clutched at his pullover. 'You're not going to leave me, are you?' Her voice rose raggedly. The Italians watched in silence. 'Where are you going?'

'I'm only going to ride your bicycle back to the hotel. We can't leave it here.' He gave her an encouraging hug. 'I won't be long.'

When Paul got back to the hotel, the bar was empty. He found Claudia and Franco in the bedroom, sitting on separate beds, drinking beer.

Franco got up as soon as he came in. 'I'm sorry, she won't sit downstairs. She says she don't feel safe. I don't know if this decoy plan is very good idea,' he added reproachfully. 'Is a big shock to her.'

'I'm fine now,' said Claudia. 'It's just that I wasn't expect-ing—' She caught Paul's eye and broke off. 'Thank you for keeping me company, Franco.'

'For you, *cara*, is a pleasure any time. You leaving tomorrow?' Paul nodded. 'Is a good thing, I think.' He kissed Claudia on the cheek. 'Goodbye, *cara*. Eternal regrets. I look forward to our next incarnation.' Paul raised his eyebrows. Franco held out his hand. 'Goodbye, Paul. Good luck.'

Paul shook hands. 'Thank you for the diversion.'

'Next time we won't be there,' said Franco sourly. 'Try not to get her killed.'

The door closed behind him. Paul and Claudia looked at each other. Paul sat down beside her and put his arm round her.

'He's right. It wasn't a good idea. I'm sorry.'

'It doesn't matter. I'm all right now.'

'It never crossed my mind that someone would show up with a knife. This whole thing is getting out of hand. I don't know what's going on.'

'And we still don't know who it is. We're no further forward.'

'You didn't recognize anything about him? His voice, for instance?'

She shook her head despondently. 'I think his voice was

disguised. There was no accent, no intonation, nothing.'

'Nationality?'

'No idea.'

'Height, build, any physical features?'

'He was shorter than you, I think. Broader, definitely. Well-built, in any case. Good muscles. My ribs are still aching. And my jaw, where he dug his fingers into me— Wait. There was something.' She was silent for a minute, frowning. 'His hand on my mouth. It felt, I don't know, odd. Sort of ridged.'

'A scar across the palm?'

'It could be, yes.'

'Which hand?'

'Left. He was holding me with his left arm, and he had the knife in his right hand.'

'Have you seen him before, do you think? Was anything familiar?'

'No to both questions. I don't think he was any of the people we've been seeing around. Not the American, definitely. And not that little German guy either. He was too solid for either of them.'

'What about the legionnaires?'

'Are they still here? I haven't seen them all day.'

'That doesn't mean they aren't here.'

Claudia shivered. 'Actually, it would make sense if it was one of them. Whoever the guy was, he's done this kind of thing before. The way he was using that knife was much too slick. He knew exactly what he was doing with it. He could have slit my throat before either you or Franco had time to make a move.'

Part Four

Excluded Areas

The road rose steeply through the mountains, and a warm, dusty breeze blew gently through the open sides of the bus. Claudia stretched her cramped legs and glanced at her watch. Quarter to bloody three. Eleven hours since they had left Pagan. They were supposed to reach Taunggyi, their destination, at three o'clock, but presumably that didn't include the time it had taken to repair the three bloody punctures they had had during the journey. God knows what time they were going to get there. She only hoped it would be before the sun went down. She had never been as cold in her life as that morning in Pagan, and it would be even colder up here in the bloody mountains.

There was no room to move her legs between the back of the seat in front and the luggage they had shoved on the floor under her feet. Burmese leg room only. Although she wasn't tall by Western standards, she was finding it a squash, and God knows how Paul with his long legs was managing. She glanced sideways at him, which was difficult since they were crammed in so tightly. The bus contained four narrow bench seats spanning its whole width. It was clearly designed for undernourished Burmese, not Westerners on a reasonably balanced diet. Paul's eyes were closed. As far as she could tell, the bastard had gone to sleep sitting up. Part of his bloody professional training, no doubt. She hoped he was finding this whole bloody marathon worthwhile. She still hadn't worked out why they were heading east into Shan State instead of north to Mandalay. Not that Shan State didn't sound exciting. By the sound of it, the whole damn place was knee-deep in smugglers and warlords and opium traffickers, and the icing on the cake was a tribe called the Inthas who lived in houses built on stilts in the middle of a lake and cultivated vegetable fields that floated on the lake's surface. Highly picturesque, no doubt, and considerably more wholesome than the spies and ghosts and contract killers who hung out in the temples of Pagan.

But right now, she was beginning to think of Pagan with nostalgia. Oh, to be shuffling round a temple in the dark dodging the ghost of Narathu instead of being thrown around in the back of a clapped-out old bus, enduring dust, thirst, boredom, back ache, leg cramps, and a few other things she couldn't be bothered to enumerate. Why the hell had she agreed to come on this trip? Two thousand pounds wasn't that much. Knowing her, she'd get back to London and fritter it away inside a week. Offer it all to Nick for a night of unrequited passion. She considered hysterics. Stop the bus, I want to get off. No, it wouldn't work. One, there was no room to do a decent job, and two, nobody would understand her. Except Paul, who would presumably pretend not to.

Oddly enough, the one thing she didn't feel was fear. Last night she had been scared out of her mind, but today her fear of the assailant in the temple had given way to rage. She hadn't come to Burma to be ignominiously set upon by some thug with good arm muscles and a handy piece of steel. Paul had asked her again last night if she wanted to leave, but she had refused. If they ran up against Narathu again, she wanted to find out who he was and what he thought he was doing. She had a feeling Paul was more perturbed by the attack in the temple than she was. Probably it was messing up his plans, whatever they were. He had told her in Paris she wouldn't be in danger, and she was pretty sure he hadn't seen this coming. Whatever else he was, he was a man of honour. He had offered to pay her everything he had promised if she decided to opt out and go home.

She stole another sideways glance at him. A man of honour, but what else? He opened his eyes and smiled at her.

'All right?'

'No,' said Claudia.

'Not much longer.'

She didn't answer. Their bodies were pressed side by side on the narrow bench, and there was a Burmese on each side of them. Today at least there was no shortage of human warmth. Funny how you never wanted things when you finally got them. They rounded a bend and arrived in what passed for a village. The bus slowed and pulled into a tumble-down forecourt. Hens, sacks, tables and a petrol pump.

'What now?' said Claudia irritably.

'Teatime,' said Paul.

Claudia grimaced. 'Do they do room service? I don't think I can get out of this bus. I may have to spend the rest of my life here.'

A wrinkled old man shoved past her with a caustic comment and leapt nimbly to the ground.

'Come on, grandma,' said Paul, and helped her solicitously out of the bus. 'Can you walk, or should I ring for a wheel-chair?'

'A stretcher will do.'

Their fellow passengers were already trooping into the café, ordering refreshments, calling to each other in loud voices. The driver was retying his *longgyi* and contemplating the heap of sacks with an official air. No doubt they would find all that under their feet too when they got back on. They were the only Westerners on the bus. Paul put his arms round her.

'Cheer up. We're not going all the way to Taunggyi. We're getting off before that.'

'Don't tell me. We're going camping in the jungle. Or do we have a secret rendezvous with an opium smuggler somewhere?'

'Both.'

'That's what I love about this trip, there's never a dull moment. You never know what's coming next.'

Paul kissed her cheek and let her go. 'Order me some coffee, will you? I'm going to talk to the driver.'

'That should be interesting, since he doesn't speak a word of English,' said Claudia sourly, but she ambled over to the café with her morale a notch or two higher. Maybe it would be more productive to spend her earnings on a night with Paul. If she could induce him to let go of whatever he was holding on to, it would be interesting to see what kind of explosion was produced.

'They left,' said Michael, 'the desk clerk confirms it. They took the bus to Taunggyi at quarter to four this morning.'

Barbara went on pencilling in her eyebrows. 'My heavens, what an hour. Where on earth's Taunggyi?'

'It's due east of here. Over towards the border with Thailand.'

'What does one go there for?'

'It's one of the jumping off points for Lake Inle.'

'Oh, Lake Inle, right.' She laid down her eyebrow pencil and picked up the brown mascara. Then, after a moment's thought, she selected the blue one instead. Michael had disappeared into the bathroom; she raised her voice to make sure he heard. 'So they're not going to Mandalay after all?'

'We can't assume that.' Michael came out of the bathroom, zipping up the case that contained his shaving kit. 'After what happened in the temple last night, we can't assume anything at all. Hurry up, sweetheart, we got to start packing. There's a taxi coming in half an hour. We're going to follow them to Taunggyi.'

The bus dropped them at a road junction in the middle of nowhere. Well, not quite nowhere. Closer inspection revealed two cafés, a walled enclosure that appeared to contain a market, two parked buses, a number of horse-drawn carriages, and a fair number of people engaged in meaningful occupations such as heaving sacks around, squatting in the dust, and chewing betel. This was Shwenyaung, said Paul informatively. They had to change buses here because they were going to a place called Yaunghwe. Right on the shores of Lake Inle, Liebling. Convenient for visiting the lake.

Claudia considered him sceptically. They were sitting in the bus for Yaunghwe waiting for it to start. Claudia was wedged behind the driver's cab, with Paul next to her. From time to time, someone wandered over from the market across the road and clambered aboard with an unwieldy sack of vegetables.

'That's what we've come here for, is it? To visit the lake?'

'I believe it's worth seeing.'

'Really? Well, I suppose it might be useful for pushing people into.'

'Who are you planning to push into the lake?'

'Narathu for one.'

'An eye for an eye?'

'Two eyes, if I can.'

Paul began to laugh. 'He's really made himself an enemy. It would be better for his sake if he didn't show up.'

'Of course he'll show up. All he has to do is ask at the hotel and the desk clerk will tell him the bus for Taunggyi came to pick us up this morning. Easy. I don't understand why we didn't take a taxi instead.'

'Because that would have made it harder for him.'

Startled, Claudia turned her head to look at him. 'What?'

Paul smiled at her. 'Look at it this way. If anyone we

recognize from Pagan suddenly pops up in Yaunghwe, it means that Narathu has lost his ace.'

'Especially if he has good muscles and a scar on his hand. Well, aren't you clever! What about Tony? Does Franco know where we've gone?'

'It was Franco's idea that we should come here,' said Paul sardonically. 'I forgot to mention we were stopping off in Yaunghwe, mind you. He said he'd tell Tony we'd gone to Mandalay.'

'Are you sure we can trust Franco? I still don't understand why he changed sides.'

'I gather Tony's a little short on management skills. Franco got tired of being treated like an errand boy. That was one reason.'

Someone else squeezed on to the end of the bench, pressing her and Paul even closer together. Burmese buses were definitely the place to go if one was feeling lonely. A young woman in a red *longgyi* came and sat on the floor at their feet, with her sack of vegetables clutched on her knees. The man opposite stared at them unwaveringly.

'And the other?'

'The other was you. I gather you turned him down.'

Claudia went scarlet. Then she said, 'I told you, I don't sleep with Italians. What does that have to do with it? Why does that make him decide to do us a good turn?'

'He was doing himself a good turn. If you'd played ball, it might have suited him to have us around for a day or two longer. Since you didn't, he figured he might as well get rid of us and get Tony off his back at the same time.'

'Is he going to tell Tony what happened last night?'

'Of course not. All I told him when we were setting it up was that someone had frightened you and we wanted to find out who it was – well, you heard me. He knows now that there was more to it than that, but he doesn't know what. Can you see him explaining all that to Tony?'

'Tony would want to know why he hadn't found out the whole story.'

'Exactly. Why don't you sleep with Italians?'

'Jesus, Paul, what kind of a question is that?'

'I'm just curious.'

'My father's Italian. I told you that.'

'You really don't like him, do you?'

'No I don't. He's screwed up my mother's life, he's screwed up mine. And he's put me off Italians for good.'

'At least until your next incarnation,' said Paul.

There was only one tourist hotel in Yaunghwe, and by the time they got there it was full. None of the other guests appeared to fit the role of Narathu and there was no one they recognized from Pagan. They were given a cubicle in the bamboo-built annexe across the courtyard. There was no furniture apart from two single beds, no bathroom, and no insulation. By eleven o'clock that night, the temperature had dropped to zero. Claudia lay in the dark shivering. She was wearing socks, a T-shirt, a sweatshirt, and a pair of black cotton leggings she had sneaked into her luggage when Paul wasn't looking, and still she was cold. The hotel provided only one pitifully thin blanket per bed. Her benefactor Mrs Gloves-and-Hairnet had never been to Yaunghwe, which was a pity, because right now Claudia would not have turned up at her nose at the cosy winceyette pyjamas she would undoubtedly have worn.

On top of everything, she was feeling distinctly queasy. With a sigh, she got up, fumbled around for her jeans and prepared to make the trip across the courtyard to the loo that she had been postponing for the last half-hour.

She returned ten minutes later, trembling with cold, to find Paul, dressed in a T-shirt and the tracksuit pants he wore in lieu of pyjamas, rearranging his bed so that the head was in the middle of the room away from the draughty little window. As she watched, he yanked the blanket off her bed and put it on top of his own.

'What are you doing?'

Paul took her pillow and put it beside his. 'I think we'd be better off in the same bed tonight, if you don't mind. Tomorrow we can ask for extra blankets. Which do you want: wall or corridor?'

'Corridor,' said Claudia, after a pause.

Paul got into bed and held open the blankets for her. Claudia hesitated. After ten days of proposition and innuendo, was she finally being taken at her word? If there was one thing she really didn't want tonight, it was sex.

'It's all right,' said Paul. 'I'm not Italian. It's perfectly all right to share a bed with me.'

'It's not that,' she lied. 'I'm going to keep you awake all night. I don't feel too good. I must have eaten something.'

Paul looked at her more closely. 'You don't look too good either. Come on, get into bed. If you don't keep warm it makes it worse.'

Resignedly, Claudia got in.

'My God,' said Paul, 'you're freezing.' He put his arm round her, and after a moment's hesitation she put her head on his shoulder. It fitted there quite well. Paul stretched out an arm and put the light off. They lay silently in the dark. Claudia felt the warmth slowly returning. Paul made no further move to touch her. She began to relax. Her stomach cramps were abating. Maybe he was right about keeping warm.

'So, Claudia. Tell me about your father.'

Claudia went rigid. 'I don't want to talk about him.'

'You have to. How else am I going to believe you about Franco?'

She was on the point of snarling back that whether he believed her or not was entirely his problem.

'Come on,' said Paul cajolingly, 'tell me.'

The rooms in the annexe were separated by flimsy bamboo partitions that gave very little privacy. Their neighbours on one side had spent most of the evening counting their money in German. On the other side there had been a deep American voice and some flirtatious giggling. But now everyone seemed to have gone to sleep. Apart from the occasional snore, creak or sigh, there was no sound anywhere. No one was awake but them, whispering in the dark, in an almost post–coital intimacy.

She decided to hedge. 'I don't usually talk about it.'

'That's bad. You should never keep things bottled up inside you like that.'

'You're very motherly all of a sudden. Keep warm. Tell me your troubles.'

'Everyone needs someone to look after them now and again. Even you. Come on, tell me what happened. Did he walk out on you?'

'Oh no. He never walked out on us. He was never there in the first place.' She hesitated and then decided that having said that much she might as well tell him the rest. 'My father is married, you see. He always has been. Not to my mother. His wife is an Italian from a fancy bourgeois family. It was more or less an arranged marriage, and they both went their own way from the start. Giulia supervised the maids and sat on charity committees. Alberto had his mistress. My mother. For the past twenty-five years, he's been having an affair with my mother.'

'Mm hm. Go on.'

'Well, that's about it, really. The affair started a couple of years before I was born. For all I know it's still going on. He used to call her whenever he came to London, and I suppose he still does. There,' she announced dismissively. 'Now you know all about my father.'

But it seemed he was hungry for more. 'What happened last summer? When you were in Italy?'

Claudia didn't answer. Last summer was something she did her best not to think about. You thought you had a person figured out, you thought you knew what they were all about, and what they would do and what they wouldn't, but it wasn't true. Human beings were capable of things you couldn't even imagine. Even someone who had been betraying you all his life still had reserves to draw on, still had it in him to deal the final crippling blow that would finish you off for good.

'Come on,' said Paul, as she remained stubbornly silent, 'tell me. It can't be as terrible as all that. Let me guess. Rape? Incest? Did he try to murder you?'

'No, of course not.'

'What then?' he persisted, and so Claudia started reluctantly to tell him what had happened last summer. To begin with, she wasn't sure if she was going to get to the end of it or not, but the tale had its own momentum, and after a while she found that she couldn't have stopped even if she wanted to.

'He invited me to go out to Italy for a few weeks – he has a villa on Lake Garda. Giulia wasn't going to be there, he said, she was going to somebody's Greek island or something. Normally I don't like to spend time with him, but last summer I'd just ... I hadn't ... well anyway, I was in a mess, so I decided to go. The first few days were fine. We stayed out of each other's way, went out to dinner a couple of times, had a couple of reasonable conversations. I was beginning to think we were finally getting to some kind of decent relationship. Then, after about a week, this woman arrives, about my age, maybe a couple of years older. Her name's Livia. He tells me she's the daughter of a friend of his, and it would be nice for me to have some company my own age. Okay, fine, except that she was clearly there to keep him company, not me. That didn't bother me. I'd never imagined he was faithful to my mother or anything like that. But then the day after, in the middle of breakfast, he suddenly announces that Giulia's agreed to a divorce. All along his line has been that Giulia's a devout Catholic so there's no question of a divorce. So I'm sitting there with my mouth open thinking he's finally going to marry my mother and wondering why he's telling me this in front of Livia. And then what do you think he says? He's going to marry Livia. Not my mother. Livia. And the reason he was telling me was that he wanted me to break the news to my mother.'

Okay, Paul. There it is. Now you know it all. She waited a little wearily to hear what he was going to say. The advantage of keeping things bottled up was that one didn't have to cope with other people's reactions as well as one's own. She had spent enough time condemning her father in her own mind, screaming at him, insulting him: she didn't need to hear someone else doing it too. Paul said nothing, just went on holding her against his side. The pressure of his arm was more comforting than any words could have been. Claudia felt the tension beginning to drain out of her. Ten minutes later she was asleep.

The snow had stopped falling, and now it was melting. The Embassy garden was caked with ice, and the air was sullen and cold.

'They've gone,' said Tony. 'Left for Mandalay this morning.'

'Damn,' said Adrian. 'Does that mean we've lost them?'

'Well, I wouldn't say that, dear boy. Foreigners aren't exactly unobtrusive in this country, you know. Won't be terribly hard to find them again.'

He stopped. Adrian waited.

'Thing is, who's going to go looking for them? My chap in Pagan can't really follow them up there. Matter of fact, he flatly refuses to do so.'

'Yes, no, of course not. That's quite understandable. I never meant, in fact this is exactly why I—'

'Yes, I know. Thing is, I don't think the arrangement you set up is going to work out. No good having him looked after by amateurs, not with the situation we seem to be facing now. We need a professional.'

Adrian sighed. Tony had sent him a signal relating the business with the dead German monk. 'Well in the circumstances, I can see that—'

'If I could, I would send someone up there to find out where he is and keep an eye on him. Unfortunately, I have nobody to send.'

Adrian was silent. Outside his office window, the sky was darkening and a greasy, sleety rain had begun to fall.

'I'll be absolutely honest with you,' said Tony. 'I don't care for this situation at all. We're dealing with a British diplomat. Formerly of the Rangoon Embassy. Masquerading as a German tourist. Travelling round Burma. Paying calls on the wrong kind of person. No intention of ever going home. Tricky situation, dear boy, and that's not all. One hasn't the faintest idea what this chap has in mind, but one can't exclude the possibility that his plans may trigger off a major crisis with the Burmese.'

'Well, I suppose we can't—'

'They've chucked out three of our people in the past couple of years already. Pretty flimsy pretexts, but that doesn't bother them.'

'Well, I can certainly understand—'

'One doesn't want to provide any more grist to their mill, does one?'

'You have nobody at all who could go up to Mandalay for a couple of days?'

'No one at all.'

Adrian sighed. Jill was going to hate this.

'You know, dear boy, I really hope that no word of this little escapade gets back to the Ambassador, because if it does there'll be hell to pay.'

'I'll fly out to Bangkok tonight,' said Adrian.

★

Claudia was woken by the thud of the bedroom door slapping shut against its wooden frame. The room was empty, but the bed beside her was still warm. Paul couldn't have been up long. Her stomach pains had disappeared; she felt rested and full of energy. She got briskly out of bed and started to dress. By the time Paul came back from the courtyard, shaved and shivering, she was fully clad in a T-shirt, a shirt and two sweatshirts. It was back to Parisian-style dressing again, with everything one owned on one's back.

'How are you feeling?' said Paul. 'Did you sleep all right?'

'Like a log.' She grinned at him. 'You were right. There's nothing like throwing a few skeletons out of the cupboard to get a good night's sleep. What's for breakfast?'

The dining room contained a single, large round table. Two guests were already having breakfast. They looked up as Paul and Claudia came in. Oh shit, just what they needed. The postcard writers from Pagan. The desk clerk, who seemed to double as waiter, cleaner and cook, shuffled off to cook some more eggs. Paul and Claudia sat down. There was an exchange of stony stares. For a moment, Claudia thought they were all about to take up where they had left off in the bus office in Pagan.

Then Paul started talking to them in German. Claudia was taken aback. Despite the claims of his passport, it hadn't occurred to her that he might really be able to pass as German, but by the sound of it he was pretty good. As far as she could make out, he was apologising to them for the scene in the bus station, explaining that he had been in Pagan several years ago with his sister, who had since died, that painful memories had impelled him to leave as soon as possible, and that this was why he had looked at the ticket clerk's chart, observed that two empty seats on the bus remained, and insisted on taking them. He didn't point out that the other two, who had been ahead of them in the queue – hence the dispute – could have looked at the chart and staked a claim themselves, but perhaps they had figured this out in the meantime, because they accepted his apologies with good grace, explaining that they had come here in a taxi, and that it hadn't been as expensive as they had feared. Claudia wondered if it had been them counting their money the previous night. Then they all introduced themselves, there were smiles and handshakes, and the temperature over the table rose several degrees in spite of the freezing air coming in through the glassless windows. The Germans were called Thomas and Christa Huber, and they were students from Würzburg. Thomas turned to Claudia and made some remark she didn't understand. She shook her head and said, *'Ich verstehe nicht.'*

'Meine Frau ist Engländerin,' said Paul, looking slightly startled at his wife's linguistic proficiency, and Thomas repeated his remark in English. The trip had been pleasant, though tiring, and the scenery was magnificent, especially between Thazi and Shwenyaung. Did she not agree? No she did not, said Claudia vehemently, and gave them a brief account of the rigours of the bus trip. As for the scenery, she had no idea what it was like, since Burmese buses were designed for maximum wind chill and minimum visibility.

'I can tell you, we did you a favour, pinching those seats from under your noses. I wish you'd taken them, then we could have travelled luxuriously in a taxi too.'

'Well, I do not know if it was really luxury,' said Thomas.

'We must keep stopping all the time,' said Christa. 'Twice for punctures, three times for water, four or five times for oil—'

'More than that,' said Thomas. 'Every half hour. We have shared the taxi with some Canadian people. They wanted to hurry to Taunggyi, and they didn't like it when we must stop all the time, but of course there was nothing they could do. In Asia, it is better never to be in a hurry,' he concluded sagely.

The outside door slammed, and two more guests appeared.

To her surprise, Claudia recognized the bearded American she had met on her first morning in Rangoon. He was accompanied by a boy of about fourteen in a black Los Angeles Raiders baseball cap.

'Morning,' said the American to the room at large. 'Hi there,' he added casually to Claudia. 'Sleep okay?' he asked the Germans.

'It was cold,' said Thomas feelingly.

'Damn right, it was. We were cold even with our sleeping bags, right, Greg?'

'Right,' said Greg.

'We're thinking we might move to Taunggyi tonight. Better hotel. So how are you today, beautiful?' he went on, turning to Claudia. 'Enjoying your trip?'

'I'm finding it very interesting,' said Claudia primly. 'I'd like you to meet my husband.'

Paul was sitting with his back to the door. He turned round to greet the new arrivals. He and the American looked at each other.

'Paul Miller,' said Paul, getting to his feet. 'It is nice to meet you.' His German accent was about three times more marked than usual.

'Hi, Paul. I'm Austin Maclaren, and this is my son Greg.' Ponderous handshake. 'Er, what did you say your name was, beautiful?'

'Claudia.'

'Well, that's a mighty pretty name.' He gave her a long, thoughtful stare, and then his gaze shifted back to Paul. A frown flickered across his face and was gone. He sat down, the desk clerk appeared with another pot of coffee and he ordered eggs for himself and Greg. Paul sat down and buttered his toast. Thomas poured more coffee, Christa explained that she and Thomas had met Austin and Greg on the local bus the previous night. Claudia looked round the table. Five bland untroubled stares. No one seemed to have noticed the short shocked pause when Paul and Austin first set eyes on each other. So had she imagined it or what?

Austin and the Germans were talking about a market in a place called Heho. Paul was sitting with hunched shoulders, concentrating on his toast and taking no part in the conversation. Claudia shifted in her seat, her knee brushed against Paul's leg, and he jumped about a foot in the air. No, she hadn't imagined it. Paul had met Austin in a previous incarnation. Whether as cockroaches or not, it was impossible to say, but he was definitely not pleased to see him again.

Heho market was like nothing Claudia had ever seen before. The merchandise was laid out on bamboo-covered stalls, and the ox-carts that had been used to bring it to the market stood in the parking lot behind. They wandered round, examining the wares. Knives, blankets, bales of material. Women with sewing machines running up the latest Shan fashions while their clients chewed betel nuts and spat and gossiped. Tomatoes, oranges, chillis, onions. Plenty of vegetables, but no meat and no poultry. Dried fish was the only protein in sight. No wonder they were all so thin. The market was crowded. People pushed past, carrying sacks and baskets on their heads. Shans wearing *longgyis* mixed with the hill tribes in their black clothes and bright headdresses. There were even a few pairs of jeans to be seen. They were closer to Thailand here, explained Paul, when Claudia commented on this deviation from the standard Marxist-Buddhist dress code, and there were more smuggled goods available. In any case, people paid less attention to the central government up here. Under British rule, Shan State hadn't even been part of Burma Proper. Along with most of the other mountainous, less governable parts of the country, it had belonged to what were delicately referred to as the Excluded Areas.

'Excluded from what?' demanded Claudia.

'Why, the benefits of British civilization. School uniforms

and Sunday lunch. You know the kind of thing.'

They walked slowly round the market, photographing the vegetable stalls, poking through the displays of Chinese tin mugs and basketware, but buying nothing. It was not a tourist market, and the goods on sale were not souvenirs but the basic necessities of life for the country people of the Shan State. Claudia kept an eye open for the legionnaires, but there was no sign of them anywhere. One of the stallholders called out to her and held out a length of material. She smiled uncomprehendingly. He repeated his remark more insistently.

'I think he thinks you're unsuitably clad for a nice Burmese girl,' said Paul. 'He's trying to sell you a *longgyi*.'

'He thinks I'm Burmese?'

'Maybe not.' Paul examined her critically. 'You don't have the right features. But you could certainly pass for Shan or something. Buy one if you like,' he added off-handedly. 'It'll make his day.'

'Can I?'

'Why not. It would make quite a useful addition to your usual wardrobe.' She looked at him warily, but he was laughing at her. She picked up the length of cloth and inspected it.

'Not that one,' said Paul. 'Not you at all. Ask to see some of the stuff he's got piled up in the back there. I'm going to take a photo of the giraffe women over there. I'll be back in a minute.'

Claudia followed his gaze to where two women with brass rings round their elongated necks were in the process of unloading their baskets. He was right: it would make a marvellous photo. She turned her attention back to the *longgyis*. The stallholder pulled out bales of material with growing enthusiasm, and a few bystanders gathered round to watch. Claudia made her choice and looked round for Paul. The giraffe women were still there, but he was nowhere to be seen. Fortunately, he had given her some kyats, and she had enough to pay for the *longgyi*. The stallholder wrapped it carefully in a piece of newspaper and presented it to her with a big grin. The bystanders murmured and giggled.

'Goodbye,' said one of them, bolder than the rest. 'Where you from?'

'England.'

'Where you go?'

'I'm going to look for my husband.' It was odd how easily the word had begun to trip off her tongue. A word, a name and separate beds, except when the cold got too bad. Handled like that, marriage was easy.

'Hi there,' said a voice behind her, and she found Austin at her elbow with a cowboy hat and a camera. 'Quite something, isn't it?'

'It certainly is. Did you see the giraffe women just now? The only people I haven't seen yet are the opium smugglers.'

'You won't see them,' said Austin. 'You're in the wrong part of Shan State. Poppy-growing areas are further north.'

'Pity. I'd have liked to visit a poppy field.'

'You need connections to do that. They aren't too keen on visitors up there. You also need a mule.'

'Why?'

'To get up the mountain. Or you can walk, of course.'

'You mean there aren't any buses? It must really be the back of beyond.'

'It is,' said Austin. 'That's the whole point.'

He sounded as though he knew what he was talking about. Claudia considered asking him if he'd been up there himself, but thought better of it.

'I'll just have to talk to Tourist Burma about it,' she said lightly. 'They do buses, I expect they can manage mules. You haven't seen my husband, have you? He went off to take a picture of the giraffe women, and I don't know where he's got to.'

'They probably sent him off with a flea in his ear,' said

Austin. 'Padaungs don't take kindly to having their photographs taken.' His eyes roamed over her thoughtfully. Not undressing her, the way Franco had, looking for something else. His gaze halted for a moment on her wedding ring and moved back to her face. 'So what have you been doing these last few days, beautiful? You weren't in Rangoon, were you?'

'We went to Pagan.'

'Ah yes, Pagan. Bunch of old temples, right? Is it worth a visit, would you say?'

'It depends what you're interested in,' said Claudia non-committally. And who's following you. And what you have to hide. Austin's attention had wandered. He wasn't looking at her any more. Claudia followed his gaze past an onion-seller, sitting cross-legged on the ground with her onions and garlic spread out around her. Thomas and Christa were standing next to a display of cigars talking to another couple of Westerners. Even from the back, they were immediately recognizable. Ms Designer Dust and her husband from Pagan.

'Well, well,' said Paul, 'it's a small world.' He had come up behind them unobserved.

'Sure is,' said Austin. Paul put his arm possessively round Claudia and Austin looked him over with a mixture of amusement and distrust. 'Always bumping into people when you least expect to.'

'Where else is there to go?' said Claudia innocently. 'It's a bit short on tourist attractions up here.'

She looked idly across at Thomas and Christa as she spoke. Thomas caught sight of her and raised a hand in greeting. The American woman saw her too, and said something to Thomas. Claudia switched her attention back to Paul and Austin.

'Yeah, well, there are tourists and tourists,' said Austin.

'Especially this far south,' said Paul.

Both men were grinning broadly. Claudia eyed them in puzzlement. She had been angling for a reaction and she had got it. Unfortunately she wasn't quite sure what it was.

Greg appeared by his father's side. 'Hey, Dad, come over here. There's something I want to show you.'

'See you later,' said Austin. 'They sell Mandalay rum in the hotel, I noticed. How about a drink this evening?'

'I thought you were moving to Taunggyi,' said Paul.

'We may not bother,' said Austin. His glance swung past them to where Thomas and Christa were standing with the Americans.

'Okay,' said Paul. He wasn't bothering with his German accent, Claudia noticed. 'See you later, then.'

'What was all that about?' said Claudia, when they were out of earshot.

'An old acquaintance,' said Paul. 'Did you buy the *longgyi*? Show me.'

The brief exchange with Austin seemed to have reassured him. The worried look he had worn all morning disappeared; he kissed her cheek, told her he couldn't wait to see her in her new clothes, and kept his arm round her to steer her through the crowds and out of the market.

CRUSH ALL DESTRUCTIVE ELEMENTS said the sign across the street from the café. All very well in theory, but in practice how did you decide which elements were destructive and which were not?

'What do you want to drink?' said Paul.

'Coffee, please. Is there anything to eat here?' said Claudia, glancing round. The café was a large square gloomy room with blue-painted walls and a concrete floor. A few dingy display cabinets contained Lux soap, toilet paper, salt, candles and tinned fish. In the background, the radio was playing an old ABBA song from the seventies, sung in Burmese. A boy of about ten came and wiped the table and stood waiting for their order.

'Hungry again?'

'You know me, Paul. Spying gives me an appetite. What about some of those cakes over there? Can we try those? *Kaffee* and *Kuchen*, just like *zu Hause*.'

Paul gave her a sharp look, but transmitted the order without flinching.

'You didn't tell me you spoke German,' he said, when the boy had gone.

'You didn't ask,' Claudia pointed out. 'Don't worry, I don't speak much. I did A-level five years ago, and I've forgotten most of it by now.'

'Hm.' He put his chin on his hand and looked at her reflectively. 'Why did you drop out of university? I guess I didn't ask you that either.'

'No you didn't, and if you had I wouldn't have told you.'

'So tell me now.'

'I don't know about that. You might let something slip to the wrong people.'

'I'll be careful, I promise.' He took her hand under the table. 'Come on, Claudia, you can trust me.'

Claudia pretended to hesitate, and then, because she had rarely seen him in such a good mood, because the sun had come out and she had taken off both her sweatshirts, and, most of all, because she knew he was telling the truth when he said she could trust him, she told him the whole tacky little story. Nick and Racine and Bérénice, tutorials on the nature of passion, smouldering looks across the office. Andromaque clinging to the memory of her dead husband, Phèdre killing herself for love. The first-year student Claudia met leaving his flat one Saturday night when she'd told him she was going home for the weekend, the trip they had been meant to be taking to Provence which died from inanition, the application for the job at Birmingham that she found on his desk, the lies, the omissions, the misunderstandings, the gradual breakdown of communications.

Paul heard her to the end in silence. When she had finished

her grisly little recital, she gobbled down two of the dry little cakes in swift succession and waited for the inevitable question. Everyone she had told had said exactly the same thing: Why didn't you hang on one more month and take your Finals? To which the answer was that there was no point, she would have failed them anyway.

Paul said, 'I can't help thinking that if you were identifying with Phèdre or Bérénice, you must have known from the start it was never going to work out.'

Claudia drank her coffee. Paul poured the green tea that was served automatically in Burmese cafés into two small handleless cups. Across the room, a tough-looking Shan wearing a leather jacket and straw hat with his *longgyi* and sandals ate little cakes with surprising delicacy.

'Yes, I suppose I was,' she said in the end. 'No one's ever accepted me in my life. There was no reason why he should be any different.'

'Claudia—'

'Let's face it,' she told him, in the most aggressive tones she could manage, 'I'm a misfit. Half-Chinese, half-Italian, illegitimate on top of everything . . . I don't belong. I don't fit in, and people don't like that. It makes them uncomfortable.'

There was a pause and then Paul said lightly,

'What you need is someone like me. Half-English, half-German, a misfit and a spy. I knew the first time I saw you that you were the girl for me. We're soulmates, Liebling. We can make people feel uncomfortable together for the rest of our lives.'

Claudia laughed aloud. Not from amusement. From gratitude, at being rescued from the resentful little corner she had painted herself into. 'Then you admit you're a spy?' she demanded.

'Certainly not. But you spend so much time telling me I am one that I'm beginning to believe you.'

'So who do you spy for? England or Germany? Are you really half German?'

'Yes. My mother was German, and I lived there for several years as a child.'

'But your father was English? Come on,' she added, as he showed signs of hesitation. 'You've got all my skeletons out of me. It's your turn now.'

'My father was English,' he agreed reluctantly. 'My parents met in Germany after the war, and settled in England. My mother never got used to England, and she took me to live in Germany when I was seven.'

'Then you grew up in Germany?'

'Only till I was fifteen. My mother died and I had to go back to England to live with my father.'

'But you didn't want to?'

'No. I was used to Germany by then, and I didn't get on too well with my father. He'd remarried and they had a two-year-old daughter. I didn't see how I was going to fit in.'

'And did you fit in?'

'It took a while. I missed my friends in Hamburg, and it was a long time before I made any English friends of my own age. Then, just as I was beginning to settle down, there were more upheavals. The summer I finished school, my uncle died, and my father decided to move back up to Edinburgh to be near his sister. We'd been living in Sussex, I'd been accepted at Cambridge, and then I had to spend vacations in Edinburgh.'

'So you lost all your friends a second time? That must have been tough.'

'Yes.'

She watched him stare into space over the edge of his coffee cup. All those convulsions, all those lost friends. And now you have no friends at all, do you, Paul? It's safer that way. Aloud she said, 'Where do you live now?'

'I don't have a proper home in England. Caroline and I sold the house in Edinburgh when my father died. Working for the diplomatic service, one spends a lot of one's time abroad, you know.'

He shot her a swift, doubtful glance, as if wondering if he had said too much, and moved the conversation back where it had been before. Plainly he was more at ease with her skeletons than with his.

'What are you going to do when you go back to England? Go back to Nick?'

'Hardly. He doesn't want me, remember?'

'He might have changed his mind.'

'I doubt it. In any case, it wouldn't work. He's ambitious, is Nick. I didn't realize that at first. He needs a nice little wife to flatter the department head and organize wine and cheese parties for the students. He doesn't need an outcast like me – and I reckon I don't need him either.'

'So it's finished?'

'I guess so. Heart-whole and fancy free, that's me, and ready to set my sights at that divine bit of rough trade over there. If he's not an opium smuggler, I don't know who is.'

'VCRs, more likely,' said Paul, turning to look. 'Too far south here for opium.'

'That's what Austin told me, yeah.'

'Austin did? Well, he should know.' Paul smiled mysteriously to himself. 'Do you want some more tea? No? Well then let's go back to Yaunghwe and take a look at the lake. With a hat like that your friend's probably an Italian anyway.'

'I really don't know what you're doing this for,' said Jill.

'I told you already.' Adrian picked up an armful of polo shirts and carried them over to the bed. 'Philip's been acting very strangely recently. He's sold his flat, he's transferred the contents of his bank account to my parents. I don't know what this trip to Burma is all about. If you want to know the truth, I think he's heading for a nervous breakdown.'

'For God's sake, Adrian, Philip can look after himself.' She was leaning against the bedroom door, not quite in and not quite out, arms folded in a posture of disapproval. 'If he chooses to go off to Burma for a few weeks, it's no one else's business. Not even yours. He won't thank you for showing up unannounced like this.'

'He's sold his flat, Jill! It's not just a few weeks we're talking about here.'

'Months, then, what does it matter? It'll probably do him good.'

Adrian paused in the act of dumping a pile of socks into his travelling bag. 'What on earth do you mean by that?'

'Philip isn't having a breakdown now. I mean it's not something recent. He's been broken down for years, if you see what I mean.'

'No,' said Adrian coolly, 'I can't say I do.'

'Philip has been unhappy with himself and his life ever since – well, ever since I've known him.'

'Nonsense! It was when Lucy died that he started going to pieces. He's never come to terms with her death.'

Jill uncrossed her arms and sat down. 'Adrian, listen to me a minute. Let me tell you something. I know you adored Lucy, and she adored you, I know how close you were, the twin thing and all the rest of it, but the truth is that she and Philip did not get on. They were all wrong for each other, and they both knew it. If Lucy had lived, I'd have been surprised if that marriage had lasted.'

'That's nonsense, Jill. I really can't accept that.'

'I know you can't. But I think you should give it some thought.'

'I never saw any evidence that their marriage was in trouble.'

'No, because they were both too busy keeping up appearances. Lucy was, anyway. And I suppose Philip was too, in his peculiar way. I've never understood the first thing about

Philip. I used to look at him and wonder what on earth was going on in his mind.'

'Well it's true that Philip isn't a very outgoing person. He's always been very self-contained.'

'He's not just self-contained. It's more than that. It's as if he's trying to hide part of himself. Do you honestly know what Philip is really like? Because I don't.'

'You read too many horror stories,' said Adrian, with a perfidious glance at the pile of science fiction on the bedside table.

'This is nothing to do with horror stories. We're talking about an identity crisis.'

'Don't be ridiculous. He has an identity!'

'Of course he does,' said Jill patiently. 'But I don't think it's the one he wants.'

Narathu had not followed them to Lake Inle. At least, not yet. Although they got back to Yaunghwe to discover that no less than three couples from Pagan were now in residence, the temple ghost was not among them. Or so Paul concluded, after an evening spent studying the newcomers at close quarters. Due to the dearth of restaurants in Yaunghwe, a lot of the guests had elected to eat in the hotel. Dinner consisted of traditional Shan dishes and was surprisingly good. The puppet show that followed wasn't bad either. Everyone ate sitting cross-legged in a circle on the floor of the lounge, a vast, bare room with white walls and a polished teak floor. Paul made a point of inspecting the hands of the three men who had come from Pagan, but none of them had a scar on his left palm.

When the puppet show was finished, Austin, true to his word, ordered a couple of bottles of Mandalay rum and invited everyone to have a drink. Paul suspected that the bottles would go on expenses. He hadn't yet worked out who Austin's target was, and he didn't much care. As long as they kept out of each other's hair, there should be no friction. Austin was a pro, you had to hand it to him. Paul doubted he had ever been to Burma in anything but an official capacity before, yet he was engaging in the usual tourist chat – where have you come from, where are you going to, how did you get here, how are you getting there? – with practised ease. Once a deceiver, always a deceiver. Paul sighed. At least with Austin, he knew where he was. It was impossible to tell which of the rest of them were deceivers and which were authentic.

His gaze wandered idly round the circle. Thomas and Christa, who were travelling round Asia for six months before starting work. Michael and Barbara Buckley, who were Canadian, not American, owned a hotel on an island near Vancouver and were taking advantage of the off-season to spend a few weeks travelling. Pierre and Mélanie Turenge, a pair of French teachers currently working in Peking, whom he had seen from a distance wandering round the temples in Pagan. The only people they hadn't encountered before were two young Australians, Keith and Angus, who had come to Lake Inle directly from Rangoon. What country have you come from, where are you going next, how long have you been travelling? Six of the people in the room had been in Pagan at the same time as himself and Claudia. Any of them could have found out from the hotel where they had gone and followed them.

Or else their presence could be sheer coincidence. From Pagan, the Burmese tourist circuit offered two main choices. One was Mandalay, and one was Lake Inle. Michael was confiding to Thomas that he and Barbara had just spent a fortnight in Thailand and were going on to India after this. Christa was telling Pierre that they were planning to go down to Malaysia where they knew someone who had a boat. Austin was giving Barbara a lengthy account of the vacation he had taken in Vancouver the year before last. Greg was explaining to Mélanie that his father was on sabbatical and the whole family had taken a year off to travel round the world. Right now his mother was back in California on a visit, but she would be meeting up with them in Bangkok. Paul smiled to himself. Austin had the kid pretty well schooled. Claudia was sitting slightly apart from the rest of the group, talking to the two young Australians. They were too far away for Paul to hear what they were saying, but as he watched, a sudden peal of laughter went up. Claudia's face was alight in a way he had never seen before. Paul felt suddenly old and excluded and vaguely guilty. She should be travelling with people like that, kids her own age, doing what she wanted to do, having a good time, instead of trailing round with a middle-aged man, pretending to be something she was not . . .

'What about you?' said Barbara. 'Have you been to Mandalay yet or are you going there next?'

Paul looked at her and smiled. Now this was more his age group. Early forties, well-tended, barely wrinkled flesh, smooth hair, perfume. 'No, we haven't been there yet. Actually, we might give it a miss.'

'Mandalay? Really?'

'I think so, yes.' He kept his smile in place. *They have hot water at the hotel in Taunggyi, you said so yourself. Why would a nicely groomed lady like you want to come and stay in a dump like this, even if it is more convenient for excursions on the lake?*

'I was already there,' he explained, 'and I didn't find it a very nice place.'

'Oh, you've been to Burma before?'

'Yes, I was here with my sister a few years ago.'

'Your wife hasn't seen it then? Doesn't she want—'

Claudia cut in smoothly. He hadn't even realized she was listening to the conversation. 'I've seen Paul's photos from his other trip. He's right, you know, it really doesn't look anything special.' She gave Paul a look that left nobody in any doubt that when Paul said jump, his adoring young wife would waste no time jumping. Paul began to feel a serious dislike for himself.

'We thought we might go to Sandoway instead,' he told Barbara. 'It's some kind of seaside resort, apparently.'

'A Burmese seaside resort,' said Michael. 'That should be interesting. Do they swim in their *longgyis*, or what?'

'I bought one in the market this morning,' said Claudia, 'just in case.' There was a general laugh, Austin passed round the bottle of rum, the French teachers got up to go to bed, someone started complaining about how it was impossible to see everything on a two-week visa. The rum ran out and Greg was dispatched to the reception desk to get another bottle.

'It is so annoying to spend so much time to work out how you can go from one place to the next,' said Christa.

'The guy at the desk handles travel arrangements,' said Keith, the older and more assertive of the two Australians. There was a chorus of interested queries. 'Buses, planes, whatever you need. Someone goes up to Tourist Burma in Taunggyi and arranges it all.'

Greg returned with the news that there was no more rum.

'What about beer?' said Austin.

'Only mineral water.'

'Well, hell.'

'Ask if they've got any opium,' said Claudia. 'This place would make a great opium den.'

'You didn't find any smugglers in the market this morning?' said Austin.

'I saw a guy who looked just like one, but we didn't manage to get into conversation.'

'Opium!' said Christa disapprovingly. 'Isn't that what they use to make heroin?'

'I'm not suggesting we should all shoot up,' said Claudia hastily. 'Just smoke a pipe, or whatever you do. I've always wanted to try opium.'

'Sounds interesting,' said Michael.

'My God!' said Christa.

'Hey, come on, Christa, there's nothing wrong with smoking opium,' said Keith. 'Don't confuse it with heroin. They've been using opium in Asia since the seventh century. Never been any social ill-effects worth speaking of. Up until World War Two, it was a perfectly normal practice.'

'There you are,' said Claudia. 'How about now? Does it still go on?'

'There's less opium use. People are switching to heroin. I believe there's at least one heroin addict per family in the north of Shan State.'

'Is that right?' said Barbara. 'My goodness.'

'Well, that's okay,' said Michael. 'That'll make sure they go right on growing it. Keep the balance of payments in good shape. As long as they don't hog it all themselves.'

'Don't worry,' said Keith. 'These days they produce about twenty times the amount it takes to keep the whole of the United States supplied. I don't know how much you need in Canada, of course.'

'Oh, we try to keep our end up.'

'What about the DEA?' said Thomas. 'I thought they were making a big drive to stamp out opium cultivation.'

'What is the DEA?' said Christa.

'DEA stands for Drug Enforcement Agency,' said Austin. 'The narcotics squad. It's a branch of the U.S. Department of Justice. Well, yeah, they tried, but they didn't get very far.'

'Why not?'

'The hill tribes who grow the opium are extremely poor. They can get more money for opium than for any other kind of crop, so it's kind of pointless trying to persuade them to grow anything else.'

'And that,' said Keith, 'is entirely the Burmese government's fault. The poverty, I mean. They've never wanted to spend money developing the mountain states. All the state's resources have always been allocated to the central plain, where the ethnic Burmans live. Contrary to those slogans you see pasted up all over the place, the only solution for Burma is to become a federation. The nationalities have to have equal rights, and equal money too.'

The tone was categorical: they all gazed at him respectfully.

'In other words,' said Michael, 'solve the nationalities problem and you solve the narcotics problem too?'

'Right,' said Keith.

'Sounds good,' said Michael.

'Yeah, well, it's not quite as easy as that,' said Austin.

'What do you mean?' said Keith, taken aback.

'You're forgetting one thing. Corruption. As things stand now, you've got half Burma on the take. Local Tatmadaw commanders, police officers, customs officials—'

'Tatmadaw?' said Barbara. 'You mean the Burmese army is involved?'

Austin gave her an enigmatic smile. 'It always has been. How do you think they get the opium down from the hill villages to the heroin refineries?'

'Well, I'm sure I don't know, I—'

'Mule trains,' said Austin. 'Big ones. Not just two or three mules, hundreds of them. Not exactly hard to spot, but Tatmadaw never intercepts them. Now why do you think that is?'

'They've been bribed,' said Keith. 'Well, yeah, I guess you're right, but ...' He began to muster his counter-arguments.

Claudia got quietly to her feet and padded rapidly across the room. Tonight they were sleeping in the main building. Given the low outside temperatures and the lack of heating, Paul doubted they would be much warmer than the previous night, but at least they now had their own bathroom. Something about the urgent way Claudia had got up and left made him suspect that this was just as well. The bedrooms all led off the central lounge where they were sitting. Claudia opened the door and slipped rapidly inside.

Paul turned his attention back to the heroin discussion, but it was beginning to run down. Austin was clearly unwilling to reveal the full extent of his knowledge, and Keith was getting the better of the argument. With the exception of Michael, who was listening intently, the group was losing interest. Barbara was examining her nails, Angus was talking in a low voice to Christa, and Greg had got up to go to bed.

'You guys sound pretty well informed,' said Michael, looking from Austin to Keith and back again.

Austin shrugged. 'Not really. Read a few books, that's all. There was a big piece in the *L.A. Times* just before we came out.'

Michael switched his attention to Keith. 'What about you?' and Keith explained that he had just completed a doctoral thesis about the influence of geopolitical factors on the economic development of South-East Asia. He gave them a complacent smile and looked around for acknowledgement.

'Well how about that,' said Barbara.

'Interesting subject,' said Austin.

'The one man in Australia who doesn't lie on the beach and drink beer all day long,' said Angus.

'And are you an Asian specialist too?' said Thomas, but Angus, it seemed, was a musicologist with a particular interest in Brahms.

'Goodness,' said Claudia, rejoining the circle, 'what a coincidence. Your favourite composer, isn't he, darling?'

'You know something?' said Michael. 'I don't think they know who we are or anything about us. I think they're in Burma for some reason that has nothing to do with us.'

'Really?' Barbara rummaged among the pots spread out on the bed for her night cream. The room they had been given was even worse than the one in Pagan. Not only was there no bathroom, there wasn't even any indoor plumbing. And naturally there was no mirror. She squinted into her little compact mirror. 'Then you think it's true what he said about Mandalay?'

'If it's the desk clerk who handles onward bookings, we'll soon find out. But even if it's true that they aren't going to Mandalay, it doesn't change the nature of the problem. Since he spent all that time poking round the gallery, we have to assume that whatever he's doing is likely to affect us.'

'How can you be so sure?' Barbara ran a finger anxiously down her cheek. This dry climate played havoc with one's skin texture.

'Burma. The link is Burma. No one comes here by chance. Like you said the other day, you got to want it. In any case, whatever that guy is, he's not an ordinary tourist. Don't forget what happened in the temple. That was a set-up. Your little brother had a narrow escape.' Michael yawned. 'God, I'm tired. Are you planning to come to bed any time soon?'

'Yes, honey, I'm nearly finished.' Barbara screwed the top back on the night cream. Michael watched her put it away in her make-up case.

'Still got our tube of toothpaste?'

'Well, of course I have. Every time we walk into an airport that thing scares me to death.'

'If they didn't find it at Kennedy, they're not going to find it here. I told you already, there's nothing to worry about.' Michael took off his shoes, pulled back the covers and got into bed.

'Aren't you getting undressed?' said Barbara, disconcerted.

'I am not. It's like an ice-box in here. Reminds me a bit of the time you took me home to Alberta to meet your folks.' Barbara didn't answer. 'Sorry, honey, I forgot you don't like to be reminded of the farm.'

'You're not usually too anxious to discuss your roots either,' she retorted.

'Hey, come on, we got nothing to be ashamed of. Couple of country hicks made good. The folks back in Alberta and Vermont would sure be surprised to see us now. Just shows you can go places with an education and a couple of bright ideas.'

'And a friend with the capital to set up an art gallery.'

'The capital, yes, but not much else. If it wasn't for me, that gallery would still be in SoHo. It's me that has the ideas, it's me that puts them into execution, and it's me that makes the money.'

'Honey, I wasn't criticizing you,' said Barbara soothingly. 'Curtis relies on you, you know that. Listen, what did you make of the American guy?'

'Austin? Nothing. California left-wing intellectual taking a little liberated interest in the drug trade.'

'You don't think that might be a cover for something else?'

'Like what? If he was from the DEA he wouldn't be going round showing off all he knows about narcotics, would he? And I doubt he'd have brought his kid along either.'

'Well, I certainly hope not.'

'You can forget Austin. The person we need to be concerned about right now is Miller.'

Anawrahta's Revenge had returned triple-strength, and Claudia spent most of the night huddled in the bathroom wishing she was dead. Paul gave her some pills to take but it was several hours before they took effect. Not until the end of the night, when the moon went down and the bells from the pagoda across the road fell briefly silent, did the cramps ease sufficiently for her to fall into a troubled sleep. And then only an hour or two later, the daylight began to filter through the dusty windows, and she was aware that Paul had got out of bed and that water was running in the bathroom. Time to get up. She opened her eyes and looked around. The room that had seemed so bright and pleasant the previous afternoon, with the sun streaming over the white walls and rush matting, was forlorn and dismal in the grey morning light. And cold – God, was it cold! The temperature had dropped like a stone when the sun set, and investigations had revealed a broken window pane and a draught down the chimney. Claudia pulled the tangled bedclothes up to her chin and wondered what they were going to do today. Her stomach hurt when she moved. She hoped Paul's plans didn't involve buses. Paul came out of the bathroom with a towel round his waist and looked at her. One hundred pounds a day. Claudia tried to look business-like.

'What time is it?'

'Quarter to eight.'

Oh God, then it was definitely time to get up. 'I don't think I want any breakfast,' she said brightly. 'Why don't you go ahead without me and I'll get dressed while you're eating. That way we won't be too late leaving.'

'Leaving? Where do you intend to go?'

She looked at him, startled. 'I don't know. Wherever we . . . Where are we going today?'

Paul came and sat down on the bed beside her. 'I'm going to Taunggyi. You're staying here.'

'Why?'

'Because you need to rest, that's why.' He ran a finger gently down her cheek. Without warning, Claudia's stomach flipped over in a way that had nothing to do with cramp.

'Did you get any sleep at all last night?' said Paul.

'Yes, no, I don't know. Not a lot, I guess.' She tried to pull herself together. 'What are you going to do in Taunggyi? Are you sure you don't need me?'

'Quite sure.' He went back into the bathroom to get dressed. Claudia pulled ineffectually at the bedclothes. Now what was going on? For the past two weeks, she hadn't felt the slightest twinge of anything at all as far as Paul was concerned. So why this sudden onslaught of lust? Surely she was too ill for stuff like this? She tugged irritably at the sheet and it came adrift from its moorings.

'Damn!'

'Here,' said Paul, 'let me do that.' And he smoothed out the bedclothes and tucked her in, brought her some tea and a couple of extra blankets when he came back from breakfast, and gave her strict instructions about staying in bed, keeping warm, and trying to sleep. Surprised and rather touched by all this solicitude, Claudia did what she was told. The sun was beginning to shine through the dusty windows and warm the room. Claudia drifted peacefully off to sleep.

Adrian took the Myanma Airways morning flight from Bangkok to Rangoon. In-flight service consisted of a cup of sweet milky tea, two boiled sweets and a face flannel. His eyes were gritty, his mouth was stale, and he felt as if he hadn't slept for a week. Tony was waiting for him at the airport. The two men shook hands.

'Glad you're here at last,' said Tony peevishly. 'I've been losing sleep over this, quite honestly.'

He looked fresh and rosy and rested. Adrian eyed him sourly. Worried in case the Ambassador found out, was he?

'Couldn't manage to get you a flight to Mandalay today,' Tony continued, 'so I booked you on the overnight train instead. This afternoon we're going to talk to Rebecca Elliott. They were close during the time he was stationed here.'

'Yes, I've met Rebecca.'

'Have you? Good. Then you know she's a little, ah, forgetful. We're going to see if she knows anything we don't.'

Adrian gave Rebecca a brief account of the contents of the intercepted mail. She listened with a tolerant smile.

'My goodness, how terribly dramatic. Are you really quite sure about all this?'

'Well yes,' said Adrian, taken aback. 'It seems fairly cut and dried to me.'

'I suppose you know other things that you aren't telling me—'

'No,' said Adrian, 'I've told you everything.'

'Then I frankly don't see why you think it's all so frightfully sinister. There's no reason he shouldn't sell his flat, is there? He doesn't spend much time there, does he? As for the money he paid your parents, it might have been a loan or something.'

'I asked them,' said Adrian. 'It wasn't.'

'No? Well . . .' Rebecca shrugged. 'I really didn't get the feeling he was planning anything desperate, quite honestly. Especially with that tarty little piece along. In any case, why would he bother sending a signal to Berlin if he has no intention of ever going back there?'

'He sent a signal to Berlin?' said Adrian.

'He did what?' said Tony.

'Berlin never said anything about that when I talked to them.'

'Are you saying you allowed him to enter Embassy premises and—'

'Ooops,' said Rebecca, 'I seem to have let the cat out of the bag.'

They took her through it step by step. He needed to send a message to Berlin. They had met outside the Embassy on Sunday at nine p.m. They had gone first to her office. She had unlocked the signals room, he had sent his message, and they had left.

'He does seem to have had himself a busy evening,' said Tony. 'I wonder what other little surprises we're going to turn up. I'll check the message was sent and decipher what it contained. That's all, is it, Rebecca? Nothing else happened while you were there?'

'Well, at one point he got in a mess with the machine and asked me to come and give him a hand,' said Rebecca, so they made her describe the incident in detail, back and forth and inside out, until it transpired that he had been alone in her office for a few minutes while she was dealing with the machine. So what might he have done in those few moments alone?

'Quite honestly, darling, your guess is as good as mine, especially as we'd been in there for hours already while he looked at all those bloody tapestries. He'd had plenty of time to do whatever he wanted then.'

'He looked at the tapestries? Min Saw's tapestries?'

'That's right. They were piled up in my office, remember?'

'The tapestries that Min Saw's been driving us all crazy about all week?'

'Yes, obviously – oh lord! You mean the one that's gone missing, it might have been Philip that pinched it? Goodness, I never thought of that. What on earth would he want to do that for?'

'You mean it never even occurred to you that he might have taken it?'

'No, why should it? I mean, he was avoiding Min Saw at the party. I thought he was just kicking himself because he missed the chance of buying one.'

'For God's sake, Rebecca, tell us what you're talking about,' snapped Tony, so they took her through the events of the party a few times, and then when they were convinced there was nothing more to be learned, they started to consider what it might mean. They reached no conclusions. It was getting on for four, and the train for Mandalay left at five. The only thing was for Adrian to get up there, check the hotels, find Philip and figure out what he was up to. The two main tourist joints, said Tony, were the Mandalay Hotel and the Mya Mandala. It was unlikely he would have gone anywhere else.

'Unless of course he's checked straight into a monastery,' he added perfidiously.

'Philip in a monastery?' said Rebecca in disbelief. 'You know, darling, I hardly think so.'

'Because if he has, then we're in trouble. Mandalay's full of them.'

When Claudia awoke, it was mid-afternoon. She turned over and saw Paul in the doorway. He was carrying a bottle of mineral water and a packet of biscuits. Instinctively she sat up and held her arms out to him, and to her joy and relief he came straight into them, saying nothing, just holding her. 'Kiss me,' she commanded, and he did so. Not a fake Hollywood kiss like the one on the set at Pagan to keep her quiet and fool the ghosts. A real kiss, private not public, just for the two of them. Not a consolation prize, not a game, not a convoluted way of making her keep her distance. A serious kiss. Then he drew back and smiled at her and made her eat some biscuits and drink some water, to keep her strength up, and held her hand while she did so.

'How was Taunggyi?' said Claudia through a mouthful of biscuit.

'Nothing special. I just went to Tourist Burma, bought our tickets and came straight back again.'

'Are we really going to Sandoway?'

'No. We're going to Mandalay.'

'Why did you—' She stopped and changed her question. 'Who did you want to hide it from?'

'I don't know. But I don't want to take any chances. We have to consider the possibility that, since Narathu hasn't shown up, someone else is standing in for him. With luck we'll find out who it is before we get to Mandalay.'

'When are we leaving?'

'Day after tomorrow.'

'Not till then?'

'There were no seats on the plane tomorrow. We could have taken the bus, but I didn't think that was a good idea.'

'Because of me? I'm screwing up all your plans, aren't I, with my stupid stomach?'

'No,' said Paul, but she persisted, unconvinced, until he explained with chilling matter-of-factness, 'Right now, we can afford to wait. Otherwise I'd have had you on the bus to Mandalay this morning, ill or not.'

For a moment she stared at him, unsure whether he was joking, and when it became plain that he wasn't, she tried to pull him to her, to bury herself in him and forget that he was scaring her, but his words had reminded him of his own darker purpose and warned him against her. He stood up and moved restlessly across the room. Desperate not to lose him, she said the first thing that came into her head.

'Did you come here with Caroline?'

There was a long pause. Well done, Claudia, first prize for tact. He turned round and looked at her, weighing her up. In the end, he said cautiously 'No,' and made it sound like a question.

Grimly Claudia plunged on. 'I wondered why you told Thomas and Christa about her the other day.'

Another pause, while he registered that she had understood the conversation in German and evaluated the extent of her knowledge. Then he shrugged and came back to sit on the end of the bed. 'Why not? It's not important. It's always better to stick as close to the truth as possible.'

'What were you doing in Burma?'

'It was after Lucy died. My wife. Caroline decided I needed a change of scene, so she announced that we were taking a trip to Asia. India, Thailand and Burma. She made all the arrangements, bought the tickets, made the reservations . . . Normally, it was me who had to look after her, but that time it was the other way round.'

'She must have been very young,' said Claudia after a while. 'Your wife, I mean.'

'Thirty-five.'

'You said it was cancer?'

'Yes. It was a form of cancer that spreads very rapidly. There was nothing they could do about it. We were on holiday in Ibiza, she wasn't feeling too good, so we thought she'd caught some kind of virus and came back a couple of days early. She collapsed getting off the plane. Six weeks later she was dead.'

'Jesus.'

'The worst of it was that I'd been on the brink of leaving her. During the holiday I'd made up my mind that I was going to move out when we got back to London.'

Claudia said hesitantly, 'If the cancer was as fast-spreading as you say, it wouldn't have made any difference. I mean, there was probably nothing else you could have done for her anyway.'

Paul looked at her sombrely. 'I can't be certain of that. If I'd been paying her more attention, I'd have realized earlier how ill she was. If she'd seen a doctor earlier, maybe they could have done something . . .'

'Maybe they could have dragged out her life a little bit longer, made her suffer more for a longer period of time.'

He let out a long slow breath. 'That's what Caroline said.'

'And she was right.'

'I know. But it doesn't change anything. It doesn't stop one feeling guilty.'

'Perhaps not. But you have to come to terms with it.'

'One has to atone,' he said, so low that he could hardly hear him.

'Bullshit,' she snapped, suddenly furious with him. 'One does not. At least not for ever. How long has your wife been dead? Six years, isn't it? Isn't that long enough? No, wait a minute. There's something else, isn't there? Your sister. Caroline. I suppose you're busy atoning for her too. So what happened there? Weren't you paying enough attention to her either?'

His hand clenched and for a moment she really thought he was going to hit her.

'I'm sorry, Paul. I shouldn't have said that. But you

shouldn't blame yourself. It's not your fault she got hooked on heroin. People go to hell in their own sweet way. You can't stop them being the way they are. There's nothing anyone can do about it.'

Paul was shaking his head. 'It's not just that she was an addict. That's not the whole story.'

'Then tell me the whole story,' said Claudia, and to her surprise he needed no further prompting. Probably he had been keeping the whole lot bottled up for years – unless he had poured it out to his lady friend in Rangoon, but she somehow had the feeling he hadn't. One couldn't unburden one's soul to someone as well dressed as that.

'When we got back from Asia,' said Paul, 'I was posted abroad. I'd had a desk job in London for a couple of years, and they decided it was time I went back into the field. So they sent me to Berlin.'

So who was 'they', Claudia wondered, but as usual it was not the moment to ask.

'For the first few months, things were pretty quiet. I went back to London a couple of times. Caroline seemed fine. She'd got a new job as receptionist in a Bond Street gallery that specialized in Indian art. She'd had trouble holding jobs in the past, she tended to get bored after a couple of months, but she'd developed an interest in the East after our trip to Asia and she seemed more motivated this time. She took me to the gallery and showed me round and introduced me to her boss. He was a bit too smooth for his own good, but she seemed to be enjoying herself, so I let it pass. That was the last time I saw her. It was over a year before I went back to England.'

He stopped. Claudia waited.

'The gallery was holding a reception for the opening of something or other. She called the police and then she . . .'

It took Claudia a moment or two to understand what he meant.

'Do you mean her death wasn't an accident?'

'She took a deliberate overdose.'

'Jesus.'

'I had no idea she was taking drugs. None at all. She never wrote letters, but I talked to her occasionally on the phone, not often and never for very long, she was hard to get hold of, and always rushing off somewhere, but she sounded normal. I never realized anything was wrong.'

'How could you?'

'I should have guessed. Emma, her flatmate, sometimes sounded a bit strange when I called and asked for Caroline, but it never occurred to me to ask her if something was wrong, and she never volunteered anything.'

'You know, a lot of addicts do what she did. It's really not uncommon. They know they'll never kick it, they get to the stage where—'

'I just had no idea what was going on.'

'Paul, you mustn't blame yourself.'

He shook his head. 'You don't understand. She knew I was coming home on leave. She killed herself the week before I was due to arrive.'

So of course it was all his fault. She hadn't been able to face seeing him, so she'd taken the route she would have travelled sooner or later anyway. One would think she might have had the consideration to leave a note behind explaining this – surely she must have realized how he was going to react – but she was such an empty-headed little butterfly that it hadn't even occurred to her to do that. As far as Claudia could see, it was rank ingratitude. Paul had more or less brought up Caroline from the age of thirteen, when her mother died and their elderly father found himself unable to cope, and later she had gone to live with him and Lucy in London. He had been bailing her out for years by the sound of it, but as soon as he turned his back, the silly bitch got hooked on heroin, realized this was one place that big brother couldn't rescue her from, and chose the only solution that was left. Not bothering to leave a thank-you note, nor even to check that her timing was convenient. Because to cap it all, he had missed the funeral. He had been away when she died, they had been unable to reach him, and he got back to find that his father's sister had organized the funeral without him, and Caroline had already been cremated.

Which left Paul locked up in his monastery, all alone with his hair shirt and his guilt. First Lucy, now Caroline. All because of him. Claudia gazed at him in exasperation. She could see from the look on his face that there was no point in saying any of this: he was too far away to hear it. She considered putting her arms round him and drawing him into the bed beside her, but rejected the idea. Atonement brooked no comfort.

She was still wondering what to say when there was a knock on the door. Paul looked at her and raised his eyebrows. She shrugged. He opened the door.

'Hi there. Hope I'm not disturbing you.' It was Austin.

'No.' Paul's tone was as welcoming as barbed wire, but Austin either didn't notice or paid no attention.

'How's Claudia?'

'Much better. Should be up and about tomorrow.'

'You're not leaving tomorrow, are you? Good. We ought to have a little talk at some point, and there hasn't been much chance so far.'

'Mm. You'd better come in a moment.' Paul stepped back to let him enter the room. Claudia was well covered up in her sweatshirt and leggings, but she drew the blankets protectively up to her chin. In the company she was keeping these days it was wisest to reveal as little as possible.

'Hi there, beautiful,' said Austin. 'How ya feeling?'

'Better, thanks.'

'We can talk now if you want,' said Paul, but Austin, perhaps inhibited by Claudia's presence, or else scenting the room's already charged emotional temperature, declined.

'The hotel's organizing a boat to go down the lake to the floating market and the pagoda tomorrow. Market's only held every five days, you shouldn't miss it. That's what everyone's been hanging round here for. Are you guys going to come along?'

'Why not?' said Paul noncommittally. 'Do you think you'll feel up to it, darling?'

Claudia wasn't sure if she was supposed to say yes or no. 'Even if I don't, you could go on your own,' she suggested. That way he could refuse to leave her bedside if he didn't want to go. 'You don't have to stay here all day.'

'Great,' said Austin, 'then I'll sign you both up.' Business completed, he backed purposefully towards the door. 'Sorry to interrupt, guys. I'll see you later. The Mandalay rum man's been by, so if either of you feel like a drink, we're in business.'

The train from Rangoon arrived in Mandalay early in the morning. Adrian took a taxi to the Mandalay Hotel. The city looked more prosperous than he remembered from his previous visit. Fewer horse-drawn carriages and more re-conditioned Japanese cars. The narco-kyats were pouring in and the local economy was thriving. There was even enough spare cash to repaint the walls that surrounded the former royal palace. Adrian remembered them as a faded but elegant pink, but at some point in the past few years they had been transformed into a sinister beetroot red.

The Mandalay Hotel stood right across the road from the old walls. It was the biggest hotel in town, a charmless, Chinese-built tourist factory. Adrian booked himself a room and asked if a friend of his, a Mr Miller, was staying there. The receptionist checked her files with ill grace, and said that he wasn't. Adrian insisted. Mr Miller was tall and blond, and his wife was half-Burmese. As he had guessed, this got her attention. Caroline had once told him that she had been mistaken for Burmese when she came here with Philip, and he was pleased with himself for remembering this detail. Nevertheless, the receptionist maintained that Mr Miller was not in the hotel. Confident that she would remember the unlikely pair if they did come her way, Adrian slipped her two dollars and asked her to let him know if Mr Miller checked in. As an afterthought, he asked her when the palace walls had been repainted. She cast an uninterested glance across the road, and told him to ask at the Tourist Burma office on the other side of the lobby. The state didn't pay her to dispense that kind of information.

The room they had given him was dark and noisy with dirty, pale-green paint and dusty shelves. The bathroom was none too clean either, but at least the water was hot. Adrian stood under the shower for a long time and considered taking a nap. He hadn't slept properly for two days. Instead, he took two tablets of Vitamin C, changed into clean clothes and went out to do the rounds of the hotels. With no idea what Philip was planning, nor how much time he had, it was best to track him down as soon as possible.

Part Five

Lake Inle

The floating market was held halfway down the lake in the village of Ywama. The village consisted of a couple of shops built on stilts and a ruined pagoda, and the market took place in the space in between. As its name implied, it was entirely water-borne. The boats, long and narrow, slid alongside each other, moving forward in apparently undirected, seemingly effortless motion. Everyone had something to sell, everyone had something to buy. Some of the boats were laden with firewood, others with flour, or vegetables, or cooked dishes. No money changed hands. Everything was bartered: firewood for vegetables, flour for cigars. A boat offering lacquer work and other curios nosed alongside, and the vendor, a sharp young man in khaki trousers, began passing things over for the tourists to inspect.

'Too big,' said Paul, confronted with an antique lacquer box. 'Do you have smaller ones?'

'No, nothing small,' said the vendor, and Paul shrugged and began examining a set of opium weights instead.

'What do you think of these?' said Barbara, holding up a set of small silver boxes.

'How much do they want for them?'

'We're offering a calculator, but the guy doesn't seem to think it's enough.'

There were ten of them in the boat. With the exception of the French teachers, who had left for Rangoon, it was the same group that had been drinking rum in the hotel the other night, plus the boatman and an English-speaking guide. It was mid-morning and the sun was high above the lake. The locals wore flat straw hats for protection against sunstroke, and the tourists had produced an unglamourous assortment of scarves, baseball caps, and cowboy hats. The boat was surrounded on all sides by curio sellers by now, and bargaining was in full swing.

'Come on, honey, isn't there anything else we can give him?' said Barbara, and Michael reluctantly proffered his watch.

'Rolex?' said the vendor hopefully.

'No way,' said Michael. 'You think I bring my Rolex to a place like this?'

The wizened old lady in the next-door vegetable boat tapped Paul on the shoulder and held out a small lacquer box.

'News travels fast,' said Claudia.

'Look over there, there's another one on its way,' said Thomas.

Angus examined a sword and decided he couldn't afford it. Austin paid dollars for the opium weights. Paul exchanged a T-shirt for the smallest of the lacquer boxes. There was not much point buying things he would never be able to enjoy, but it would look odd if they didn't buy something. He would give it to Claudia as a souvenir.

'You sure your watch is going to hold out for the rest of the trip?' said Michael to Barbara.

'Of course I am. I've had this watch for years.'

'This not enough. You got whisky? Perfume?'

'Oh for God's sake. Honey, do we really need these things?'

'Come on, sweetheart, they're real cute. They'd look really good on that small table in the corridor.'

'How are you feeling?' said Paul to Claudia. She was looking a lot better today. She had been fast asleep when he came to bed the previous night, and the rest had clearly done her good.

She smiled at him. 'I'm fine. I'm glad we came. This is fun, don't you think?'

'Yes,' said Paul. Or it would be if I could figure out which of these bastards are here for the fun and which are here because I'm here. Michael and Barbara, complaining of the cold and the lack of hot water and making no attempt to move on. Thomas and Christa, who came in the same taxi from Pagan. One couple goes to Taunggyi and the other to Yaunghwe and they all meet up in Heho market to compare notes. It's perfectly feasible. And then there's Austin, the wild card in the game, moving round the tourist circuit on some mysterious undercover mission. So here we are, all laughing and joking and bargaining together. Since Narathu hasn't appeared, someone else must have taken over. It's time to set a trap. Put out some bait and see who takes it.

Keith bought some large thin pancakes that resembled papadums and passed them round. Angus, egged on by Claudia, changed his mind and bought his sword. The guide announced that if everyone was ready they were going to move on to the shop which sold traditional locally woven textiles. The boat nosed slowly out of the mêlée, still surrounded by curio sellers. Michael took a pack of chewing gum out of his pocket and began to unwrap it. The man with the silver boxes saw it and his eyes lit up.

'You give me chewing gum and watch and calculator and I give you boxes.'

'Thank God it's not like this back home,' said Barbara as they pulled away. 'Imagine bargaining for an hour every time you go to the store to buy something.'

'They don't go shopping as much as we do,' said Christa a little too tartly, and Paul eyed her thoughtfully. Barbara the hedonist and Christa the puritan were an unlikely combination. Maybe the taxi was just a coincidence.

They left the market behind and headed for the weaving workshop. The edge of the lake was overgrown with silt and weeds and tangled water hyacinths. Houses on stilts hovered a few feet above the surface of the water. A few boats went past, heading for the market, and the boatman called out a greeting to them. Further out in the middle of the lake, a lone fisherman trawled the surface of the water. He was balanced on one leg on the stern of the boat, his other leg was twisted round a single long oar, and he was rowing through the shallow water. His head was bent, and he held a tall, conical net ready to drop to the lake bottom at the slightest sign of movement. Everyone grabbed their cameras. Greg scrambled to his feet in his anxiety to get a good picture and set the boat rocking dangerously.

'Careful now,' said Barbara.

'Sit down,' said his father, 'what do you think you're doing?'

'Don't turn the boat over, if you don't mind,' said Paul. 'I can't swim.'

Austin glanced at him sharply. Claudia opened her mouth and shut it again.

'Is that right?' said Barbara.

'We're not far from the shore,' said Thomas reassuringly.

'Far enough,' said Paul, casting a nervous glance behind him.

'Sorry,' said Greg, and sat down again.

The weaving workshop sold the kind of simple check and flower-patterned textiles that the Burmese used for their *longgyis*, plus some fairly garish Shan shoulder bags. Claudia took one look and was preparing to wait outside till everyone had finished, but Paul grabbed hold of her arm and started telling her that they ought to buy something for your mother and my mother and Tante Monika in Heidelberg, and was there anyone he had forgotten, and did she see anything here that would do. Claudia was inclined to think he was over-doing it a bit, until she looked up from the flowery material they were pretending to consider for Tante Monika, and saw that all the other married couples in the group were engaged in the same kind of discussion. If this was the proof of the marital pudding, it was just as well she hadn't married Nick. They had nearly come to blows one evening over what kind of flowers to take to someone's dinner party.

Paul caught her eye and she said carefully, 'You know, darling, I'm not sure this is really your aunt's kind of thing. I think she might go more for a lacquer box, or something like that.'

'You should have told me that in Pagan,' said Paul, hitting just the right note of restrained irritability, and she smiled at him admiringly.

'I know, but you can find lacquerware in Rangoon too. We saw some in the market, remember? What about one of those shoulder bags for Katja?'

'Katja?' said Paul cautiously.

'Not your aunt Katja, your niece Katja. She could use it as a school bag or something.'

'Good idea, yes, let's go and look at them.' He put his arm round her waist to escort her to the other side of the shop. The shoulder bags were not particularly enticing. Maybe they're too bright, said Claudia, maybe Katja will get into trouble at school. Nonsense, said Paul airily, she can use it at weekends, I think we should take it. He kissed her cheek, and then her mouth. Why hadn't he woken her up when he came back from his drinking session with Austin last night? He went off to pay for the bag, and she wandered outside. Thomas was sitting on a bench overlooking the lake, and she sat down beside him.

'Your husband must have a very big family in Germany,' said Thomas inquisitively. 'In which city do they live?'

Claudia eyed him warily. 'Oh . . . here and there. All over.

He has an aunt in Heidelberg.' She paused and tried to think of another German town. 'Munich, there's a brother in Munich. With a little girl, well, not so little really. The one we're buying the shoulder bag for.'

'How old is she?' asked Thomas.

'Fourteen,' said Claudia, after a pause. She was aware that Michael was hovering in the background, fiddling with his camera. She wasn't sure if he was listening or not.

'Really? I too have a sister of fourteen. What is she called?'

A name, oh God, a German name. 'Heike,' said Claudia, remembering the name of a penfriend she had had at school. 'And his mother's in Hamburg. That's where the family came from originally. That's where he grew up.'

'I know Hamburg well,' said Thomas happily. 'Where in Hamburg does his mother live?'

What? For Christ's sake, what kind of a question was that? Claudia had never been to Hamburg in her life. Would it look odd to say she had never visited his mother? Yes, it would. She glanced round anxiously for Paul, but he was talking to Austin in a corner of the shop with his back half turned towards her. 'Actually she just moved. I'm not really sure what the new address is. She moved into Paul's sister's old flat,' she went on, talking much too fast, before Thomas had time to ask what the old address was. 'Her own flat was much too big now that Paul's father's dead and all the family's moved out, so when . . .' she pretended to falter '. . . after the accident, she decided to take over her daughter's flat.'

She looked sideways at Thomas to make sure he remembered Paul's defunct sister with whom he had visited Pagan. With luck he would now have the delicacy to shut up. But Thomas, whether or not he remembered, was too intent on the topography of Hamburg to bother with delicacy.

'But did you never make a visit to the sister in her flat?'

'No,' said Claudia desperately, 'because she hadn't been living there, she'd been living in London.'

'Is that so?' said Thomas, side-tracked at last. 'Both the brother and the sister at the same time, that's very interesting. Is the family perhaps part English? Your husband speaks very good English.'

There was a clicking noise behind them as Michael adjusted the shutter of his camera.

'No, no, it was just coincidence. She was just over for a few months brushing up her English.'

In a minute she would turn round and ask Michael what he was photographing. She couldn't stand much more of this conversation.

'Ah so, was she then taking language lessons?'

Claudia hesitated. Was she or wasn't she? No she wasn't. He would only want to know the name of the language school. Stick to the truth wherever possible, Paul had told her. 'No. She found a job as a receptionist in an art gallery and she—'

There was a sudden crash behind them. Claudia broke off. She and Thomas both turned round. Michael, white-faced, was kneeling a few yards away retrieving his expensive Nikon camera from the boards of the jetty.

'You dropped your camera?' said Thomas. 'My God.'

'You dropped it?' Barbara appeared from inside the shop with a package in her arms. 'Oh, honey, how could you do that?'

'Is it all right?'

'What happened?'

In the confusion, Claudia eased herself away from Thomas, but her prudence was unnecessary. A potentially damaged camera was a serious affair, and he had forgotten about her. Outwardly, the camera was intact, but this would not be known for sure until the device could be taken to a specialist and thoroughly inspected. Barbara was reproachful. Michael, after the first abashed apology – 'It just slipped through my fingers' – was grim and silent. The guide announced that it was nearly lunchtime, but first they were going to take a quick look at a pagoda. Claudia was in no state to catch its name.

The pagoda was a large, bare room on the edge of the lake. A Buddha statue squatted in the middle of the room and a sign saying Ladies are Prohibited warned off the unclean. Christa was indignant, made Thomas take a picture of the sign, and looked round for sisters to share in her outrage, but both Barbara and Claudia were engaged in intense discussion with their husbands in opposite corners of the room. The guide shrugged apologetically, Angus and Keith made a couple of snide remarks. Christa stalked off pointedly on her own.

'What happened?' said Barbara. 'Why did you drop the camera?'

'Do you remember Caroline?'

Barbara frowned. 'No, who's she?'

'The receptionist at the London gallery. The one who took an overdose a year or two back.'

'Oh that Caroline. Well, yes, of course, I mean I never met her, but—'

'I never met her either,' said Michael impatiently. 'That's not the point. Do you remember what happened to her?'

'Not really, no. She'd been getting the stuff off Roland, hadn't she?'

'Yeah. Damn stupid thing to do, but try telling that to Roland. Arrogant son-of-a-bitch. Anyway, one fine day she's had enough and she ODs. There's a big opening on, the gallery's full of people, there are police swarming all over the place and a lady stuffed with heroin in the basement.'

'How'd the police get there so fast?'

'She had the foresight to call them before she shot up.'

'She did? You never told me all this. Did she leave a note too?'

'She certainly did. Fortunately, Roland kept his head and sent Graham over to her apartment right away. Graham found the note and destroyed it. Just as well, or you and I wouldn't be here now. She knew exactly how everything worked and she implicated all three galleries.'

'I don't believe it.'

'That's not all. Caroline had a brother who worked for the Foreign Office. Or so she said. He was out of the country for long periods, so it could have been true, but she let drop a couple of remarks that made Roland think he might actually have been SIS.'

'Oh my lord.'

'So naturally Roland was a little worried what the brother, who was presumably some kind of trained investigator, might make of all this when he showed up. And so of course were we. But it all went off very well. The guy was devastated by his sister's death, said he hadn't even realized she was on drugs. Roland said neither had he: true she'd been a little unreliable lately, but she'd told him it was man trouble, and he'd seen no reason to disbelieve her. So the two of them went out for a drink to console each other, and that, according to Roland, was that. But guess what I just found out? Roland was wrong. The guy was too clever for us. He left the London gallery alone and carried out his investigations in New York instead.'

'Michael, I do not believe this. Are you trying to tell me that the brother is Paul Miller?'

'Hush, not so loud.'

'Oh my God, what are we going to do?'

'He knows about the galleries, ' said Michael grimly. 'Since Min Saw is the only Burmese artist who bases his work on the Glass Palace Chronicles, he knows about him. Maybe he even has a copy of the fucking suicide note, maybe he knows about the whole damn set-up.'

His voice was rising. 'Calm down, honey, calm down,' said Barbara. She cast an anxious glance over her shoulder, but the group was beginning to drift out of the pagoda, and they were almost the only people left. 'Don't forget we still have the upper hand. We know who he is, but he doesn't know who we are. Did you ask the desk clerk where he's going next?'

'Yes, but he didn't know. Miller went up to Taunggyi himself. Said it was to ask about flights to Sandoway. What do you bet it was to book himself on a flight to Mandalay without anyone finding out?'

'Excuse me, you come please now? We go lunch in very nice restaurant just next door to this pagoda.'

'Great, we'll be right there,' said Michael.

The guide moved out of earshot. 'You think Miller's going to Mandalay after all?' said Barbara.

'Of course he is, it stands to reason.'

'But what's he going to do when he gets there? You think the British secret services might be mixed up in this too?'

Michael thought about it. 'I don't know about that. I get the feeling this is more likely to be a spot of private enterprise. With the girl along too ... She's no professional, that's for sure. Thomas was asking her questions about Miller's family, and she was making it up as she went along.'

'Then what's he going to do?' said Barbara again.

They began to walk towards the door of the pagoda. 'I don't know, Barbara, and I don't propose to wait around and find out. My feeling is that it would be better for all of us if he never got to Mandalay.'

Lunch was a choice of chicken curry or beef curry. So what else was new? Barbara said she was getting to the point where she'd sell her soul for a slice of pizza, and Greg agreed. Austin asked the waiter if they did enchiladas.

'How about a steak?' said Michael. 'Medium rare with fries, and a salad on the side.'

'Lasagne,' said Claudia.

'Weisswurst,' said Thomas.

The waiter giggled nervously. 'Beef curry, chicken curry. Very nice.'

Back to reality. They sighed and made their choice. Beef

curry for Michael and Austin, chicken for the others, straight rice at Paul's insistence for Claudia.

'You must not fall sick again, Liebling.'

'Husbands!' said Claudia across the table to Barbara. She had made sure that she and Paul were at the far end of the table from Thomas and Christa. They had talked enough about Paul's family antecedents for one day. 'Does yours boss you around like this too?'

'He likes to think he does,' said Barbara, and they exchanged all–girls–together smiles.

Paul put his hand on Claudia's knee under the table. For a few minutes, her mind wandered. The restaurant was on a floating platform at the edge of the lake, with an awning to keep the sun off their heads. A cool breeze ruffled the waters of the lake, and bells tinkled faintly in the distance. The waiter banged dishes down on the table. Chicken curry, beef curry, rice, salad, chillis, sauces, cutlery in a bowl of hot water, napkins to dry the cutlery and wipe one's fingers. Michael and Austin were discussing yachts. Barbara announced that the first thing she was going to do when they got to Thailand was get a manicure. Greg complained that the batteries on his Walkman had gone flat. Angus got out his sword and tested the blade.

'What will you use that for?' said Christa, eyeing it disapprovingly.

'Killing bandits,' said Angus. 'I'm going to Vietnam after this. I've heard they're pretty rough on tourists out there.'

Christa turned away in disgust. Claudia hid a smile. Angus didn't say much, but when he did, he had a nice line in sharp comments.

Barbara put her silver boxes on the table and began to examine them.

'Nice,' said Keith, picking one up to inspect it.

'Expensive,' said Michael.

'Do they come filled and ready for use?' Austin spooned

curry over a sticky mass of rice, and added a generous helping of chilli sauce.

'What?'

'They use 'em for opium, those little boxes. Didn't you know?'

'Is that right? Oh my.'

'What do you say, sweetheart? How about a side trip to the hill villages to fill them up?'

'Don't worry,' said Austin, 'you'll find what you need in Mandalay.'

Michael looked up sharply. 'What the hell do you mean by that?'

'Surely they don't grow poppies in Mandalay?' said Thomas, surprised.

'Hell, no, Mandalay's a transit point. See, what you need to convert opium into heroin is a chemical called acetic anhydride. It's manufactured in India. The only way to get it up to the refineries in the Golden Triangle is through Mandalay. And that means the military commander of Mandalay, the customs people, the police, and a few assorted bureaucrats are all lining their pockets nicely too.'

'Great,' said Michael. 'So if we see any military trucks in Mandalay, we'll know what's in them.'

'That's right. You want to pass me the chilli sauce, Greg, please?'

'Oh my. If we didn't have to be in Mandalay tomorrow, I'd say give it a miss. It sounds like a dangerous place to go.'

'Dad, one of these days you're going to die of internal combustion.'

'Not just yet awhile, son. So what happens tomorrow in Mandalay, Barbara? Peking Opera coming to town?'

'Oh why nothing, I just—'

'She has an appointment with her hairdresser,' said Michael easily. 'Or was it your dress designer, honey? I just hope these guys take kyats. Can't afford to pay dollars for a designer *longgyi*.'

'But if this all is taking place in Mandalay, why doesn't the government put a stop to it?' said Christa.

'She's right,' said Thomas. 'I always thought that the trafficking goes on in frontier areas that the government cannot control.'

Keith and Austin exchanged glances.

'Well that's certainly what the government likes people to think,' said Keith.

'All that stuff about powerful rebel armies that are a law unto themselves is kind of a convenient myth,' agreed Austin.

'Apart from the actual cultivation, they control pretty well everything these days. They rent out military vehicles to run the stuff down to Rangoon, they take commission from the traffickers to allow them to drive trucks of opium and heroin across the country without being stopped—'

'Are you saying the government is in league with the traffickers?' demanded Christa incredulously.

'Christa, they are the traffickers. It's not just a question of kicking out a few corrupt bureaucrats. You want to put a stop to the drug trade, you got to get a whole new government first.'

'It's impossible.'

'Since SLORC took over in 1988, Burmese heroin production has doubled.'

'But why would a government want to get involved with drugs?'

'Hey,' said Michael, 'an idealist.'

'They need money,' said Austin, 'that's why. Drug money is the only thing keeping the economy of this country afloat at the present time.'

For a moment or two, no one spoke. Claudia poked unenthusiastically at the dry rice on her plate. Austin took a third helping of hot sauce. A sudden gust of wind ruffled the surface of the lake and blew a couple of paper napkins to the floor. Briefly, the pagoda bells chimed louder.

'How come you know so much about all this drug stuff?' said Michael to Austin. 'Are you an expert on South-East Asia too?'

'Me?' said Austin. 'Not yet, no, but I'm working on it.'

'Why are you so interested?'

'Thought I might write a piece about it, that's all. Well, okay, the truth is I thought it might be possible to get out into the insurgent areas and take a look at what was going on.'

'You mean you're a journalist?'

'Yeah. I can see now that I was being a trifle naïve. I didn't realize everything was so tightly controlled, and I hadn't bargained for there being so few foreigners around. We stick out like a sore thumb. Can't do anything without attracting attention.'

'What about Greg?' said Barbara disapprovingly. 'You were going to take him into the rebel areas too?'

'No way. What I planned to do was take a look around this trip, go back to Bangkok, leave him with his mother, get a new visa and come back on my own. But I reckon I won't bother. I'm just not skinny enough to pass for Burmese.'

'You can penetrate the rebel areas from the Thai side of the frontier. That's what most journalists do,' said Michael.

'Exactly,' said Austin. 'That's what all journalists do. I wanted to do something different.'

'A scoop?' said Keith.

Austin grinned ruefully. 'Like I say, I was naïve. Another thing I thought I might look into was the possibility that the DEA officials stationed here were taking a cut of something too.'

'Be surprising if they weren't,' said Michael.

'That's what I figured. Tried to do some poking round in Rangoon and ran up against a lot of blank walls. This ain't a good country for investigative journalism, I can tell you.'

Michael and Barbara exchanged glances. The waiter came

to clear away the plates. Dessert was bananas. Paul gave his to Claudia.

'I don't like bananas.'

'Eat it. You hardly touched that rice. You have to keep your strength up, Liebling.'

'Pretend it's cheesecake,' advised Barbara.

'Or a brownie,' said Greg.

'Pecan pie,' said Austin.

'It's lemon tart,' said Paul. 'Your favourite.'

'I'm going to take a photo,' announced Greg. 'Can you all move a bit closer together so I can get everyone in.'

'Don't you want to be in it too?' said Austin. 'Why don't I take it instead?'

'No, Dad, I want you in it. You never let me take any pictures of you. No one's going to believe we went round the world together.'

'Some of us are more photogenic than others,' said Austin, patting his stomach.

Claudia sensed Paul stirring beside her. On an impulse she got to her feet. 'Why don't I take it? I don't feel very photogenic today either. Here.' She got up and walked over to where Greg was standing. Paul was another one who didn't like to be photographed. It was time she had a picture of him as a souvenir. She would get Greg to send her a copy.

'You look through here,' said Greg, 'and you press this button here.'

He went over to rejoin the group. Claudia looked through the viewfinder. What a picture. Angus and Keith had wandered off to take another look at the pagoda, but all the rest of them were there. All the conspirators and anti-conspirators smiling at the camera with various degrees of unease. Some had brought their cloaks and daggers with them, and others were sufficiently sure of themselves to do without. Austin had managed to position himself so that his face was three-quarters concealed by his son. Paul had moved backwards so that his face was in shadow. Thomas was grinning broadly. Michael had put his arm round Barbara and she had tilted her face up into what was presumably her best profile. They were used to being photographed together, and practice had made them pose-perfect. Claudia's hands suddenly froze on the camera. She had seen that pose before. It was the one they used in New York, in front of the Statue of Liberty, with out-of-town visitors.

She realized she was staring. Barbara was beginning to look puzzled. She forced herself to frown.

'Barbara, there's a funny kind of shadow, could you move just a little bit to the left. Yeah, great, that's much better. Say cheese, everybody.'

Click. Okay, that's it. Hand the camera back to Greg. Smile, act normal. Pick up bag, put on sunglasses to hide stunned expression, walk nonchalantly towards the boat, pretend you have nothing more pressing on your mind than the next pagoda, which the guide says is a big deal, and hope to God it has some quiet corners to talk in.

'They're not Canadians, and they don't have a hotel. They're Americans and they own an art gallery on East Seventy-second Street in New York. The Rajasthan Gallery. The one that gives exhibitions of Min Saw's tapestries.'

Paul turned his back to the room and put an arm lovingly around her. No hint of a quiver: he was perfectly calm. The second pagoda was even bigger and larger and emptier than the first. In one corner a youth in jeans and a leather jacket was absorbed in a set of prayer beads. In another, a monk was reciting prayers over a family who had brought baskets of vegetables as an offering. The guide was explaining that the five huge golden Buddhas in the centre of the pagoda were taken somewhere in a procession during some annual celebration.

'How do you know?'

'Min Saw showed me a photo of the three of them taken in New York and told me who they were and the name of the gallery – oh Jesus!'

Paul lifted his camera and aimed it at the praying youth. 'What's the matter?' He sounded almost bored.

'I've just remembered something.' The inscription on the shop in the rue de Miromesnil, gold against the black Paris night. The label on the tapestry at the bottom of Paul's bag. 'There's a Rajasthan Gallery in London too, isn't there?' She paused: Paul said nothing. 'Come on, Paul, tell me! That's where Caroline worked, isn't it?'

'Calm down,' said Paul. 'Don't look so agitated. Yes it is.'

'Oh shit, that's torn it. I've gone and given the whole thing away. No wonder he dropped his bloody camera.'

'Don't cry,' said Paul urgently. 'Try and act normal. Please. Is that what happened at the weaving shop? You told him my sister worked in a Bond Street gallery and he dropped his camera?'

'I was talking to Thomas. He must have overheard.'

'We have to walk round a little. Admire the Buddhas. That's what we're here for. Here, give me your hand. Try to smile. Make one of your silly comments about cockroaches. That's better.'

'I'm sorry, I didn't think. Thomas was being so nosy, asking all those stupid questions about names and addresses—'

'Maybe he was trying to trap you into giving something away.'

'You think they're working together?'

'Perhaps. Anyway, don't worry, it doesn't matter. They must have suspected something already or they wouldn't have followed us from Pagan. You just gave them the confirmation they were looking for. Have you seen the size of those Buddhas? The procession must be quite something. Maybe we should come back to see it in September.'

'Paul, please stop talking about Buddhas. What are we going to do?'

'No,' said Paul, and there was an odd gleam in his eye as he turned towards her, 'that's not the question. The question is, what are they going to do?'

The sun was sinking lower and the temperature was dropping. The boat turned back up the lake in the direction of Yaunghwe. It was five o'clock: time to change into evening wear. Hats and sunglasses were stowed away, and the socks and sweaters that had been discarded earlier in the day were put back on. Halfway up the lake was an abandoned pagoda and at Michael's request they stopped to take a closer look at it. The bells tinkled in the twilight and an immense ruined Buddha glowered over the darkening lake. Cameras snapped, recording the pagoda, the houses on stilts, the floating gardens. As the boat pulled away, Paul stood up to get a wide-angle shot of the pagoda with the houses in the background.

'Good idea,' said Michael, 'that'll give a nice shot,' and he followed suit.

'Look at the little boy over there,' cried Barbara, and everyone's head swivelled away from the pagoda to watch a small boy trying to manipulate an oar with his leg in the traditional way. Thomas took a photo. The boy overbalanced, lost his oar, and gave them a big apologetic grin.

'Isn't he cute?' said Barbara. 'Do you think we could get him to pose again?'

Her voice was a shade too high-pitched and insistent. The boat was gathering speed. Some sixth sense made Claudia turn away from the boy and look back towards the pagoda. Michael and Paul were both still upright in the boat. Paul was holding his camera, about to take a photo. Michael was bending down, putting his camera on the floor of the boat. Suddenly Michael appeared to stagger. He fell hard against the back of Paul's legs. Paul was pushed violently off balance. For a few seconds, they both lurched dangerously in mid-air. The next minute they both toppled over into the water. First Paul, and then Michael. There was a huge splash. Claudia screamed. The boat was already several yards away. Paul couldn't swim. She could see Michael's head above the water, but there was no sign of Paul. The others were turning to look, there were cries of alarm and confusion, the guide was yelling at the boatman to stop. Where was Paul? Why hadn't he come up? Claudia began to get to her feet, ready to plunge in after him, but then she was shoved aside, someone said brusquely, 'Stay there,' and the next minute Angus had pushed past her and dived in.

He was a good swimmer, that much was clear. With a few fast powerful strokes, he reached the spot where Michael and Paul were floundering. Michael semed to be panicking. Angus elbowed him aside and disappeared underwater. Claudia waited, clutching the edge of the boat. No one spoke. They were all holding their breath. After what seemed like a long time, Angus reappeared at the surface, holding Paul in what looked like an expert grip. A subdued cheer went up. The boatman had already turned the craft around and was manoeuvring back towards them. Angus brought Paul along-side the boat, with Michael following a few yards behind. Keith and Austin reached down to pull them into the boat, one after the other. Claudia crawled down the boat and bent over Paul. He retched and spluttered, apparently unharmed. Between splutters, he mumbled something in German. Claudia didn't understand. It was Christa who answered him.

'Is he all right?' said Barbara.

'He'll be fine,' said Austin. 'Hey, Angus, want a ride?'

'Don't let's forget the noble rescuer.'

'Give me your arm. That's right. Sorry, Claudia, move over a bit, can you?'

Claudia shifted obediently. Between the legs of the rescuers, she caught sight of a hand sticking up out of the water. The skin across the palm was defaced. It stretched in an ugly ridge from one side of the hand to the other. Claudia stared, mesmerised. Did Michael have a scar after all? How could they have failed to notice it. A head appeared after the hand and Angus was hauled dripping into the boat.

'There you go, mate. Enjoy your swim?'

'Now, Michael. Up you come.'

'Is that it, or are there any more out there?'

'Is everyone all right?'

'What on earth happened?'

'It was all my fault,' said Michael. 'I lost my balance.'

'You've been having quite a day, Michael. First the camera, and now this.'

'I'm really sorry. Is Paul okay?'

'What a good job Angus was here,' said Thomas. 'He has more quick wits than any of us.'

'Oh he's done life-saving classes,' said Barbara. 'He's used to it.'

'Lucky for Paul,' said Keith.

Paul said something else in German, and again it was Christa who answered.

'What's he saying?' said Michael.

'He asks what has happened, and I tell him you overbalance.'

She went on talking to him in German. Barbara looked curiously at Claudia.

'You don't speak German?'

'Not much, no.'

'Maybe you'd better learn it if he's going to relapse into German every time he gets a shock,' said Keith.

'Maybe he could just take swimming lessons,' said Austin. 'Okay now, can anyone spare some clothes for our swimmers here? If they stay like that we're going to have three cases of pneumonia on our hands.'

'We have blankets here, sir. Please take.'

'Great. You're pretty well prepared, I see. I guess it's not the first time this has happened.'

'Oh no. Sometimes we have accident. Always on water people will fall in.'

Nothing to worry about, no reason to be suspicious, just par for the course. The 'swimmers' peeled off their wet clothes, pulled on donated sweatshirts and pullovers and wrapped themselves in the blankets produced by the guide, the same calibre as those that the hotel put on its beds, but better than nothing. The boat got underway again. Paul hauled himself up next to Claudia on the bench. Michael and Angus were sitting opposite.

'You're sure you're okay?' said Michael solicitously.

'I'll be fine.'

'Well thank God for that, you're speaking English again!'

'But my camera's on the floor of the lake.'

'Shit, I hadn't thought of that. I guess mine is too.'

'No, yours is here,' said Austin, holding it up. 'You must have dropped it as you went in.'

'Yeah? I don't remember. Well, that's a lucky break. I'm real sorry about yours, though, Paul. You must let me reimburse you for it.'

'The camera don't matter. It is an old one. But I have in it a roll of film nearly finished. That is the pity.' He put his arm round Claudia, and she huddled closer to him and buried her head in his side. It was a good excuse not to have to look at First Murderer and Second Murderer sitting calmly on the other side of the boat chatting about cameras. 'Don't worry, Liebling.' He softened his peevish tone, and his lips grazed the top of her head. 'It is over now. I promise I will take swimming lessons when we get back to London.'

'Good idea,' said Austin. 'Angus here might not be around to fish you out next time.'

★

The hotel was in the middle of a power cut, and there was no light but a faint radiance filtering in from the windows across the street. Claudia slammed shut the door of their room and turned the key in the lock.

'What's wrong?' said Paul, dropping his borrowed sweatshirt on the floor.

'Angus has a scar across his left palm. I saw it when he was climbing back into the boat.'

Paul stopped halfway out of his jeans. 'You mean he's Narathu?'

'He must be. He has the right build. It never occurred to me to connect him with Narathu because we never saw him in Pagan.'

'Well, clearly he was there.' Paul shivered suddenly. 'God, I'm freezing.'

'But why would he save your life, that's what I don't understand. If Michael was trying to drown you, why would Angus jump in and stop him?'

'I don't know and right now I'm too cold to care. Is that door locked?'

'Yes.' Claudia put her hand against his chest. 'Jesus, you really are cold. Why don't you take a shower to warm you up – oh God, I forgot, there's no hot water in this stupid hotel.'

'No there isn't.' Paul took her in his arms. 'I'm afraid you're going to have to do it all on your own.'

'I can't believe you'd be so fucking stupid,' said Angus. 'Trying to drown the guy in full view of a whole boatload of people. Shit. I've seen some pretty stupid things in my life, but I don't think I've ever seen anything as half-assed as that.'

'You cut that out,' said Michael. 'It would have worked fine if you hadn't butted in.'

'If I hadn't, someone else would have. Thomas or Austin. Even Claudia was all set to jump in after him. Next time you want to drown someone, Michael, try and do it more privately.'

'Come on, guys,' said Barbara. 'Let's all calm down now.'

Angus rounded on her. 'Did you know he was planning to do this? Why the hell didn't you warn me about it?'

'Well, you know, it just seemed like a good opportunity. We're all out on the lake, the guy can't swim—'

'Did either of you pause to think that probably isn't even true? Let's not forget that Miller has a history of setting traps.'

There was a dead silence.

'You think it was a trap?' said Barbara nervously.

'Of course it was. He set a trap, probably to try and figure out who was after him, and Michael fell into it. And now you guys are burned.'

'Oh I don't think so,' said Barbara. 'He was pretty dazed when he got back in the boat. He asked what had happened and Christa told him you over-balanced. He doesn't suspect a thing. He wouldn't have been bitching about his camera if he thought you were trying to kill him, would he?'

'What the hell did you fish him out for anyway?'

Angus rolled his eyes. 'Michael, for Christ's sake, think a little. Let's assume you managed to drown him. And let's assume that everyone thinks it's an accident. Have you any idea what's likely to happen when a foreign tourist gets killed in a place like this? You'll have the police swarming all over everywhere, taking statements, filling in forms. Probably none of us would have been able to move out of here for a week.'

Michael and Barbara looked at each other.

'Now here's what we're going to do. We're going to wait and see if he shows up in Mandalay, and if he does we'll get Min Saw to deal with it. With connections like his, he'll be able to handle it discreetly, and there'll be nothing to link it with us. Right, Michael?'

There was a long pause. 'Right,' said Michael.

Bells chimed softly in the darkness and the sound of chanting came faintly from the pagoda across the road. Closer at hand, there was the hum of voices rising and falling from the outer room. The monks were at their prayers, and the tourists were drinking rum. Claudia felt drowsy and at peace. Here, with Paul's breath warm against her neck and his arms around her, she was safe. The little white-walled room was a haven against the dangers outside: the plotters, the watchers, the murderers. Her brain cleared and the memory of what had happened on the lake cut through the haze of indolence. Somewhere in the darkness was Narathu: Angus, with the scar on his hand, the knife in his pocket, and now a sword in his luggage too. She shuddered convulsively. Paul woke up and pulled her against him.

'What's the matter? Are you cold too now?'

'Can you really not swim?'

'Of course I can swim.' She could hear him smiling in the darkness. 'Do you think I'd tell that bunch of thugs out there if I couldn't?'

'You could have warned me.'

'If I'd told you, you wouldn't have screamed so convincingly.' His hand circled her breast, and moved idly down her body.

Claudia caught her breath. 'I thought you were going to drown.'

'I nearly did drown. Michael was doing his damnedest to keep me under the water. It was lucky for me that Angus showed up.'

'Oh God, Angus ... I never for one moment thought it might be him. I thought he was fun. I liked him. And to think it was him all the time with that knife in the temple ...'

'Don't think about it.' Paul began to kiss her.

'And it means there are even more of them than we thought. Not just two, but three, maybe even four, if Keith's in with them too.'

'We'll see if they all turn up in Mandalay together.'

'Jesus, that's right, Angus said they were going on to Pagan.'

'But now we know that he's been there already. Stop worrying about it, little one, and kiss me. Now that we've found out what the Burmese do for night life, we might as well make the most of it.'

Adrian lay on the bed in his grim little green-painted lair at the Mandalay Hotel and wondered what to do next. Philip was in none of the tourist hotels in Mandalay, and none of the guest houses for Burmese travellers either. None of the rickshaw drivers at the tourist sites remembered a tall blond foreigner with a half-Burmese wife. Where could they have gone? How was he going to find them? Despite Tony's parting gibe, he had no intention of checking the monasteries. He was pretty sure he had been wrong about that. The theft of the tapestry suggested that Philip's trip to Burma was a great deal more purposeful than he had at first supposed. But Philip's preoccupations, whatever they were, had not brought him to Mandalay.

So where had they taken him?

It occurred to Adrian that Tony's contact in Pagan might have some additional information. He went down to reception and asked them to call the Irra Inn.

The call came through at half past ten in the evening. By then Adrian had given up and gone to bed. He threw on some clothes and stumbled downstairs to take the call at the reception desk. Room telephones were a refinement unknown in Mandalay hotels. The line was very faint and the receptionist at the Irra Inn seemed not to understand a word of his bawled inquiries after Franco Masiero. After five minutes Adrian hung up. Even if he managed to get hold of Masiero, there was no way he would be able to extract any useful information from him.

There was no reason for him to stay in Mandalay. Tomorrow, he would fly to Pagan and talk to Masiero in person.

Part Six

Mandalay

As Claudia had surmised, once Paul decided to let go, an explosion of sorts took place. The sex was quite different from what she expected: neither friendly nor polite, and very little to do with human warmth. There had been nothing like this since she met Nick. (If she were perfectly honest, there had been nothing like it with Nick either. Nick was a self-absorbed bastard: she was well rid of him.) Nor had she ever been able to talk to Nick the way she and Paul were talking. A barrier had burst in both their minds, and it was all coming pouring out, Hamburg and Hong Kong, Lucy, Nick and Caroline, all inextricably entwined, because in a way his childhood had been her childhood and his past had been hers.

It seemed to Claudia that she had never talked so much in her life. She could tell him anything, and he would understand. She could tell him things she had never told anyone, such as the day in school when her teacher had held up a picture of a Chinese woman in wide blue trousers and a peaked straw hat kneeling in a rice paddy and informed the class, 'Claudia comes from China.' The weeks of gibes about 'Where's your hat?' and 'What did you have for dinner last night?' that followed. The poring over postcards sent by Aunt

Susan from Hong Kong, trying to spot the rice fields between the skyscrapers ... There would be no raised eyebrows, embarrassed silences, retreats, withdrawals. She could tell him things she would never have dreamed of telling Nick, about growing up as an illegitimate child in a conventional suburban neighbourhood, with a mother who worked for her living and cooked chop suey instead of sausages for dinner, and a father who rolled up unexpectedly with an armful of champagne and silk blouses and then disappeared again for weeks on end. Paul knew it all already: he had been there himself. He had been turned out of the house by the father of a schoolfriend who had spent three years in a German prisoner of war camp, asked in his A-level history class for his personal view of the Holocaust, and watched How-we-beat-the-Hun films every week on television.

The only difference was that Paul had given in to them. He had allowed them to decide the way he behaved and the way he talked. What he said and how he lived. Paul had honed off his un-English edges and protruding thoughts and turned himself into a carbon copy of a perfect Englishman. It wasn't healthy. Claudia was aware that her own operating mode, that of the professional outcast, didn't have much to recommend it, but it seemed preferable to that of full-time undercover agent that Paul had chosen. There was a lower risk of schizophrenia, for a start.

'Don't you ever find it a strain?' she asked doubtfully. 'Trying to be something you're not all the time? Or are you just so used to it that you don't notice it any more?'

She half-expected him to evade the question, but tonight he seemed prepared to answer anything. 'Of course I notice it. I feel it more and more as time goes on. It's getting very obvious that I've made a lot of wrong choices. The wrong job, the wrong woman.' He paused, and then went on. 'Quite frankly, my life's a mess. I'm forty-two years old, and I don't have anything to show for it.'

For a moment Claudia was too startled to speak.

'Jesus, Paul, are you serious?'

'Yes.'

'There's still time to change,' she told him firmly. 'You can always do something else.'

'I don't think so. Years ago I took a wrong turning, and now it's too late to go back.'

'It's never too late. What would you have chosen to do if you hadn't decided to ... er ... '

'To be a spy, you mean?' She could hear the amusement in his voice. 'It's all right, you can say it out loud, there's only us here. I don't know, little one. That was partly why I joined the service in the first place. I didn't know what else to do. I had a friend who'd been recruited through his uncle, he passed on my name to them, they were interested in my German skills ...'

'So you thought this was your big chance to redeem yourself by serving England.' She felt him move convulsively against her and added guiltily, 'Sorry, that was a bit brutal. I shouldn't have said that.'

'You have this habit of hitting the nail right on the head. It's a little alarming at times.' He sighed and rolled over on his back. 'That was exactly what I had in mind – though I didn't realize it till much later on, of course.'

'I'll have to see if I can think of an alternative career for you. We can't have you wasting the rest of your life on Queen and Country now you've finally seen the light. What did you want to be when you were little?'

'That's easy. I wanted to be the first man on the moon.'

It was as if a door had opened and admitted him to another world. A world of warmth and light and colour and abundance that he had known existed, had even occasionally glimpsed, but never set foot in until today. Maybe he had just been choosing the wrong kind of women all his life. Women who would keep their distance and allow him to keep his. Under normal circumstances, he would have steered well clear of someone like Claudia, sensing instinctively that here was someone who would violate his withdrawals, trample on his silences and batter down his protective barriers. And so he had been making do all his life with second-best: the stintingness of Lucy, the capriciousness of Rebecca, the polite circumspection of nearly all his other sexual relationships. In bed, as elsewhere, he had been holding back, playing a role, experiencing life at one remove. How ironic that only now should he realize what he had been missing.

It was an amazing sensation. He could say what he wanted, do what he wanted. Whatever he said, whatever he did, it would be all right. She knew what he was like without having to be told, and she took him the way he was without having to be convinced. He had no need to watch for her reactions and adjust his behaviour accordingly. He could tell her things he had never told anyone, not even himself, and then discover that he hadn't needed to tell her because she knew them already.

He had never felt so free. Free to make love to her any way he wanted, knowing that she would follow him, even anticipate him: free to talk to her as he had never talked to anyone about his lonely childhood, his pointless career, his failed marriage, and his whole wasted, useless life. For his sixteenth birthday, his father had bought him a copy of the *Republic*, and made sure that he read it. Being with Claudia was like approaching the mouth of Plato's metaphorical cave, and seeing the real world clearly through the flickering flames at last.

They had talked about his childhood, his schooldays, his job. His father, who read Herodotus in the original and wrote monographs on Greek military history, who had come to collect him in Hamburg when his mother died and not spoken a word during the whole flight home. The months of misery he had then endured. His growing attachment to little Caroline, who expressed no objections to his German accent, odd tastes in food and un-English manners. The only one they hadn't talked about was his wife.

'What about Lucy? Was she a misfit too?'

But Lucy, it appeared, had been a model of conformity. Roots as long as your arm, English through and through. A house in Oxfordshire which had been in the family for God knows how many generations. Her father, like his father before him, had been the local solicitor and her mother was the vicar's daughter. Solid rural gentry. Lucy had kept the friends she had made in primary school, and her whole world was made up of people she had known all her life. She worked in London and went home every weekend. Her twin brother was the Cambridge friend who had put Paul in touch with the spies, which meant that her uncle must have been a big wheel with same. Serving their country, every damn one of them.

'Why didn't you have children?' she asked. 'Not very patriotic of you, was it?'

'Don't laugh,' said Paul. 'One or two people actually made remarks like that. The truth was that we both realized fairly soon that we'd made a mistake. We never actually discussed whether or not we were going to have children: it was just taken for granted that we weren't.'

'Why didn't you get a divorce?'

'There were several reasons. One, it wouldn't have done my career any good. Two, it would have caused a huge outcry in Lucy's family. Three, neither of us had any alternative plans. Lucy didn't like sex much – in fact, she didn't like men. As long as she had someone to take along to dinner parties and weekends, she had no reason to want to get married again.'

'What about you?'

'I didn't want to get married again either. I had a few affairs, nothing much. But in the end, as I told you yesterday, I got to the point where I couldn't handle living with her any longer.'

'It sounds rather sad.'

'It was very selfish. On my part especially. If I'd insisted on a divorce she'd have had to look round for someone else, and she was pretty sure to have found someone more temperamentally suited to her, who would have looked after her better. I really blame myself for what happened.'

Yes, thought Claudia, we know that already. And you're determined to take all the blame that you can, even if it means depriving Lucy of her fair share. She could see exactly how he had argued himself into such an irrational corner. He had married Lucy because he coveted her roots, her solidly built little niche, her belonging. He had thought that by marrying her, he would succeed in belonging too. And then he had got disillusioned with it all, but before he could make up his mind to ditch her, she had died, and he had managed to convince himself that it was all his fault because he had fallen in love, not with her, but with the social stability he thought she offered him. Oh dear, oh dear.

She kissed his cheek and held him tight. The first grimy light of dawn was beginning to creep through the unwashed windows of the little white room. 'You should never have married her. She was all wrong for you.'

'Yes,' said Paul. 'I made the mistake and she paid the price.'

Across the road, bells began to chime and the sound of chanting rose raggedly into the thin morning air. The monks were up and about and doing penance.

At five o'clock in the morning on the bus to Mandalay, it was as dark as hell and as cold as Siberia. It was a goddammed nuisance there hadn't been any room on the plane. The Buckleys had taken the morning flight to Mandalay, but there had been no seats left for Austin and Greg. With all the money SLORC was raking in from narcotics, you'd think they could trade in their lousy little Fokkers for some serious flightware. Greg wrapped his towel round his head and his sleeping bag round his shoulders and announced at frequent intervals that he had never been so cold in his life. Austin didn't pay much attention. He had too much on his mind. He just hoped to God the guy in Mandalay would pick out the Buckleys at the airport and see where they went and who they met. They sure as hell weren't going to the hairdressers. Occasionally, Greg asked if they would be able to find new batteries for his Walkman in Mandalay. Austin fervently hoped they would. Get some for the Game Boy too while they were at it. Greg was a good kid, but he was only fourteen, and Burma was pretty rough going. You couldn't expect too much at that age. It wasn't surprising he was starting to whine now and again.

When it got light, Greg tried without much success to read the guidebook.

'So what's there to see in Mandalay anyway?'

Austin looked at him reflectively. What indeed? A lot of Chinese, sneaking in illegally from Yunnan province trying to get rich. A lot of army officers building themselves fancy houses with their illegal incomes from heroin smuggling. A lot of trucks, some military, some not. Some carrying opium southwest to the new refineries they'd set up on the banks of the Chindwin river. Some carrying acetic anhydride northeast to the old refineries up on the Thai border. Some carrying refined heroin down to Rangoon.

'Well, you know, there's Mandalay Hill. A pagoda or two. The palace walls.'

'Doesn't sound very exciting.'

'Depends how you look at it,' said Austin. In a sense, the kid was right. There was a lot happening in Mandalay, but not all that much to be seen for it. What was more, any excitement that blew up during their stay would probably not be taking place on the tourist circuit. Today, Michael and Barbara Buckley had an important engagement, and Austin was praying it was an appointment with their heroin supplier. He wouldn't mind finding out who that was. He'd been chasing round Burma for a week after those two jerks, and so far he had nothing to show for it. Meanwhile, it might be a good idea to get Greg out of the way before the shooting started. He had catalogued Buckley as the kind of upwardly mobile, white-collar criminal who would avoid getting his hands dirty, but it looked as though he had underestimated him.

'Actually you're right, Greg. You can see Mandalay in one day, and I reckon that's exactly what you're going to do. After that I'm going to put you on the plane back to Rangoon. You can stay with Marty for a couple of days. He won't mind.'

'Why? What's the idea?'

'Things are hotting up.' He looked round to make sure that Thomas and Christa, who were travelling on the same bus, were out of earshot. 'You saw what happened last night.'

'Did Michael push him deliberately?'

'Reckon so.'

'Why?'

Austin shook his head. He would gladly trade his expense account for the answer to that question. He had spent all day yesterday trying to find out what Miller was up to in Burma, but without success. The guy was so tight-lipped he made clams look amateurish. The incident on the lake had established that there was a link between Miller and Buckley. Buckley wanted Miller dead. But why was anybody's guess.

'Why can't we go to Pagan?' said Greg mulishly.

'We've been to Pagan.'

'Oh yeah, half a day.'

Austin shrugged. It wasn't his fault if they had got to Pagan only to find that the Buckleys had left for Shan State two hours earlier.

'Come on now, Greg. I warned you this might happen.'

'What am I supposed to do in Rangoon?'

'Hang out. Swim in the pool. Wait for me to show up.'

'And what are you going to be doing?'

'Hey, kid,' said Austin. 'You know better than to ask me that.'

Mandalay was the last royal capital of Burma. According to the guidebook, it had been founded in 1857, and conquered in 1886. British troops had overrun the city, sent the king into exile, and moved the capital south to Rangoon. For a time, the royal palace was used as military headquarters, but it burned down during World War Two. All that remained were the walls surrounding the palace compound, four massive red-brick walls, each one over a mile long, built in a perfect square, dominating the city even to this day.

'What's in there, anyway?' said Barbara, as they came out of the hotel.

'Mandalay Fort,' said Michael. 'As far as I know it's still used as military headquarters, and I think it's a prison too.'

'It gives me the creeps. That awful blood-red colour.'

'We're going to have to hurry,' said Michael. 'Min Saw's expecting us at two.'

Min Saw lived in a big wooden house on a quiet residential street. The house stood in a vast, dusty garden, surrounded by trees. By local standards, it was distinctly opulent. The workshop was at the front of the house. Double doors opened on to a shady porch and three low wooden frames had been set out in the open air. Large squares of black velvet were pulled taut on the frames, and two or three girls sat on the ground around each one, working at embroidery and beading on different parts of the tapestry. They looked up as the Americans approached, then went back to their work. They were clearly used to seeing foreigners come and go. A well-dressed woman, who had been sitting on a chair a little further away, got up and came to greet them.

'Hello.' Michael gave her his most urbane smile. 'I'm Michael Buckley from the Rajasthan Gallery in New York, and this is my wife Barbara. I believe U Min Saw is expecting us.'

The woman gave them a dazzling smile. 'He not here.'

Michael frowned and glanced at his watch. 'When will he be back?'

'He Rangoon. He come Mandalay tomorrow.'

'Tomorrow? But we were supposed to have an appointment today.'

'Many problems Rangoon. He drive to Mandalay tomorrow only.' She raised her hand to her mouth and giggled.

'I see. Then maybe we could come by tomorrow evening?'

Min Saw's wife stopped giggling and displayed unexpected firmness. 'No. You not come tomorrow. He come late. He come very night. You come morning only. You come morning after tomorrow. You come Thursday.'

Paul and Claudia reached Mandalay by plane in the early evening. They sat side by side in the taxi from the airport, watching the streets roll past. After the archaism of Pagan and the wildness of Shan State, it was strange to be back in an approximation of the twentieth century. Paved roads, brick-built houses, and the same blue taxis as in Rangoon. But then, on a street corner, Claudia saw a group of people clustered round a large water tank conducting their ablutions, men and women together, all chastely clothed in their *longgyis*, pouring buckets of water over their heads, soaping themselves, washing their hair. Modernity went no deeper than the taxis – running water and electric light were out of reach, civilization was an illusion. She put her hand on Paul's knee and he gave her a distant smile. Before she could wonder what that meant, her attention was caught by a sign by the side of the road that said BE KIND TO ANIMALS BY NOT EATING THEM.

'That's a bit different from their usual line,' she observed. 'Is vegetarianism supposed to help keep the Union intact?'

Paul's mind was clearly elsewhere. 'What? Oh, that's just because Mandalay is the spiritual centre of Burma. SLORC's trying to empathize with the monks.'

'Ah.' So they were back among the monks, were they? Not a good sign. She removed her hand and folded her arms chastely across her chest.

The hotel was a new one called the Innwa Inn, which Paul had found on a previous visit to Mandalay. It had yet to be discovered by the Western guide books, and they seemed to be the only tourists there. They were taken across a dusty lawn to a green-roofed bungalow with a verandah overlooking the garden. In the car park, a man in chauffeur's uniform was washing a car. A teenage boy wearing a T-shirt, jeans and Converse trainers sauntered past. The verandah of the adjoining bungalow was occupied by three young men drinking Pepsi-Cola and listening to Burmanized Rod Stewart on an outsize ghetto blaster. They were deep in the heart of official, affluent Westernized Burma. No sign of the Buckleys, nor of Angus and Keith. The perfect place to go to ground. The bellboy accepted a ballpoint pen and closed the door behind him.

'What now?' said Claudia warily.

To her relief, Paul dropped his bag on the floor and gave her a kiss like a normal, flesh-and-blood human being.

'First we'll have dinner. And then we're going to go for a little drive.'

The hotel restaurant was Stalinist, square and functional, with net curtains, fluorescent lights, and a raised platform for Marxist-Buddhist orators to harangue the guests at official functions. A waiter offered them a choice of Chinese dinner or European dinner. This wasn't the kind of hotel where people could be fobbed off with Burmese dish. The only other clients were a small group of men at the other end of the room. Their table was invisible beneath a vast amount of empty soft-drink bottles.

'Who are they?' said Claudia curiously.

'Government officials, I imagine. This place is full of them.'

'What's the big celebration in aid of? Has the Tatmadaw finally won the war?'

'No,' said Paul, 'it's payday. They just got the monthly heroin kickback.'

She laughed in relief. For the time being, it was still all right.

'Here comes the food. My God, what's this?'

'That's your European dinner. Steak, just like you ordered.'

'It's not steak, it's hamburger. No, it's not that either. It's a new kind of animal.' She poked dubiously at the hybrid lump of meat. The steak had been ground up just enough to allow the cook to mix a suitable amount of chilli peppers into the meat. European food for Burmese palates.

'You should have waited till you got back to England,' said Paul sardonically.

'England?' said Claudia, taking a tentative mouthful. 'Oh well, yes, I suppose I should.'

He gave her a suspicious glare. 'You are going back to England after this trip, aren't you?'

'Yes. I expect so. Sure.'

'That business at the consulate. That was just a passing mood?'

'Oh yes, of course. That was just ...' What were all these questions for?

'You can stay with your mother while you look for a job, can't you?'

'Jesus. I haven't lived at my mother's since I was eighteen – Well yes, sure, after all, why not?'

'Claudia, what are you going to do?'

She looked up and smiled at him. 'Darling, I told you already, I'm never going back to England. I'm staying in Burma for ever and ever, remember?'

She could tell from the expression on his face that it wasn't the right thing to say.

'Ah yes, so you are,' he said irritably. 'Doing what, may I ask? Running an opium den?'

'Why not? It might be quite fun. I can ask Austin where to get supplies.'

'Great idea.'

'Anyway, don't worry about me. I'll think of something.' She pushed the remains of her steak decisively aside. 'What about you? Are you going back to Berlin, or wherever it was?'

'Do you want anything else to eat,' said Paul, 'or can I ask for the bill?'

Michael and Barbara were eating dinner in the restaurant of the Mandalay Hotel when Austin and Greg walked in.

'Well, hi there,' said Barbara. 'We wondered when you guys were going to arrive. How was the bus?'

'Gross,' said Greg.

'Let's say it was an interesting experience,' said Austin.

'Then maybe it'll give you some good copy,' said Michael.

'I did consider a piece on travelling in Burma, but my editor would never believe it. Maybe I could sell it to the Vancouver — hell, what's your local paper up there called again?'

'*Vancouver Sun*,' said Barbara.

'Right, yeah, the *Vancouver Sun*. So what's for dinner?' he went on, glancing critically over Barbara's plate.

'They have Chinese food here. It's not bad at all.'

'Seen anything of the Millers?' asked Michael.

'No. Thought they were going to Sandoway. Did they change their minds?'

'I just wondered.'

'What about Keith and Angus? Are they here?'

Michael and Barbara exchanged glances. 'Didn't they go to Pagan?' said Barbara.

'Did they?' said Austin. 'Well, never mind. I'm pretty sure

we'll run into eveyone sooner or later in one of the pagodas. It's a small world.'

Min Saw's house was as imposing as Paul remembered. The double doors leading to the workshop were tightly shuttered, and no lights were visible on the ground floor. Paul wondered whether to undertake a few preliminary investigations, but decided not to take the risk. According to Rebecca, Min Saw was leaving for Rangoon tomorrow morning. It was safer to abide by the timetable she had given him.

The rickshaw driver had stopped pedalling. 'Don't stop,' said Paul. 'I just wanted to see where it was. We'll come back tomorrow.'

The man yelled an instruction to his colleague a few yards behind, who was driving Claudia. 'Does friend of you live there?'

'A friend?' said Paul startled. 'Oh no, he's not a friend.'

'Then why you visit him?' The driver was in his mid-twenties, with an intelligent face and an infectious grin. Paul was amused rather than offended by the inquiry.

'We heard he makes tapestries.'

'*Kalagas?*'

'Yes.'

'Is better you buy *kalagas* somewhere else. I take you good place tomorrow. This man here very bad man. He make good *kalagas*, but he very bad man.'

'Really?' said Paul. 'Why's that?'

There was a pause. 'He make many *kalagas* for government people.'

He shot Paul a careful sideways glance.

'Then he must be very rich,' said Paul. 'Government people have a lot of money, but the ordinary people are poor.'

'Yes, that is right, sir. Ordinary people are very poor, especially Shan people.'

'Are you Shan?'

'Yes I am.' He hesitated a moment more, and then it all came pouring out. 'I study to be engineer, but they say to me, you cannot study any more. Now I must work as rickshaw driver.'

'Why don't they want you to study?'

'Because I fight against them in 1988. Many students fight against government in 1988. You know this very big uprising? My brother and I both. They kill my brother, and they say I cannot study any more.'

'Why stay in Mandalay? Why don't you go with the other students to the jungle and fight with the MTA?'

'Because my father and mother they are old and cannot work. I must make money for them to live. My brother is dead, and now I am alone to make them live. They are very sorry because my brother is dead and because I cannot be engineer. I cannot leave them.'

'I understand.'

'Where you go tomorrow? You do sightseeing? You want we drive you, me and my friend? We take you see *kalagas*, very good *kalagas*.'

'Why not?' said Paul. A Shan ex-student, apparently hostile to SLORC, might be a good contact to have. It could be useful to play along, pretend to be a tourist, sound him out, see where it led.

'What's your name?' he asked.

'Sai Thawda. And my friend is Sai Pan. He is Shan too.'

'Okay, then. Come and fetch us at nine at the hotel. We'll start with Mandalay Hill.'

One of the sights of Mandalay by night had presumably been Min Saw's house. Claudia didn't ask: she didn't want to know. She was beginning to get a pretty shrewd idea why they had come to Mandalay, and it scared her to death. She was reassured by the purposeful way Paul locked the door of their bungalow and drew the curtains. The countdown had started, the hours were numbered, but for a little while longer they could forget about everything but each other, their bodies coming together, seeking each other out, taking up where they had left off in the little white room in Yaunghwe, shutting out the smugglers and the killers and the ghosts, and the whole lost, dusty city of monks and traffickers.

She had been afraid too that in this city of monasteries, he might have regretted forswearing his old ascetic vocation, but it was clear that, for the time being at least, he had no inclination to return to his former celibate ways. It was all right. In fact it was even better than the night before. When it was over, they lay silently together, dazed and languorous. Claudia wondered how on earth she could have thought that sex was not Paul's thing. She had had enough intimations of the violence underlying that controlled surface: she should have realized a long time ago that she was wrong. She wanted to hug him, to thank him, to tell him that this was what she had been looking forever since she had allowed the father of a schoolfriend to seduce her, at the age of fourteen, one Thursday afternoon on the living room sofa when her mother was at work, but she didn't think it was the kind of thing he wanted to hear. Not yet. Not here in Mandalay where there was business to be done. For a while she drifted off to sleep, until the sound of the ghetto blaster coming through the wall dragged her back to wakefulness.

'Oh God, what the hell's that, what time is it?'

'Just after nine.'

'Too early to ask them to turn it down.'

'If you ask them to turn it down, you get offered alternative accommodation in Mandalay jail.'

'Papa the Party official comes waddling out of the restaurant and throws us into a Black Maria?'

'That's right.'

Claudia laughed and stretched and returned to her original position against his side. After only two days, their bodies were already developing habits and customs of their own, and all kinds of niches and hollows were starting to slot together as if they had been doing so all their lives.

'Why aren't you always like this?' she demanded. 'It suits you.'

'I am always like this.'

'Then you hide it very well. I want you to know that even if you get me carted off to jail tomorrow, tonight has been one of the best nights of my life. Last night too.'

'Mine too. I wish—' He broke off.

'What?'

'I wish I'd met you somewhere else. Under different circumstances. Earlier.'

'You did meet me earlier,' Claudia pointed out. 'But you turned me down.'

There was a pause. 'Well, you know how it is,' said Paul lightly. 'I was afraid you might find me a bit dull after all your . . . excitement in Paris.'

Claudia went rigid. Jesus, the bastard, how could he say such a thing? It was exactly the kind of remark Nick could be relied on to produce at particularly tender moments. And now Paul too. They really were all the bloody same.

'Good heavens, what an idea,' she said brightly. 'I do assure you, Paul, you have absolutely nothing to worry about.'

'I'm sorry, I shouldn't have said that. It's not what I meant.'

'You are paying for it, after all. One shouldn't lose sight of that.'

'Please, I didn't mean to imply that—'

'Oh yes, you did.'

'It's not what I meant. Claudia, please, I didn't want—'

Next door the radio was abruptly silenced. His voice rang out loudly in the sudden hush and he broke off, startled.

'Nine thirty,' said Claudia, looking at her watch. 'Burmese bedtime. Don't worry, Paul, I know what you're trying to say. I realize this isn't going any further. We leave Burma at the end of the week, fly back to Europe and go our separate ways. After Saturday, I promise you'll never see me again.'

Keith and Angus were staying in a guest house near Zegyo Market, on the far side of town to the Mandalay Hotel. Michael and Barbara went there by rickshaw, making sure that no one saw them leave the hotel. For safety's sake, they stayed in the guest house to talk.

'Take a seat,' said Keith.

He and Angus sat on one bed, and Michael and Barbara sat on the other. The room was hot and airless. The only window opened onto the corridor and the washrooms were at the end of the hall. Barbara opened her mouth to exclaim and then shut it again. They had decided from the outset that Keith and Angus should keep out of sight and avoid the tourist hotels. Yaunghwe had been an exception, since there was only one hotel in the whole town. Poor guys, they had probably been staying in dumps like this all the way across Burma.

'So how did it go ?' said Angus.

'There's a bit of a problem.' Someone padded down the corridor, and Michael lowered his voice to avoid being heard through the bamboo walls. 'He wasn't there. Got held up in Rangoon, apparently. We've got another meeting scheduled for Thursday.'

'Thursday?' said Keith. 'That's a bit tight. What time?'

'Thursday morning. We can go early if you want. What time's your train to Rangoon?'

'Three o'clock.'

'Well, that shouldn't be a problem, should it?'

'Not if we can get everything wrapped up in one meeting. You're sure he's going to go for the idea?'

'Of course I'm sure. I wouldn't have come all this way, otherwise. He's a greedy little bastard. He's not going to raise any objections.'

'What are you guys doing when you get to Rangoon?' said Barbara.

'Leaving the country,' said Angus. 'No reason to stay, is there?'

'What about us? You're supposed to be watching our backs.'

'Once you've seen Min Saw you won't need us any more,' said Keith reassuringly. 'In any case, our visas expire Friday. We got here before you did, remember? We're flying home Friday evening.'

'You're flying straight back to the States? Both of you? But what about Miller?'

'What about him?' said Angus. 'Explain the problem to Min Saw and let him handle it.'

'But we don't even know if he's here or not. No one's seen him.'

'If he's not here, then there's nothing to worry about,' pointed out Keith.

'Of course he's here,' said Michael. 'Where else would he be?'

Mandalay Hill had been a sacred place for thousands of years. According to legend, the Buddha himself had even passed this way. Despite this, or perhaps because of it, the site possessed neither the calm radiance of the Shwedagon, nor the archaic ferocity of Pagan. The covered stairway leading to the top of the hill was equipped with stone seats to sustain the flesh during the climb, and shrines to sustain the spirit. A multitude of astrologers, palm-readers, souvenir peddlers, and photographers were on hand to provide the faithful with tangible proof of their spiritual pilgrimage. The atmosphere was frankly commercial and the decor was Buddhism at its tackiest. Lourdes-on-the-Irrawaddy, Caroline had called it. The best thing about the place was the view. As you climbed higher, Mandalay unrolled before your eyes, piece by piece, like a giant jigsaw puzzle. First the white Kuthodaw Pagoda at the foot of the hill, then the Sandamuni Pagoda next to it. Then the palace moat, the walls, and finally the grounds. The golf course, which was probably where the residents of the Innwa Inn were spending the day. Finally, as you neared the summit, the whole countryside spread out before you: the Irrawaddy to the west, the Shan plateau to the east, and further south the dim, pagoda-studded hills of Sagaing.

As he climbed higher, Paul's exhilaration grew. He felt like a long-distance runner within sight of the finishing line. He knew where he was going, and nothing could stop him getting there. Oblivious of Claudia by his side, he gazed silently out over the landscape. The sky was a clear, cloudless blue. A high light wind swung through the courtyards. As far as he could remember, he was standing in exactly the same spot he had stood with Caroline. The wheel had come full circle, and the momentum of its movement had brought him exactly where he wanted to be. He felt a sudden surge of confidence. Everything was coming together. It was all going to work out perfectly.

He turned abruptly to the girl by his side. It was time to explain why he had brought her all this way and brief her on the role he intended her to play. 'Let's go and sit down somewhere. We have to talk.'

They found a café in a shady courtyard, with low tables and blue wooden chairs. Paul selected a table half-hidden by a large statue of the Buddha which commanded an unimpeded view of people going up the steps and people going down. Most of the other tables were empty, and the inevitable Burmanized pop music was playing in the background. They could not be overheard. He ordered Pepsi-Cola for Claudia and beer for himself. They waited in silence for the drinks to arrive. Claudia sat impassively in her chair, uncharacteristically silent. Paul barely looked at her. It was all so clear it was perfect. Everything was coming together, sweeping him forward out of his failed, passionless life into a higher, purer realm of sacrifice and achievement.

He took a long gulp of beer and began to speak.

There was something in the air of Mandalay. Maybe the spiritual effluvia of all those monasteries. Ever since they got here, Paul had been moving further and further away from her, and this morning he seemed barely aware of her presence. He had spoken to her twice: the first time to tell her where they were going, the second to ask what she wanted to drink. Claudia had never been so scared in her life. She had reached the far end of the world, and any minute now she was going to fall off the edge. She ordered Pepsi-Cola, which seemed to be the chic drink around here, because it was plain that this was the equivalent of the condemned man's last breakfast.

Paul began, as she had expected, with Caroline. Alpha and Omega. The beginning and the end.

The first thing to arouse his suspicions after Caroline's death was the fact that she had left no note. 'She wouldn't have done that,' he said flatly. 'She knew I— She wouldn't have gone without leaving me a message. It's unthinkable.' Emma had found the flat in chaos when she got home that night, and he was convinced someone had been sent over to destroy any incriminating evidence that might be lying around.

The second thing to attract his attention was Caroline's choice of location, presumably no coincidence.

'But what really made me suspicious was when Emma told me that Caroline kept on working at the gallery until the day she died. Heroin addicts are known to be incapable of holding down a job, but Caroline went to work every single day. I had talked to Roland, her boss, and he had admitted that she wasn't a model employee. She came in late, her work wasn't always up to standard, she forgot things. But he said it had never crossed his mind that she might be on drugs.'

He paused. Claudia concentrated on her breathing. In and out, in and out. He had turned into a monk for real this time, exchanging signs of fraternity with a passing brown-robed colleague, casting off flesh and emotion, moving back to that graveside where she could not reach him.

'I decided he was lying. The only place heroin addicts go regularly is to see their dealer. I realized then that Roland must have been Caroline's supplier. I set up a watch on the gallery, I saw who went in and who came out, and I followed some of them. They were dealers, there was no doubt about it. They were going to the gallery to collect their supplies. At that point, I needed to get inside the gallery to ask questions, look at the things on display, and try to work out how the heroin was actually being smuggled. But I couldn't, because they knew who I was. So I went to see the galleries in New York and Paris instead. In any case, I needed to know if they were involved in narcotics smuggling too. It was clear that they were. One interesting thing I noticed was that all three galleries had a lot of Burmese artwork. Because of this, I felt fairly sure that the drugs were coming from Burma.'

'So you got yourself posted to Rangoon?' said Claudia, and he frowned because she was disturbing the rehearsed, chugging progress of his narrative, but agreed that yes, he had. It was obvious that he wasn't taking questions, but she asked another anyway. There was no point letting oneself be pushed off the edge of the world without a struggle.

'Why didn't you ask the police to investigate and get the galleries closed down?'

'I was just getting to that. They took the London gallery apart after Caroline died and they found nothing. So I decided to track down the supplier instead. I managed to obtain a posting to Rangoon. As soon as I arrived, I started going round the local art dealers, trying to find out who sold what, who sent what abroad, and so on. For several months I got nowhere. Then I had a stroke of luck. I was taking a few days' leave to visit Mandalay and the Ambassador asked me to check on the progress of a tapestry that had been commissioned for the Embassy. I went to the artist's house and saw his work-shop. The tapestries were very distinctive. I recognized them immediately. I'd already seen some of them in the Rajasthan Galleries. The artist explained to me that everything he did was based on the Glass Palace Chronicles. That was the title of an exhibition I had seen in the London gallery when Caroline showed me round a few years earlier. It all came together. The artist was using those tapestries to smuggle heroin to the West.'

'Min Saw,' said Claudia, though it was fairly obvious who they were talking about, and Paul nodded expressionlessly. 'Yes, but that's only circumstantial evidence, you know. How can you be sure it's him?'

'He has a big house in a nice part of town and an army of people working for him. There's no way a mere tapestry designer, even one with an international reputation and regime backing, can afford to live in a house like that. The only people in Mandalay with that kind of lifestyle are government officials and army officers. People who supple-ment their regular income with kickbacks from the heroin traffic. Min Saw is doing exactly the same thing. He doesn't make that kind of money just by selling tapestries. But just to make sure, I asked Jürgen to check up on him.'

'Jürgen?' said Claudia blankly.

'The monk who died in Rangoon. The one they wrote about in the paper. I'd known him for years, and it was partly on my suggestion that he came to Burma. He wasn't exactly reliable, in fact he was anything but. He'd been the despair of his family for years, never had a steady job, continually moving around, he'd done alcohol, drugs, God knows what else. But he was grateful to me for putting him on to the monastery, and he used to write me long letters about how meditation had changed his life, so I thought if I asked him to see what he could find out about Min Saw he probably would. Unfortunately, he seems to have done more than that. Jürgen never had any sense of what he could do and what he couldn't. Whenever he got himself into trouble, he was invariably surprised. He never ever saw it coming.'

He paused for a moment. 'I'll never know exactly what happened to him, but I think he must have decided to purloin a tapestry, even though I specifically warned him against it, and someone found out about it. There were two men hanging round in front of his hotel when I went there: I think they must have been watching him. Maybe they were from the police, maybe they worked for Min Saw. It doesn't matter. I think he panicked and swallowed the sachets to hide them.'

Claudia caught sight of a familiar baseball cap coming down the steps from the top of the hill. The Los Angeles Raiders, with the Hubers hard on his heels, and his father, camera in hand, bringing up the rear.

'Careful, we have company,' she said, trying to keep the relief out of her voice.

'Well, yes,' said Paul, turning to look. 'This is the main tourist site in Mandalay, you know.'

'Oh really? I can see why you chose it for a quiet chat then.'

'All tourists come here,' said Paul. 'It's good cover. Besides,' he added distantly, 'I came here with Caroline on our first trip to Burma.'

There was a sudden flurry of nudging and pointing and waving. They had been seen. Paul lifted a hand in greeting, Claudia waved energetically back.

'But, of course, you're right,' said Paul. 'I have no proof, and without that there's nothing I can do. That's what we've come here for. To get that proof.'

Well, hey, look who's here! Haven't we seen you guys some-place else? Small world, huh? When did you get here, what happened to the beach, what have you seen, where are you staying?

'Kind of kitsch up here, don't you think?'

'At least it is not so cold as Lake Inle.'

'We all have to sleep in the Mandalay Hotel. Everything else is full.'

'Where did you guys sneak off to?'

Changed any money here, what's the black market rate, where are you going next, what are you doing tomorrow?

'Mingun's supposed to be worth seeing. Biggest bell in the world, apparently.'

'Or else there's Ava and Amarapura. The old Burmese capitals, before they moved to Mandalay.'

'You might be interested in Amarapura, Claudia. That's where they wrote the Glass Palace Chronicles, you know.'

'Yes I know,' said Claudia. 'I'd really like to go there. We haven't decided what to do yet.' Actually, Christa, I think we have other plans. Burglary, by the sound of it, and there's a nasty glazed little look in Paul's eye that makes me think murder could also be on his list of things to do.

'Not much is left of the actual Glass Palace, but the foundations are still there. I think it might be interesting for you.'

'Paul, I would stay away from Mingun if I were you,' said Thomas. 'You can only get there by boat.'

'Yeah, that's right,' said Austin. 'Take some swimming lessons first. Michael and Barbara were looking for you last night, by the way. Wanted to know if anyone had seen you here.'

'Really?' said Paul. 'Well, I expect we'll run into them sooner or later.'

Greg finished his Pepsi and began to show signs of restlessness. 'Come on, Dad. If I have to get on a plane this afternoon, I want to see the rest of Mandalay first.'

'You are leaving?' said Paul.

'Just him,' said Austin. 'I'm staying on for another couple of days. It sounds like there's enough to keep one busy. Don't you think, Paul?'

Paul picked up the thread of his narrative as soon as they were out of earshot. Whatever sentimental or symmetrical associations had brought him back here, the interruption had made him aware that he had no time to lose. He had been waiting over a year already. Shortly after tracking down the smuggler who kept the Rajasthan Galleries supplied with heroin and was indirectly responsible for the death of his sister, he had been transferred out of Burma and back to Germany. For a year, he had been biding his time, growing his hair, sharpening his knives and plotting his stratagem. Burglary and murder. Much as Claudia had suspected.

'Min Saw leaves for Rangoon today,' he explained. 'He'll be gone till Friday. That gives us three days. Next week, he's going back to Rangoon with a consignment for New York. That's the one we're looking for. The tapestries will be finished already. They'll be hanging in his workshop ready to go.'

Claudia said nothing.

Paul gave her a sidelong glance, and changed pronouns. 'While he's away, I have to get into his workshop and get hold of one of those tapestries. That's the proof I need. One tapestry with his signature embroidered on it and a few hundred grams of heroin stuffed in the back.'

'How can you be sure they'll have heroin in them?'

'Because last week he sent nineteen tapestries to London. There was no heroin in any of them. If a whole consignment went out clean, it stands to reason the next one won't be. He needs a regular income.'

'How do we get it out of the country? Jungle route via Thailand?'

'No. Diplomatic pouch via Rangoon. That's what I want you to do. Take it down to Rangoon on the train – it takes

– 247 –

longer, but there are fewer controls than on the plane – and give it to Rebecca to pouch to London. If we take the tapestry tonight, you can be on the train tomorrow.'

'Me? All on my own?' She looked at him suspiciously. 'And what are you going to be doing in the meantime?'

'I'm going to wait till Min Saw gets back from Rangoon.'

'What for?'

'The tapestry will serve to get the three galleries investigated and closed down. The scandal might just be big enough to prevent Min Saw finding other distributors in the West. But as far as he's concerned it'll stop right there. He has very high-level protection. I can't count on the Burmese authorities to take any action against him. Why should they? They're all involved in it themselves.'

He stopped and looked at her. The glazed look she had noticed earlier was back at the edges of his eyes. Blood for blood. He said very softly, 'That means I have to deal with it myself.'

'How?' Instinctively, she dropped her voice to a whisper.

'It's easy enough to get hold of a gun in Mandalay if you know where to go. I have an address. If necessary, I think Sai Thawda might help.'

She stared at him in amazement. 'You're going to shoot him? But how . . .? I mean . . . what about the noise? Will you have a silencer? Surely the noise is going to attract attention. How are you going to get away afterwards?'

Paul didn't answer immediately. The birds were twittering in a tree in a corner of the courtyard and the radio came faintly in the background. The sun was high overhead and the air was clear and warm. Claudia felt herself breaking out in a cold sweat. There was something else, something he hadn't told her, something she hadn't guessed.

'The thing is,' said Paul composedly, 'I don't think I have much chance of getting away at all.'

*

Adrian took the bus from Pagan to Taunggyi. Franco Masiero said this was the way Philip and Claudia had travelled the previous week, and the desk clerk at the Irra Inn confirmed it. Masiero had been surprisingly co-operative. It hadn't been hard to get him to admit that he had lied to Tony about Philip's destination. Adrian hadn't bothered to ask him why. The way he had greeted Adrian when they met last night said it all. 'So you're Tony's new errand boy?' Plainly his working relationship with Tony had not been all it should. Having met Tony, Adrian could understand that.

What bothered Adrian was the sense that Franco had been holding something back. Either he had found out more about Philip than he should have, or else something had happened in Pagan that he wasn't telling Adrian about. Why else would that half-reticent, half-puzzled frown come over his face every time Philip's name was mentioned?

The whole thing was increasingly baffling. Why had Philip come to Burma? Why had he stolen a tapestry? Why had he gone to Taunggyi? And what was the nature of his relationship with the girl he had brought with him? If Masiero was to be believed, they were having some sort of sexual fling. 'Why did you tell Tony they'd gone to Mandalay?' Adrian had asked last night, and the Italian had given him a lecherous little smile and explained that it was what Miller had asked him to say. In Franco's opinion, Miller wanted to be alone with the divine Claudia, with none of Tony's spies running after them. It was understandable, no?

Adrian didn't know if it was understandable or not. He had been thinking on and off about what Jill had said before he left, and was reluctantly beginning to admit that there might be some truth in it. Obviously it was an exaggeration to say that Philip and Lucy were all wrong for each other, but it was true that there could have been areas of incompatibility. He had heard Philip complaining several times about Lucy's 'endless' dinner parties, and once he had run into Lucy spending the weekend alone with mutual friends because Philip had flatly refused to accompany her.

The bus drew up at a roadside halt and Adrian climbed stiffly out. Philip had had one or two affairs during the marriage, he knew that, but they had never seemed to last long, and Adrian was pretty sure they weren't important. Thinking about it now, he supposed it was conceivable that Philip and Lucy might have had sexual problems. He had a feeling his sister hadn't liked sex much. As for Philip ... Adrian realized that he had no idea whether sex was important in Philip's life or not. Jill was right: there were things about Philip that one simply had no inkling about.

He sat down at one of the tables outside the café and ordered a beer. Another five hours to Taunggyi. God, it was hot. But whatever the nature of his problems with Lucy, whatever the nature of his sexual needs now, the one thing Adrian could not understand was how Philip could possibly have found what he was looking for in that aggressive little black-clad trollop with the outsize chip on her shoulder. There were some things that just totally defied the imagination.

Masiero, he decided, was either stirring up trouble or trying to hide something. The whole thing was too implausible for words.

For a while, Claudia was totally speechless. He went on explaining it to her in that same cool, matter-of-fact voice. People would see him enter the house. Neighbours, passersby. You couldn't do anything in Burma without everyone knowing about it. In any case, some of Min Saw's family and workers were bound to be there. They would hear, perhaps even see, him fire the shot. As a foreigner he was hopelessly conspicuous. He had practically no chance of getting away afterwards. He had thought through the consequences and accepted them. He was sorry she had to be involved, but he needed her to get the tapestry to safety. It was the only way he could be sure of getting the galleries closed down. Naturally, he would take no action till Saturday, till he was sure she was out of the country. He had already made arrangements for the money he owed her to be paid into her bank account in Kingston.

Claudia found her voice again. 'You didn't tell me it was blood money. Thirty pieces of silver, is that what you've paid me?'

He looked slightly put out. 'Thirty pieces of silver? Is that really an appropriate analogy? After all, it's not betrayal we're talking about here.'

Isn't it? Well it's true that I'm not betraying anyone. But you are. I trusted you, Paul. Fuck you, I trusted you. I thought that between them Nick and my father had taught me all there was to know about betrayal. Well, I was wrong. There was worse to come. Because with them, I was never stupid enough to trust them in the first place. But I did trust you, and now look where it's got me.

Aloud she said, surprised and slightly impressed by her own cool tone, 'I think maybe it is. Is this really what Caroline would have wanted?'

From the dazed way he looked at her, she thought for a moment she had scored a hit, but she was wrong. 'No, I don't think she would,' he said thoughtfully. 'Caroline wasn't the revengeful type. It's for me that I'm doing this.'

'Why?'

'Because ultimately revenge is always for the person carrying it out. Not for the victim. That's just the pretext. Since Caroline died, I've had only one idea in my head, which is to get revenge on the people who caused her death.'

'But, Paul—'

'I know you probably think it's a little . . . primitive. I know it's not what rational people are supposed to want to do.'

Claudia gritted her teeth.

'You're quite wrong,' she said calmly. 'I think it's perfectly normal that you should want revenge. What I don't understand is the hara-kiri side of it. Why put your own head in a noose at the same time? There must be other ways of dealing with Min Saw.'

'It's impossible. He's too well-connected.'

Claudia made an impatient gesture. 'So they won't put him on trial here. What does that matter? It isn't as if he never left Burma. An accident could be arranged for him on one of his trips to the West. Mugged in Central Park, for instance. Something that doesn't implicate you.'

There was a long silence. Then Claudia said, 'I've got this wrong, haven't I? You want to be implicated, don't you?'

The glazed look she had noticed earlier was back at the edge of his eyes. Blood for blood. 'Yes,' said Paul. 'I want him to know where this is coming from.'

'High noon? Shootout at the OK Corral?'

'Don't trivialize it. That's unworthy of you.'

'It's unworthy of you to throw your life away for someone like Min Saw. He doesn't deserve it.'

'Not for Min Saw, for Caroline.'

'You just admitted she wouldn't have wanted this.'

'Shut up, Claudia! May I remind you that in the final analysis this is none of your business. You're being paid to do a job and that's it.'

'You didn't tell me the job involved burglary, murder and suicide!'

For a moment they sat glaring at each other. Paul sighed.

'Claudia, I know this isn't easy for you, but please try to understand. Since Caroline died, I haven't thought of anything but getting revenge on the people responsible for her death. Literally nothing else. Let's assume I manage to do all I set out to do: get the galleries closed down, get Min Saw disgraced, neutralized, whatever... What do I do then? I have no family left, I've drifted apart from most of my friends, my job doesn't interest me any more, I have no wife, no children, no home. I sold my flat and disposed of the proceeds. I spent the last of my savings on preparing for this trip, paying you, buying the air tickets out here. I really don't have a lot to go back to.'

'You're tired of the way you've been living, yes, I understand that. But you don't have to go back to being what you were before.'

'Claudia, it's too late to change. I told you that already. I don't have the courage, I don't have the energy, I don't have the ideas. I don't know where else to go.'

Claudia stared at him. Oh God, what was she supposed to say now? Why hadn't he told her all this in the privacy of their hotel room, where she might have stood a chance of saving him by physical means, ripping his clothes off, dragging him into bed and if necessary raping him, pulling him back to reality with her body. But he had timed his declaration well. A large Burmese family were busy installing themselves at the next table, with a lot of fuss and giggling, and two Western couples they hadn't seen before were stalking energetically across the courtyard in full safari rig. It was neither the time nor the place for a major sexual initiative, and she had no other weapon at her disposal. Or did she? Wait, of course she did.

She got abruptly to her feet. 'Let's go.'

Paul put a pile of kyat notes on the table and followed her. They went back down the steps without a word. The two rickshaw drivers were waiting at the bottom of the hill. The plan that had been hatching in Claudia's head began to take shape. They stopped to put their shoes back on.

'I'm sorry,' said Paul. 'I realize this must be a shock. I'm sorry I had to—'

'I want to go back to the hotel,' said Claudia. 'I need some time on my own.'

*

Once you knew what he had in mind, it all fell into place. The final piece of the jigsaw that made sense of all the rest. Why he hadn't wanted to sleep with her. Why he had carefully reminded her last night of the business nature of their relationship. Even the revelations about his past and his feelings of guilt over Caroline and his wife, which she had taken for signs of increasing intimacy – they all turned out to have an underlying purpose. Claudia realized she was crying. Impatiently, she rubbed the tears away. This was no time to worry about herself and her own hurt feelings. The call to Rangoon would be coming through soon. It was important to work out what she was going to say to Tony, bearing in mind that the hotel receptionist and any number of SLORC phone-tappers would be listening to every word.

She went to the bathroom and splashed cold water on her face. There was no light in either the bathroom or the bedroom. The electricity went off from nine in the morning until six at night. She rummaged round in the dimness until she found a paper and pencil. Then she sat down on the bed and began to make notes.

An hour later, the call had still not come through. Wait in your room, the reception clerk had said, we'll fetch you as soon as we have the number. There were no phones in the rooms: all calls had to be made from the lobby. Or maybe they had just forgotten it. She cast an anxious glance at her watch. Paul had gone to look round the handicraft shops – cover, he said, for their forthcoming visit to Min Saw's house tonight. She had no idea how long he was going to be.

The reception area was deserted, except for a solitary clerk reading the newspaper.

'Excuse me. I asked you for a call to Rangoon about an hour ago.'

'Yes, madam.' He gave her a bland smile. 'Unfortunately the lines are all busy.'

'Oh. So how long is it going to be?'

'I cannot say at all. There is not so many lines between Mandalay and Rangoon and there is much traffic. Sometimes it may take many hours. If you will care to wait in your room, I will tell you when the call come.'

He returned to his newspaper and switched off his smile. Shaking, Claudia turned away. Many hours. Oh God, what the hell was she going to do? Paul would be back in another two hours at most. How on earth was she going to contact Rangoon? If there were no telephones, there were no faxes. There were probably no telexes — not that she would be able to get at one if there were. Maybe she should jump on a plane and take the message herself. Wait, the plane, Greg, this afternoon — She stopped dead in the middle of the garden. Greg, that was it! She would get Greg to take a message. She looked at her watch again. Quarter past one. Austin had said the flight left at four. It wasn't too late.

Austin and Greg ran into the Buckleys in the lobby of the Mandalay Hotel. Greg was carrying a large backpack and Austin a smaller one.

'Well, hi there,' said Michael. 'Are you guys leaving already?'

'Just me,' said Greg. 'Mom's arriving in Rangoon tomorrow, so I'm going to meet her. Dad's staying on here for another couple of days.'

'Is that so?' said Michael.

'Oh my,' said Barbara, wide-eyed, 'does this mean you're going off—'

Austin made a shushing gesture.

'Oh, I'm sorry.'

'No point selling seats ahead of time,' said Austin.

'He got a hot tip,' said Greg.

'Yeah, well, nothing may come of it. Stay tuned, huh?'

'Come on, Dad, let's go. I don't want to miss the plane.'

'Have a good trip now,' said Barbara.

Michael and Barbara climbed the stairs to the first floor and turned on to the gallery that ran along the front of the hotel, overlooking the main entrance, the road outside, and the palace walls.

'Do you think he's really going off into the jungle?' said Barbara, as they turned on to the outside corridor leading to their room.

'God knows. Some people are crazy enough for anything.'

'Wish it was me leaving today. With an onward connection to Bangkok. You got the key?'

'Just another two days, honey. Tomorrow we see Min Saw, and after that we're out of here.'

'Wait a minute. Take a look down there. Isn't that Claudia with Greg and Austin down by the gate?'

'It certainly is. So they are here. I was beginning to think I was wrong.'

'They must have found another hotel.'

'Yeah,' said Michael thoughtfully. 'I wonder ... Look, honey, here's the key. You go and rest for a bit. I'm going to follow her, see where she goes.'

'Be careful now,' said Barbara anxiously. 'Don't do anything ... well ...'

'Don't worry. I won't do anything to upset Angus. I'll just find out where they're staying and come straight back.'

Greg gave Claudia's message to Marty Freedman as soon as he reached Rangoon.

Marty took one look at it and shook his head.

'Can't do anything with this. It's a book code. Look there. All in three-number sequences. The first number is the page, the second is the line, the third is the word. If you don't know what book she's using and you don't have exactly the same edition, it's unbreakable. Is it important?'

'Dad seemed to think it was.'

'Well, I'm sorry, but ...'

'What about the letters? There are some letters in there too.'

'Yeah, ' said Marty. 'Letters, but no words. RAJ, WA, DA. Can't do anything with that. Doesn't mean a thing.'

'I guess not.'

'You ever see her reading anything in particular?'

'I never saw her with a book at all. We were always travelling round looking at things, you know? Pagodas and stuff.'

'Too bad. Can't be helped. We'll have to let the Brits keep their little secrets to themselves. Did you figure out what they're up to in Mandalay?'

'No,' said Greg. 'I guess Dad was hoping this message would tell us that.'

Paul had been prepared for an afternoon of scenes, tears and pleadings, but when he got back to the hotel he found Claudia composed and distant. She sat on the verandah reading Albert Camus and made no further attempt to argue him out of his decision. Paul told himself that it was all to the good. They were going to pay a visit to Min Saw's workshop that night, and he needed her co-operation. He told her in detail what he wanted her to do. She listened intently, asked a few questions, and returned to her book.

They ate dinner in silence and arrived at Min Saw's house at eight o'clock. Lights shone out from the upper floor, but the workshop doors were closed and the whole of the ground floor was dark and silent. The workers had gone home, and only the family remained on the premises. Paul was confident he could persuade whoever opened the door to let them look at the tapestries. He had met Min Saw's wife on his last visit and judged her none too bright, while the children were too young to know about their father's business sidelines. The small backpack he had brought with him contained, among other things, a selection of suitable bribes: a bottle of perfume, a clock-radio, a watch.

The house had a European-style bell. Paul pressed it and waited. Footsteps sounded almost immediately from inside the house. The door opened. Paul felt the blood drain from his face. Min Saw himself was standing on the doorstep.

The revered national arsehole had gone snivelling to his highly placed friends about the loss of his tapestry, and the Foreign Minister had summoned the Ambassador to lodge an official complaint.

'Good God,' said Tony. 'What damned cheek.'

'Quite,' said the Ambassador icily. 'Do we have any idea what happened to the bloody thing?'

'Actually, it's rather a mystery, sir.'

The Ambassador sat down at his desk and drummed irritably with his fingers on the polished surface. Not at all his usual style. Tony wondered what the Foreign Minister had said to him.

'All right, maybe it's better you don't tell me. What I want to know is if there's any chance of getting it back?'

'I have the matter in hand,' said Tony prudently.

'Glad to hear it.' The fingers drummed harder. 'Right, Mansell, let's just get one thing straight. Our job here is to represent the British government to the best of our ability. To this end, we must avoid undue friction with our host country. I take it you agree with me on this?'

'Yes, of course, sir.'

'If we don't get this tapestry back, there could be serious repercussions. We've lost enough staff members already. I don't want them kicking anyone else out.'

'No, indeed.'

'Make this your top priority, Mansell. I want that tapestry back as soon as possible.'

It wasn't possible. He must be seeing things. How could Min Saw be here? He was supposed to be in Rangoon. Paul opened his mouth, but no sound came out.

Min Saw's face began to cloud over in puzzlement.

'U Min Saw,' said Claudia. 'How lovely to see you again. I do hope we're not disturbing you. It's not too late, is it? You do remember me, don't you? Claudia Miller. We met at Rebecca Elliott's house in Rangoon last week.'

Min Saw peered more closely. Claudia smiled at him. 'Yes, I remember you,' he pronounced finally. 'And this?'

'My husband. Didn't you meet him last week? Well, never mind, now you have.' She giggled cheerfully. 'Gosh, it's super to be here in your workshop at last. It was so nice of you to invite us to come and see where you work. May we come in for just one moment?'

Without waiting for an answer, she stepped past him over the threshold. The door led straight into the workshop, empty and silent at this time of night. The long row of frames, each with its half-worked square of black velvet, stretched back into the darkness. Along the far side of the big room, on sliding rails, hung a long row of completed tapestries. The shipment for New York.

'Oh, how wonderful.' Before Min Saw could stop her, Claudia was across the room looking at them. 'That's exactly what we came here to see.' She pulled at one and it slid away from the wall into the room.

'Please don't—' Min Saw took two steps across the room towards her, then remembered Paul still lingering on the threshold, glanced over his shoulder and took an uncertain step backwards.

'We've come to buy a tapestry, you see,' Claudia informed him. 'Do say you have a little, tiny one somewhere that we can have. Rebecca says you only work to commission, but I'm sure that's not true, is it?' She flashed him her most brilliant smile and turned back to the tapestry. 'Tell me, this must be Areindama?'

'The spear of Anawrahta,' agreed Min Saw. 'Yes, you are right.'

'It's wonderful.'

'Artistically, this is a most great challenge. No human figures, just spear and hand of Anawrahta in top right-hand corner.'

'You've succeeded brilliantly.' Claudia slid the tapestry back into place and pulled out the one behind it. Paul entered the workshop and closed the door behind him, deliberately making as much noise as he could. Min Saw, halfway across the room now, glanced back over his shoulder, but kept on going.

'Excuse me, madam—'

'What about this one? It's not a portrait of Anawrahta himself is it? Do you know, I always wondered what he looked like. Are there any existing portraits of him? Or descriptions? Or did you create the likeness from your own artistic spirit?'

She held his eyes, waiting for an answer. Paul waited, forgotten by the door. Instinct told him to stay where he was, to let her handle this. She listened with a serious little frown while Min Saw explained the creative processes which had enabled him to give birth to a true likeness of the first Burmese emperor, and then switched on her smile again and told him how wonderful he was.

'Unfortunately,' said Min Saw, 'I cannot show you these tapestries tonight here. They go all to New York, where I have big exhibition two months' time. And so I must ask you, madam, please not touch.'

'Oh I'm so sorry.' Claudia withdrew her hand as if stung. 'All of them? Oh how disappointing. They look simply gorgeous. And they're all going to New York? Now, you know, U Min Saw, that's really not fair. Why don't you send them to London instead? We'd just love to have them!'

She put her hand on his arm and laughed into his face. Min Saw, as far as Paul could tell in the dim light, was actually blushing.

'Well, I won't touch them any more if you don't want me

to,' declared Claudia, 'but you really must show them to me before they go. I'd never forgive myself if I left without having seen them.'

Min Saw hesitated, torn, Paul judged, between vanity and caution. He decided to give him a push in the right direction.

'Darling, maybe we should come back another day. We don't want to be a nuisance. I'm sure U Min Saw has better things to do than entertain us.'

'Am I being a nuisance?' Claudia picked up the cue immediately. 'Oh no, I am so sorry, I really didn't mean to bother you if you have other things to do.' She put her hand on his arm again. 'My husband's right, maybe we should come back another day.'

Min Saw gave an irritated little shrug. 'Please. It is no bother. It is always pleasure to show works to true connoisseur of my art. You too, sir,' he added grudgingly.

'It's really very kind of you.' Paul shuffled obediently across the room to join them. Claudia winked at him behind Min Saw's back. With a mixture of reluctance and conceit, the tapestry-maker went down the row of tapestries, pulling them out one by one, answering Claudia's questions, drinking in her admiration, but refusing steadfastly to sell her any of them, or even to send them to London. Paul stayed in the background, making vague appreciative noises and casting discreet glances round the workshop for signs of anything untoward. Min Saw had switched on the lights to show off the tapestries. The whole room was clearly lit, but there was nothing unusual to be seen: no packets of heroin lying on the table, no bottles of acetic anhydride standing in corners, no strange smells in the air. He turned his attention to the sliding rails where the tapestries were hung. By the look of it, the tapestries were simply attached to their rails by two clamps, one in each of the two top corners. It should be easy enough to detach them and substitute the tapestry he had brought with him. It wasn't padded, but one or two of these had no padding either. With luck Min Saw would not notice the substitution immediately: possibly he wouldn't even notice it at all. For all his claims about never doing the same design twice, a lot of the tapestries seemed to Paul to differ in minor details only. All he needed to effect the substitution was two minutes alone.

They neared the end of the row of tapestries, and Claudia, having found Min Saw intractable on the subject of selling them any of the finished tapestries in the workshop – 'For my personal clients, I insist always on personalized artistic concept that reflects their innermost strivings and reality' – began to discuss the logistics of buying a commissioned tapestry.

'Madam, there is nothing easier,' Min Saw assured her. 'I will be here in Mandalay until Saturday, and I will be happy to discuss it with you whenever it is your desire.'

Claudia caught Paul's eye. 'Until Saturday? Why, that's wonderful.'

'Yes,' said Min Saw, 'it is very fortunate indeed. You see, madam, it was not at all my intention to be in Mandalay at the present time. If my plans had not been unexpectedly thwarted, I would have today been in Rangoon.'

'Oh dear,' said Claudia, 'your plans have been thwarted, have they? I'm so sorry to hear that.'

'Only a very small problem, madam, I assure you. But perhaps you know about it already from your good friend Miss Elliott?'

'We haven't been in touch with Rebecca since we left Rangoon. The telephone, you know, it isn't easy. I hope it doesn't have something to do with the consignment you were sending to London?'

'As a matter of fact it does,' said Min Saw peevishly. 'The British Embassy has been most careless. One of the tapestries I left in their care has been lost. I suspect theft, madam, to tell you the truth.'

'Oh no, how dreadful. Do you have any idea who might have taken it? Surely no one in the Embassy—?'

'No, no, please rest assured that I do not question the honour of your fine diplomats. But certain Burmese persons are also employed in the Embassy, in a menial capacity, you understand.' He pursed his lips disapprovingly. 'Well, suffice it to say that I had to spend a great deal of time last week on this disagreeable matter. I question the efficiency of your Embassy's security methods, madam, I regret to say.'

'Oh my goodness,' said Claudia, 'I'm terribly sorry.'

'It was an extremely valuable tapestry. A priceless work of art. Well, here we are at the end of the row, madam. I am afraid I have nothing more to show you.'

He replaced the final tapestry with an audible sigh of relief.

'Thank you so much, U Min Saw. That was a really marvellous experience to see all those beautiful works. It's such a privilege to be able to see the place where an artist works, where he draws the sources of his inspiration. You really have a very nice house here. I don't think we've seen anything like it since we've been in Burma.'

'I have also a quite remarkable collection of Burmese antiques. I would be honoured for you to come upstairs and see my antiques and meet my wife.' He waved the way eagerly towards the stairs leading up to the first floor.

'That would be absolutely super.' Claudia started for the stairs, Paul lingered by the unfinished tapestries on their frames. 'I expect you have a lot of old lacquerware, don't you? We saw some nice pieces in Pagan, but unfortunately a lot of it was damaged. But I expect you know places to go where tourists don't have access.' She began to mount the stairs. Min Saw followed, and then realized Paul was still bent over the embroidery frame, ostensibly absorbed in an intricate pattern of beading.

'Please, sir, you must come too.'

'Go ahead, I'm just looking at this, I'll be right with you.'

'Excuse me, I wait for you.' Min Saw retraced his footsteps and positioned himself at the foot of the stairs. 'One moment please, madam. Your husband is not quite ready.' Claudia stopped halfway up the stairs. Cursing inwardly, Paul abandoned his study of the embroidery and moved across the room to join them. Clearly Min Saw was not going to allow him to stay down here on his own.

He was halfway across the room when there was a peremptory ring on the doorbell. Paul and Claudia exchanged glances. Who was this late visitor? Michael Buckley, come to pay a discreet call on his heroin supplier? Min Saw had tensed perceptibly. The bell rang out again. With seeming reluctance, he moved towards the door to open it.

The man on the threshold was tall for a Burmese and heavily built. He was in full military uniform. Paul realized that he was a general. He took two steps into the workshop, saw Paul and Claudia, and shot a question at Min Saw in Burmese. Min Saw's agitation redoubled. Paul couldn't understand the answer, but the tone was unmistakable. Apologetic verging on the obsequious. The general rapped out some kind of order. Claudia came back down the stairs. Paul moved instinctively towards her. Min Saw turned towards them.

'I so sorry, comrade general and I have meeting tonight, I forget, cannot make comrade general to wait, please excuse, come back other time, antiques other time, not now, not now.'

In his agitation, his English was deserting him. The general smiled derisively. Claudia took charge of the situation.

'Please don't apologise, U Min Saw. You've put yourself out more than enough for us tonight as it is. Again, thank you so much for showing us your exquisite tapestries. It was a true privilege. We'll come back some other time when you aren't so busy and discuss our commission.' She gave him a dazzling smile and then switched her attention to the general, who was regarding her with interest. 'Goodnight, comrade general. It was a pleasure to meet you.'

*

So where the fuck had Miller disappeared to? What had he done with the tapestry? Why hadn't Ferguson managed to find him? Why hadn't that damned girl got a message to him?

Tony marched irritably up and down the fine Shiraz carpet on the floor of his study. The Ambassador getting wind of this was a catastrophe. In a day or two he would start demanding results. At the very least, he would want to know the truth. And then, what the fuck was he going to tell him?

The bell rang. Tony looked at his watch. Ten past nine. Not a usual visiting hour in Rangoon. He opened the door and his eyebrows rose in astonishment. Standing on the doorstep was Marty Freedman of the DEA, accompanied by a scrawny teenager with a back to front baseball cap.

'Hi there,' said Marty. 'Sorry to trouble you at this hour. Greg here has a message for you, from a lady called Claudia Miller.'

Tony looked at him in disbelief. Good grief, that's all we need. A week's silence, and then what do we get? A message hand-delivered by the DEA, no less. Might as well rent air time on Rangoon bloody Radio, make sure the whole world knows what's going on. He got rid of the pair of them as soon as he could and locked the door of the study. When he unfolded the message, a long list of numbers and letters met his eyes. His irritation began to abate. At least she had had the sense to use the code he had taught her. So that was why Marty's offers of help had been so insistent. They had tried to decode it themselves and got nowhere. Smiling sourly to himself, Tony got out his copy of *Pride and Prejudice* and began to decipher the message:

'mind saw sends heroine in calico pictures to three RAJ gallery stop Darcy sister attended London gallery endured irremediable heroine excess stop Darcy considers mind saw responsible sister fate stop plans termination with irremediable prejudice stop send help inn WA inn man DA lay'

Obviously, it wasn't the ideal text to use to send this kind of message. In one or two places, she had been obliged to use letters to make up for the deficiencies of nineteenth-century vocabulary and the lack of Burmese names, but he doubted Marty would have been able to make sense of them. RAJ, WA, DA – no, there was nothing to be learned from that. Otherwise, take off a letter here and there, and it was clear enough. The calico pictures would be Min Saw's tapestries. Darcy was the code name they had agreed on for Miller. His sister must have worked in the Rajasthan Gallery, her fate was presumably a heroin overdose, and Miller's plan for Min Saw was assassination.

Tony's first reaction was anger. Miller must have gone right out of his mind to even contemplate something like this. Travel all the way to Burma to take out a heroin smuggler like some Sicilian hitman. The man needed a psychiatrist. If he managed to put his crazy little plan into practice, the Burmese were likely to expel half the Embassy and maybe even close it down altogether. Didn't the stupid bastard realize that his true identity was bound to come out? Didn't he know what kind of connections Min Saw had? It was unprofessional and irresponsible behaviour. When all this was over, Tony promised himself, he was going to write a full report on the affair. If they got Miller out of Burma alive, he would make damn sure the man never worked for the service again.

And another one he wouldn't fail to mention in the report was Adrian Ferguson. Unjustified use of official property, unjustified procurement of official documents . . . First he had colluded with Miller and then he had blown the whistle on him. If Miller had taken leave of his senses, Ferguson had never had any in the first place. Given his family connections with Miller, he must have known all about the sister, where she worked and how she died. If he had only passed on that information at the beginning of the week, Tony would have put two and two together a long time ago. If Ferguson had briefed him properly, they could have grabbed Paul Miller and had him safely back in Bangkok by now. God damn the pair of them. The only one who seemed to have half a brain was the babysitter. She had taken her time about it, but at least she had come through with the goods.

The phone rang. That would be Ferguson. He had called earlier in the day to say he was following the trail to Taunggyi. Tony picked up the receiver. That one had better get up to Mandalay to talk some sense into his good friend Miller before all hell broke loose.

At the Innwa Inn, all was calm. The reception clerk looked up and nodded as they passed. The garden was deserted. Lights shone out from the restaurant and from some of the bungalows. As soon as they opened their door, they heard the muffled thud of the ghetto blaster from the neighbouring room. Paul felt a headache coming on. In the darkness outside Min Saw's house, Claudia had flung her arms round his neck and they had embraced with a mixture of exhilaration and relief. But his euphoria had evaporated in the chilly night air on the ride back to the hotel. True, they had got in and out of the lion's den unscathed, but they were no further forward. He closed the door of the bungalow and turned the key in the lock.

'Right,' said Claudia. 'I'm pretty sure there's heroin in those tapestries.' She settled herself on the bed and folded her legs into the lotus position like a small, self-contained female Buddha. 'One, they were very heavy. Two, you saw how he reacted when I tried to touch them.'

Paul let himself drop on the other bed. He felt tired and discouraged and totally at a loss. 'I think you're right. But we're not going to be able to get near them. He's going to be there till Saturday. And on Saturday our visas expire, and we're supposed to be on the plane back to Bangkok.'

'Can we stay on illegally?'

He shook his head. 'We won't be able to stay in a hotel and we won't be able to use any regular means of transport. Where are we supposed to stay, and how are we supposed to get around?'

'You said Sai Thawda was involved with the dissident movement in 1988. Would he help us?'

'I think he'd probably be too frightened. In any case, it could get him into serious trouble. I wouldn't want to ask. The best thing would be to go back to Bangkok and renew our visas, but by then the tapestries won't be here any more, they'll have taken them down to Rangoon.'

'And they'll be going out through the American diplomatic pouch, right? Isn't there any chance of getting at them while they're still in the American Embassy?'

'Since his spot of trouble at the British Embassy, Min Saw will be paying extra attention to security measures. I doubt one would be able to get near them.'

'Doesn't Rebecca have a friend there?'

'Rebecca's friend works for the Country Office of the DEA in Rangoon.

'Then surely that's even better!'

'I don't know. Co-ordination between the DEA and the Embassy is sometimes pretty bad.'

He put his head in his hands. On Mandalay Hill this morning, it had all seemed so clear and straightforward and inevitable. But now it had all fallen apart, and he didn't know how to put it back together again. The finishing line had been moved, and he couldn't see where it had gone.

'What are you going to do now?' said Claudia.

He shrugged helplessly. His head was full of fog and he couldn't think. 'I haven't the faintest idea.'

There was a silence. Claudia watched him, clearly puzzled by his disarray. At last she said hesitantly, 'One solution might be for me to go back tomorrow night on my own – he seems to like me – and see if—'

Paul glared at her. 'You do that, yes! He'd enjoy that. That would really make his day.'

'That's not what I meant. In any case, you know perfectly well he wouldn't look at me. Not in that way. I'm not Burmese.'

'You can pass for it.'

'Outwardly, maybe I could.' She sounded as if she was humouring a fractious child. 'With my *longgyi* and some of that white stuff they put on their faces. But that's all. I don't have the right kind of soul – no that's not right, Buddhists don't have souls, do they? Anyway, you know what I mean.' Her composure broke. 'For God's sake, Paul, don't be so obtuse! You know it's you I want, not Min Saw!'

There was a sudden brisk tapping on the door. 'Telephone, madam.'

Claudia frowned. 'Telephone? For me?'

'Your call to Rangoon.'

She got up and went to the door. The receptionist was standing outside. 'Your call to Rangoon has come through, madam.'

'I'm sorry, there must be some mistake. I didn't ask for a call to Rangoon. Did you place a call to Rangoon, Paul?'

She turned to look at him. He shook his head. Her eyes were wide and guileless. The sluggishness fell away, his mind began to function normally again. He could tell she was lying.

She turned back to the receptionist. 'It's a mistake. It must be for someone else.'

'No, no, is for you.'

'Okay, fine. It's for me. Well, I don't want it any more. Please cancel it. All right? Thank you very much. Goodnight.'

She closed the door, rolled her eyes, and went back to sit on the bed again. 'God knows what all that was about. I hope I haven't cancelled someone else's long distance call.'

Paul watched her fold herself back into the lotus. She knew

no one in Rangoon except the people she had met at Rebecca's party. Franco was in Pagan, Min Saw was here in Mandalay. That left Rebecca herself, but it seemed unlikely that she would be phoning Rebecca. Or else it left Tony. Who had taken her aside and made a pass which had left her annoyed and upset. If it was really a pass he had made. Tony had other ways of annoying and upsetting people. What if Claudia had been given the same treatment as Franco? What if she too had been set up to spy on him? No, that didn't work. If Tony had sounded her out, she would have told him. Or perhaps Tony had no need to sound her out. Perhaps she was already in place. But if that was the case, there was only one person who could have put her there. And that meant that . . .

Claudia was back in her Buddha position, looking straight ahead, waiting for her cue.

'Tell me something,' said Paul slowly. 'What were you really doing in that bar in Paris when I met you?'

She jerked round to look at him as though she had been stung. Her eyes widened, and an expression of surprise and guilt crept over her face.

'I told you. I needed the fare back to England.'

'Ah. And how much did you earn from your client the previous night?'

'A thousand francs.'

'Very generous. You can get a one-way air ticket to London for a lot less than that. Why were you in that bar? Why weren't you back in London already?'

Silence.

'Claudia, I'm waiting for an answer.'

'I'm sorry, I can't tell you.'

'Tell me.' He knew he had the ability to frighten her: briefly her eyes met his and slid away again.

'I don't want to talk about it.'

'I don't care whether you want to or not. Tell me.'

'All right, I will.' She unfolded herself from her lotus

position and pulled her knees protectively up to her chin. He remembered her sitting in the same way on his bed in Paris, the night he had asked her to come to Burma with him.

'When I met you, Paul, I was at rock bottom. I had no money, nowhere to go, and no one to go to.' Her tone was level and matter-of-fact, and so was her gaze. 'It was the only way I could fight back.'

'What was?'

'What I was doing in that bar. You see, I'd always told myself I could do anything I wanted. I was on the outside, so I had no obligations to anyone, there were no rules I had to respect. I could do exactly what I wanted. What was more, I had to. It was a question of survival. No one was going to help me. If I was going to make it, I had to do it all on my own.'

She paused. Paul wanted to stop her, he had heard enough, but it was too late. She had turned her head so he couldn't see her face, but her voice was cool and self-possessed.

'I was trying to find out how much of all that was really true. I wanted to find out exactly where the outer limits were. How far I could go. How much I could force myself to do. For money, of course. Do you understand now?'

She turned back to look at him with the sweet, enigmatic smile of half the Buddhas in Burma. Paul was unable to speak. The ghetto blaster was abruptly switched off. Burmese bedtime. The silence deepened. His eye fell on the pile of books by her bed. She had given up on Jane Austen and started reading *L'Etranger* before they left for Min Saw's. The Outsider. Oh yes, there was a pattern to all those books. He'd been a fool not to notice it before.

'You're not going to go back to your mother in Kingston, are you? Ever?' She didn't answer. 'What are you going to do instead?'

'What do you care?' said Claudia. 'You're going to be sitting in some Burmese prison waiting to be hanged, or whatever they do to people here. You'll have enough on your mind without worrying about me.'

Her eyes met his across the gap between the beds. People go to hell in their own sweet way, there's nothing you can do to stop them. The gap between them might have been ten miles wide instead of just a few inches. He wanted to reach out and touch her, but she was too far away and there was no way he could get to her. She had kissed him spontaneously in Min Saw's garden, but no doubt she regarded that as part of her business commitments. As he himself had incautiously pointed out, not once but twice in the past twenty-four hours, she was getting paid for it. She swung her feet on to the floor and stood up.

'I think I'll take a shower before I go to bed if those sods next door haven't pinched all the hot water.'

She picked up her towel. Paul searched desperately for something to say to keep her with him. Once she got behind that bathroom door and turned on the water they would have nothing left to say to each other. She tied her hair on top of her head. He opened his mouth, maybe with some vague idea of explaining that the receptionist's mistake with the telephone had given him a sudden notion she might be spying on him, though he knew perfectly well that such an admission was unlikely to improve matters, but he was interrupted by the sound of footsteps on the gravel outside. Someone trod confidently across the verandah and knocked on the door.

'Well, hell,' said Austin. 'I sure choose my time to come visiting you guys. Or do you live like this all the time?'

He stood in the doorway, his bulky frame taking up most of the space, self-confidence unshaken, amused rather than abashed by the fact that he had arrived in time to witness the end of a major confrontation.

'How ya doin', beautiful?' he asked Claudia, who had opened the door to him. She was standing next to him, hand still on the doorknob, barefoot, towel in hand, looking far from pleased to see him. 'No, on second thoughts, don't answer that.' He came into the room and closed the door, then put his arm round her and gave her a brief hug. 'Come on, cheer up, it can't be as bad as that.'

'I'll leave you two alone to talk.' Claudia dropped the towel on a chair and looked around for her shoes. 'Let me know when you've finished. I'll be in the garden.'

'You stay right here,' said Austin soothingly. 'This concerns you too.'

She glanced uncertainly at Paul. 'I'd like you to stay,' he said.

Scowling silently, she sat down on top of the towel, arms folded. Austin produced a small transistor radio and switched it on. He took the other chair. Paul stayed on the bed.

'How did you know where we were?' said Paul.

'Followed you,' said Austin succinctly.

'From where?'

'Ah well, that's what you'll have to tell me. I know where the house is and I know that the homeowner has a pretty eclectic collection of visitors. You guys. Mr and Mrs Buckley. The deputy commander of the Mandalay Military Division. But I don't know why people are queueing up to get in there. Not yet. You want to tell me about it?'

'Why should I?'

'Because we have interests in common,' said Austin. 'And if you'd only come out and admit it, we might be able to help each other out. I'm interested in the Rajasthan Galleries. You're interested in whoever lives in that house. So are the Rajasthan Galleries. So come on, tell me. What's the connection?'

'Do you have local back-up here?'

Austin thought about it. 'A couple of guys, yeah,' he admitted. 'One of 'em followed the Buckleys from the airport. That's how we found the house.'

'If you have local people, you must know who lives there.'

'Okay, so maybe I do. A tapestry maker. Min Saw. Exhibits regularly in New York, Paris and London. Exclusive contract with the Rajasthan Galleries.'

'He's the source of the heroin coming out through the Rajasthan Galleries.'

'Figured he might be. But I don't see how they do it.'

'It's hidden in the tapestries.'

Austin frowned. 'How?'

'Look.' Paul reached for his backpack and pulled out the tapestry. 'This is one of Min Saw's tapestries. See these figures here? Often they're padded in this type of tapestry. This one isn't, unfortunately, or I'd be home and dry already.'

Austin's eyes widened in understanding. 'They pad 'em with heroin. Then they take it out when it gets to New York and put rags or something in instead. Neat, very neat. But what about customs? Sniffer dogs, all that stuff?'

'They go through the diplomatic pouch. Min Saw has high level connections.'

'Beautiful,' said Austin admiringly. 'What a great little set-up. Must have made them millions.' He picked up the tapestry, turned it over and examined the backing. It was made of plain black cotton, sewn loosely round the edge. 'Easy enough to take this off and put it back again without anyone noticing. So where did you get this from, if I may ask?'

'The British Embassy. It was part of a consignment due to be shipped to London. I hoped I might find the heroin right there, but there was nothing in any of them.'

'Why did you take this one?'

'Because I need a tapestry with heroin in it as proof of what's going on. I was hoping to steal one from his workshop. But after that, I have to get it as far as Rangoon, to the Embassy, and then out of the country before the alarm is raised. Travel facilities being what they are in this country, all that takes the best part of two days. I figured that if I was able to substitute a tapestry for the one I took, there was a better chance of the theft going undiscovered for a few days at least.'

'Makes sense.'

'Unfortunately, I didn't reckon with Min Saw making a final check on the tapestries before they were crated and shipped to London. My informant told me he'd counted them already, but apparently he decided to do a recount. He found there was one missing, and stayed in Rangoon most of last week trying to find out what had happened. The result is that he's here in Mandalay now, at a time when I thought he was going to be safely out of the way. I don't mind admitting that it puts me in something of a dilemma.'

'What's your interest in all of this?'

Paul met his gaze. 'Much the same as yours, I imagine. You're interested in the Buckleys, right?'

'Right,' said Austin. His gaze slid carefully from Paul to Claudia and back again. 'Not just them, mind you. Their bodyguards too.'

'You mean Keith and Angus?'

Austin raised his eyebrows. 'How did you know about them?'

Paul hesitated.

'That night in the boat, Barbara gave herself away,' said Claudia, opening her mouth for the first time. 'She said Angus had done life-saving classes. How would she know that unless they were more than casual acquaintances?'

'Oh you noticed that, did you? In fact he's her younger brother.'

'But he's Australian.'

'Oh no he's not. He's Canadian like she is. He stabbed someone in a brawl when he was seventeen and he's wanted in Canada for manslaughter. He fled to Australia several years ago and he's been living there ever since. Until last October when he suddenly showed up in San Francisco.'

'Wow,' said Claudia. Her eyes met Paul's. So she had been

right about Narathu's dexterity with the knife. 'What about Brahms, then? I suppose that was just cover.'

'Actually that happens to be true. Angus really is a musicologist, and his friend Keith really does have a doctorate in political science. We're moving in pretty cultivated circles here.'

'Is Keith Canadian too?'

'No, Keith's Australian. His parents own a gallery in Melbourne. We figure he and Angus are fixing to set up a branch of the Rajasthan Gallery in San Francisco. Meanwhile, the situation here is that Michael and Barbara have been travelling round South-East Asia for nearly four weeks, and Keith and Angus have been following them. At a distance. We figure their job is to make sure the Buckleys aren't under surveillance.'

'Are they here in Mandalay? Keith and Angus, I mean?'

'Guess so, but no one's spotted them yet. Probably they'll all show up at Min Saw's sooner or later. But that's not going to do us any good. The Rajasthan Galleries exhibit Min Saw's work, and there ain't no law against buying a tapestry. I reckon you had the best idea, Paul. What we need is a tapestry with heroin in it. Now how are we going to get us one?'

Paul shook his head wearily. 'Your guess is as good as mine.'

'My guess,' said Austin briskly, 'is that my "go-fer" might be induced to undertake a spot of burglary.'

Min Saw did not sleep well. The conversation with the General had been disquieting. Fortunately, his good friends Mr and Mrs Buckley from New York City came by early the following morning, and that took his mind off things. As always, he was a little overwhelmed by the American and his wife. They were so tall, so sleek, so imposing, with their nice Western clothes and their blond hair and their white teeth. Even here in Burma, where Western people soon fell into Burmese ways – not quite dirty, but not quite clean either, just a little dusty and rumpled, because after all this was a primitive, backward country by their standards – even here, Michael and Barbara were so smooth and clean and smart, just as they had been in New York City when they took him on the boat to see the Statue of Liberty.

'Good to see you again,' said Mr Buckley, shaking his hand, and smiling a big, friendly white smile.

'How was your trip back from Rangoon?' asked his wife, smiling too.

And then they introduced the two young men they had brought with them, who were called Keith and Angus, Mrs Buckley's brother and his friend, who were not so clean and nice as Michael and Barbara, but after all they were young, they would learn. Min Saw apologized for his unfortunate absence on Tuesday, and ushered all the Western visitors into his study on the first floor, where he kept his designs, his accounts and some of his finest antiques. The visitors sat down, glancing around with evident admiration, and his eldest daughter brought Chinese tea.

'Nice place you have here,' said Mr Buckley. 'Curtis told me about it, but his description didn't do it justice.'

Min Saw smiled proudly and explained to them how many workers he had, how many servants, how many rooms. How many of his own and his wife's elderly relatives he was able to house. How much he had paid for his reconditioned Japanese car and his seventeenth-century bronze statue. Americans liked to know things like that.

'Must cost a bomb to keep all this running,' said Mr Buckley casually.

Min Saw bowed his head in acknowledgement. 'Naturally, were it not for our agreements, things would be more difficult. I am sorry, incidentally, that our friends in London have been obliged to interrupt our arrangements.'

'Yeah, well Roland's been under a lot of pressure. He's had the police nosing round the gallery ever since his receptionist snuffed it. Not a good situation to be in. And now we're beginning to have the same problem in New York too.'

Min Saw put down his cup in alarm. Some of the liquid sloshed on to the lacquer table. 'You too in New York, sir? Oh no, that is most distressing. Does this mean that you too are planning to interrupt our deliveries?'

'No, we don't want to do that,' said Mr Buckley. 'Can't afford it, can we, Barbara? What we want to do is cool the New York end of operations for a while. Keep the heroin coming, just route it some place else.'

'But how, where—?'

'This is where Keith and Angus come in. We're planning to open a new gallery in San Francisco. You know where that is, do you? Good. It'll be nothing to do with the Rajasthan Gallery, it'll have a completely different name, and the merchandise will be different too. Less Indian, more South-East Asian. We're going to call it the Monsoon Gallery. Angus and Keith here are going to be running the place.'

'But me, how can I—?'

'This won't affect you adversely in the slightest. In fact, it'll be better for you, because it'll give you an extra outlet in the States. You'll be able to sell more tapestries this way. Regular tapestries to us in New York, and special consignments to the address I'm going to give you in San Francisco. Everything through the pouch, same as in the past. Sound okay to you?'

'Yes, I think so.' All this was going a little too fast. 'I do not think there would be any problem, but . . .'

'Good,' said Mr Buckley briskly. 'Now can we assume your supplies are going to be able to keep up with the new arrangement? Last time we met you mentioned you were having some problems. That's all sorted out now?'

'Oh yes, of course,' said Min Saw. The tone was confident but, remembering his conversation with the General last night, he was unable to suppress a shudder. The American saw it, and exchanged a glance with his wife. 'That is to say, things are getting a little difficult with my friend the General. However, another possible source has come to my attention, and if the General and I are unable to reach an agreement, then I will switch immediately to this other alternative.'

'This is another officer who has contacts with the insurgents?' said Mr Buckley, and Min Saw nodded assent, even though he did not actually know of any such officer and had so far made no attempt to find one. It would be easy enough to do when the time came. How the General would react to being cut out of such a profitable arrangement was another matter. He would have to tread very carefully indeed, but there was no point telling any of this to the Americans. As long as they got their consignments on time, they weren't interested in his problems. With the Americans, their own interests always came first. He sniffed in self-pity and offered them more tea.

'Right,' said Michael. 'Now we're going to have to leave shortly because Keith and Angus have a train to catch, but before we go there's something else we need to deal with.'

'Something else?' said Min Saw apprehensively. He was beginning to feel as if he had been run over by one of the tanks that sometimes carried out manoeuvers in the grounds of Mandalay Fort. Why were Americans always in such a hurry?

'The London receptionist we mentioned just now. Caroline Hamilton. We wanted to warn you that her brother's in Mandalay. He knows what happened to his sister, and we believe he intends to pay you a visit.'

'Hamilton?' said Min Saw. 'No, I have seen no one of that name. Last night, however, I received the visit of a Mr Miller and his wife.'

The Kaunghmudaw Pagoda lay six miles outside the town of Sagaing, on the far side of the hills beyond the river. The pagoda was round and white. According to legend, its shape was a copy of the perfect breasts of someone's favourite wife. Vast, quiet white courtyards led one into the other and finally out into the fields at the back. Paul and Claudia had the place to themselves. There was no one around but two men grooming a cow in the field behind the pagoda, and a young monk showing round an older couple who might have been his parents.

They found a bench under a tree in one of the courtyards and sat toying with the rudimentary picnic lunch they had bought in Sagaing. Neither of them was hungry. Afterwards, Claudia wandered off to explore a covered gallery at the far end of the courtyard. Paul leant his head on the trunk of the tree and closed his eyes. For the time being, Austin had taken over. It had been his idea that they should take a trip outside Mandalay, to avoid the risk of being spotted by Michael or Angus, while he contacted his 'go-fer' and set up the burglary. There was nothing to do but wait. The sun moved slowly across the sky and the air grew heavier. What was the use of it all? Even if Austin's burglar succeeded in breaking into the workshop and removing a tapestry, what good would it do? Even if the Rajasthan Galleries were closed down and their owners imprisoned, even if Min Saw were dead, what was the point? Caroline was dead, and it wouldn't bring her back. Nothing could bring her back, not justice, not revenge, not even self-sacrifice. So why bother? How much easier it would be to simply let go, stay here for ever in this quiet, white-walled courtyard, shave his head, pick up a begging bowl . . .

He opened his eyes and looked around. The courtyard was empty. The young monk and his parents had gone. There was no sign of Claudia. She had been calm and remote all day. To all intents and purposes, she was waiting quietly for the moment when he would give her the stolen *kalaga*, put her on the train to Rangoon, and walk out of the station with Sai Thawda on his way back to Min Saw's house. She was no longer a lover, not even a companion, simply a messenger. Their relationship had attained at last the business footing to which he had originally aspired. Everything comes to him who waits. Even his long-sought vengeance seemed at last to be within reach. The mission that he had thought would give his life a meaning was close to completion. Then why was he so tired? Why had he stopped caring? He closed his eyes again and let the silence overwhelm him. To sleep, forget it all, wipe it all out. To drop easefully, unresistingly into the muffling, white cotton-wool sea of oblivion . . .

Later, he realized that he must have dozed off for a few minutes. He was woken by the sound of voices. Two monks, deep in discussion, were heading towards the shrine at the heart of the pagoda. Paul shook his head to clear it of sleep, took a swig of mineral water, and looked at his watch. Three o'clock. He stood up and went in search of Claudia.

She was sitting on the ground behind the pagoda, with her face turned up towards the sun. Her eyes were closed, and there were tears on her lashes. She hadn't heard him approaching. He stood looking down at her. Her hair was pulled back in a scruffy knot and there was a smudge on her cheek. He hadn't thought he was capable of wanting anyone so much and so badly. He hadn't thought he had it in him any more. After years of paralysis, the blood had begun to roll in his veins again, the sap was rising in his dried-out body, revitalizing all the nerves and ligaments and muscles and bones.

She opened her eyes and looked up at him with a wide, startled stare. A flicker of anguish swept across her face and was gone. She snapped into business mode, wiped the back of her hand briskly across her face and made as if to stand up.

'I'm sorry, were you looking for me? Is it time to go?'

'No.' Paul dropped to his knees beside her and pushed a strand of hair back off her face. 'We have plenty of time. All the time in the world.' He drew her against him. She leant her head against his shoulder with a long, shuddering sigh. The men and their cow had disappeared. There was no one else in sight. What was it she had said last night? *You know it's you I want*. It had been there all the time, if he had only been listening.

He pulled her head gently back and began to kiss her. He had lost his indifference, he realized, that was the trouble. He just didn't want to die any more.

This time, Angus had no reservations. Miller was dangerous: they had to get rid of him. He and Michael worked out the plan between them. It was a pity Angus with his greater experience would not be around to help carry it out, but Michael was confident he could manage it on his own. They sat Min Saw down at the table and made him write a note for the Millers. A servant was summoned and told where to take it. It was lucky Michael had spotted Claudia the previous day and found out where they were staying.

When that was done, they took Min Saw down to the workshop to check the layout and discuss the preparations. All they needed was a syringe and an adequate quantity of heroin, plus something to stun the victims beforehand. They wouldn't be expecting to find Michael there: it would be easy for him to position himself behind a door and hit them over the head as they came in. First Paul, then Claudia. And then send them off the same way as the sister – what could be more fitting? Heroin addiction was on the increase in all Burmese cities. As far as Min Saw knew, it had been confined to Burmese, not tourists, so far, but any day now the word would get around and the junkies would start pouring into Mandalay for a cheap fix. Sure, the police might notice that the two European overdose victims been knocked out beforehand, but what were they going to do about it? No one would link the dead couple with Min Saw, the internationally renowned artist, and if they did, they wouldn't dare bring an accusation against him.

By midday, preparations were complete. Keith and Angus left to pack their bags and catch their train. Michael and

Barbara went to visit a pagoda Barbara had read about in the guidebook. Before leaving, Michael reminded Min Saw to make sure his family and servants were all out of the way by seven o'clock. They didn't want unnecessary witnesses hanging around. He and Barbara would return at half past seven to make sure everything was ready for the guests' arrival at eight. This time, nothing could be allowed to go wrong.

Paul was back with her again. In both mind and body. Claudia still didn't know what had happened in the pagoda, but somehow he had escaped from his strange, monachal vision of atonement and repentance. They sat waiting for the Mandalay bus to leave, shoulder to shoulder, thigh to thigh. It was very hot. Outside a boy was shouting on a high, flat monotone – Mandala, Mandala, Mandala – and there was a large red-and-white message from SLORC to the people of Sagaing which read: DON'T LET THE UNION DISINTEGRATE BECAUSE OF YOU. The dust blew through the open windows and the inside of the bus grew stuffier as more and more people piled in.

Claudia was barely aware of them. Part of her was still in the field behind the pagoda. She had never realized it was possible to feel like that. The expression 'to make love' had never been part of her vocabulary. 'Fuck,' 'screw' or, in more constrained circumstances, the euphemistic 'sleep with' had served her linguistic needs perfectly well up till now. But this afternoon, Paul hadn't fucked her, he had made love to her. For the first time in her life, she understood that the words could have a literal meaning. For the first time in her life, she felt as though she was no longer an outcast.

There were two messages waiting when they got back to the hotel. The first was from Austin to say he had been delayed and would drop by around nine. The second was a note from

U Min Saw inviting them to come to his house at eight for a drink.

'A drink?' said Claudia blankly. 'What does that mean? Cocktails with the Burmese Army?'

'No, we're invited to look over his antiques collection. With apologies for the interruption last night. Oh, and to buy a tapestry. He's decided he's willing to sell us one of those we saw last night.'

Claudia stopped dead in the middle of the path. 'It's a trap.'

Paul studied the paper detachedly. 'It could be, I suppose.'

'Michael tried to kill you once already.'

'Why would Michael have anything to do with this?'

'They must have been to see him by now.'

They reached their verandah and sat down. The sun was setting. In another half hour, it would be dark. After the hot, dusty drive through Mandalay, it was pleasantly cool out here.

'Michael doesn't know we have any connection with Min Saw,' said Paul.

'He knows about Caroline and the gallery.'

'Yes, but that's all. He doesn't know I'm on to Min Saw as well.'

'Perhaps, but I still don't like it.' What the hell was Tony doing? She had asked him for help, why hadn't he sent someone to help her? How was she supposed to deal with this all on her own?

'We can't afford to turn down the invitation. Austin's burglary plan might not work.'

'I suppose so.'

'You don't have to come if you don't want to.'

'Maybe I won't then.' Go and get yourself killed if you want, but why the hell should I? She stared blindly out over the garden. So much for the interlude behind the pagoda. Rest and recreation, that was all, and she had just been the nearest available comfort girl.

'Claudia.' He reached over and touched her cheek. 'Don't

be angry. You know I'd rather stay here with you.'

'Would you?'

'Yes.'

The sound of the radio blared out from the other side of the building. Rod Stewart and Pepsi Cola: the traditional evening ritual.

'Paul, why can't we—'

'What?'

Why can't we just run away? Get on the train, go back to Rangoon, go anywhere, just get away from this doomed city. She stared at him hopelessly. Of course it wasn't possible. Paul wasn't going to run away. Not with her, not with anyone. He had chosen his course a long time ago, and there was nothing she could say to make him change his mind.

'Let's go inside,' she said.

There had been a delay of some kind in Heho airport, and it was already dark when Adrian's plane touched down in Mandalay. He sat on in his seat, too exhausted to move, as the other travellers disembarked. The plane was travelling on to Pagan and Rangoon. He was sorely tempted to do the same. He had been chasing round Burma for nearly a week, trying to save Philip from himself. First Mandalay, then Pagan, then Taunggyi, and now back to Mandalay again. The flight attendant looked at him sternly and he rose reluctantly to his feet.

Part of it was the fault of that Italian idiot in Pagan, who had twice sent him off on a wild goose chase, but if only the girl had got a message to Tony a bit faster it would have saved a lot of time and energy. He trudged across the tarmac to the airport building. So far, he had failed to find any sign of Philip anywhere. He hoped this time he would be luckier. Not that he had any idea what he was going to say to Philip when he did find him. What did one say to a person who for over two years had been quietly plotting to kill someone? Yes, Jill was absolutely right: there were things about Philip that were simply beyond one's understanding.

He joined the end of the queue at the Immigration desk and waited irritably for the official to write down his name, passport number and all the other details he had already supplied on embarking at Heho. Did the fools think one might have changed identity during the flight? Of course, part of it was Tony's fault too. If he had only bothered to mention the name of the gallery the tapestries were routed to in London, Adrian would immediately have made the connection with Caroline, worked out that Philip would at some point make contact with Min Saw (though not necessarily to kill him, for God's sake), and stayed on in Mandalay to wait for him.

The Immigration official waved him out of the airport and Adrian plodded wearily off to find a taxi. What was the name of this hotel? The Innwa Inn. He hoped to God they would have a room there for him too. He was tired out, he had a long interview with Philip ahead of him, and he had no desire to go looking for a place to stay when they had finally finished talking.

They left late for Min Saw's house. By the time they had made love, dozed, been woken by the Bee Gees in Burmese coming through the wall, taken a shower in the cold water left by the golden youths, and dressed, it was already eight o'clock. Paul didn't care. He had no particular desire to spend an evening with Min Saw. Under the shower, it occurred to him that he didn't much care whether he managed to get hold of a tapestry either. All he could think of right now was Claudia. Maybe he could phone Min Saw to say they couldn't come. No, he couldn't do that, he couldn't just walk away from it all. Not yet. He came out of the bathroom and stopped dead at the sight of Claudia.

'What are you wearing that for?'

She smoothed down her *longgyi*. 'Don't you think it's a good idea?'

'No I don't.'

'I do.' She gave her hair a final pat in the mirror. 'I'm hoping he'll be so smitten with lust when he sees me like this that he won't be able to aim his revolver.'

'Oh for God's sake.'

'Seriously, Paul. It's going to throw him off balance, and one never knows how that might come in useful. I've got a bad feeling about tonight. I don't think we ought to go.'

'The way you've done your hair too.' He ran a finger wonderingly down her face. 'You really could pass for Burmese.'

'Well it's certainly having an effect on you.' She reached up and kissed him. 'Why don't we forget the whole thing and just go back to bed?'

Gently Paul disengaged himself. 'Later.' He scribbled a note for Austin to leave at the reception desk. 'Come on, it's time to go.'

Min Saw's house was a twenty-minute ride away. The rickshaws pedalled one behind the other through the empty streets, Claudia ahead, and Paul behind. It was very dark and very quiet. There were no street lights. Occasionally a shaft of light from a house or tea room fell across the dirt road. Here and there, open fires burned. The atmosphere was heavy with smoke and dust, blurring light and muffling sound. Sometimes another bicycle loomed up out of the shadows in the opposite direction; once or twice a car went past. For most of the journey, there was no sound but the whirr of the bicycles, and intermittent strains of voices from the houses fronting directly on to the street.

Paul was beginning to regret not having phoned to cancel. Why spend an evening listening to that self-obsessed idiot mouthing complacent platitudes when all he wanted was to be in bed with Claudia. God knows, he had wasted enough time already. He watched the back of her head a few yards ahead, barely visible in the dimness. From time to time Sai Pan sneaked an incredulous sideways look at her and her Burmese disguise. When she came out of the hotel, neither of the rickshaw drivers had recognized her. They had to talk, he had to tell her he had changed his mind, they had to decide what to do next.

They rounded a corner and Sai Thawda let out a muffled exclamation. The rickshaw halted abruptly. Ahead, looming up out of the fog, was an inchoate mass of lights, noise, activity. Cars blocking the street, people swarming all over the place. Paul knew without being told that it was coming from Min Saw's house.

There was a traffic jam, of all things, in the middle of Mandalay. The taxi was held up for a good five minutes while a squadron of police cars went past, and then it seemed there were roads cordoned off, and the taxi had to make a detour. Adrian wondered vaguely what was happening, but he was too tired to bother questioning the taxi driver. He was saving his energy for the confrontation with Philip.

He reached the Innwa Inn at half-past eight. Not bad timing, all things considered. The Burmese ate early and retired early. There wasn't much in the way of night life in Mandalay: Philip and Claudia were probably back in their hotel room already.

The clerk at the reception desk looked up as he approached.

'I'm looking for Mr Miller I believe he's staying here.'

'Yes, sir. He stay here.'

At last! Adrian's tiredness began to fall from him. After all this time, he had finally tracked them down. His euphoria was shortlived.

'Which is his room?' he asked and the clerk shook his head sadly.

'He not here. He go out just small time ago. He go in rickshaw. Just small time before you come.'

Paul went on foot to investigate with Sai Thawda, leaving Claudia with Sai Pan. As they approached the house, Paul was more and more perplexed. What on earth could have happened? Had Austin's burglar got caught? It seemed unlikely. There wouldn't be five police cars, God knows how many unmarked cars, and a huge spotlight glaring down on the house and half the grounds, for a mere burglary attempt. The crowd thickened and Paul realized that he was getting some curious looks. Sai Thawda touched his arm.

'Is better you wait here, sir. I go see.'

The Shan slipped away into the crowd and Paul moved back into the darkness. What could have happened? It was impossible to make out what was going on from back here. A lot of shouting, someone wailing hysterically, people rushing round, but no clue as to the reason for all this agitation. He checked his watch. Twenty-five-past eight. It would have taken a while to summon the police cars and set up the spotlight. He and Claudia would have been arriving here at eight o'clock, just about the time it would all have been starting up. He had an uneasy feeling that the timing was not a coincidence.

After what seemed like a long time, Sai Thawda appeared at his side, tugged at his sleeve and gestured in the direction of the rickshaws. They walked swiftly back the way they had come. Claudia and Sai Pan were waiting where they had left them. Sai Pan appeared nervous and fidgety, but Claudia was sitting calmly in the rickshaw, her arms wrapped round her Shan shoulder bag. A police car started up and came slowly down the road towards them. Sai Thawda cast a nervous glance over his shoulder and pushed Paul unceremoniously backwards into the shadow of a tree.

'Do not move at all, sir!'

Sai Pan asked a question in Shan, and Sai Thawda answered. Sai Pan exclaimed incredulously, his voice rising in panic, and cast a fearful glance in Paul's direction. Sai Thawda said something reassuring. Sai Pan subsided. The police car drove past. The Burmese lady and the two rickshaw drivers turned their heads to watch it go. Sai Thawda mounted his bicycle and signalled to Paul to get into the rickshaw.

'Come quickly. Is very dangerous here.'

'What's happening?'

'I explain soon. Not speak English here. Very dangerous.'

They went back the way they had come, away from Min Saw's compound, and plunged almost immediately into a maze of side streets and alleys, some of which were barely wide enough to pass through. Each time they had to cross a main road, Sai Thawda waited for several minutes to ensure that no one was in sight before riding rapidly across the road and plunging into another little alley opposite. Away from the main streets, it was darker than ever, and there was a rank stench of old cooking smells. Puddles of stagnant water splashed up as the rickshaws crashed through. They rode past broken fences, dark courtyards, empty verandahs. There was no one to be seen. The whole of Mandalay had gone to ground. For the first time since he had arrived in Burma, Paul was afraid.

At last they rode up a potholed alley into an unlit courtyard. Sai Thawda parked the rickshaw against the wall, and Sai Pan drew up behind him. Sai Thawda knocked softly on the door at the head of the alley, and Sai Pan danced around nervously, waiting for the door to open. Claudia stood immobile beside the rickshaw, still clutching her shoulder bag. No one spoke. The door opened a crack and there was a low, muttered conversation. Finally, the door opened wider, Sai Thawda stood back with an air of relief, and Sai Pan gestured urgently to Paul and Claudia to go inside.

The house was fairly comfortable by Burmese standards,

with cane-backed teak armchairs, a low table covered with the remains of a meal, and a television in one corner. A woman and two children aged about ten and twelve disappeared through an inner door and closed it behind them. A Burmese pop singer continued to sing in bright, wooden 1950s style on the television screen. They had interrupted a quiet family evening.

'This is Sai Lek,' said Sai Thawda. Another Shan, but broader and burlier than the two skinny rickshaw drivers. He shook their hands solemnly.

'I am please to meet you. I have van.'

Paul stared at him, unsure of the significance of this remark.

'He drive tomorrow to Chiang Mai. He take you there,' said Sai Pan eagerly.

'Chiang Mai? But that's in Thailand! What—'

'You must go very very fast,' said Sai Pan. 'Fast is best.'

'But why—?'

'You see, he is dead,' cut in Sai Thawda.

'Who's dead?'

'Min Saw,' said Claudia. 'Obviously. But what does that have to do with us?'

'Min Saw wife she say foreigner come to house. He tall, yellow hairs. She say yellow hairs foreigner kill husband.'

The eyes of everyone in the room were drawn to Paul. Tall and blond, and invited for cocktails at eight o'clock sharp. As he had guessed, it was a trap. If they had arrived at Min Saw's house on time, they would have walked right into it.

Part Seven

Golden Triangle

It was clear enough what had happened. Sai Thawda had talked to Min Saw's next door neighbour, who had been sitting on her porch about seven o'clock, and had seen the murderer arrive. Since the man was a frequent visitor to the house, she thought nothing of it. She knew why he came and assumed it was a routine call. She had been mildly surprised when he left after less than five minutes, but it was none of her business, was it? She hadn't heard the shot – or if she had, she wasn't admitting it. Nor was she going to mention the visitor's name, though it was unlikely that anyone in an official position would ask her for it. No one was going to suggest that a high-ranking army general might be implicated in a murder case, and no one was going to provide an alibi for the person he had set up to take the rap for him: not the desk clerk who had seen Paul arrive at the Innwa Inn at six and leave again at eight, nor the rickshaw drivers who had picked him up at the hotel at eight and driven him to Min Saw's house. Paul knew that without asking.

The only hope was to make a run for it. Sai Lek was an antiques smuggler. He was leaving early in the morning for Thailand, and he was willing to take passengers concealed in the back of his van. He did the run regularly, he said. Mandalay, Meiktila, Taunggyi, Chiang Mai. Paul grimaced. Right through the middle of the Golden Triangle. The van could be intercepted by the Tatmadaw or Shan insurgents, held up by bandits, requisitioned by opium smugglers. The Tatmadaw, he knew, would shoot on sight. He wasn't sure about the others.

'Won't you be searched at the checkpoints along the way?' he asked, and Sai Lek laughed indulgently. Judging by the nonchalant way he offered his services, he was clearly used to having fugitives aboard. He knew all the soldiers at all the checkpoints along the road, he explained, and they knew him. He made regular payoffs to everyone concerned. Why should they search his truck? Of course, he added hastily, that didn't mean there was no risk involved, and Paul nodded. Sai Lek would want to negotiate his terms.

'We are going to go with him, aren't we?' said Claudia apprehensively. 'You don't want to stay here and ...' Her voice trailed off.

'Oh yes, we'll go with him,' said Paul. Setting up his own trap was one thing: falling into someone else's was another matter. Since learning that Min Saw was dead, his head had cleared. He was thinking faster and more lucidly than he had done for weeks. Their passports had been left behind at the hotel, but that didn't matter. On this route, no one would want to see them before they got to Thailand, and they could get new ones from the British Consulate there. The only safe conduct they would need for the next few days was money, and that he had with him. Dollars in the money belt he wore under his clothes, kyats in the back pocket of his trousers. What was more, the gadgets he had taken to Min Saw's house last night were still in the bottom of his backpack. His watch was gold, as was his wedding ring. If they ran into trouble along the way, they should be able to bribe their way out of it.

Sai Lek settled for $1000 and the bottle of perfume. The journey to Thailand, he explained, would take at least three days. More if the van broke down. During the day they would be locked in the back of the van, forbidden to talk or make any kind of noise that would betray their presence. At night, Sai Lek would park somewhere safe and they would be able to get out.

'What do you think?' Paul asked Claudia.

'What choice do we have?'

'I have none. But you do. It's me they're looking for, not you. If you go back to the hotel—'

'Oh no, sir, hotel is dangerous,' interrupted Sai Thawda.

'Is better she go too,' said Sai Pan.

'Don't be ridiculous, I'm not staying here,' said Claudia.

Sai Lek's van was already loaded for the journey. In the wavering beam of his torch, it looked like Ali Baba's cave: a treasure trove of lacquer chests, Victorian mahogany furniture, carved wooden statues, and God knows what else. He settled them among the loot with blankets, bottles of water and containers of food. They were on opposite sides of the van, unable to see or touch each other. The doors slammed, the engine started. Paul's spirits rose. Claudia was there in the darkness a few feet away. He was free and alive and on his way to Thailand.

Within ten minutes of reaching the scene of the crime, the police officer charged with investigating Min Saw's murder knew exactly what had happened, and why. But his gloom began to lift when the widow of the deceased remembered that a tall, blond foreigner had been twice that week to see her husband, and his depression vanished completely when she decided that one of those visits had coincided with the time of her husband's death. Min Saw had been found lying on the floor of his office at quarter to eight. Death had occurred less than one hour previously. Maybe the foreigner had been three times, said Suu May thoughtfully, and the officer nodded understandingly. They could iron out the details later, once the foreigner had been arrested. Arresting a foreigner was not a good career move, but it was better than trying to apprehend the true criminal and finding himself supervising mine-clearing operations on the frontier of Kachin State.

He told his assistant to take five or six men with him and check the main hotels where the foreigners usually stayed. The Mandalay, the Mya Mandala. The man had to be tall and blond. It shouldn't be too difficult to find someone who corresponded to that description. By Burmese standards, nearly all foreigners were tall and blond.

Neither Michael nor Barbara slept much that night. With Min Saw dead, their network had fallen apart. Min Saw's artistic talent combined with his impeccable government connections had made him the perfect source of supply. Where were they going to find such a combination again? Barbara stared bitterly up at the ceiling. There was no point opening the gallery in San Francisco now, and they might even have to close the gallery in New York. The profits from the sale of South-East Asian art alone were barely enough to offset the costs of renting on the Upper East Side. The first thing that was going to suffer was their lifestyle, that was for sure. The extension she had been planning to the house in Greenwich would have to wait, and she was going to have to forget about the new Mercedes she'd had her eye on. They might even have to sell some pictures. Who would have thought that jerk Paul Miller would ignore the invitation for eight and barge in there like Rambo a whole hour earlier?

'Goddammed motherfucker,' said Michael occasionally in the dark. 'If we see him in town tomorrow, I'll hand him over to the nearest policeman.'

Barbara didn't answer. He knew as well as she did that it was the last thing he could afford to do. Their best plan was to lie low tomorrow morning, take the train to Rangoon tomorrow afternoon, and get the first plane they could back to Bangkok. Not that there was anything to link them with Min Saw's death: as soon as they saw the body on the floor, they had gone right back through the open front door, and returned to the hotel. They had seen no one, and no one had seen them. No one but Min Saw had known they were coming. Still, in a place like this, one couldn't be too careful. Barbara hoped Michael wasn't going to insist on travelling to India as they had originally planned, to give credence to their story that they were just Canadian tourists on holiday. She was sick of Asia, just sick of it. She wanted to go home.

Towards dawn, they were finally beginning to doze off when they were awakened by the sudden muted tramp of feet in the corridor. Several men, by the sound of it, quiet but businesslike. The footsteps stopped right outside their door. The was a couple of seconds of total silence. Then someone knocked on the door, in the same quiet, businesslike fashion.

Barbara jerked bolt upright, her hand going to her mouth to stifle a scream. Michael sat up too, but more slowly.

'Who's there?' he asked.

The voice that came back through the door was calm and authoritative and spoke surprisingly good English.

'Open the door please, Mr Buckley. This is the police.'

Adrian was awoken by a gentle tapping on the door of the bungalow. He sat up and looked around. Light was beginning to filter through the flimsy cotton curtains. It must be nearly dawn. The room was empty. Philip was still not back. He must have fallen asleep waiting for him. The door handle began to turn. It hadn't occurred to him to lock the door. Was this the hotel clerk, come to throw him out? But the man silhouetted against the grey morning light was too tall for a Burmese. Too large as well. The man took a step forward and turned on the light. He had a scruffy beard and a creased safari jacket, and he was carrying a package under one arm. He scowled at Adrian suspiciously.

'What are you doing here? Where are the Millers?' The accent was American, and the face was vaguely familiar. 'Wait a minute. I remember you. Bangkok, wasn't it? A year or two back. What's your name again?'

'Ferguson. Adrian Ferguson. And you're——?'

'Austin Maclaren,' said the man, extending his hand. 'Good to see you again, Adrian. They're not here, I take it?'

'No. They haven't been back all night, actually.' The American had a piece of paper in one hand. 'You don't have any idea where they might have gone?'

'Well, yes and no. I can tell you where they went at eight o'clock last night, but where they are now is anybody's guess.'

He passed the paper over. Adrian read it. 'Thursday, 20.00. Our friend invited us over for a drink. Back by eleven. Paul Miller.'

'Found this at reception. Guy's flat out, so I was just tiptoeing past when I happened to notice it on the desk.'

'This is Min Saw they're talking about? But surely they're not still there?'

Maclaren dropped his package on the other bed and sat down next to it, ignoring the dishevelled state of the sheets. Adrian had been chagrined to discover that, of the two beds in the room, one was neat and unslept in, while the other was rumpled and messy and bore clear signs of recent love-making. Unbelievable though it seemed, Masiero's assertions were apparently correct.

'I doubt it, Adrian. You see, Min Saw's dead.'

'Dead? Oh God, no!'

'He a friend of yours?' Maclaren looked at him oddly.

'Min Saw? No, of course not, I didn't even know him, but Paul ... Then they've arrested him, I suppose, and that's why——'

'So far they haven't arrested anyone. They're out trawling

the hotels right now to see what they can catch.'

Adrian stared at him blankly.

'See, the real criminal is above the law, unfortunately,' said Maclaren, and told him what had happened. 'Only thing no one seems to know is whether the General was demanding too big a share of the profits from Min Saw, or whether Min Saw was getting greedy and withholding commission from the General,' he concluded. 'But I guess that's academic at this stage.'

Adrian was barely listening. He was conscious of an immense feeling of relief. 'Then it wasn't Paul who killed him?'

Austin's eyes opened wide. 'Why would Paul kill him?'

'Oh well, no reason at all. Sorry, I'm not quite awake yet. I just dozed off, you see, waiting for them to come back.'

'Sure,' said the American amiably. 'Well anyway, Paul didn't kill him. But he must have thought he'd be suspected of it. My guess is, he's gone to ground.'

The van rolled steadily southward. After a few hours, the dawn came up and faint rays of light began to seep through the cracks in the floorboards. The sun rose, and the interior of the van began to warm up. Claudia stopped shivering and rolled her blanket into a back rest. For a while, she was marginally more comfortable. The morning wore on, the sun beat down on the metal sides of the van, and the temperature got steadily higher. Fortunately there was enough air coming through the cracks in the floor to ward off asphyxiation. Her body ached from the jolting of the van over the pot-holed roads, and her legs were cramped from being drawn up under her chin. There was a wooden elephant's trunk poking into her ribs, and the knob of a Victorian chest of drawers sticking into her spine. Compared to this, the bus they had taken on their first visit to Shan State was the height of luxury.

The van shuddered to a halt. Sai Lek turned off the engine

and shouted out a greeting. Another checkpoint. They had been through three or four by now, and she had stopped worrying about them. The first one, on the outskirts of Mandalay, had been the worst. There was the danger that the police might have set up road blocks to prevent anyone from leaving the city. But everything had passed off normally. No orders were rapped out, no questions barked. Somebody laughed, the voices rose in a crescendo, the engine was turned back on, and the van moved forward.

At the other checkpoints, the procedure had been much the same. As Sai Lek had said, they knew him and they let him through without difficulty. This time was no exception. He was already climbing back in the cab, ready to leave. So far, there was no sign of a nationwide manhunt. The authorities must still be searching for Min Saw's murderer in Mandalay. She wondered what Paul was feeling now? What was going through his head now that Min Saw was dead and somebody else had killed him? What was he going to do next? How was he going to get his vengeance, now that his plans had been short-circuited?

One thing was sure: as soon as they got to Bangkok, she was going to leave him. She couldn't take any more of this. Whatever Paul felt for her, and she was willing to believe that yesterday in the pagoda he had felt something, he was too bound up with his vow of revenge and sacrifice for anything to come of it. What they had was sex – good sex, admittedly – but that was all. It would wear off, it always did, and then what would be left? The mad monk with his obsessive lust for vengeance, and the nymphomaniac playing crazy games in sleazy bars. Not a great base on which to build. She didn't know where the death of Min Saw had left Paul, and she didn't want to have to deal with whatever peculiar form his reaction was going to take. Life was too short. She had other things to do. She had just emerged from one disastrous affair; the last thing she needed was to get embroiled in another. Last night had opened her eyes. They had reached the point where they had nothing to say to each other and the only thing to do was go to bed. Exactly the same pattern she had fallen into with Nick.

The van slowed again, Sai Lek called out of the window, and then braked and cut the engine. This had happened several times already: presumably he was exchanging news and greetings with his mates along the road. What was more, one of these days Paul was going to find out what she had really been doing in that damn bar. He was no fool, he had come close to the truth once already, and sooner or later she was bound to give herself away. No, better to leave now while they both had some part of their illusions intact. Better to turn her back on him, let him go, remember only the good times, the little white room in Yaunghwe, the field behind the pagoda in Sagaing . . .

The knob was sticking painfully into her back. She was about to try and change position when she realized that the van was still immobile. If she moved, she was going to make a noise. What the hell was going on now? She was pretty sure this wasn't another checkpoint, it was too quiet for that, and the conversation, now that she paid attention, didn't sound like the usual idle exchange of gossip with roadside cronies. Claudia listened harder. Sai Lek was carrying on a long discussion in a low monotone with someone by the side of the road. She detected a clear note of urgency. Oh God, had something gone wrong? Were they going to search the van?

But Sai Lek got back into the cab and the engine started up again. The van moved off. Thank God, it must be all right. No, it wasn't. Instead of regaining speed, they were slowing, turning a corner. They had left the main road and entered a town. She could hear street noises, cries, car engines. There was another sharp left turn. The engine was cut. Sai Lek got down from the cab. The door slammed. She could hear his footsteps receding.

After that, there was silence. The noise of the traffic had been left behind, and she could hear birds twittering. Sweat poured down Claudia's face, the knob ground into her spine, she had acute cramp in her left leg. She didn't dare to move. The silence went on and on. Surprisingly, the van didn't heat up as much as it usually did when they stopped moving. They must be parked under a tree. They weren't at a military checkpoint, then, nor at the police station. Could this be the house of some bribe-taking official? Had Sai Lek run into trouble? Was he about to double-cross them?

It was half an hour before she heard the sound of footsteps returning. Not just one set. At least two people. The doors at the back of the van were flung open. The light poured in. The air smelt of dust and chilli peppers. A cultured English voice said, 'I'm afraid we have to ask you to come out now. The road is dangerous. Sai Lek can't take you any further.'

They had wrapped up the murder investigation by noon. Min Saw's widow had no hesitation in identifying Michael Buckley, a Canadian passport holder, as the tall, blond foreigner who had come to the house three days earlier asking for her husband. He had even given her his name: there was no possible doubt about the identification. Three of Min Saw's workers remembered seeing him on the same occasion, and one of them had seen him again the previous morning. Min Saw's neighbour had seen him on both occasions, and had also seen him the night before about seven thirty. The investigating officer filled in the forms charging the prisoner and authorizing his transfer to Mandalay Fort. The four other 'tall blond foreigners' who had been picked up during the hotel raid were put back in police vans and returned to their hotels, with apologies for the inconvenience caused. One of them was Thomas Huber, who was able to give a brief account of events to his wife and Barbara Buckley, who were waiting anxiously together in the lobby of the hotel, before

Barbara was ushered into the police van too and driven away.

After interrogating Barbara Buckley, also a Canadian citizen, the investigating officer decided against charging her with complicity. Foreigners were a lot of trouble, but their wives caused even more problems. And the trouble-causing potential of this one seemed extremely vast. A search of her luggage had failed to reveal the tapestry that had vanished from Min Saw's workshop during the night, so there was no reason to accuse her of theft. The officer concluded that the best thing to do was to send her to Rangoon under armed escort. There she would be delivered into the custody of her Embassy, pending her expulsion from the Union of Myanmar at the earliest possible date.

They had driven right into the middle of a full-scale military alert. The Wa tribe, who were supposed to have signed a ceasefire with Rangoon, had attacked a Tatmadaw position near Taunggyi. The army was on full alert, there were extra checkpoints on all the roads leading in and out of Taunggyi, and it was highly probable that Sai Lek would be stopped and searched.

He had turned for help to his relative in Kalaw, a town forty kilometres before Taunggyi. Khun Nawng was a stocky Shan of about Paul's age. He wore a well-pressed *longgyi* and a black satin bomber jacket, and he held a degree in philosophy from Cambridge. 'Good grief, what next?' muttered Claudia. Sai Lek assured them that Khun Nawng was a good man, and drove apologetically away to take his chances with the Tatmadaw. Khun Nawng led them across the yard into his house. Paul squeezed Claudia's arm reassuringly and she gave him a brief, apprehensive smile. He could see she had been crying, but whether from fear or some other emotion it was impossible to tell.

Khun Nawng's house could have belonged to a colonial governor one hundred years earlier. Sombre wall-hangings, heavy dark furniture, Persian carpets. A servant was sent scurrying off to fetch tea, and their host began to describe his credentials as a philosopher. He had been at King's College in the early seventies, and he had studied Sartre, Spinoza, Heidegger, Hegel ... Something began to stir in Paul's memory. He stopped worrying about alternative routes to Chiang Mai and leaned forward intently.

'You know, it's odd ... I think I remember you.'

Khun Nawng opened his eyes wide. 'You are a Cambridge man too?'

'Yes. I was at Trinity from 1969 to 1972, reading history.'

'Is that so? I had many good friends at Trinity College. What is your name please?'

Paul barely hesitated. 'Philip Hamilton,' he said.

Barbara Buckley was allowed to spend five minutes with her husband before he was removed to Mandalay Fort. The meeting took place in a small, bare room with two armed guards on either side of the door.

'Go straight back to New York,' said Michael. 'Change your ticket, don't bother going through Vancouver. Get Curtis onto it right away. He has the name of a lawyer who handles cases like this. Talk to Angus as well, he might have some ideas. I don't want to spend any more time here than I have to. It's a clear miscarriage of justice. All we have to do is prove it.'

'Oh God, Michael, I just hate to leave you here like this. This awful place. It's so filthy here, I just hate to think what the prison's going to be like.'

'Don't worry about me. I can handle it. The other thing you have to do is find Paul Miller. He's the key to it all. He must have killed Min Saw and taken this tapestry they're making such a fuss about. He has to be made to swear an affidavit explaining what happened. And, obviously, he has to produce the tapestry as evidence of what he's saying.'

'I'll find him,' said Barbara.

'You may need private detectives to track him down.'

'Don't worry, I'll look after it. I'll make him swear the affidavit and hand over the tapestry. And after that, I'll get even with him.' Barbara smiled for the first time that morning.

Amazing who you ran into in the backwoods of Burma. Warlords with degrees in philosophy and spies without their cloaks on. Claudia sat back in her chair and let the flood of reminiscence wash over her. They hadn't actually known each other, but they had known a lot of the same people. Whatsisname who wrote a book about Spinoza, whosit who runs an advertising agency. Do you remember the professor of ancient history at whatsit college, did you really know old so-and-so? Do you remember thingummy whose girlfriend turned up for the May Ball in a short evening dress? Did you ever go to the pub round the corner from wheresit after meetings of the something society? Khun Nawng had asked her politely if she had been at Cambridge too, and when she said no, immediately lost interest. Claudia didn't mind. Khun Nawng, she decided, as he and Paul discovered yet another old acquaintance in common, would do whatever he could to help them out of their predicament. If the house was anything to go on, his capabilities were probably quite vast. The Cambridge mafia to the rescue.

Ten minutes later, when the reminiscences were dying down and they were both staring misty-eyed into the past, Khun Nawng said abruptly, 'Sai Lek tells me you need to go to Thailand. Tonight I will drive you to Kengtung.'

'Why, that's very good of you,' said Paul, as calmly as if he was being offered a lift home from the pub.

'No need to thank me. I have business to do there anyway.'

'What about the military controls?'

Khun Nawng waved his hand dismissively. 'They know me. Everyone knows me. The Tatmadaw, the MTA, the Wa

. . . I travel this road all the time, at least three or four times a month. They know me, they know my car. If I have a passenger, no one will ask any questions. My presence is guarantee enough.'

Paul looked sideways at Claudia. 'Fine.'

'Nevertheless, we will take some precautions. You will dye your hair black and wear Burmese clothes. It won't deceive anyone who comes too close to you, but from a distance it will serve its purpose. You will sit beside me in the passenger seat. You will wear a blanket round your head and blow your nose a lot. If anyone asks, I will tell them you have a cold.'

'Fine,' said Paul again. 'What about my wife?'

Khun Nawng scratched his nose reflectively. 'To take a woman on a trip like this . . . I'm sorry but I don't think it can be done. People would think it strange.'

'So what am I going to do?' said Claudia, alarmed, but he had it all worked out. Since she could pass for Burmese, there was nothing to prevent her from travelling openly to Rangoon on the train. There was a bus leaving in an hour for Thazi, where she could pick up the night train from Mandalay. His wife would escort her down to Thazi, buy her ticket, and put her on the train.

'The journey overland is too dangerous for a woman,' he explained to Paul. 'Especially after Kengtung. I have a relative there who will accompany you to Thailand, but once you are out of my protection, the safety of Mrs Hamilton cannot be guaranteed.'

Mrs Hamilton? She caught Paul's eye, noticing that he was looking mildly taken aback at the unexpected form of address. A Mrs Hamilton was of course a different proposition to a Mrs Miller, and sat a lot less easily on the tongue and in the mind.

'Yes,' said Paul, 'I understand. I suppose you're right.'

'You will see each other again in Thailand,' said Khun Nawng nonchalantly. 'Mrs Hamilton will wait for you in Bangkok.'

Claudia smiled demurely. Taking this for assent, Khun Nawng bore her off to prepare for her journey. His wife looked her over, re-did her hair, made her replace her English lady's tropical T-shirt with a traditional Burmese blouse, smeared her cheeks with a white paste called *thanaka*, which the Burmese used to keep the sun off their faces, gave her an ancient plastic holdall filled with rags to pass as her luggage, and sent her back to say goodbye to Mr Hamilton. She found him sitting at Khun Nawng's mahogany dining table counting his money into little piles. Three piles of dollars, three piles of kyats. Some for him, some for her, and some for Khun Nawng, who had not made his offer of safe-conduct through the jungle merely for old times' sake. Paul pushed a large pile of kyats and a small pile of dollars towards her.

'This should be enough to pay your train fare. When you get to Rangoon, go straight to Rebecca's, get her to arrange a new passport, and leave the country as soon as possible. Here's where to go when you get to Bangkok.' He scribbled something on a piece of paper and held it out to her. 'Learn the address off by heart and destroy it. This is a friend of mine. He's a journalist, not a diplomat. Call him when you get to the airport. He'll look after you.'

Claudia looked at the paper without taking it. 'Thanks, but I won't need this. I'm not planning to stay in Bangkok.'

He looked up at her, surprised. 'What do you mean? Where are we going to meet up again?'

Claudia remained standing, keeping the table between them. 'Is it really necessary for us to meet up again?'

There was a short silence. Paul folded his arms and gave her one of his best and chilliest monk's stares.

'It's not *necessary*, no. Not if you feel that way.'

'You hired me to do a job, Paul. For two weeks. And now the two weeks are up and it's time to go our separate ways. Wasn't that the deal?'

'That was the deal.'

'As regards our personal relationship, I realize that things developed in a way that wasn't entirely planned and, well, it was fun while it lasted, but I don't really think that as a long-term—'

Their eyes met and she broke off.

'You know that's not true,' said Paul quietly.

'I think it is. You've been very nice to me, considering the circumstances in which we met, and I appreciate that, but—'

'Look I told you I was sorry for what I said the other night. I didn't mean—'

'I know, it's all right, I understand why you said it. I don't hold it against you.'

'Then why—?'

'But I think it's better if we don't see each other again.'

Paul heaved a sigh of exasperation. 'What are you going to do when you get to Bangkok?'

'My mother has relatives in Hong Kong.'

'Your aunt, right. Is that where you plan to go?'

'Maybe, yes. I don't know. Why not?'

He looked at her closely and sighed again. 'Whatever you decide to do, you'll need money.'

'I know. Don't worry, I'm not going to pick up where I left off in Paris.' She smiled perfunctorily. 'I'll get the bank to transfer the money you gave me.'

'You'll have to wait for them to do that. It might take a day or two.'

'Well yes, but—'

'Then wait for me too.'

'Why? Why do you want me to wait for you? So we can fly to New York and take out Michael Buckley?'

'No. I've given up on revenge. I don't want it any more.'

'Just like that?'

'In the pagoda the other day, I think I knew already that I wasn't going to kill him.'

Claudia didn't know what to say. He was pulling the rug

slowly from under her, destroying all her arguments, one by one. She stared obstinately down at the table.

'If you don't want revenge, what do you want? What are you going to do with the rest of your life?'

He smiled at her then, the same tender, caressing smile that she had first seen in Rebecca's house in Rangoon. This time, she had an uneasy feeling that he wasn't play-acting. 'I want you. I don't want you to disappear from my life when we get out of here. I can't work for the service any more after this, so I don't know where we're going to be, or what we're going to be doing. I just know I want you to be there.'

'Paul, it wouldn't work. We got off on the wrong foot together. There's no going back on that. You can't just wipe it out. For God's sake, your name isn't even Paul.'

'Actually, it is. I was christened Philip Paul. You can go on calling me Paul if you want to.'

'But if no one else does—'

'That's just the point. No one else does. Only you.'

There was a knock on the door and Khun Nawng appeared in the doorway. 'Are you ready to leave?'

'She's just coming,' said Paul. 'Look, Claudia, we need to talk—'

'There's nothing to say!'

'Yes there is.' He got up and went round the table towards her. 'Please. Wait for me in Bangkok. Let's at least talk about it. Then if you still feel you don't want to see me again, we'll call it a day and go our separate ways. Will you do that?'

'I don't think—'

'I'm sorry,' said Khun Nawng, 'but we really ought to go.'

'Surely I have time to kiss her?' Paul demanded, and Khun Nawng shrugged gracefully. Claudia wanted to resist, but with Khun Nawng looking on, she couldn't very well push him away. So he took her in his arms and kissed her, the same way he had kissed her in the field behind the pagoda in Sagaing, and she felt the last of her resolve melting. She looked at him uncertainly.

'Paul, there's something else. Something you don't know about me. I ought to tell you that first.'

'Mrs Hamilton, if you wish to catch the bus, you must leave immediately!'

'You'll have to tell me in Bangkok. Will you go to Geoff's and wait for me?'

'All right.' She took the paper with the address and tucked it in the waist of her longgyi. 'If you want me to.'

'Yes I do want you to.'

She couldn't resist. 'And will I be Mrs Hamilton or Mrs Miller?'

'It might have to be Mrs Hamilton, I'm afraid. If you want it to be legal.' He leant forward and kissed her cheek one last time. 'I love you.'

'Paul—?' He had spoken the words so softly she wasn't sure she had heard correctly.

He smiled at her. 'Don't forget your shoulder bag.'

With an effort Claudia pulled herself together and smiled back.

'I don't need it, darling. That's for you. Just so you don't forget me between here and Bangkok.'

Adrian spent the morning with Maclaren and his go-fer trying to track down Philip and Claudia. They found no trace of either of them. They were in none of the hotels in Mandalay, and in none of the police stations. Given the state of their bedroom, they were probably not in a monastery either. It looked as though Maclaren's theory was right, and Philip had left overland with the tapestry that had gone missing from Min Saw's workshop. Adrian decided to go back to Rangoon on the afternoon train. Maclaren had given him the tapestry Philip had taken from the British Embassy: there was nothing more he could do. Maclaren declined to accompany him, saying he would hang on a bit longer in Mandalay in case anything came to light.

Mandalay station was in chaos. The departure of the Rangoon train was clearly the big event of the day. The platform where the train was standing was sealed off in a kind of cage, accessible to passengers only. A soldier with a rifle slung over his shoulder guarded the entrance to the cage. Adrian showed his ticket and found his seat. The crowd flung itself against the cage with the desperation of the inhabitants of a besieged city watching the last train depart. Adrian stared at them with a growing sense of unreality. He found it hard to understand why he had come here, and what he had been trying to do.

The car was filling up. The train was due to leave in ten minutes' time. Suddenly, Adrian's attention was caught by a Western woman being marched down the platform with a policeman on each side of her. Even by the inelegant standards of Western tourists, the woman was in a dishevelled state. Her T-shirt was grubby and wrinkled, her hair uncombed and her face smudged with dirt. Adrian wondered idly if she had run out of money. Odd, when you saw the kind of luggage she had with her.

A young Western couple standing on the platform looked up as she went by. The woman gasped in amazement, and the man took a step forward. 'Barbara,' he began, 'what are they doing—' He broke off as one of the policemen shoved him roughly to the side. Adrian went on watching. This must be the wife of the man they had arrested for Min Saw's murder. The prisoner and her guards climbed into the next car but one. The two young Westerners followed, talking animatedly in a language that sounded like German. Five minutes later, the train pulled out.

As soon as the front door slammed behind Khun Nawng and Claudia, Paul turned his attention to the shoulder bag. It was heavier than he expected. He put his hand inside, and drew out a piece of dark cloth. He guessed immediately what it was. His heart began to thump. He glanced instinctively at the door. It was closed, but anyone could come in at any minute. Seeing a key in the lock, he crossed the room and turned it. Then he went back to the table and took the tapestry out of the bag. As he unfolded it, the sunlight gleamed and shimmered on the beads and spangles and gold-threaded embroidery. Areindama. The spear of Anawrahta. In the daylight, it was even more impressive than it had been in the dim light of Min Saw's workshop.

But how on earth had she got hold of it? The night they had visited Min Saw, she had had no opportunity to take anything. Unless it was when the General arrived and distracted his attention? No. She had been standing on the stairs, well away from the tapestries. The next day they had spent in Sagaing. That left the previous night, when Min Saw had been killed. He had left her alone with Sai Pan for over half an hour while he and Sai Thawda went to see what was happening. He remembered the way she had been sitting in the rickshaw when they got back, her arms wrapped firmly round the shoulder bag, an odd little smile on her face, and Sai Pan dancing up and down with nerves. Somehow she must have got into the workshop and taken it.

No, she couldn't have. It was impossible. All those people, lights, policemen all over the place. Someone would have seen her and stopped her.

Or would they? According to Sai Thawda, the house had been in chaos. Policemen rushing round giving contradictory orders, Min Saw's wife having hysterics, servants wailing and moaning, onlookers clustering round the body. Min Saw had been killed in his study, which was on the first floor of the house. With all the excitement taking place elsewhere, maybe the workshop had been empty. Maybe no one had noticed an ordinary Burmese girl slipping inside the workshop and unhooking a tapestry in the dark. But, good God, what an amazing risk to take.

Using his pocket knife, he unpicked the stitches that held the backing of the tapestry in place. On the inside, the back of the spear was covered with another piece of cloth. Patiently, taking care not to tear anything, he unpicked that too. And then, hallejulah, there they were at last. The little plastic sachets he had been looking for for so long. The spear was full of them, so was the moon on the left-hand side of the tapestry, and so was the sun on the right-hand side. At a rough guess, the tapestry contained around five hundred grams of heroin. $250,000 worth at current New York street prices. No wonder Michael Buckley had been prepared to kill for it.

Khun Nawng's wife had decided that Claudia would be safer travelling to Rangoon in Upper Class, the preserve of foreigners and the better-off Burmese. In the cosy, cramped proximity of Third Class, people were more likely to try and engage her in conversation, whereas in Upper Class they would leave her alone.

Big mistake. The first person Claudia saw when she boarded the train was Thomas Huber. He and Christa were down at the far end of the car, fiddling around with mineral water and sweatshirts, and casting attentive glances in Claudia's direction. She shrank back in alarm. Surely they couldn't have recognized her? She had hardly recognized herself when she looked in the mirror before leaving Khun Nawng's house. A policeman appeared in the doorway beside her, and she flinched back into her seat. Jesus, this was it. They had come to arrest her. The policeman yelled something at the top of his voice. A second policeman rose from his seat halfway down the car and came to join him. The two of them conferred in low voices. Claudia relaxed. Nothing to do with her. She glanced cautiously back at Thomas and saw to her horror that he was sidling determinedly down the aisle towards her.

But he stopped a few rows ahead of her. Right next to the seat just vacated by the policeman.

'Barbara? Are you okay? What they are doing to you? Where's Michael? Do you need anything?'

That was Barbara travelling alone to Rangoon with a policeman? Claudia's mouth fell open. She leaned forward to hear better. Fortunately, Barbara had a clear carrying voice and she had no difficulty overhearing her answers to Thomas' questions. It was good news, no doubt about it. Barbara was being deported and Michael was in Mandalay Fort. Michael had no reason to murder anyone, Barbara went on, it was a clear miscarriage of justice, and she was going to hire the best lawyer she could just as soon as she got back to New York. New York? repeated Thomas, giving Barbara an odd look, but before she could answer, the policeman came rushing back up the aisle, told Barbara to be quiet, and ordered Thomas back to his seat. Barbara subsided into her corner and Thomas slunk back to the far end of the car. The second policeman disappeared and the train started to move. Claudia pushed her seat into the reclining position and put her feet on the footrest.

It really couldn't be better. Michael had fallen into the trap that had been set for Paul. The hunt had been called off. The danger was past.

To Austin's disgust, the police had impounded all of Min Saw's tapestries – with the exception of the one that had unaccountably gone missing. Austin wanted that tapestry, and he wanted it badly. He needed concrete evidence to get those damn galleries closed down. A tapestry full of heroin marked 'Rajasthan Gallery, New York' would fit the bill perfectly.

Unfortunately, no one in Mandalay seemed to know where the damn thing was. The police didn't have a clue, and neither did anyone else. Austin had two hypotheses, and they were both pretty shaky. One, Paul Miller had taken it, but how had he got hold of it? Two, the Buckleys had it, but where had they hidden it? The police had taken both their luggage and their hotel room apart. Where else could those fuckers have put it?

He took a rickshaw over to the market, where the go-fer ran an antique stall, to tell him he was leaving and pay him what he owed. Night was falling, and the dust was rising. Fog here was worse than San Francisco. Either the tapestry was out in the middle of Shan State with Paul Miller, or else it was on its way back to Rangoon in the false bottom of Barbara Buckley's luggage. It wouldn't be hard to organize a chat with Barbara once he got back to Rangoon, but he felt in his bones that it wasn't she who had it. His money was on Miller.

But where the hell was Miller now? And where was that goddammed tapestry?

Unlike his compatriots, Khun Nawng liked to drive at night. They left Kalaw shortly after eight, when the rest of the traffic on the road was pulling up and looking for somewhere to shelter from the evil spirits that ruled the darkness: the *balou*, the *leipya*, the *teye* and the *song*. His jeep, of course, was better maintained than most of the others, and should he chance to break down by the roadside, the assorted guerrillas, soldiers, bandits and smugglers who roamed the jungle by night would be more inclined to leave him alone. Even the evil spirits would probably recognize a Cambridge man and go elsewhere.

Khun Nawng knew the road like the back of his hand. He forged confidently ahead, barely slowing to take the bends. The jeep seemed to be the only car on the road in the whole Shan State, with the forest wild and dark and groaning outside the cosy yellow circle of the headlights. On the outskirts of Taunggyi, they stopped at a Tatmadaw checkpoint. Paul drew his blanket round his head and waited, curious but not alarmed, to see what would happen. Taunggyi was a big garrison town, and with the Wa alert on, they were likely to be nervous. The two soldiers on duty saluted Khun Nawng and the commanding officer arrived to pay his respects. He bent to peer through the window at the passenger. Paul drew the blanket closer round his face and mimed a fit of coughing. Khun Nawng made a derisive-sounding remark, the officer straightened up and saluted, the soldiers stood back to let them pass. The same thing happened on their way out of Taunggyi, except that this time there was a fairly lengthy conversation with the commanding officer. Paul couldn't understand a word, but it sounded as though the officer was giving Khun Nawng some kind of instructions. The discussion ended and the officer handed over a small bundle of banknotes. Khun Nawng pocketed them before Paul had a chance to identify them. He guessed they were dollars: the businessmen of Shan State were unlikely to trade in kyats. Khun Nawng restarted the engine and accelerated into the dark. He made no comment on what had passed. Paul asked no questions.

The road climbed through the mountains and the night grew colder. Khun Nawng turned up the heating and began to tell Paul about the evil spirits that haunted the night, the ogres who fed off human flesh and the ghosts undergoing punishment for past acts of wickedness. Paul moved his feet till he felt the outline of his backpack containing Claudia's tapestry on the floor beside him, and hoped the spirit of Min Saw was not in the vicinity. But of course, Khun Nawng went on, all that was superstitious nonsense, because obviously God did not exist and neither did the spirit world.

'Mind you, Philip, this is just as well. I wouldn't care to think of Heidegger and I spending the afterlife as ghosts together.'

Paul looked at him. Heidegger and I?

'Why Heidegger, you may wonder? Well because I feel there is something of a parallel between a philosopher who supported the Nazi party and a philosopher who supports SLORC.'

'Oh really?'

'Not ideologically, of course, certainly not. In that, I differ from Heidegger. But by certain of my actions, I fear I am making their task easier. Inversely, other actions may put spokes in their wheels. In the final analysis, I hope it will all balance out.'

He shot Paul a sharp, sideways glance. 'I'm sure it will,' said Paul.

They drove for a mile or two in silence. Abruptly Khun Nawng pulled over to the side of the road and stopped the car.

'This is a rendezvous point. Please put the blanket round your head and say nothing.'

They waited for about five minutes. Khun Nawng left the headlights on. There was no sound but the wailing of the wind. Then something moved in the shadows. A moment later the jeep was surrounded by men coming silently out of the darkness. Two of them approached the driver's side of the car, and Khun Nawng wound down his window. Someone bent and squinted through the window at Paul. He stared straight ahead. There were two or three others in front of the car, just out of range of the headlights, and doubtless others behind it. They were all wearing green uniforms similar to those worn by the soldiers at the last checkpoint. Was this an additional Tatmadaw control point set up because of the Wa? Paul doubted it. Khun Nawng was talking through the window in a brisk, businesslike tone, and Paul didn't think the language was Burmese. One of the men standing in front of the jeep moved briefly into the headlights and he caught a glimpse of the flashes on his shoulder. As he had guessed, these men were not Tatmadaw. They belonged to the MTA, the Shan insurgent army, and Khun Nawng, the rich, British-educated, well-connected Shan patriot, was giving them an impromptu briefing on the state of Tatmadaw readiness just up the road. Or else he was passing on whatever the Tatmadaw officer had told him to tell the Shans. Balancing things out.

One of the two men standing by the car asked a question. Khun Nawng answered. The man nodded, satisfied. Another wad of notes was handed over. This time, Paul was sure they were dollars. The man sketched a salute and melted back into the shadows. Looking round, Paul saw that all the others had gone too. Khun Nawng started the engine and they drove on.

After an hour on the train, Claudia was getting seriously hungry. Vendors of various kinds had been marching up and down the car since they left Thazi, offering fruit, sweets, nuts and hot meals. She was beginning to regret turning down Khun Nawng's wife's proposal to buy food for the journey in Thazi. When the chicken and rice went past for the third time, and the fat Burmese across the aisle ordered his second portion, she couldn't resist any longer.

Obviously, she shouldn't have done it. Indicating what she wanted in sign language was easy enough. The problem was trying to pay. She couldn't understand how much money they wanted. The man repeated the amount in what seemed to be several different languages. The party boss across the aisle began to stare. Claudia got more and more flustered. Finally, the vendor indicated the amount with his fingers. Claudia took out her wad of kyats. Since they had been here, Paul had paid for everything: she barely even knew what denomination the bloody notes were. She was fumbling with the unfamiliar money when Barbara Buckley went past. Hearing a voice say 'excuse me' in English, Claudia looked up. Her eyes met Barbara's, she saw Barbara frown in puzzlement, and then the moment was over, she counted out the right amount of kyats, the vendor moved on to the next passenger, Barbara disappeared into the loo, and the fat Burmese began to concentrate on his supper. Claudia subsided into her corner and waited for her pulse rate to return to normal before starting on her meal.

The chicken was surprisingly good. She considered ordering another portion – it was the first decent meal she'd had in two days – but decided it was better to let them all forget about her as quickly as possible. Barbara Buckley gave her another long stare as she returned to her seat, but Claudia flung a chicken bone through the open window with gay Burmese abandon and pretended not to see.

The train sped onwards and the sun sank into the mist like a Chinese water-colour. Claudia's spirits rose. Michael was in prison, Barbara was under escort, Paul was on his way to Thailand, and she was on her way to meet him.

So what was Claudia doing disguised as a Burmese on the train to Rangoon?

Barbara closed her eyes and tried to concentrate. The car had filled up in Thazi and nearly all the seats were taken. After it got dark, the conductor had come round and made everyone put the blinds down. The vendors had disappeared, the passengers had wrapped themselves up in pullovers and blankets for the night, and the atmosphere was frowzy with sweat and sleeplessness. Beside her, the policeman was snoring. The train was taking her further and further away from Michael, crammed into some evil-smelling little cell in Mandalay, with God knows how many other prisoners, maybe sleeping on the floor, for a crime he hadn't committed—

Barbara's eyes snapped open and she jerked upright in her seat. That was it. Of course. The real murderer was Paul Miller, who was now presumably in hiding somewhere. If Claudia was returning alone to Rangoon, it could only be because she was carrying the tapestry the police had been searching for that morning. Barbara turned her head cautiously until she could see the rack above Claudia's head. Yes, she had a bag with her: a battered plastic holdall. It must be in there.

One of the tapestries that should have been dispatched to New York next week, with several thousand dollars' worth of heroin inside it. Money that by rights belonged to her. When she got back to the States there were going to be lawyers' bills to pay, household expenses to meet, mortgage payments to make, and until she worked out some kind of arrangement with Curtis, no money coming in. Nothing. For a moment, she saw the house repossessed, the pictures and furniture sold, herself on the street, no roof over her head, nowhere to go except the farm in Alberta, the neglected yard, the filthy kitchen, the nightly Bible-readings— No! She got a hold on herself. It wasn't going to come to that, she wouldn't let it. She was never going back to Alberta, whatever happened.

Meanwhile, she had to be realistic. She had no chance of getting her hands on that tapestry, but she was damned if she was going to let Claudia get away with it either. Barbara thought some more. Then she woke up the snoring policeman and began to talk to him in a low intent voice.

The train was late arriving in Rangoon. It had stopped about an hour earlier at a station in the middle of nowhere, and stayed there for a long time. Barbara's police escort had got out and disappeared into the station building. He was gone at least twenty minutes. Arranging for a police van to collect Barbara at the station, Claudia surmised. The train set off as soon as he got back.

The confusion in Rangoon station was even worse than Thazi. Everyone poured off the train with their bags and parcels and spread shrieking over the platform. Claudia was in no hurry. She had reached her destination unchallenged. The fat Burmese had waddled off up the platform. Barbara and her escort had de-trained without a sideways glance. The Embassy was a mere taxi-ride away. She got her bag down off the rack and followed the last passengers out of the car.

They were waiting for her on the platform. She saw them

as soon as she reached the door. Four policemen bunched together in a tight serious group. Barbara and her escort standing beside them. She heard Barbara say, 'That's her,' and the policemen began to fan out round the door. Without hesitating, Claudia flung her bag straight at the face of the nearest policeman, jumped down from the train, dived past him, and began to run.

She didn't get far. There were too many people and too much luggage. She tripped over a bundle, cannoned into someone, stumbled again and nearly fell. One of the policemen grabbed her from behind, and jerked her to her feet. Another one came pounding up to help. They held her one on each side and turned her back in the direction she had come. She found herself looking straight into the eyes of a thin, brown-haired man with a tired face. He stared at her, mildly baffled by all the commotion. She grabbed desperately at his arm.

'Help me!'

He raised his arm to brush her off, one of the policemen gave her a shove forward, she realized he hadn't recognized her, and then in the nick of time she remembered his name.

'Adrian!' she yelled. 'It's me, Claudia. Help me, for God's sake!'

Help was useless. All they could do was let things take their course. That was the view Tony expressed over breakfast on the terrace, and Adrian was disinclined to argue with him. The encounter with Claudia was going to be awkward. He would rather put it off as long as possible.

'How long are they likely to keep her?' He poured himself more coffee.

'Until they find out who she is.' Tony buttered a piece of toast. 'Usually takes a few hours. We'll just have to wait until they call us to come and take charge of her.'

'If we called them ourselves, wouldn't they release her earlier?'

'Not in this country,' said Tony. 'Everything has to go through the proper bureaucratic channels. Mind passing me the jam, dear boy?'

'This Fortnum's strawberry here?'

'Right. Brought it back on my last leave. Try some, it's good. Thing is, if we intervene too soon, it's going to draw attention to her. Don't want them to think she's important. We definitely don't want them to think there's any truth in what Mrs Buckley had to say about her. It's a blessing she didn't have this tapestry stashed in her luggage.'

'That reminds me.' Adrian got up and went into the house, re-emerging a moment later with the tapestry Austin had given him.

'Good God,' said Tony, 'don't tell me it's you who swiped the damn thing?'

'Actually, no. This is the one that was taken from the Embassy.'

'Oh, is it? Well that's nice. Don't know what we're going to do with it, mind you. With Min Saw dead, I don't suppose the Ministry gives a damn any more. Maybe I'll put it in the loo as a souvenir.'

'Good place for it,' said Adrian. 'Mind if I have some more coffee? Haven't tasted anything this good since I got here.'

'That's Fortnum's too. I like to stock up when I go home. One needs one's little comforts in a place like this. You know, dear boy, this business has turned out a great deal better than I expected. It looks as though Miller's completely in the clear as far as Min Saw's concerned. From what you say he didn't do it, and with this Canadian in Mandalay Fort, he isn't even going to be accused of it. We really couldn't have hoped for a more favourable outcome.'

'We don't know where Philip is now,' Adrian pointed out.

'Yes, but the beauty of that is that he's travelling on a

German passport. It's the Germans' problem, not ours. Oh, you mean is he all right? Well, yes, I'm sure he is. Probably on his way overland to Thailand. Maybe he even has this tapestry, who knows? Even little Claudia hasn't come out of it so badly. At least she's not in jail.'

The Immigration Office. If Claudia hadn't been so unnerved by the hysterical venom of Barbara Buckley's accusations, she would have laughed at the sheer idiocy of it. Without a passport, she didn't exist. She had fallen off all their duplicate and triplicate lists and dropped into administrative limbo. Until they had decided who she was, they could not accuse her of murder, complicity to murder, fraud, burglary, breaking and entering, tapestry-theft, or any of the other crimes that Barbara was trying to convince them she was guilty of.

The Immigration Office was a square, white, modern building, with the familiar nondescript ugliness of half of London. She was interrogated by a crisp little lady official wearing a white uniform jacket, an ankle length navy skirt, and nifty little black shoes and socks. When had she arrived in Burma, where had she come from, what nationality passport was she travelling on? Where had she travelled to inside Burma, was she travelling alone or accompanied? Claudia told them as much of the truth as she could. She had had a row with her husband in Mandalay, she explained, and caught a lift to Thazi with some people who were going to Pagan. No, sorry, she only knew their first names, Georges and Monique, and she thought they were French, or possibly Belgian. It was only when she reached Thazi that she realized she had left her passport in the hotel in Mandalay. That was why she had decided to disguise herself as Burmese for the trip to Rangoon. It had been a silly thing to do, she realized that now, and she really was terribly sorry to put them to all this inconvenience.

The lady immigration officer wrote it all down using a scratchy little pen that might originally have belonged to some

Dickensian clerk. When she had finished, she blotted her page, screwed back the top on her bottle of ink and conducted Claudia downstairs to the basement. They went down a long, dimly lit corridor lined with battered wooden doors. She opened one of the doors and ushered Claudia inside.

'You will wait here while we contact your Embassy.'

'How long will it take?'

'I cannot say.'

The officer locked the door and Claudia heard the sound of her neat black-shod feet retreating down the corridor. She looked round the room with distaste. The floor was concrete and the walls were unplastered brick. There were no furniture or fittings beyond a dim light bulb hanging from the ceiling and a bucket in one corner. Yes, Claudia, you've got what you asked for. Heroin smugglers, spies, assassins, and for dessert a real live Burmese prison cell. She sat down reluctantly on the dirty floor. Never mind. It wouldn't be long before Adrian and Tony came to get her out of here.

They arrived towards the end of the afternoon, cool and trim in their lightweight shirts and gabardine trousers, and Tony signed a paper guaranteeing that she would remain in the custody of the British Embassy until a court hearing could be arranged for her. In the absence of any greater crime, the Burmese authorities had decided to charge her with over-staying her visa. She had overrun by twenty-four hours. The penalty was deportation.

The Embassy car was parked outside and they drove her across Rangoon to Rebecca's, where she was to spend the night. It was getting dark. She had been incarcerated in the basement of the Immigration Office for nearly twelve hours. Her head was spinning from hunger and exhaustion. She felt filthy and humiliated and perilously close to tears.

'Where's Paul?' said Adrian, as soon as the car was moving.

Well, yes, of course. If they hadn't needed an answer to that embarrassing little question, they would probably have left her there all night. Biting back her resentment, she gave them a full account of everything that happened since Thursday night. Why and how they had left Mandalay, why they had stopped off at Khun Nawng's house, why she and Paul had parted company.

'By now he should have reached Kengtung,' she went on. 'Khun Nawng was going to pass him on to a relative of his who runs a network of clandestine guides. One of them will take him to the Thai border. If all goes well, he should be in Chiang Rai tomorrow or the next day, and in Bangkok as soon as possible after that.'

They glanced at each other dubiously. Tony made a face, and Adrian scratched his head.

'This man Khun Nawng. Can't say I ever ran into him at Cambridge. Another one of Philip's oddball friends, I suppose. Does the name mean anything to you, Tony?'

'No, but there are a lot of people like that out there, who are into everything and just travel round as they please. You have to understand that they all know each other, the soldiers and the guides and the Tatmadaw and the MTA. They're all in each other's pockets, they all do business together. My guess is that this fellow is some kind of intermediary between the Tatmadaw and the Shan insurgents. If that's the case, he'd be virtually untouchable – until the day when one side or the other suspects him of double-dealing, and then . . .'

'Well I hope it works out,' said Adrian dourly.

'Oh, it might, you know, there have been cases. Chiang Rai by tomorrow is a little over-optimistic, naturally, but, well, if his money holds out . . . As soon as we hear anything, I'll keep you informed.'

'It's a pity things had to come to this,' said Adrian, staring coldly at Claudia over the back of the seat. 'If you'd only got a message to us sooner, none of this need have happened.'

So they were blaming her now, were they? With difficulty,

she held on to her temper. 'I sent you a message as soon as I knew what he was planning. I couldn't get through to Rangoon by phone. It was lucky I knew someone who was able to hand-carry a message.' Resentment got the upper hand and she added bitterly, 'For all the help I got, I might just as well not have bothered.'

'Gosh now that's jolly unfair. I got there as soon as I—'

'You should try having to deal with someone hell-bent on committing hara-kiri. It's no fun.'

'It took me all day to get on a plane. Furthermore, I've just spent a week running round Burma after you two and I thoroughly resent your insinuation. If you'd bothered to keep us informed of your itinerary—'

'How? How the hell was I supposed to do that? You told me not to let him find out I was reporting on him. How was I supposed to contact you? By carrier pigeon?'

'Well, really, there's no need to—'

'If I'd known what you were letting me in for, I'd never have come.'

'For all the good you did you might just as well have stayed in the gutter where I found you!'

'Come now,' said Tony soothingly. 'All this is quite unnecessary. We both know Claudia did the best she could in the circumstances.'

'Fucking right I did,' said Claudia, but they had reached Rebecca's and neither of them was listening to her. Rebecca came downstairs to greet the rescue party and make a big fuss of them for being brave boys and snatching away poor Claudia from the jaws of the Immigration people.

'Goodness me,' she went on, casting a desultory eye over Claudia, who had climbed out of the car and was standing sulkily in the background, 'I hardly recognized you. What on earth has Philip been doing to you? You'd better have a bath right away and I'll see if I can find you some clothes.'

Possibly she smelled, or maybe they just wanted to get her out of the way while they held their council of war. It didn't really matter. Claudia poured a generous helping of Yves Saint Laurent *bain moussant* into the bath and took her time. Rebecca's bathroom was well stocked. She washed her hair with Revlon shampoo and rubbed Estee Lauder body lotion generously over herself. Her skin felt like sandpaper. It was a wonder Paul had been able to get near her. Oh God, Paul – No. She took a firm grip on herself. She was not going to think about him. She was not going to let those bastards get to her. She dried her hair and put on the clothes Rebecca had laid out for her. A faded black T-shirt and black jeans with a hole in the knee. Jesus, it felt good to be back in black. What a good thing Rebecca hadn't known about that. She turned up the hem of the jeans, picked a belt out of Rebecca's drawer to cinch them in at the waist and wandered barefoot into the sitting room where they were waiting for her.

They looked up as she came in. Adrian drew his breath in sharply, Rebecca narrowed her eyes. Tony was the only one who didn't react, but that was because he spent more time practising his technique than they did. Claudia deduced that she was looking good.

'That was heavenly,' she announced, dropping into a chair. 'Just what I needed. I must say, if I'd known what Burmese bathrooms were going to be like, I'd never have come.'

Rebecca's eyebrows shot up, Adrian turned puce. 'Yes, I think it's time we got you back to civilization,' said Tony urbanely. 'Rebecca called the airport while you were in the bathroom, and we've managed to get you on a plane to Bangkok tomorrow afternoon.'

'Wonderful. Do I get a Scotch too, by the way? But I thought they had to deport me first.'

'The hearing's been set for tomorrow morning. The flight to Bangkok is at four, and the onward connection to Paris leaves just after midnight. You'll have to wait a few hours in the airport, I'm afraid, but aside from that it should all work out very nicely. Adrian will travel with you to Paris, to keep you company. Then when you get to Paris, he'll put you back where he found you, and we'll pretend none of this ever happened. That suit you, Claudia?'

'Tony, it sounds perfect. The only thing is, I was supposed to be meeting Paul in Bangkok.'

'Ah yes,' said Tony, glancing round at the other two, 'we were wondering if you'd arranged anything like that. Fact is, dear girl, I don't know if that's a terribly good idea at this point. For one thing, he might not make it to Bangkok within quite the kind of time frame you were mentioning in the car earlier on, and I don't suppose you want to hang around waiting for ever, do you? The other thing we have to consider is your own safety. We ought to get you right away from the firing zone as soon as possible. Is it really necessary, would you say, this meeting?'

'Well, no, I suppose not. Thank you, Rebecca, that's gorgeous. Cheers, everyone. Not really. It just seems a bit, well, callous, to go rushing off like that without making sure he gets out all right. I would like to say goodbye to him, it's only normal.'

'Oh we can pass that on to him, no bother at all,' said Tony reassuringly.

'Can you?'

'If you have a particular message, we can see he gets that too.'

'I don't think there's anything in particular I need to say to him. Maybe I could just write him a note, to say goodbye and so on, and you could see that he gets it?'

'Sure,' said Tony amiably. 'No problem.'

Since Canada did not have an embassy in Rangoon, Canadian diplomatic interests in the Union of Myanmar were represented by the British Embassy. Barbara had expected to find herself billeted on a pair of toffee-nosed Brits for the night. Instead, for reasons that were not quite clear to her, she found herself in the custody of the American cultural attaché and his wife. They were polite but uncommunicative, and clearly considered her presence undesirable. A Burmese house boy brought her meals to her room and turned the key in the lock when he left. Although she was, all things considered, relieved by the lack of social contact, Barbara was puzzled not to be treated as befitted the wife of an unjustly imprisoned Canadian national. Her own passport was genuine: surely they had no means of knowing that Michael's was not?

She found out the reason for her host's lack of cordiality towards the end of the afternoon, when Austin paid her a visit.

'Hi, Barbara, how ya doing?'

'Austin?' Barbara had been sitting on the bed reading. She looked up in surprise. 'What on earth are you doing here? Where's Greg?'

'I just thought I'd drop by and see if there was anything I could do. I'm on my own at the moment, Greg's back in Bangkok. Your host is an old buddy of mine, so when I heard you were here . . .'

'It's nice of you to come, but there's nothing I really need right now. I have to go to court to be officially deported tomorrow morning, and then I'm catching the plane to Bangkok tomorrow afternoon. And after that, I'm going to get on the first flight back home. I have to get some lawyers moving on Michael's case. It's a gross miscarriage of justice. I have to get him out of there as soon as possible.'

'Sure,' said Austin sympathetically. 'I understand. Jack said you had some problem with a lost tapestry too?'

'Not lost,' said Barbara, 'stolen. It belonged to us and Claudia Miller took it. I suppose they told you what happened on the station this morning? Thieving little bitch.'

'Well, I don't know about that. I gather she didn't have it after all.'

'Of course not. She must have left it with that husband of hers. You don't happen to know where he is?' she added craftily.

'No idea,' said Austin off-handedly. 'Nothing else you want to tell me?'

'Tell you?' Belatedly Barbara remembered who she was talking to. 'Look, Austin, if you're looking for a story, forget it. The last thing I want to do right now is talk to the press.'

'No? You don't want to talk about the Rajasthan Gallery in New York?'

'What is this? How did you know about that? I mean—'

'Then you don't deny it?'

'I don't know what you're talking about!'

'Oh I think you do.'

She stared at him apprehensively. 'You've been lying to us. You're not really a journalist, are you?'

'Afraid not.'

'What are you? DEA?'

'Something like that.'

'I have nothing to say to you. I am a Canadian citizen, and I do not have to talk to a representative of the US government. Please leave.'

'You're an American citizen too. By marriage. You were married on July 12 1979 in New York City.' He paused, watching her face. 'Your present address is 1619 New Hampshire Drive, Greenwich, Connecticut.' Another pause. 'You drive a 1992 Mercedes, colour red, registration BARB 100.'

'What do you want?' It came out as a croak.

'To offer you a deal. If you agree to go on record concerning the contents of this famous tapestry that everyone's combing Burma for, my agency might be in a position to intercede in your husband's case.'

'The contents of the tapestry? What on earth do you mean by that? They pad those things with rags, everyone knows that.'

'Sure,' said Austin. 'Now what about it?'

'Even if I knew what you were talking about, there's no reason for me to make a deal with you. Michael doesn't need your help. He's innocent. He had nothing to do with the murder.'

'He's been framed,' Austin agreed. 'But I wouldn't really say he was innocent. He didn't commit this particular murder, but he's committed enough other stuff in his time.'

'How dare you—'

'Makes you think there might be some justice in this world after all.'

Paul's new guide was called Noom Pan. He was allegedly the star of the stable of illicit frontier-crossers run by Khun Nawng's 'relative'. Paul distrusted him on sight. His appearance was unprepossessing and his manner was shifty. He had a broken nose and two missing front teeth. His clothes were dirty and he smelt unwashed. He avoided meeting the eyes of both his boss and his client. Paul considered objecting, but Khun Nawng had already left and his 'relative', sensing Paul's reticence, assured him that Noom Pan was their most experienced guide, to whom he would not hesitate to entrust even his own life. Paul had no choice but to go with him.

His days of travelling in style in the passenger seat were over. Noom Pan made Paul lie down on the floor at the back of his jeep and covered him with a skimpy red and white striped blanket.

'This isn't enough,' Paul protested. 'They're going to see there's someone on the floor right away.'

Noom Pan laughed derisively, revealing an array of betel-stained teeth. 'They know that already,' he said, and started the engine. 'They must not see you foreigner, is all.'

Paul reflected gloomily that he was probably telling the truth. The Excluded Areas were a small, incestuous, inter-locking world. Everyone knew everyone else: the soldiers knew the guides, and the Tatmadaw knew the MTA. Khun Sa visited selected government officials in Rangoon, and high-ranking Burmese military officers dropped in on Khun Sa's headquarters out here in the jungle. Noom Pan probably did the Kengtung-Tachilek run three or four times a month, and everyone along the road knew why, and who he had with him, and probably even how much he earned for doing it. Paul just had to hope that none of their delicately balanced little agreements were going to break down with him in the middle.

They got through the guard post on the edge of Kengtung without difficulty. If they knew he was there, they didn't care. There would be no more checkpoints till they reached the immediate vicinity of the frontier. So far, so good.

Sunday in Rangoon was Deportation Day. Claudia arrived at the Law Courts with a four-man escort: Tony, making it very clear that he was In Charge, Adrian, along for the ride, and a couple of Burmese go-fers, the Embassy lawyer, and the Embassy translator. Austin's term slid naturally into her mind, and she found herself wondering where he was now. Whoever he was, she liked Austin. He was a nice guy, in spite of all his ulterior motives. He must have had to call off his burglary. Had he been to the Innwa Inn and waited for them on the night they left Mandalay? And then they turned the corner into the corridor outside the courtroom, and she stopped dead, for there in the middle of a small group of people was Austin himself. And Barbara Buckley too. It was a small world. What on earth was Barbara doing here? She had expected her to be halfway to New York by now.

Austin gave her a big smile and came to greet her with a hug and a kiss on the cheek. 'Well, hi there, beautiful. Fancy meeting you here. Hi, Adrian, how ya doing?'

He drew her aside and looked her over. Tony watched them suspiciously.

'What are you doing here?' said Claudia.

'Oh, I'm just hanging out. Seeing what gives. So how are you today?' He examined her with something that was a lot closer to concern than anything else Claudia had encountered lately.

'Fine.'

'You don't look it. Where's Paul?'

'I don't know. I ...' She forced herself to smile at him before someone noticed something. 'On his way to Chiang Rai, I hope.'

'Yeah? That's what I figured. How's he planning on getting there?'

'He found someone to take him to Kengtung. That part of it should be okay. After that, I don't know. He has to find a guide, and then ...' She shrugged blindly. 'Maybe he'll be there by tomorrow, maybe not.'

'Don't worry.' Austin patted her shoulder reassuringly. 'He'll be okay. He knows how to look after himself. He's got the tapestry with him, I take it?'

'The tapestry?' Claudia suddenly realized that Barbara had edged nearer and was listening avidly. 'No, he doesn't have a tapestry. Why should he?'

'Well, there's one missing, you know.'

'Is this the one she was going on about yesterday?' Claudia jerked her head in Barbara's direction. 'I don't know anything about it.'

It was obvious that she was lying.

Austin didn't altogether blame her. With Barbara Buckley listening, he would have done the same. Apparently, they had damn near come to blows in the station yesterday.

He would call Bangkok as soon as they got out of here, he decided, and get someone from the Country Office there to meet him at the airport with a car and a couple of Brownings. He had booked a seat on the same flight as Mrs Buckley, but once they got to Bangkok, she would just wave her Canadian passport at him and tell him to fuck off. Someone could pick her up when she reached the States. Between here and New York, she wasn't going to get into trouble. His time would be put to better use trying to get hold of the tapestry. It was a good job Marty had put Greg on the plane to Bangkok yesterday morning. There was nothing to stop him leaving directly for Chiang Rai. If they drove all night they could be there by six or seven in the morning. It was unlikely Miller would get there any sooner. They could intercept him and the tapestry as soon as he crossed the border.

Twenty minutes out of Kengtung, the jeep veered off the road and jerked to a halt. The blanket was pulled off Paul's face, and the guide leant over him.

'We stop now. You get out. I go back to Kengtung.'

Paul pushed himself into a sitting position. 'What do you mean? What's going on?'

'It too dangerous. I go no further. Many Tatmadaw patrols here. If they find Western man in my car, they shoot me. You too,' he added as an afterthought.

'Your boss says it's not dangerous.'

The man sneered. 'My boss he know nothing. He sit in office and count his money. No danger for him, oh no. Only for me.'

So that was it. Paul glanced around. They had turned off the road and parked in some kind of forest glade. The jeep seemed to be entirely surrounded by trees. A nice secluded spot for a little highway robbery.

'How much do you want to take me to Thailand?'

'You show me what you got. I say if enough.' He raised a hand to his mouth and tittered.

Resignedly, Paul dug in his pocket and handed over his remaining kyats. He wouldn't be needing them in Thailand anyway. Noom Pan counted rapidly through them.

'This very good. Now show me bag.' He gestured towards Paul's backpack. 'What you got there?'

Paul began to open it.

'No, no. You no open. Give to me.' A knife appeared in his hand: Paul passed him the backpack. He took out the contents and examined it, item by item. One Sony clock radio, one Swiss watch, one half used tube of sun cream, one *longgyi*, one penknife, three ballpoint pens, two disposable lighters, one tapestry full of heroin. Paul watched, his mouth suddenly dry. Tossing aside the *longgyi* and the sun cream, the guide put everything into a large canvas bag he had produced from under the seat. Everything but the tapestry. He unfolded it, grimaced, and shoved it disdainfully back in the backpack.

'This no good to me. Only for tourists. You keep. Souvenir of Burma.' He tittered again, and zipped his bag briskly shut. 'Good, very good. Now you give me dollars, and we go to Thailand.'

'I've given you everything I've got.'

'No, you not give me dollars. All Western people have dollars. You give me.'

Paul turned out his empty pockets. He had discarded the longgyi in Kengtung and was wearing his own cotton trousers again.

'No dollars left. I gave them all to your boss.'

'No, this is lie. You tell me truth, or—' He made a plunging motion with the knife. Paul hesitated. What was he going to do when he got to Thailand with no money and no passport? On the other hand, judging by the gleam in this maniac's eyes, if he didn't produce any dollars, he would never get to Thailand.

'Round you waist. You Western people carry money round waist. I know this. You show me please what you got round waist.'

Reluctantly Paul reached under his trousers and pulled his money belt into sight.

'Ah yes, you see, I am right. You lie to me. Show me what you got.'

Claudia was glad to get out into the damp, spicy air of Rangoon again. The Law Courts had been built under Victoria and, judging by the number of spiders' webs, not cleaned since. They had waited three hours in the corridor, but the hearing itself had only taken five minutes. First Barbara and then her. A bored-looking judge decked out in a black coat, white hat and rather grubby *longgyi* listened perfunctorily to the evidence, informed her that she was convicted of having remained in the Union of Myanmar illegally after entry, for which she was liable to deportation under section something something of the Union of Myanmar Immigration Emergency Provision Act, and fined her the equivalent of two hundred dollars. Claudia looked duly chastened, Tony paid the fine, and they were free to go.

Outside, Tony exchanged a few words with the go-fers. Claudia looked around at the dishevelled buildings and pot-holed roads with a faint stirring of regret. Now that she was on the point of leaving Burma, she felt almost sorry to be going. In spite of everything, she would remember it kindly.

When they were in the car, Tony held out a printed form. 'Mind signing this, dear girl?'

'What is it?'

'Repayment of the fine, that's all.'

Claudia read it through. 'I'm not signing this. Why the hell should I? It's not my fault if I overran my visa. Make him pay it.'

'Me?' said Adrian.

'Well yes. Who else? You got me into this, remember?'

It was odd, but the resemblance to Caroline had gone. Three weeks ago, when Adrian had seen her walking down boulevard Haussmann in the lunchtime crowds, the likeness had stopped him dead in his tracks. Yesterday in the station, he had totally failed to recognize her. Even today, dressed in the clothes that Rebecca had loaned her, she looked nothing like the waif he had met in Paris. What had reminded him of Caroline, aside from her physical appearance, was the lack of direction he had sensed underneath the aggressivity and the chip on her shoulder. But somewhere along the line, it had disappeared. Two weeks in Burma had somehow given her a new self-assurance. She knew where she was going now. He wondered idly what she would do when she got back to Paris.

When the plane was in the air, he took the envelope he had prepared for her out of his inside pocket. He hadn't intended to hand it over before they reached Charles de Gaulle airport, but he had been feeling guilty ever since yesterday about their little altercation in the car, and this would be as good a way as any of making amends. She was sitting beside him in stony silence, as well she might after some of the things he had said to her. It was going to be a long trip: if a semblance of normal relations could be restored, things would be easier for both of them.

'This is for you,' he said. holding it out. 'The amount we agreed.'

To his surprise, she made no move to take it. 'You don't have to give me that. Paul's paying me too, you know. There's no reason I should get paid twice over.'

'You've earned it,' said Adrian firmly. She raised her eyebrows. 'Well, yes, it's true that I wasn't entirely fair to you in some of my comments yesterday, and I want to apologise for that. I do appreciate that this hasn't been an easy trip for you.'

'You can say that again.'

He gritted his teeth and pressed on with the apology. 'I'm afraid I rather lost control of myself, but I hope you'll understand that I've been under rather a lot of strain. Paul's been a friend of mine for over twenty years, and of course my brother-in-law for many years too, part of the family—'

'Your brother-in-law?'

'Well, yes. I thought you knew that.'

'How could I know that? You didn't tell me, and there's no reason Paul would.'

'Oh, well, I just thought maybe . . . Since you were . . . er . . . well, anyway, I thought maybe he'd mentioned it.'

'Paul doesn't know I've ever met you, Adrian.'

'Oh, well, yes, that's true, I suppose. Anyway, here, please take it.'

She shook her head. 'I can't take it. You're Paul's,' she hesitated, 'friend, you got me into this out of friendship for him. I don't want to take your money for that.'

'Please,' said Adrian, 'take it.' It was suddenly important to him that she should. This had to remain a purely financial transaction. 'If you must know, it's not my money. The service has a kind of, well, slush fund, I suppose you could call it, for situations like this.'

She stared at him unblinkingly. The cabin staff were moving down the aisle with the food trolley, and the passengers were snapping down their tables and sitting up expectantly.

'The political repercussions could have been really quite unfortunate.'

She smiled at him. It wasn't a very nice smile. 'Well, Adrian, since you put it like that, I won't deny that I really do feel I earned this money.' She stowed the envelope neatly away in the pocket of her jeans. Adrian relaxed. She hadn't needed much persuading. As he had thought, money was all that really interested her. It was a good job she wouldn't be seeing Philip again. This was the sort of person who was only out for what they could get.

As soon as they were out of the way with that damned food trolley, Claudia made her way to the toilets at the rear of the cabin. She splashed cold water on her face and looked at herself in the mirror. She couldn't see the label on her forehead that said WHORE in scarlet letters, but apparently it was there. In the presence of people like Adrian, it lit up and started to glow. After that illuminating little conversation she at least knew why Adrian had been so hostile ever since they came to get her out of jail yesterday. Austin must have told him about her and Paul. He wouldn't have liked the idea of her taking the place of his bloody sister. Especially since it was him who had acted as pimp.

There was a queue waiting when she finally came out. At the end of it was Austin. She had caught a glimpse of him and Barbara in the airport, so she knew he was on the plane. He touched her arm as she drew alongside.

'Adrian tells me you're both flying back to Europe tonight.'

Claudia regarded him warily. 'That's right.'

'I've got a car waiting for me in Bangkok. I'm going to drive up to Chiang Rai tonight to see what your husband plans to do with that tapestry of his. You set on going back to Paris, or do you want to come along?'

Paul would not have been surprised to find himself thrown out of the car between Kengtung and Tachilek, with or without his throat cut, but Noom Pan seemed to think that he had driven a satisfactory bargain, and they reached the Thai frontier without further incident. There was honour of a kind among thieves. Once or twice they were stopped by patrols, but Paul stayed out of sight on the floor and no one bothered to pull the blanket aside and see what it was concealing. Shortly after three, they turned off the road and struck off into the jungle. It was too dangerous to cross the frontier by road. The last few kilometres had to be done on foot, and around five in the afternoon, when the water was at its lowest point, they would wade across the Mekong into Thailand.

'You get off floor now,' said Noom Pan, and Paul climbed thankfully up on to the back seat of the jeep. The sky was completely hidden by a blanket of dark green foliage, and it was suddenly dark. The trail plunged steeply down a thickly forested ridge and Paul had to crouch low in his seat to avoid being scratched by overhanging branches. They reached the bottom of the ridge and Noom Pan turned to the right. For about ten minutes, the jeep rattled slowly on, following the stream that ran along the bottom of the valley, and then the guide abruptly ran the jeep into the undergrowth and switched off the engine.

'Now we must walk.'

'How far is it to the frontier?'

'I not know. Three kilometre, maybe four.'

The jungle was a labyrinth. The way lay along a narrow path that twisted in and out of dense bamboo thickets, past giant teak trees, over an endless series of low ridges. Without a guide, one would be lost in five minutes. The paths branched endlessly in all directions. Noom Pan's pace never faltered. He glided soundlessly along with a fast, fluid rhythm, looking continally left and right into the undergrowth as he went. It was hard going over the uneven ground, and Paul had trouble keeping up. Beneath the canopy of trees, there was no wind and the heat was stifling. His shirt was soon soaked with sweat. From time to time he wiped the perspiration out of his eyes with the back of his hand. And then, cresting a ridge, he found himself standing on the edge of a vast landscape of deep, intense green, stretching on endlessly as far as the eye could see, with no sign of human habitation anywhere. He stopped for a moment to gaze out over the unexpected panorama.

'Please, you must hurry. Soon it will be dark.' The guide's anxious whisper urged him onwards. He turned back on to the path and the guide set off again at the same rapid pace. Trying not to fall too far behind, Paul kept a watchful eye open for snakes and land mines. The Burmese side of the frontier had been mined in places by the Tatmadaw. It would be a pity to get blown to bits having got this far. A week ago, he wouldn't have cared, a week ago, he might just have gone plunging heedlessly downwards into that sea of green, but now—

They rounded a corner and came face to face with four men in green uniforms, standing silently in a clearing waiting for them. One of them had his rifle raised, already pointing in their direction. They had walked right into a Tatmadaw patrol.

After two weeks in Burma, the ultra-modern, air-conditioned cleanliness of Bangkok airport came as a welcome relief. Barbara felt her spirits reviving. Now that she had got back to civilization, everything seemed possible again. All she had to do was take the right measures and pay the right people. The spectre of the farm in Alberta receded.

She was afraid Austin was going to insist on sticking with her when they got to Bangkok, but to her relief he gave her a curt nod when they got through Passport Control, told her that as a Canadian citizen she was free to go wherever she wanted, and turned on his heel. Barbara collected her bags and made her way to the domestic terminal. She kept a sharp lookout, but saw no sign of him. He had finally accepted that there was nothing he could do to her. Good.

At the Reservations counter, a violet-clad, silkily smiling clerk told her that the last flight of the day to Chiang Rai had already left. After a moment's hesitation, Barbara made a reservation for the following morning. Claudia wasn't expecting Paul to arrive before tomorrow at the earliest. She would still be in time.

There was a six-hour wait for the flight to Paris. Adrian and Claudia walked along several miles of shiny corridors, Adrian toting his canvas travelling bag and Claudia marching empty-handed beside him, and settled themselves in the transit lounge. Adrian read *Time* and Claudia read *Newsweek*. A cleaning lady waxed the floor under their feet. Two or three Western backpackers with long hair and travel-stained jeans sprawled in attitudes of exhaustion on the other side of the lounge. The loudspeaker announced departures to a variety of exotic locations. Penang, Singapore, Phnom Penh, Ho Chi Minh-Ville.

Claudia dropped her magazine on the seat beside her and stood up.

'Do you know where the loo is in this place?'

'I believe it's downstairs,' said Adrian. 'Over there.'

'Thanks.' She thrust her hands into her pockets, and sauntered slowly in the direction he had indicated. Down the stairs, along the corridor. The ladies' room was deserted. Without bothering to go into one of the cubicles, she took the money Adrian had given her out of the envelope and counted it. He was honest, if nothing else. She put it back in her pocket and went back up the stairs. The transit lounge was not visible from here, and there was no sign of Adrian. Well, why should there be? There was no reason for him to be suspicious. As far as he knew she had babysat Paul for the money, fucked him for the same reason and, having been paid, was now anxious to get back to her own squalid little concerns. She smiled briefly to herself as she made her way towards the long row of glass booths housing the immigration officials. According to the loudspeaker, a flight had just arrived from Hong Kong. Making a mental note of the flight number, she began to fill in an immigration form. Claudia Miller, British citizen, airport of embarkation Hong Kong. Tony had made out her passport in her *nom de guerre*, to avoid unnecessary complications with the Burmese. The Thai immigration official, bless his heart, gave her a covetous look, read her form, stamped her passport and let her through.

She marched briskly through the airport. Look, no hands. Nothing to declare. No handbag, no backpack, no profession, no past. Claudia Miller, arriving from Hong Kong. Heart whole and fancy free. Well, that wasn't quite true. Tony might order her to expunge the past three weeks from her memory, but he was powerless to put her heart back the way it had been beforehand. Fortunately, he didn't know that. She cast a glance over her shoulder, but there was no sign of pursuit. She caught sight of the Hertz counter and made her way towards it.

'Well, here you are at last, beautiful,' said Austin cheerfully. 'I thought you were never coming.'

So this was it. It was all over. Too bad if he had decided he wanted to go on living after all. The decision had been taken out of his hands and his life was going to end here on a hillside in an obscure corner of Burma. No one would ever find his body, no one would ever know what had happened to him, he would never see Claudia again.

One of the soldiers rapped out a question. The man with the rifle took aim. The guide answered, his voice high and frightened.

The patrol commander turned his attention to Paul. 'Which country?'

'England.'

'Where you coming from?'

'Mandalay.'

'What you—?' The man broke off and shot a question at his companions. No one seemed to know the answer. They all looked at each other with blank faces. The commander frowned. Paul guessed they had run out of English.

'You come with us,' said the commander, and added something in Burmese to the guide. To Paul's surprise, Noom Pan turned and ran back the way they had come. Why had they let him go? From what he had heard of the Tatmadaw, it wasn't the way they usually worked. One of the soldiers went past him, signalling to him to follow, and he got a closer look at the insignia on the uniform. He realized with a slight shock that it wasn't the Tatmadaw. The insignia were Shan, not Burmese. He had been captured by Shan insurgents from the MTA.

'Sorry it took so long,' said Claudia. 'I didn't want him to get suspicious.'

'No problem,' said Austin. 'Had to make a few phone calls anyway.'

He steered her out of the airport and into the parking lot. A mild-looking man with crewcut hair and a small moustache was waiting for them behind the wheel of a Nissan Patrol. They were going to travel up to Chiang Rai in style.

'This is Tom,' said Austin.

'Hi, Claudia,' said Tom. 'Nice to meet you.'

'Thank you for waiting for me,' said Claudia, although she knew that basically Austin was just doing himself a favour. Some kind of subtle trade was in the air. He was taking Claudia up to Chiang Rai to offer to Paul, and was hoping to drive back to Bangkok with the tapestry in exchange.

'How long will it take to get to Chiang Rai?'

'Twelve hours. Tom and I will spell each other at the wheel. You can just stretch out in the back there and go to sleep. You'll find a rug there somewhere if you need it. Tom's brought along a picnic, or we might stop for a meal somewhere, depending on what kind of time we make.'

He gave her an avuncular smile. 'Great,' said Claudia. All very cosy and efficient. Too good to be true, in fact. Austin was a nice guy, but no philanthropist for all that. There was more to come. She kicked off her shoes and waited.

'And now,' said Austin, 'how about telling me just what you and Miller and Ferguson and the rest have been getting up to in Burma all this time?'

*

They took him along another jungle path, much the same as the one he had come along with Noom Pan. More hillocks, more rattling bamboo thickets, more gnarled roots clutching at his ankles, more mosquitos biting him through his shirt. There were two soldiers ahead of him and two behind. A sudden wave of exhaustion swept over him. The three days on the road, the lack of sleep, the hours of walking through the jungle were beginning to take their toll. After a while, he began to walk on automatic pilot, not even bothering to wipe the sweat out of his eyes, impervious to the branches scraping past his face and battering his head, the thorns scratching him, the sodden shirt sticking to his back. Each clearing in the forest looked identical to the one before. He wondered raggedly if they were simply walking him round in circles to exhaust and confuse him.

Finally they emerged into a clearing bigger than the others. Paul saw two or three flimsy bamboo huts and a few soldiers in the same green uniforms sitting or crouching on the ground. They stopped talking and got to their feet. Paul was led across the clearing and into one of the huts. An officer was sitting behind a wooden table writing. He looked up as Paul came in and his eyes widened in surprise. There was a brief exchange with the soldier who had been commanding the patrol, and then the soldier disappeared and they were left alone.

The officer had a round, childish face and an air of disillusion. Paul judged he was about twenty-five. It couldn't be much fun sitting out here in the jungle for weeks on end. He wondered suddenly if the patrol had simply brought him back for entertainment purposes. A foreigner to interrogate to break the monotony for a while.

The officer looked him up and down like a jaded child offered a new plaything. 'What you English doing here in jungle?'

'I want to get to Thailand.'

'You go to Rangoon, take plane to Bangkok.'

'I lost my passport.'

'Ah yes.' The officer smirked cynically. 'You go embassy, get new passport.'

Paul was too tired to play games. 'I have to leave overland because the police are accusing me of murdering someone. I didn't kill him, but I have no way of proving my innocence.'

The officer was suddenly flustered. 'Please, you say again.' Paul repeated it, using simpler words and shorter sentences. The officer clearly didn't believe him.

'Who you kill?'

'A Burmese man. A tapestry-maker.'

'Tapestry?'

'Kalaga.'

'Ah yes, *kalaga.*' A pause while he looked Paul over again. 'You got dollars?'

'What?' It was Paul's turn to be taken aback.

'Dollars. You give me dollars.'

Well, why not? He should have seen it coming. This was still the Golden Triangle. The same rules applied in a Shan army command post as in the drawing rooms of Kalaw and the offices of Kengtung. What a pity he hadn't had the foresight to stow his dollars in different places instead of leaving them all in the money belt for the robber guide to find.

'I don't have any dollars. My guide robbed me. He took everything.'

Again that world-weary *moue*. Paul pulled out the money belt and showed him. 'No money,' he said, suddenly exasperated with the whole bloody lot of them. 'No camera,' he went on, opening his backpack. 'No radio, no kyats, no nothing. Sorry, old chap, you're too late. I've been cleaned out.'

'What that?'

'That's nothing. That's just a *kalaga.*'

'Oh, *kalaga.*' He looked Paul over carefully and his gaze

fastened on his wrist. 'You got watch. Let me see.'

Paul took off his watch. As an afterthought, he slipped off his wedding ring and held it out too. 'Here, it's gold. They're both gold.' The man took them eagerly, and he watched them go without regret. The ring was the last symbol of his union with Lucy, and the watch had been her present for his thirtieth birthday.

The officer was clearly encouraged by this show of co-operation. 'Good, very good. Now give me dollars too.'

'I told you. I don't have any.'

'No dollars?' The Shan officer rubbed his nose dispiritedly and gazed at Paul in evident perplexity. It was evidently a delicate situation. How not to lose face before his troops with such meagre spoils of war. He picked up the watch again and looked at it. Drummed his fingers thoughtfully on the table. Added two or three words to the report he was writing. Considered Paul again. And then his glance went to the Chinese-made Kalashnikov leaning against the table, and it occurred to Paul that if he was to be of any entertainment value to them at all, they might have to shoot him.

No. He had got this far, the frontier couldn't be more than a kilometre or two away, he was not going to be shot now.

Paul didn't hesitate. He took the Spear of Anawrahta out of his backpack and laid it flat on the battered teak desk, turning it over so that the backing was uppermost. Nothing was visible: he had borrowed a needle and thread off Khun Nawng and sewn everything back in place before leaving Kalaw. He looked up at the Shan officer who was watching with interest.

'Give me a knife.'

The drive up to Chiang Rai was fast and uneventful. They reached the airport, their first stop, at quarter past six. At this hour of the morning it was deserted. The first flight for Bangkok was at ten thirty. Might as well go into town and take a look around, said Austin, so he and Claudia left Tom on guard in the airport and drove into town.

Chiang Rai was bigger than Claudia had expected, and possessed none of the exotic mountain charm she had been hoping for. It was a tourist factory and that was all. Featureless concrete streets lined with hotels, restaurants, banks, shops, and endless tourist agencies offering one-day excursions to the Golden Triangle. It was cold, Lake Inle weather, and she pulled the anorak Austin had lent her closer round her neck. How on earth were they going to find Paul in this labyrinth?

'Wouldn't we do better to go on to the frontier?' she asked doubtfully, and Austin shook his head.

'No, because we don't know exactly where he's going to cross. All the guides have their favourite places for crossing the Mekong, and we don't know exactly where he'll arrive. But he'll wind up here sooner or later because there's nowhere else to go. After that, I'm assuming he'll make for the airport and get on a plane, but we should keep an eye on the bus station too, just in case he decides to take the bus to Bangkok.'

Paul was not in the bus station either. They would go and find some breakfast, Austin decided. After that, they would hang around town for a while, to see if they could spot him, and then return to the airport in time for the plane to Bangkok.

Barbara was at the airport in plenty of time to check in for her flight to Chiang Rai. She had no luggage, but her capacious Vuitton shoulder bag contained everything she would need for the trip. Including the gun. As she knew from her previous travels in Thailand, they rarely bothered to check the hand luggage on internal flights. She boarded the plane without difficulty.

She had spent the night in the airport hotel. Not sleeping, preparing. She had put through a call to Curtis in New York, told him what to do, asked him to contact Angus, and warned him that she might not arrive back for another three or four days. She had some business to attend to first, she told him, but did not go into detail. Things like that were best not discussed over the phone.

After that, she had assembled the gun. First she took the barrel out of the tube of toothpaste where it had lain concealed since they left New York and cleaned it. Then she took the other pieces out of the bag containing Michael's camera equipment and fitted them together. They were all in the same moulded black plastic as the lenses and light meters and no one had looked at them twice. Her familiarity with guns was the one thing she could thank her childhood in Alberta for. She had gone hunting and trapping with her brothers ever since she was small.

The plane took off on time. Looking down from her seat by the window at the featureless fields surrounding the airport, Barbara felt a surge of determination. She had not been to Chiang Rai during the two weeks she had spent in Thailand with Michael. She didn't know how big it was, or how easy it would be to find Paul Miller. All she knew was that it was her only chance. Once he got back to Bangkok, he could just disappear. The city was so big and sprawling, she would never find him again. She could get detectives working on it, as Michael had suggested, but that wasn't the way she wanted to do it. She wanted to confront him, face to face, and punish him for what he had done to Michael. And to her. Above all, she wanted the tapestry back. Claudia had lied about it to Austin yesterday, that was for sure. Paul had that tapestry. And it was rightly hers.

Paul sat in the bus to Chiang Rai, crammed in among the sacks and the vegetables and the hill tribes in their elaborate costumes. He had spent the night in an Akha village on the Thai side of the border and walked into Mae Sai, the town on the Thai side of the Mekong, to take the bus as soon as it was light. The Shan officer, delighted with the contents of the *kalaga*, had detailed two soldiers to escort him across the Mekong, and had even left him two sachets of heroin to pay his way on the other side of the border. So far, he hadn't needed to use them. Examining his money belt in the village last night, he discovered that Noom Pan had left him his credit card and the bahts remaining from his stay in Bangkok. He had had just enough money to pay the bus fare. No matter. Chiang Rai was only sixty kilometres away, and in Chiang Rai there were banks, automatic telling machines and an airport with regular flights to Bangkok. Since getting rid of that damned tapestry, his luck had changed. Everything was working out splendidly.

Barbara's flight landed at twenty to ten. She had taken the precaution of tying a scarf round her head and she was wearing sunglasses. She didn't want Paul to see her coming. Tom, at his post in the main hall of the airport, saw her disembark. He watched her for a moment or two. With the Raybans and the expensive clothes, she stood out from the other tourists who had come here in search of local colour, or heroin, or a ride on an elephant.

A tall blond man walked past, and he took the photo Austin had given him out of his pocket to check the man's features against those of Paul Miller. No, it wasn't Miller. Too young and too fleshy. He glanced idly over the other people in the group with Miller and put the photo away again. It didn't occur to him to make any connection between the taut, subdued woman in Raybans and the blonde with the confident smile on the shores of Lake Inle.

Paul didn't linger in Chiang Rai. He withdrew some money from the nearest automatic teller and took a taxi to the airport. Checking the departure board, he saw there was a plane for Bangkok at ten thirty. He bought a ticket and headed for the phone. For once there was no delay in getting through to

Rangoon. Rebecca was in her office at the Embassy and she picked up the phone on the first ring.

'Philip, what a relief! Are you still in one piece, darling? Where are you? Have you been having lots of adventures?'

'I'm in Chiang Rai. Where's Claudia? Did she arrive safely in Rangoon?'

'Well, more or less. It's rather a long story. Actually the Burmese deported her. She flew out yesterday with Adrian.'

'With Adrian? My brother-in-law Adrian? What was he doing in Rangoon?'

'Your brother-in-law is a treasure,' said Rebecca. 'He's been terribly worried about you. That's why he arranged that Claudia should travel with you, as a kind of babysitter, you know.'

'He arranged what?'

'Didn't she tell you? Apparently Adrian set the whole thing up, the meeting arranged to look like an accident, and so on. Philip? Are you there?'

'Yes, I'm here. So are they both in Bangkok now, or has Adrian gone back to Paris?'

'No, they've both gone back to Paris. They took the plane yesterday evening.'

'They both went back to Paris? Claudia too?'

'Oh yes. She was thrilled at the idea of getting back to civilization again. I think she's had it with adventure for a while, poor lamb. Actually, she left you a note. Hold on, let's see if I can find it. Yes, here we are. Dear Paul, Sorry to rush off like this. Hope you made it through the jungle. Thanks for everything. Call me if you're ever in London. Best, Claudia.'

'That's all?'

'Yes, that's all. Look, Philip, I'll tell you what. If you have nothing better to do, why don't you hang around in Bangkok for a few days and I'll come over for the weekend? Maybe I could even get away a day or two earlier—'

Paul hung up. He closed his eyes and leaned his head against the cool metal side of the phone booth. The loudspeaker announced the departure of the flight to Bangkok. Paul ignored it. He was in no hurry to go to Bangkok any more. He was in no hurry to go anywhere.

Barbara followed him at a discreet distance as he walked out of the airport and across the parking lot. It had taken her a while to spot him with his hair dyed black, but she had finally seen him talking on the phone. She wasn't sure she would have had the nerve to go up to him and stick the gun in his ribs in the middle of the crowded concourse. It was a stroke of luck that he had come out here. There was an altercation of some kind taking place just outside the airport building between a fruit vendor, his client, and one or two unidentified others. The travellers and taxi drivers and assorted idlers who hung out in all the airports of Asia had drifted over to watch, and the parking lot was deserted. It was the perfect place for a quiet talk.

Paul had gone as far as he could go. He leaned against the wire netting on the far side of the car park and stared into space. He didn't see her come up to him.

'Why, Paul,' she said. 'It's a small world, isn't it?'

He turned his head slowly to look at her. He seemed to have difficulty focusing. She wondered briefly if he was ill. 'Barbara. What are you doing here?'

'I was waiting for you.'

'Oh.' He frowned, obviously puzzled. Then he asked, 'Where's Michael?'

'Where's Michael? He's in jail in Mandalay, you bastard! Don't tell me you didn't know! Where you should be!' He went on gazing at her blankly, so she spelled it out for him. 'They charged him with murder, Paul. The murder you committed.'

'Me? You mean Min Saw? I didn't kill Min Saw, the general did.'

'What are you talking about? What general?'

'The deputy commander of the Mandalay Military Division. Min Saw's heroin supplier.'

'It wasn't you who killed him? Then what . . .? Oh God, I don't understand!'

He was lying to her, he must be. It didn't make sense. In any case she couldn't think about it now. She had to get back on track.

'I'm sorry if they've arrested Michael.'

He was looking at her with what might have been pity. She didn't need pity from Paul Miller. Her head cleared and she remembered what she had come here for.

'You're sorry? That's wonderful, that's just wonderful. Well, you're going to make amends for it, don't worry. For a start, I want that tapestry back.'

He looked at her in silence for a moment, and then to her outrage, he smiled. 'I'm sorry, Barbara. I don't have it any more.'

'Then you don't deny it was you who stole it?'

'No.'

'So where is it now?'

'I got ambushed by Shan insurgents near Tachilek last night. I had to give it to them.'

'I don't believe you,' said Barbara flatly. 'Show me what's in that backpack.'

He unzipped the backpack and held it in front of her. It contained a *longgyi*, a half-used tube of sun cream and two sachets of heroin.

'What's this?'

'That's the consolation prize. It's all they left me.'

'Well I'll take this for a start, if you don't mind. This belongs to me.' She stuffed the sachets into her shoulder bag. 'And now tell me what really happened to the tapestry.'

'For Christ's sake, I just did.'

She pulled the gun out of her bag and pointed it at him. 'Paul, I want the truth.'

'I told you the truth.'

A car turned into the parking lot and pulled up a few yards away from them. Barbara held the shoulder bag in front of her to prevent anyone seeing the gun.

'I don't believe you.'

'Why should I lie to you?'

'Why should you tell me the truth?'

He was beginning to reply when a voice cried, 'Paul!'

Paul swung round. Barbara looked over to where the voice had come from. Austin and Claudia were getting out of the car that had just pulled in.

'Claudia!' Paul was already moving towards her.

Barbara pointed the gun at him. 'Don't move or I'll shoot,' she cried, but he flung her an abstracted backward glance and went on walking.

'Hold it right there, Barbara!' Austin had produced a gun of his own and was pointing it across the roof of the car. His glance slid sideways towards the airport building and he yelled, 'Tom! Over here!' Barbara felt events skidding out of her control. She hadn't expected this. How many of them were there? She had thought it would be just her and Paul. She hadn't planned any of this. Paul was already several yards away. What should she do? There was a sudden roar from the engines of the Bangkok plane standing on the tarmac a few hundred yards away, Paul fell like a stone to the ground, Claudia screamed, Barbara glanced down at the gun in her hand. She had squeezed the trigger without even realizing what she was doing. There was blood pouring from the side of Paul's head. She had never used this gun before and her aim had been way too high. He was lying face down on the ground. He was quite still. There was blood everywhere. She had killed him.

For a split second, no one moved. Then everything began to happen at once. There was too much going on, she couldn't take it all in. Claudia rushing towards Paul, Austin telling her to drop the gun, another man running round the corner of the building, the noise of the jet engines rising to a climax, Claudia flinging herself on the ground beside Paul. She couldn't think, she couldn't work out what to do next. She wanted to fire at Paul again, to make sure, finish him off before they got her, because she was done for now, she knew that, but Claudia was in the way, Claudia had thrown herself between Paul and the gun, she couldn't hit him without hitting Claudia first. She fired again anyway, but she didn't have time to see if she had hit him or not, because she felt a sudden, stunning blow in her stomach, and another in the region of her heart, and then everything went black, and she was falling, falling . . .

'She's dead,' said Tom. 'What about him? Is he all right?'

Claudia sat up shakily. No. No, he's not. He's dead too. She killed him. He went all the way through purgatory and came out the other side. He decided he wanted to live, but it was too late, they took him anyway. He's gone to join Lucy and Caroline, and now there's only me left, all on my own, and no one even to take vengeance on.

'Did she hit you too?' said Tom. 'There's blood all over your T-shirt.'

'It's not me. It's him. He's dead. She killed him.'

'Let's see. You're right, it doesn't look good. Hey, Austin, take a look.'

'Paul. Oh God, Paul.'

'Is this our man? You told me to look for a blond.'

'Scalp wound,' said Austin. 'Nothing serious.'

'But he's dead!'

'Not he's not. Just stunned. Look, can't you see he's moving? Paul? You okay?'

'Can you get up?'

'Easy does it.'

'Hold on to me.'

Between them, they got Paul to his feet. Claudia gazed at him incredulously. He was chalk-white, there was blood pouring from the side of his head, it was doubtful if he could have stood unaided, but he was alive.

'Let's get him into the car,' said Austin briskly. 'Here, Paul, hold this to your head. Come on, beautiful, don't just stand there. Grab his backpack and get into the car. You acted mighty stupid, let me tell you. Might have got yourself killed.'

'I thought she'd killed him.' The tears were sliding down her face: she was powerless to stop them.

'In that case, why throw yourself in front of the gun? Good job she couldn't shoot straight, or she'd have got you too with the second shot. Get into the car, goddammit! You want someone to come and find us all here like this?'

Claudia got into the car. Paul was slumped in the opposite corner with his eyes closed and a towel pressed to his head. She peered at him fearfully.

'Where are we going? Shouldn't we take him to a hospital?'

'No way,' said Austin. 'He came over the frontier illegally, he has no papers, and the police tend to find out about gunshot wounds pretty fast. Before we know where we are he'll find himself accused of murder.'

'She only grazed him,' said Tom. 'It looks much worse than it is. We'll take a look at him a few miles down the road. There's a first aid kit in the trunk.'

Austin drove sedately towards the exit. Claudia glanced round nervously, but there was no one in the car park but Barbara. Her body lay on the ground near the perimeter wire. Her bag had fallen open when she had dropped it and its contents were scattered beside her. Could they really drive off without anyone noticing?

'Won't someone have heard the shots?'

'Nope,' said Tom. 'Plane decided to rev up at just the right time. You run into the odd shooting victim in these parts now and again. No one will worry about her.'

Paul opened his eyes. 'She has a couple of sachets of heroin in her bag.'

'Great,' said Tom. 'They'll like that. Who is she anyway?'

'Where's the rest of the heroin?' demanded Austin. 'You've still got that tapestry with you, I hope?'

Paul began to laugh and then grimaced with pain. 'So that's what you've all come rushing up here for. I don't have it, I'm afraid. Got robbed along the way.'

Austin looked at him intently in the rear view mirror. 'You're kidding.'

'No I'm not.'

'No shit. Bandits?'

'More or less. MTA.'

'Well, fuck that. You mean we've come all the way up here for nothing?'

'Well you saved my life.'

'That's supposed to cheer me up?'

'Drop me off by the roadside if you want.'

Austin sighed deeply. 'We'll just ask Miss Niagara Falls here what she wants to do with you.'

Paul looked across at her. 'Liebling, do stop crying. Did you come up here for the tapestry too?'

'I can't. Of course I didn't. I came for you.'

'Then why did you write that note?'

'What note? Oh God, not the one in Rangoon? How do you know about that?'

'I called Rebecca just now.'

'The bitch!' She began to sob in earnest. 'I wrote that note for them, not for you. They were all determined to stop me seeing you again. I didn't think you'd ever read it. The bitch! I suppose she told you about Adrian too?'

Paul didn't answer. He closed his eyes again and his face tightened with pain.

'Lay him down flat,' said Tom. 'Put his head on your knees,

Acknowledgements

The following works were useful in preparing this book:

Burma: Insurgency and the Politics of Ethnicity, Martin Smith, Zed Books, London and New Jersey, 1991.

Land of Jade, Bertil Lintner, Kiscadale Publications, Edinburgh, 1990.

Birmanie, E. Guillon and C. Delachet, Editions du Seuil, Paris, 1975.

Pagan: L'Univers Bouddhique: Chronique du Palais de Cristal, P.H. Cerre and F. Thomas, Editions Findakly, 1987.

Thanks are also due to the U.S. Drug Enforcement Agency and the Observatoire Géopolitique des Drogues; to S. Aung, Claude Delachet-Guillon and, in particular, Nicolas Le Petit Prince, who were kind enough to put their considerable expertise on Burma at my disposal; and to David Gettman, of Online Originals, who was the first to publish this book on the Internet.

Finally, I would like to thank my husband, whose interest in Burma initially kindled mine, and who has been a source of unflagging encouragement and moral support before, during, and after the writing of this book.

The Angels of Russia
Patricia le Roy

In the cold war Soviet Union, even passion is political ...

On a study trip to Leningrad, literature student Stéphanie meets Sergei, an enigmatic young dissident. Stéphanie had fallen in love with a fairy tale image of Russia – full of palaces and aristocrats; Sergei offers to show her just how different the reality is. Even in the supposedly enlightened days of Gorbachev, Sergei is in constant danger because of his political beliefs. So when he asks Stéphanie to agree to a marriage of convenience so that he can leave the country she is unable to refuse him.

Stéphanie finds herself increasingly attracted to her mysterious new husband. But when Stéphanie introduces Sergei to her aunt Marina, a Russian who defected to Paris whilst accompanying her father on a political mission, he appears to know more about Marina's past than Stéphanie. Could Marina be the real reason why he has come to Paris? As it becomes increasingly clear that Sergei is harbouring more than one secret, Stéphanie is forced to question whether their first meeting was as accidental as it seemed...

"A sweeping contemporary historical romance...gripping, surprising...page-turner"

Times Literary Supplement

The very best of Piatkus fiction is now available in paperback as well as hardcover. Piatkus paperbacks, where *every* book is special.

☐	0 7499 3118 3	The Angels of Russia	Patricia le Roy	£6.99
☐	0 7499 3112 4	One Hundred and One Ways	Mako Yoshikawa	£6.99
☐	0 7499 3116 7	Stigmata	Phyllis Perry	£6.99
☐	0 7499 3149 3	Four Mothers	Shifra Horn	£9.99
☐	0 7499 3063 2	Fair Exchange	Lynne Reid Banks	£6.99
☐	0 7499 3167 1	Lip Service	M. J. Rose	£6.99
☐	0 7499 3108 6	Summer Storm	Siân James	£6.99
☐	0 7499 3141 8	The Reef	Nora Roberts	£5.99

The prices shown above were correct at the time of going to press. However, Piatkus Books reserve the right to show new retail prices on covers which may differ from those previously advertised in the text or elsewhere.

Piatkus Books will be available from your bookshop or newsagent, or can be ordered from the following address:
Piatkus Paperbacks, PO Box 11, Falmouth, TR10 9EN
Alternatively you can fax your order to this address on 01326 374 888 or e-mail us at books@barni.avel.co.uk

Payments can be made as follows: Sterling cheque, Eurocheque, postal order (payable to Piatkus Books) or by credit card, Visa/Mastercard. Do not send cash or currency. UK and B.F.P.O. customers should allow £1.00 postage and packing for the first book, 50p for the second and 30p for each additional book ordered to a maximum of £3.00 (7 books plus).

Overseas customers, including Eire, allow £2.00 for postage and packing for the first book, plus £1.00 for the second and 50p for each subsequent title ordered.

NAME (block letters) _____

ADDRESS _____

_____

I enclose my remittance for £ _____

I wish to pay by Visa/Mastercard   Expiry Date _____
